Helen McGrath and Toni Noble

Bounce Back!

YEARS 3–4

3RD EDITION

Contents

About Bounce Back! vi
How to use Bounce Back! vii

HANDBOOK

Chapter 1 • What is the Bounce Back! program? 1

Introduction 1
About Bounce Back! 2
The history of the program 2
Key features and benefits 4
Expected outcomes 11
References 12

Chapter 2 • The Bounce Back! curriculum 14

Introduction 14
Curriculum Units 15
Unit 1: Core values and Unit 2: Social values 15
Unit 3: People bouncing back 17
Unit 4: Courage 17
Unit 5: Looking on the bright side 18
Unit 6: Emotions 19
Unit 7: Relationships 20
Unit 8: Humour 21
Unit 9: Being safe 21
Unit 10: Success (STAR!, CHAMP!, WINNERS!) 22
Extra unit: Elasticity 23
References 24

Chapter 3 • Wellbeing and resilience 26

Introduction 26
What is student wellbeing? 27
What is teacher wellbeing? 27
What is mental health? 27
What is mental fitness? 27
What is resilience? 27
What is Social and Emotional Learning? 28
Student wellbeing at the heart of educational policy 28
Protective processes that promote student wellbeing and resilience 30
Differentiating the Bounce Back! curriculum 35
References 38

Chapter 4 • Social, emotional and coping skills for wellbeing and resilience 40

Introduction 40
Everyday and major stressors 41
Social, emotional and coping skills: Self-awareness 42
Social, emotional and coping skills: Self-management 54
Social, emotional and coping skills: Social awareness 56
Social, emotional and coping skills: Social management and relationship skills 57
Social, emotional and coping skills: Responsible decision making 57
References 58

Chapter 5 • Teaching the BOUNCE BACK! acronym 60

Introduction 60
Guidelines for teaching the acronyms 61
The key principles in BOUNCE! and BOUNCE BACK! 61
How to use the BOUNCE BACK! acronym 64
Using the BOUNCE BACK! critical question prompts 64
Ten myths and realities about resilience 65
Indicators for referring a student for professional help 67
References 67

Chapter 6 • Implementation and maintenance of Bounce Back! — 68

Introduction	68
Implementing Bounce Back!	69
Bounce Back! assessment	72
Assessing change	74
Using Appreciative Inquiry to refresh Bounce Back!	75
Advice for managing challenging situations	78
References	79

CURRICULUM UNITS

Teaching strategies and resources — 81

Circle Time	81
Safe class discussions	82
Literature prompts	86
Bounce Back! key message prompts	87
Organising students into pairs and groups	88
Class meetings and school committees	89
Teaching strategies used in Years 3–4	90
Cooperative games round robin	98
Classroom resources	101

Unit 1 • Core values — 109

Key messages	109
Being honest	110
Cheating	111
Being tactful	112
Being fair	114
Social justice	116
Being responsible	117
It's okay to be different	119
Consolidation	121

Unit 2 • Social values — 124

Key messages	124
It's important to be kind	125
Our family is kind and supports us	126
Our teachers are kind and support us	127
Being kind and supporting people we don't know very well	128
Being kind to animals	129
It's important to be friendly	130
It's important to cooperate	133
It's important to respect others	136
Self-respect is important too	138
Consolidation	139

Unit 3 • People bouncing back — 142

Key messages	142
Life has ups and downs but you can bounce back	144
Bouncing back from injury or being ill	146
Animals and plants can bounce back too	147
Losing someone or a pet you love	149
Other people can help if you talk to them – get a reality check	150
Unhelpful thinking makes you more upset – think again	152
Nobody is perfect – not you and not others	153
Concentrate on the good and funny bits when things go wrong	154
Everybody has setbacks sometimes	155
Blame fairly	157
Accept what can't be changed (but try to change what you can change first)	159
Catastrophising exaggerates your worries	161
Keep things in perspective	162
Consolidation	163

Each Curriculum Unit also has Blackline Masters, interactive tools, games and activities available in the eBook.

Unit 4 • Courage — 166

Key messages	166
Everyone feels frightened sometimes	167
We don't all get frightened by the same things	169
Everyone feels anxious sometimes	170
What is courage?	171
Animals can be brave too	173
There are different kinds of courage	173
The courage to be yourself	175
How to become braver	177
Being foolish and showing off is not being brave	178
Consolidation	179

Unit 5 • Looking on the bright side — 183

Key messages	183
Bad times don't last	184
Bright side versus down side thinking	185
Being a positive tracker	186
Being thankful and grateful	190
Being hopeful	193
Making your own good luck	195
Consolidation	196

Unit 6 • Emotions — 199

Key messages	199
Describing and understanding feelings	200
Feelings change a lot	204
Boosting positive feelings	205
You can change a bad mood into a good mood	206
Being mindful to be the boss of your feelings	208
When do you feel angry?	209
Dealing with angry feelings	210
Helpful thinking – check your facts	212
Be an intention detective	213
Dealing with disappointment	214
Dealing with jealousy	215
Dealing with embarrassment	216
Dealing with feeling lonely and being left out	217
Dealing with sadness	218
Dealing with worries	219
Developing empathy	220
Consolidation	222

Unit 7 • Relationships — 224

Key messages	224
Getting along well with others	225
Being a good listener	226
Having an interesting conversation	227
Being a good winner and a good loser	229
Making and keeping friends	230
Dealing with friendship problems	233
Dealing with friendship disagreements	234
Fixing friendship problems	237
Building bridges and saying sorry	239
Dealing with being separated from a friend	241
Consolidation	242

Unit 8 • Humour — 245

Key messages	245
Everyone has a different sense of humour	246
Humour is enjoyable and is good for your health	247
Humour helps us cope better and feel more hopeful	250
You can use humour to cheer someone up	252

Each Curriculum Unit also has Blackline Masters, interactive tools, games and activities available in the eBook.

Humour can help friendships grow stronger	253
Humour can be hurtful if it makes fun of others	255
Consolidation	257

Unit 9 • Being safe — 260

Key messages	260
Classroom organisation	261
What is bullying?	261
What is cyberbullying?	264
Bullying causes great harm	265
Bullying is not okay in our school and is everyone's problem	266
Put-downs are not okay in our school	267
If someone gets bullied, it is not their fault	269
Why do some children bully others?	270
Think for yourself – don't just follow others	271
What can someone do if they are being bullied or cyberbullied?	273
Dealing with cyberbullying	274
How can we all help with the problem of bullying?	275
Consolidation	278

Unit 10 • Success (CHAMP) — 280

Key messages	280
Train your brain for success and think like a CHAMP	281
Challenge yourself, set a goal and make a plan	283
Have a go, take a risk and believe in yourself	286
Always look for and use your strengths	288
What are your ability strengths?	288
What are your character strengths?	290
Using your strengths to help others	292
Mistakes help you learn – don't be afraid to make them	294
Use grit – persist, work hard and don't give up	295
Using willpower	298
Solving problems and being resourceful	299
Managing time and being organised	300
Managing time	300
Being organised	302
Consolidation	303

Index — 306

Each Curriculum Unit also has Blackline Masters, interactive tools, games and activities available in the eBook.

About Bounce Back!

Bounce Back! provides practical strategies to improve student wellbeing and help students (and teachers) cope with the complexity of their everyday lives. It teaches them how to 'bounce back' when they experience sadness, difficulties, frustrations and challenging times. ***Bounce Back!*** is an evidence-informed program built on Positive Psychology, Cognitive Behaviour Therapy and Social and Emotional Learning principles.

There are ten **Curriculum Units** in each level that help students to:

- develop positive and pro-social values, including those related to ethical and intercultural understanding
- develop self-awareness, social awareness and social skills for building positive relationships
- develop self-management strategies for coping and bouncing back
- find courage in everyday life as well as in difficult circumstances
- think optimistically and look on the bright side
- boost positive emotions and manage negative emotions
- develop skills for countering bullying
- use humour as a coping tool
- develop strengths, skills and attitudes for being successful.

The ***Bounce Back!*** program:

- is a single but multi-component program that communicates consistent messages to the whole school community, including families
- uses the four SAFE elements of effective programming (sequenced, active, focused, explicit) recommended by the Collaborative for Academic, Social and Emotional Learning (CASEL)
- takes a whole-school approach to build a positive school climate and embed the program into the curriculum and general life of the classroom and school
- is a universal program taught to all children
- is integrated with academic learning to encourage application of skills in context
- is long-term and multi-year to develop deep understanding and application of the concepts and skills

- uses evidence-informed teaching strategies, such as cooperative learning, thinking tools, Circle Time, high quality educational games and peer support
- is designed to be integrated with other curriculum areas, such as English through the use of quality children's literature and multimodal resources, Health and Physical Education, The Arts and other curriculum areas
- incorporates a range of assessment tools for measuring aspects of wellbeing and resilience.

The program consists of:

- ***Bounce Back!*** **Years F–2: Handbook and Curriculum Units**
- ***Bounce Back!*** **Years 3–4: Handbook and Curriculum Units**
- ***Bounce Back!*** **Years 5–6: Handbook and Curriculum Units**

Bounce Back! is recommended by KidsMatter.

Resources available in the ***Bounce Back!*** **eBooks** include:

- Tools for measuring aspects of wellbeing and resilience
- Elasticity, an extra Science and Maths **Curriculum Unit**
- Curriculum correlation charts
- Scope and sequence charts
- Suggesions on how to find resources
- Index of resources
- Resources list for each **Curriculum Unit**
- Blackline Masters (BLMs) for each **Curriculum Unit**
- Digital teaching tools and interactive games and activities for each **Curriculum Unit**
- Information for families

The digital resources are identified by the following icons:

 – PDF resources

 – interactive resources

How to use Bounce Back!

Each level in **Bounce Back!** consists of a **Handbook** and **Curriculum Units** plus digital resources.

Handbook

Six chapters explore the most recent evidence-based research supporting **Bounce Back!** including linkages to CASEL (Collaborative for Academic, Social, and Emotional Learning) and the Australian Curriculum, as well as suggestions for differentiation and program implementation.

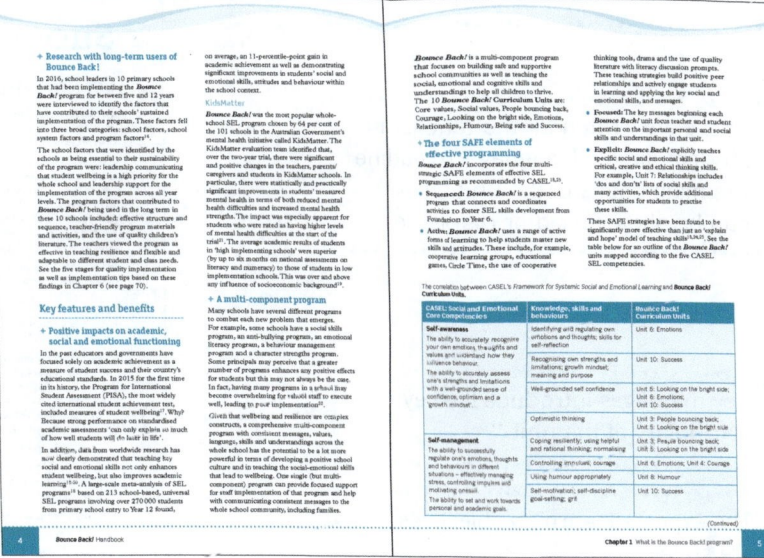

Curriculum Units

Each level begins with an introductory unit containing:

- evidence-informed teaching strategies, such as Circle Time
- literature and key message prompts
- classroom resources.

Teaching strategies and resources

Circle Time

What is Circle Time?

Circle Time is a planned and structured framework for whole-class discussion. The whole class sits in a circle so they can see and hear each other, and everyone is included in the Circle Time activities and discussion. Being in a circle means the group is more engaged and distractions are less likely. Everyone has the opportunity to speak and be listened to. Circle Time works best on chairs, although some teachers have younger students sitting on the floor in a circle. Circle Time is used in every **Bounce Back!** Curriculum Unit. It builds classroom community, positive relationships and teaches Social and Emotional Learning (SEL) skills.

What happens in Circle Time?

A typical Circle Time discussion in **Bounce Back!** follows this format:

- a reminder of the Circle Time rules (see below)
- a reminder about the talking prompt that you are using (see page 82) – only the student who has the prompt can speak
- an introductory game (optional), energiser or simulation
- an activity that introduces the topic for Circle Time (often reading a relevant book)
- a whole-class discussion, with students participating in a variety of ways, for example:
  - every student may be invited to speak around the circle
  - selected students may be invited to speak
  - students may be asked to volunteer to make a comment or answer a question
  - students may be asked to discuss in pairs or threes and then one person in each pair is invited to explain what they agreed on
- a final activity that closes the circle, e.g. summarising the key messages from the class discussion or a sentence completion (e.g. One thing I learnt is ... One thing that surprised me was ... One thing that was new ... I feel ...)
- a follow-up group or individual activity after Circle Time (usually).

The Circle Time rules

When everyone is sitting in the circle, begin the session by stating the rules.

1. Everyone has a turn, and when one person is talking (i.e. the person who has the talking prompt), everyone else listens.
2. You may pass if you do not have anything to say (but the teacher may come back and ask you again when you have had a bit more time to think about what you want to say).
3. No put-downs are allowed during Circle Time.

Curriculum Units

There are ten **Curriculum Units** in each level.

These are written for the teacher in student-directed language to outline the main points of the unit. They can be photocopied or displayed.

Key messages introduce the key vocabulary of the unit.

The expected learning objectives are stated.

The eBook includes a reference list of all the core resources (books, films, video clips, poems, songs, websites) referred to in the unit, as well as additional suggestions.

Each unit is structured according to topics, which can be one or more lessons. Some units also have subtopics.

Each topic begins with suggested resources to start exploring the ideas that will be taught.

Each topic has Circle Time discussions using the resources or activities as a starting point to engage with important life issues in a safe and comfortable way.

These prompt teachers to reflect on the relevance of the key messages to their own wellbeing or their teaching practices in enhancing their students' wellbeing.

UNIT 10

Success (CHAMP)

KEY MESSAGES

Think like a CHAMP.
You can train yourself for success by using the CHAMP acronym.

Challenge yourself, set a goal and make a plan.
A challenge is something that is new or hard to do. You have to work hard when faced with a challenge. To achieve a goal, start by making a plan about how you will do it. When you do achieve a goal, you will feel happy with what you have done. However, nobody achieves all of their goals.

Have a go! Take a risk! Believe in yourself.
Challenging yourself means pushing yourself to do something that you are unsure you can do. You may need to risk making a mistake or not being able to do it to begin with. Having a go shows that you believe in yourself.

Always look for and use your strengths.
The things you are best at are called your 'strengths'. Everyone has different strengths and no-one is good at everything. Usually you really like doing the things you are best at. However, you can still improve in things that are not your strengths through hard work.

There are two kinds of strengths.
We all have two kinds of strengths:
- **Character strengths** are the ways in which you behave, such as being kind.
- **Ability strengths** are things you are good at, such as reading, maths, art or sport.

Use your strengths to help others.
When you use your ability and character strengths to help others, then you are helping to make both yourself and other people happy.

Mistakes help you to learn. Don't be afraid to make them.
Everybody makes mistakes when they try to do something that is new or challenging. Making a mistake or failing is useful because you can learn from them. Try to learn from your mistakes as well as your successes.

Persist, work hard and use willpower.
Keep on trying. There will be some things you can't do YET. But you will mostly be able to do them if you persist. 'Grit' is a word we use for trying and not giving up. Using willpower is also part of grit. This means doing what you have to do or what is most important rather than just what you feel like doing.

The harder you work, the smarter you get.
Every time someone uses their brain to work hard (e.g. by thinking of new ideas, solving problems, practising new skills, creating new things), their brain gets 'smarter'.

Don't give up when you face a challenge, problem or obstacle.
Everyone faces some obstacles when they challenge themselves and try to achieve their goals. That's normal. Be clever or resourceful to solve problems – use other people or information to help you.

Manage your time and be organised.
If you want to succeed at something, then you need to manage your time and be organised, e.g. by making a plan with a timetable.

Think about yourself and your behaviour.
Thinking like a CHAMP means you learn to think about:
- what you are good at (your strengths)
- what you are not good at (your limitations)
- what you have learnt
- what was easy for you to do
- what was challenging and needed lots of hard work
- what you still need to learn
- how your mistakes helped you to learn. It helps to get feedback from others.

> **Learning objectives**
> In this unit, students will further develop their understanding of how to:
> - use their strengths
> - develop grit and use a growth mindset.

Resources list

A complete list of resources including references for core and additional books, films, video clips, poems, songs and websites is available.

Getting along well with others

Resources

+ Books

Look What I've Got
This is a modern morality tale. Jeremy has everything – a new bicycle, a pirate outfit and an enormous bag of lollipops. But he won't share anything with Sam and boasts about what he has. Jeremy's selfishness and unkindness have negative outcomes for getting along well with others.

One of Us
Roberta is starting at a new school and hopes to find some new friends. She investigates various groups but realises that she is different in some way to all of them. She begins to worry she might not fit in anywhere, but then finds a group who is happy to be all different.

Circle Time or classroom discussion

Prior to this topic, give each student a list of the names of all the students in the class. Then ask them to place a tick against the names of the people they know very well, a dot against the names of the people they know reasonably well, and a question mark against the names of those people they don't know well.

Begin the circle with a name game, for example, where students introduce themselves and then the person on their right and left. Then read one of the books and discuss the ways in which the character tried to get along with others. Use the **What Works and What Doesn't? e-activity** to introduce the skills of getting along well with others.

Then ask the students to imagine they are meeting someone for the first time. Write down:
- three things you could tell them about yourself
- three things you could ask this person to find out more about them.

Write some of the ideas on the board.

Then organise students in pairs, based on the 'Classmates I don't know well' data above so that they are carrying out a Partner Retell interview (see page 95) with someone they don't know well.

Steps:
1. One person interviews their partner and asks them three things to find out more about them.
2. The pairs reverse roles and the second person does the interview.
3. Each student in the circle shares one new thing to the whole class they learnt about their partner.

> **Teacher reflection**
> What importance does your school executive place on collegial relationships at your school? Are there any structures or processes that are designed to enhance these relationships? Are they effective? What approach to enhancing staff relationships have you seen or heard about being used in other schools?

Curriculum Units

Each topic has a range of cross-curricular activities using evidence-informed teaching strategies. The activities incorporate thinking tools and cooperative learning, and there are many opportunities for peer support.

Many units feature role-play and drama opportunities.

Each unit contains activities to create linkages between school and home.

Each unit has high quality educational games for cooperative learning.

Each unit includes ideas for successful implementation and sustainability of *Bounce Back!* across the whole school.

Each unit concludes by consolidating concepts, skills and key vocabulary.

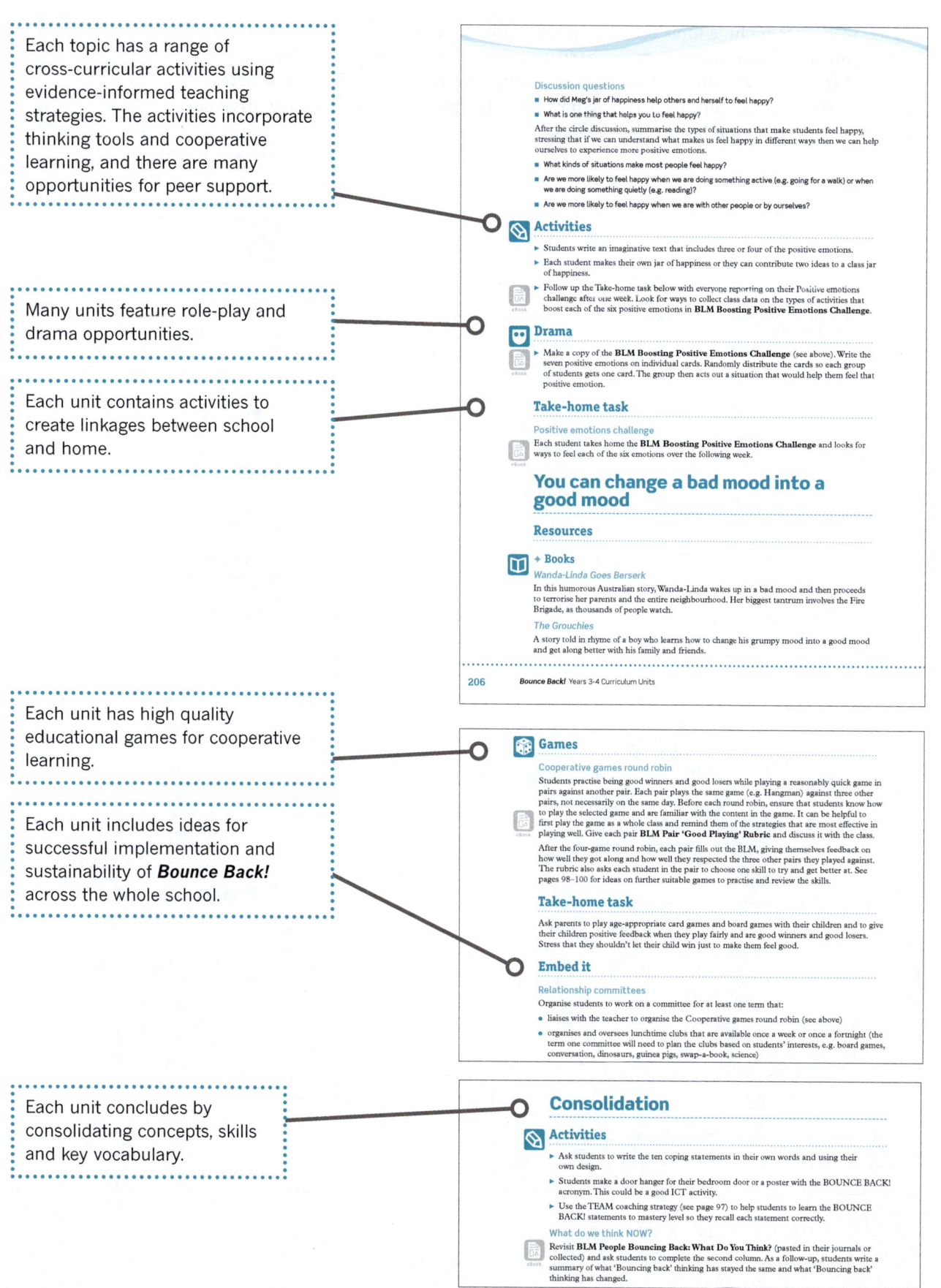

How to use Bounce Back!   ix

Digital resources

Digital resources include tools for measuring resilience and wellbeing, Curriculum correlation and Scope and sequence charts to assist with planning, an extra Science/Maths **Curriculum Unit**, tips on finding resources, an index of resources, resource lists for each unit, BLMs, teaching tools, interactive games and activities, and information on *Bounce Back!* for families.

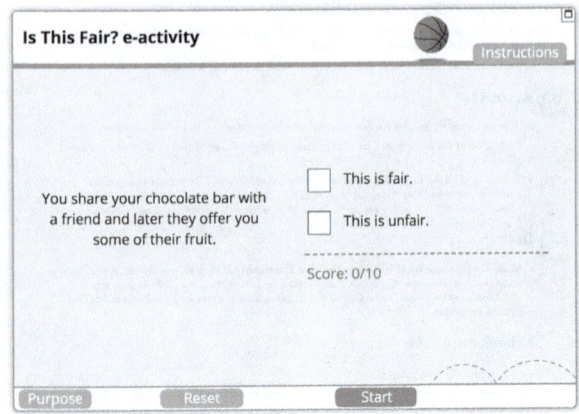

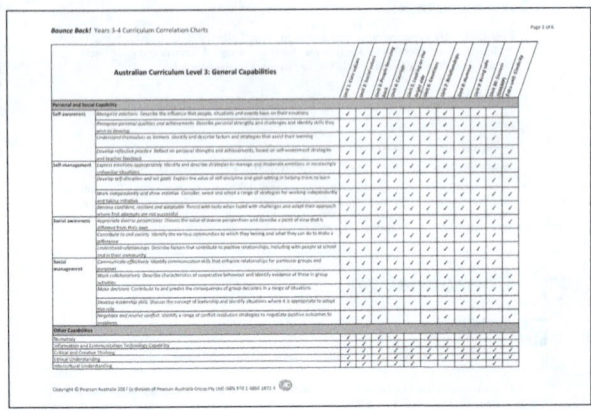

How to use Bounce Back!

CHAPTER 1

What is the Bounce Back! program?

IN THIS CHAPTER

- A review of the central role of schools in developing student wellbeing and resilience
- The history of the **Bounce Back!** program in Australia and overseas
- Details of the evidence-informed key features of the program
- The potential benefits for students in implementing the program

INTRODUCTION

Life for children and young people today can be challenging. They not only need to master the typical developmental hurdles that are part of growing up, but also manage complex and relatively new challenges, such as cyber safety, greater family mobility, higher levels of family breakdown and easier access to addictive illicit drugs and alcohol.

Global figures show that approximately 10 per cent of young people have a diagnosable mental disorder[1]. Given that approximately one-third of the world's population is under 18 years old[2] this represents over 220 million children and adolescents[1]. Over half of those who experience mental illness in childhood will also suffer from a mental illness in their adult lives[3,4]. In recognition of these challenges, student wellbeing is now an integral part of the global education agenda[5]. Governments, policymakers and educators around the world are uniting to determine how educational policy and school and classroom practices can not only help children and young people develop greater wellbeing and resilience but also thrive and lead successful and happy lives.

About Bounce Back!

The award-winning *Bounce Back!* program was developed to support schools and teachers in their efforts to promote positive mental health, wellbeing and resilience in their students. It is the world's first Positive Education curriculum program, first published in 2003, then revised in 2011. The *Bounce Back!* program has since been substantially updated and revised in this third edition.

Bounce Back! is a whole-school Social and Emotional Learning program that teaches the Social and Emotional Learning (SEL) skills advocated by CASEL (Collaborative for Academic, Social and Emotional Learning). It also includes evidence-informed coping skills identified in research studies in Positive Psychology that boost students' sense of wellbeing and help them to act resiliently when faced with challenges and adversity. *Bounce Back!* also aims to develop the optimal learning environments that help children experience joy in learning, develop positive teacher–student and peer relationships and thrive.

✦ Schools are central in developing student wellbeing and resilience

Great teachers do more than promote their students' academic learning. They teach the whole child, recognising that a focus on teaching social and emotional skills enhances students' academic outcomes as well as their capacity to form positive relationships and cope with the 'ups and downs' of their lives. Outside family life, schools are the most important social institutions for helping young people develop wellbeing and resilience.

✦ Positive Psychology and Positive Education

Positive Psychology is defined as 'the study of the conditions and processes that contribute to the flourishing or optimal functioning of people, groups, and institutions'[6]. Positive Education adopts the focus of Positive Psychology, focusing on strengths rather than deficits, on positive experiences rather than difficulties, on competency building rather than pathology and on what is going well rather than what is not working[7].

Positive Education applies the core principles of Positive Psychology in educational contexts and focuses on student resilience, wellbeing and accomplishment. *Bounce Back!* integrates the science of evidence-based practices in improving wellbeing with effective educational pedagogy and practices to help students thrive and succeed academically, socially and emotionally[8,9].

✦ Social and Emotional Learning

One of the central components of a student wellbeing program is the teaching of social and emotional skills. Social and Emotional Learning helps children and young people to understand and manage their own emotions, set and achieve positive goals, feel and show empathy for others, establish and maintain positive relationships, and make responsible decisions[10,11]. *Bounce Back!* is the most comprehensive Social and Emotional Learning program for schools globally. Acquiring these social and emotional skills and perspectives can be highly beneficial for everyday living and learning, which will continue later in life – at school, at work, in relating to others and as responsible citizens and community members.

The history of the program

✦ The first trial

The *Bounce Back!* program was first trialled in a joint research collaboration between the Drug Education section of the Department of Education in Victoria and the Faculty of Education at Deakin University[12]. Over 14 weeks, eight teachers from state, Catholic, independent, rural and urban schools implemented an early version of the program in their Year 5 or Year 6 classrooms.

All the teachers reported that the *Bounce Back!* program was user-friendly and easy to implement. And all but one of the teachers reported greater confidence in teaching the coping skills that underpin the program and expressed greater confidence in their ability to counsel and support their students. The teachers perceived that their use of the program facilitated better communication with their students, which, in turn, helped in the students' management of personal issues as well as schoolwork issues. All teachers also reported greater personal and professional resilience as a result of teaching the program. The students in the eight classes successfully learnt, understood and recalled the BOUNCE BACK! acronym (see pages 61–64).

The students achieved an average 80 per cent success rate and an increase in resilient thinking, especially optimistic and helpful thinking, when asked to solve problems in hypothetical difficult situations. In focus group interviews, many students reported using the coping skills in their own lives, including difficult family situations. Teachers also observed students spontaneously using the *Bounce Back!* statements in real-life stressful situations and in supporting their classmates and friends.

✦ The Bushfire Recovery Project

Australia is one of many countries prone to repeated natural disasters of bushfires and floods. In 2009 the state of Victoria experienced devastating bushfires with great loss of life and homes. The Bushfire Psychosocial Recovery Unit of the Victorian Department of Education and Early Childhood Development (DEECD) offered workshops on the *Bounce Back!* program for the teachers and community support staff in the seven regions most affected by these devastating fires. The goal was to develop teachers' skills in supporting their students, teaching students the skills of resilience to help them recover from the trauma that many of them had experienced, and to enhance the capacity of all students to cope with any such future disasters.

Data was collected after the implementation of *Bounce Back!* over two school terms in 18 sample schools affected by the Victorian bushfires[12]. In summary, the findings indicated that participation in the *Bounce Back!* program enhanced the capacity of many students to cope more effectively with their experiences during the bushfires and, in general, to behave more confidently, resiliently and socially.

Teachers noted that they observed students using skills or behaviours that had been taught in the program in both the classroom and playground, and that they themselves had started to incorporate the key resilience messages from the program in their own lives.

Since all children and young people experience setbacks, difficulties and failure, these findings are relevant for all schools, but such initiatives are particularly relevant for those school communities experiencing any kind of trauma.

✦ International responses
Scottish primary schools

A two-year evaluation of the implementation of *Bounce Back!* in 16 primary schools in the Perth-Kinross area in Scotland found similar benefits for both students and teachers to those obtained in the original *Bounce Back!* trial research study conducted in Australia[13,14].

The study concluded that one of the main effects of the program was enhanced student–student relationships, enhanced teacher–student relationships and increased classroom connectedness. Additionally, the Scottish study not only found an increase in student resilience and social skills but also identified a highly significant increase in teacher resilience and wellbeing as a result of their teaching the program. The results of this research were cited in the report 'After the 2012 Riots'[15] by the UK Government's Riots Communities and Victims Panel.

> The evaluation data showed increases in pupils' personal resilience, attitudes and skills in the schools where Bounce Back! had been adopted. In particular, there was a marked increase in students' awareness of control over their feelings. Pupils also commented on the positive effect of Bounce Back! on their own confidence and social skills. The Panel proposes that building character should be a central part of every school's purpose. […] it seems beyond dispute that this should be a core purpose of schools with at least as much importance as academic attainment[13,14].

This initiative was awarded a silver medal by the Perth Kinross Council for an inspired community applied project in Perth Kinross schools.

European Career Learning for at-risk college students

An adaptation of *Bounce Back!* was led by Anne Gillen, Adam Smith College, Kirkcaldy, Scotland as part of a collaborative project for European Career Learning for Lifelong Learning targeting at-risk college students in eight European countries (Austria, Belgium, Finland, Germany, The Netherlands, Poland, Scotland and Spain). The project was funded with support from the European Commission.

✦ Research with long-term users of Bounce Back!

In 2016, school leaders in 10 primary schools that had been implementing the **Bounce Back!** program for between five and 12 years were interviewed to identify the factors that have contributed to their schools' sustained implementation of the program. These factors fell into three broad categories: school factors, school system factors and program factors[16].

The school factors that were identified by the schools as being essential to their sustainability of the program were: leadership communicating that student wellbeing is a high priority for the whole school and leadership support for the implementation of the program across all year levels. The program factors that contributed to **Bounce Back!** being used in the long term in these 10 schools included: effective structure and sequence, teacher-friendly program materials and activities, and the use of quality children's literature. The teachers viewed the program as effective in teaching resilience and flexible and adaptable to different student and class needs. See the five stages for quality implementation as well as implementation tips based on these findings in Chapter 6 (see page 70).

Key features and benefits

✦ Positive impacts on academic, social and emotional functioning

In the past educators and governments have focused solely on academic achievement as a measure of student success and their country's educational standards. In 2015 for the first time in its history, the Program for International Student Assessment (PISA), the most widely cited international student achievement test, included measures of student wellbeing[17]. Why? Because strong performance on standardised academic assessments 'can only explain so much of how well students will do later in life'.

In addition, data from worldwide research has now clearly demonstrated that teaching key social and emotional skills not only enhances student wellbeing, but also improves academic learning[18-20]. A large-scale meta-analysis of SEL programs[18] based on 213 school-based, universal SEL programs involving over 270 000 students from primary school entry to Year 12 found, on average, an 11-percentile-point gain in academic achievement as well as demonstrating significant improvements in students' social and emotional skills, attitudes and behaviour within the school context.

KidsMatter

Bounce Back! was the most popular whole-school SEL program chosen by 64 per cent of the 101 schools in the Australian Government's mental health initiative called KidsMatter. The KidsMatter evaluation team identified that, over the two-year trial, there were significant and positive changes in the teachers, parents/caregivers and students in KidsMatter schools. In particular, there were statistically and practically significant improvements in students' measured mental health in terms of both reduced mental health difficulties and increased mental health strengths. The impact was especially apparent for students who were rated as having higher levels of mental health difficulties at the start of the trial[21]. The average academic results of students in 'high implementing schools' were superior (by up to six months on national assessments on literacy and numeracy) to those of students in low implementation schools. This was over and above any influence of socioeconomic background[19].

✦ A multi-component program

Many schools have several different programs to combat each new problem that emerges. For example, some schools have a social skills program, an anti-bullying program, an emotional literacy program, a behaviour management program and a character strengths program. Some principals may perceive that a greater number of programs enhances any positive effects for students but this may not always be the case. In fact, having many programs in a school may become overwhelming for school staff to execute well, leading to poor implementation[22].

Given that wellbeing and resilience are complex constructs, a comprehensive multi-component program with consistent messages, values, language, skills and understandings across the whole school has the potential to be a lot more powerful in terms of developing a positive school culture and in teaching the social-emotional skills that lead to wellbeing. One single (but multi-component) program can provide focused support for staff implementation of that program and help with communicating consistent messages to the whole school community, including families.

Bounce Back! is a multi-component program that focuses on building safe and supportive school communities as well as teaching the social, emotional and cognitive skills and understandings to help all children to thrive. The 10 *Bounce Back!* **Curriculum Units** are: Core values, Social values, People bouncing back, Courage, Looking on the bright side, Emotions, Relationships, Humour, Being safe and Success.

✦ The four SAFE elements of effective programming

Bounce Back! incorporates the four multi-strategic SAFE elements of effective SEL programming as recommended by CASEL[18,23].

- **Sequenced:** *Bounce Back!* is a sequenced program that connects and coordinates activities to foster SEL skills development from Foundation to Year 6.
- **Active:** *Bounce Back!* uses a range of active forms of learning to help students master new skills and attitudes. These include, for example, cooperative learning groups, educational games, Circle Time, the use of cooperative thinking tools, drama and the use of quality literature with literacy discussion prompts. These teaching strategies build positive peer relationships and actively engage students in learning and applying the key social and emotional skills, and messages.
- **Focused:** The key messages beginning each *Bounce Back!* unit focus teacher and student attention on the important personal and social skills and understandings in that unit.
- **Explicit:** *Bounce Back!* explicitly teaches specific social and emotional skills and critical, creative and ethical thinking skills. For example, Unit 7: Relationships includes 'dos and don'ts' lists of social skills and many activities, which provide additional opportunities for students to practise these skills.

These SAFE strategies have been found to be significantly more effective than just an 'explain and hope' model of teaching skills[18,24,25]. See the table below for an outline of the *Bounce Back!* units mapped according to the five CASEL SEL competencies.

The correlation between CASEL's *Framework for Systemic Social and Emotional Learning* and *Bounce Back!* Curriculum Units.

CASEL: Social and Emotional Core Competencies	Knowledge, skills and behaviours	Bounce Back! Curriculum Units
Self-awareness The ability to accurately recognise your own emotions, thoughts and values and understand how they influence behaviour. The ability to accurately assess one's strengths and limitations with a well-grounded sense of confidence, optimism and a 'growth mindset'.	Identifying and regulating own emotions and thoughts; skills for self-reflection	Unit 6: Emotions
	Recognising own strengths and limitations; growth mindset; meaning and purpose	Unit 10: Success
	Well-grounded self confidence	Unit 5: Looking on the bright side; Unit 6: Emotions; Unit 10: Success
	Optimistic thinking	Unit 3: People bouncing back; Unit 5: Looking on the bright side
Self-management The ability to successfully regulate one's emotions, thoughts and behaviours in different situations – effectively managing stress, controlling impulses and motivating oneself. The ability to set and work towards personal and academic goals.	Coping resiliently; using helpful and rational thinking; normalising	Unit 3: People bouncing back; Unit 5: Looking on the bright side
	Controlling impulses; courage	Unit 6: Emotions; Unit 4: Courage
	Using humour appropriately	Unit 8: Humour
	Self-motivation; self-discipline goal-setting; grit	Unit 10: Success

(Continued)

CASEL: Social and Emotional Core Competencies	Knowledge, skills and behaviours	Bounce Back! Curriculum Units
Social awareness The ability to take the perspective of and empathise with others, including those from diverse backgrounds and cultures. The ability to understand social and ethical norms for behaviour and to recognise family, school and community resources and supports.	Perspective taking; empathy	Unit 6: Emotions
	Honesty; responsibility; kindness and support for others; fairness	Unit 1: Core values; Unit 2: Social values
	Respect for others; appreciation of diversity	Unit 1: Core values; Unit 2: Social values
Relationship skills The ability to establish and maintain healthy and rewarding relationships with diverse individuals and groups. The ability to communicate clearly, listen well, cooperate with others, resist inappropriate social pressure, negotiate conflict constructively and seek and offer help when needed.	Social skills for getting along with others	Unit 7: Relationships
	Friendships	Unit 7: Relationships; Unit 8: Humour
	Resisting negative peer pressure	Unit 9: Being safe
	Conflict management	Unit 7: Relationships; Units 1–10: Relationship-building teaching strategies
Responsible decision-making The ability to make constructive choices about personal behaviour and social interactions based on ethical standards, safety concerns and social norms. The realistic evaluation of consequences of various actions, and a consideration of the wellbeing of oneself and others.	Identifying and solving problems	Units 1–10, especially Unit 3: People bouncing back and Unit 4: Courage
	Analysing situations; evaluating and reflecting	Units 1–10
	Fairness	Unit 1: Core values; Unit 2: Social values
	Ethical responsibility	Unit 1: Core values; Unit 2: Social values; Unit 9: Being safe

Source: Collaborative for Academic, Social, and Emotional Learning, 2007, http://www.casel.org/what-is-sel

✦ A whole-school approach

A whole-school program is taught to students at all year levels and involves partnerships with families and the community. A whole-school program is not just an 'add-on', but is, wherever possible, embedded in the curriculum and in the general life of the classroom and the school. When the program is embedded, the skills, concepts and understandings in the program are also linked to other curriculum areas and applied in a variety of classroom and playground contexts. Chapter 6 includes guidelines on effective schoolwide implementation of the program (see page 68).

Positive school culture and climate

Just as important as teaching the skills for wellbeing and resilience is creating and maintaining a supportive and inclusive school culture where every student feels welcomed both as a learner and as a valued peer. A whole-school program, like **Bounce Back!**, that communicates the same key wellbeing and resilience messages in age appropriate ways across the school, is more effective in developing a positive school climate and culture than a program for one or two year levels only[14,26]. A positive school climate and culture has also been shown to be significantly related to improved outcomes for students such as stronger motivation to achieve and better academic results, increased prosocial behaviour, and higher school connectedness[27,28].

Teacher wellbeing

Various international studies have shown that up to one-third of teachers are stressed or extremely stressed[29]. A Canadian study found that in elementary classrooms where teachers reported more burnout or feelings of emotional exhaustion, students had elevated cortisol levels. Higher student cortisol levels are linked to learning difficulties as well as mental health problems[30]. Teaching a SEL program has been found to lead to greater job satisfaction and higher levels of teacher efficacy and teacher wellbeing[28,29]. The *Bounce Back!* program has been found to have a significant impact on improving teacher wellbeing[14] and on teachers' perceptions of an increase in their own professional and personal resilience[12].

Education and support from home

Great importance in education is now placed on effective family–school partnerships to facilitate SEL so children use these skills at home as well as at school[31]. Implementing *Bounce Back!* as a whole-school program makes it easier to communicate the key messages to the whole school community, including families[14,16]. Home communication can be achieved through school newsletters, assembly items, school concerts and performances, student talks to families and so on[16,32]. **Information for families** and take-home information is provided, and each unit also includes homework tasks, such as interviews, which are designed for students to communicate the *Bounce Back!* messages to their families.

✦ A universal program

Bounce Back! is a universal program which means it is taught to all students, not just children identified as 'at-risk' for behaviour problems or mental health difficulties. It is designed to be delivered to all students from the first to the last year of primary school[23,33,34].

✦ Taught by class teachers

Academic improvement, as well as social and emotional improvement, is more likely when teachers (rather than external professionals) implement a SEL program[18,35]. Based on their knowledge of their students' needs, the classroom teacher is able to provide targeted support. For example, a teacher can teach the whole class about managing 'their worries' which benefits all students but may be especially relevant for highly anxious students. Teachers are also able to utilise 'teachable moments' (e.g. after a bullying incident) that can provide a real-world opportunity to teach or reinforce the program's relevant skills and values to encourage students to apply these skills in context[16].

✦ Long term and multi-year

Multi-year programs are more likely to produce enduring benefits and are more sustainable, especially when taught across all year levels as a whole-school program[32,33,36,37]. *Bounce Back!* is taught from the first year of school and then every year throughout primary school with age/developmentally appropriate activities. The 10 **Curriculum Units** are introduced in Years F–2 and then repeated in Years 3–4 and Years 5–6. This means that the key wellbeing and resilience concepts, skills and understandings in the 10 units are repeated with an age-appropriate curriculum, so that students develop a deep understanding of these concepts and therefore can apply them in their lives.

✦ Delivered to students early in their schooling

Most reviews of preventative research stress that programs that start when students are very young are more likely to be effective[32,38,39]. Indeed, by the end of primary school, students develop the habit of thinking optimistically or pessimistically[40]. The implications are that the earlier children learn the skills of thinking, feeling and behaving optimistically, the better for their ongoing mental health and wellbeing. *Bounce Back!* is designed to teach children good habits of thinking, feeling and behaving socially and emotionally from the first years of school with the aim of inoculating children against mental illness. Ideally the program should be taught from the first years of school, but there are always benefits of introducing the program at any age level.

✦ Evidence-informed psychological principles

The two main models of Psychology that underpin the *Bounce Back!* program are Positive Psychology and Cognitive Behaviour Therapy (CBT).

Positive Psychology

In 2011, the founder of Positive Psychology, Martin Seligman, challenged policy makers to develop a new measure of 'prosperity', beginning early in life:

> The time has come for a new prosperity, one that takes flourishing seriously as the goal for education and of parenting. Learning to value

and to attain flourishing must start early – in the formative years of schooling – and it is this new prosperity, kindled by positive education, that the world can now choose.[7] (p.97).

Seligman defines wellbeing in terms of five elements: **P**ositive Emotions, **E**ngagement, **R**elationships, **M**eaning and **A**ccomplishment (PERMA).

The verb 'to prosper' means to thrive, to flourish, to succeed in a healthy way and grow strong. The acronym PROSPER stands for the Science-based wellbeing components of **P**ositivity, **R**elationships, **O**utcomes, **S**trengths, **P**urpose, **E**ngagement and **R**esilience[8]. PROSPER is not a curriculum but a framework that offers schools coherence and a common language for their selection and implementation of a range of evidence-based structures and practices derived from Positive Education/Positive Psychology. These practices are linked to encouraging positivity, building relationships, facilitating outcomes and an optimal learning environment, focusing on strengths, fostering a sense of purpose, enhancing engagement and teaching resilience. *Bounce Back!* is a curriculum for student wellbeing, not a framework. The *Bounce Back!* curriculum incorporates all these PERMA and PROSPER elements.

Cognitive Behaviour Therapy (CBT)

There is more research support for the efficacy of CBT in changing feelings and behaviour than there is for any other type of therapy[41]. Originally developed by psychiatrist Aaron Beck[42], CBT is based on the understanding that 'how you think affects how you feel which in turn influences how you behave'. The key message is that by changing a person's thinking from irrational to rational and more positive thinking, they can change their behaviour and feel happier. Two specific refinements of the basic model of CBT have particularly influenced the content of *Bounce Back!* These are Albert Ellis's Rational Emotive Behaviour Therapy (REBT)[43] and Martin Seligman's Learned Optimism[44]. The 'coathanger' of the *Bounce Back!* program is the BOUNCE BACK! acronym (see page 61), which incorporates the 10 key CBT coping statements[23].

✦ Evidence-informed teaching strategies

The learning environment is a key to student success at school. Therefore, the use of effective teaching strategies in a SEL program enhances student engagement and interest while also increasing their achievement. The teaching strategies embedded in *Bounce Back!* have been informed by large scale meta-analyses of effective teaching and learning research by Hattie[45] and Marzano[46]. According to Hattie, teacher effectiveness is 'less about the content of the curricula and more about the strategies teachers use to implement the curriculum so that students progress upwards through the curricula content'[45].

Effective teaching strategies motivate and challenge students through the provision of high performance standards, opportunities for formative assessment and by providing tasks that promote higher order thinking. *Bounce Back!* includes the following high impact evidence-informed teaching strategies.

Cooperative learning

Working cooperatively helps create a sense of belonging in the classroom. The most frequently used teaching strategies in *Bounce Back!* are cooperative learning strategies that have extensive evidence[45-48] for achieving positive outcomes, such as:

- higher levels of academic outcomes
- higher levels of class engagement
- the building of positive relationships
- enhanced class cohesion
- more effective social and emotional skills.

Students learn more about social skills such as taking turns, negotiating, reaching consensus and developing positive respectful relationships when cooperative learning is used well. It also enhances literacy outcomes as students are actively engaged in social dialogue that encourages deeper understanding and promotes different perspectives and a range of acceptable responses. Teaching strategies and resources, and the **Curriculum Units** in *Bounce Back!* provide step-by-step instructions for implementing many cooperative learning structures.

Thinking tools

Giving students a challenging task that is designed to foster critical and creative thinking skills doesn't mean they will actually use these thinking skills. A student is more likely to persist at a task that is intellectually challenging if they find the task intrinsically interesting. **Bounce Back!** includes many topics that are relevant to young people today. It also includes thinking strategies that encourage students to consider different perspectives and different values on important social justice and life issues, as well as how to reach a group consensus. Many of the activities are open-ended and encourage students to develop skills in solving problems, making decisions and thinking critically, creatively, ethically and empathically. These thinking and social and emotional skills are important to employers and are crucial to coping with the complexity of life. Thinking tools from McGrath & Noble[49] are outlined in Teaching strategies and resources and are included in the **Curriculum Unit** topics depending on their relevance to the year level:

- Under the Microscope
- Ten Thinking Tracks
- Cooperative Controversy
- Multiply and Merge
- BRAIN
- PACE
- Socratic Circles
- Multiview.

Circle Time

Like cooperative learning, Circle Time builds positive relationships and a sense of classroom community, while also teaching social and emotional skills[50,51]. Circle Time is used in all 10 **Bounce Back!** units to introduce key concepts and facilitate whole-class and small-group discussions and activities. Each Circle Time discussion is followed up with individual or small-group activities that provide opportunities for students to apply the concepts in a meaningful way. See Teaching strategies and resources for more information.

High quality educational games

Games can be effective in improving student engagement and learning outcomes, as well as creating classroom energy and a sense of fun[52]. Redefining an aspect of schoolwork (e.g. revision) as a game has been found to sustain students' attention longer and makes it more likely that they are willing to 'have a go' at intellectually challenging content[53]. The rules and procedures that are a core part of any game provide both structure and limits, and make it more likely that students will behave more socially and less aggressively when playing educational games[27]. Most of the games in **Bounce Back!** require students to play in either pairs or in a small group against another pair or small group. Students then practise social skills such as being a good winner and loser, negotiating with their partner, taking turns and using perspective. Playing cooperatively also provides opportunities for practising organisational skills (e.g. recording data and time management), language skills, hypothesis testing and strategic problem-solving. Cooperative games can provide a natural setting in which to conduct assessments of the social and emotional skills of specific students. This can be the basis for further more-focused direct teaching of specific social skills in small group contexts.

Peer support

In **Bounce Back!** many activities involve older students working directly or indirectly with younger students. These activities are usually based on educational games, literacy activities or a specific children's picture book. For example, older students are encouraged to assist with creating digital stories on themes such as courage, bouncing back after a setback, and so on. Older students also gain a deeper understanding of wellbeing concepts when they teach and work with younger children. Those students who need a boost in self-confidence particularly benefit because they can feel more knowledgeable than the younger student. This can boost confidence in their own skills and abilities while also helping them relate positively to others[54]. They also gain a sense of meaning and purpose through helping someone else. This cross-age contact can be based on:

- direct classroom visits to run a game, make a craft activity or work with a buddy
- lesson preparation, or products for younger students
- using technology to develop a product to teach wellbeing concepts that may include sound, video clips, images, digital storytelling, animation, and so on.

✦ Designed to be integrated with other curriculum areas

Integrating social and emotional learning with academic content has been shown to increase program effectiveness[35]. The content of *Bounce Back!* has been developed so that it can effectively be integrated with other curriculum areas (and their key learning outcomes), such as English, Health and Physical Education, Technologies, Humanities and Social Sciences, Science, Mathematics, Religious Education and The Arts.

Where possible, links are made between aspects of social and emotional learning and common topics that are often covered in primary school. For example, concepts such as courage, persistence and dealing with setbacks can be addressed through age-appropriate literature and through the topics of explorers, inventors, those who have stood against injustice and researchers who have made great breakthroughs in Science and Medicine.

English and children's literature

The use of high-quality children's literature in *Bounce Back!* is perceived by teachers as a stand out strength of the program, as shown in two research studies (see pages 2–3 for more detail). Teachers' comments confirmed that the use of quality literature made the program easy to teach and helped them to feel more confident about teaching their students about wellbeing and resilience[16,55].

The books, films and videos used in *Bounce Back!* can be used in a range of ways:

- to introduce a key topic (e.g. being brave)
- to enable students to engage with and discuss key real life issues (e.g. friendships, kindness) in a safe and comfortable way
- to encourage students to discuss a problem that is linked to a book's character without owning that problem
- a teacher can choose a book to use with the whole class that has particular relevance for one student or a group, but do so without specifically focusing on that individual or group
- to help 'normalise' a situation such as loneliness and help a student see that they are not the first or the only person to encounter such a problem

- to encourage students to feel and express empathy for a character in a specific situation which can enhance their empathy for 'real people' in a similar situation
- to prompt self-reflection and insight
- a character can be used as a positive model when they display a prosocial value such as kindness, solve a relationship problem through a social skill such as negotiation, or get on top of a situation by using an emotional skill such as managing their anger or being courageous.

An age-appropriate critical literacy approach is adopted through discussion questions and activities. Literature prompts and wellbeing prompts that specifically focus students' attention on the social and emotional aspects of a book, film, video or poem are provided in Teaching strategies and resources (e.g. Who was the most optimistic character? Who was courageous and what risks did they take?).

Detailed Resources lists (both core and supplementary) of books, films, poems, songs and websites are available at the start of each **Curriculum Unit**.

The Arts: Drama, Music, Visual Arts

Most **Curriculum Units** in *Bounce Back!* include opportunities for students to demonstrate their understanding of wellbeing concepts through drawing, painting, constructing, modelling, singing or drama activities. These activities are developmentally appropriate and meet various outcomes for The Arts at different levels.

Music is reported to be one of the most powerful means for inducing powerful positive emotions irrespective of culture, age or time[56]. Class singing is encouraged in *Bounce Back!* as there is now substantial research to indicate that group singing enhances positive mood and attention as well as social connection and cohesiveness[56]. Many of the key SEL concepts and wellbeing and resilience messages have been incorporated into songs for Years F–4 and are available online. Regularly singing the *Bounce Back!* songs allows students to revisit the key wellbeing messages many times. This repetition makes it more likely that students will then transfer this learning to their real-life experiences and remember them in difficult situations. In Years 5–6, students are also encouraged to go 'song hunting' and bring to school songs that they believe are consistent with a key message related to wellbeing and resilience.

Health and Physical Education

Bounce Back! addresses outcomes from the Health and Physical Education (HPE) curriculum. The HPE curriculum has a strong focus on students' social and emotional development so they learn to work and play effectively with others, to understand and value diversity, to manage change and to negotiate roles and responsibilities with their teachers and peers.

Technologies

Each ***Bounce Back!*** unit includes ideas on how students might use digital technology, such as slide shows, podcasts, photographic displays, narrated photo essays, digital storytelling and book trailers, short movies, animation, visual records of their learning products, topic-related internet research and creating their own music.

Other curriculum areas

Activities in each curriculum unit also draw on Humanities and Social Sciences, Science and Maths. The Elasticity unit (available digitally) in particular relates to Science and Maths.

✦ A range of assessment tools

The evaluation of any SEL program is essential in the implementation research to ascertain what's working and what's not[11]. Documenting progress in students' understanding of the key ***Bounce Back!*** messages is not only critical to their own self-knowledge and self-management but is also important for teacher feedback. Documenting progress also creates opportunities to share outcomes with the whole school community and gain system support. ***Bounce Back!*** recommends both formative and summative assessment. The topics provide teachers with day-to-day formative assessment on students' readiness for learning specific social and emotional learning skills, their strengths and interests and their approaches to learning. A range of assessment tools for summative assessment which can be used as pre- and post-intervention measures of change in student wellbeing and resilience is also included. See Chapter 6 for more information about these assessment tools for measuring wellbeing and resilience (see page 68).

Expected outcomes

Expected short-term and long-term outcomes from *Bounce Back!*

Expected short-term outcomes	Expected long-term outcomes
• Knowledge and understanding of social and emotional skills • More positive attitudes (e.g. to self, others, learning and school) • Enhanced learning environment: classroom becomes more safe, supportive, respectful and engaging	• Enhanced social behaviour • More-positive, respectful peer relationships • More-positive school climate • More-resilient behaviour • Less emotional distress • Fewer conduct problems • Improved academic performance • Higher levels of teacher wellbeing and resilience • More-effective teacher counselling/support for students

REFERENCES

1. World Health Organization (WHO), 2003, *Caring for children and adolescent with mental disorders: Setting WHO directions*, World Health Organization, Geneva.
2. UNICEF, 2014, 'The state of the world's children 2014 in numbers', available from www.unicef.org/sowc2014/numbers.
3. Kim-Cohen, J., Caspi, A., Moffitt, T.E., Harrington, H., Milne, B.J. & Poulton, R. 2003, 'Prior juvenile diagnoses in adults with mental disorder: Developmental follow-back of a prospective-longitudinal cohort', *Archives of General Psychiatry*, 60, pp. 709–717.
4. Layard, R. & Hagell, A. 2015, 'Healthy Young Minds: Transforming the Mental Health of Children', in *World Happiness Report 2015*, J.H. Helliwell, R. Layard & J. Sachs. (eds), Sustainable Development Solutions Network, New York
5. https://www.oecd.org/australia/Better-Life-Initiative-country-note-Australia.pdf
6. Gable, S.J. & Haidt, J. 2005, 'What (and why) is positive psychology?', *Review of General Psychology*, 9(2): pp. 103–110.
7. Seligman, M.E.P. & Csikszentmihalyi, M. (eds) 2000, 'Positive Psychology – An Introduction', *American Psychologist*, 55, pp. 5–14.
8. Noble, T. & McGrath, H., 2015, 'PROSPER: A New Framework for Positive Education', *Psychology of Well-Being: Theory, Research and Practice*, 5:2
9. Noble, T. & McGrath, H. 2016, 'PROSPER for Student Wellbeing: Pathways and Policy', *Springer Brief*, The Netherlands.
10. Zins, J.E., Bloodworth, M.R., Weissberg, R.P. & Walberg, H.J. 2004, 'The scientific base linking social and emotional learning to school success', in *Building academic success on social and emotional learning*, J.E. Zins, R.P. Weissberg, M.C. Wang & H.J. Walberg (eds), Teachers College Press, New York.
11. Weissberg, R.P., Durlak, J.A., Domitrovich, C. & Gullotta, T.P. 2015, 'Social and Emotional Learning: Past, Present, and Future', in R.P. Weissberg, J.A. Durlak, C.E. Domitrovich, & T.P. Gullotta (eds), *Handbook of Social and Emotional Learning: Research and Practice*, Guilford Press, New York.
12. McGrath, H. & Anders E. 2000, 'The Bounce Back! Program', *Turning the Tide in Schools Drug Education Project*, Victorian Department of Education.
13. Axford, S., Blyth, K. & Schepens, R. 2010, 'A Study of the Impact of the Bounce Back Programme on Resilience, Wellbeing and Connectedness of Children and Teachers in Sixteen Primary Schools in Perth and Kinross, Scotland, Midpoint Report', Perth and Kinross Council, Scotland.
14. Axford, S., Schepens, R. & Blyth, K. 2011, 'Did introducing the Bounce Back Programme have an impact on resilience, connectedness and wellbeing of children and teachers in 16 primary schools in Perth and Kinross, Scotland?', *Educational Psychology*, 12 (1): pp. 2–5.
15. 'After the Riots 2012, The Final Report of the Riots Communities and Victims Panel', UK Government: http://riotspanel.independent.gov.uk/wp-content/uploads/2012/03/Riots-Panel-Final-Report1.pdf
16. Noble, T. & McGrath, H. 2017, 'Making it real and making it last! Sustainability of teacher implementation of a whole school resilience program', in *Resilience in Education: Concepts, Contexts and Connections*, Wosnitza, M., Peixoto, F., Beltman, S., & Mansfield, C.F. (eds.), Springer, New York.
17. Borgonovi, F. and Pál, J. 2016, 'A Framework for the Analysis of Student Well-Being in the PISA 2015 Study: Being 15 in 2015', *OECD Education Working Papers*, No. 140, OECD Publishing, Paris: http://dx.doi.org/10.1787/5jlpszwghvvb-en.
18. Durlak, J.A., Weissberg, R.P., Dymnicki, A.B., Taylor, R.D. and Schellinger, K.B. 2011, 'The Impact of Enhancing Students' Social and Emotional Learning: A Meta-Analysis of School-Based Universal Interventions', *Child Development*, 82, 1, pp. 405-432.
19. Dix, K., Slee, P.T., Lawson, M.J., Keeves, J.P. 2012, 'Implementation quality of whole-school mental health promotion and students' academic performance', *Child and Adolescence Mental Health*, 17(1): pp. 45–51.
20. Diekstra, R.F.W. & Gravesteijn, C. 2008, 'Effectiveness of School-based Social and Emotional Education Programmes Worldwide'.
21. Dix, K.L., et al. 2009, 'KidsMatter Evaluation Executive Summary', beyondblue, downloaded 7/1/10 from www.kidsmatter.edu.au/wp/wp-content/uploads/2009/10/kidsmatter-executive-summary.
22. Bradshaw, C. 2015, 'Translating Research to Practice in Bullying Prevention', *American Psychologist*, 70(4): pp. 322-33.
23. Collaborative for Academic, Social and Emotional Learning, 2007 [cited 18/1/10], available from www.casel.org.
24. McGrath, H. & Noble, T. 2011, *BOUNCE BACK! A Wellbeing & Resilience Program, Lower Primary K-2; Middle Primary: Yrs 3-4; Upper Primary/Junior Secondary: Yrs 5-8*, Pearson Education, Melbourne.
25. McGrath, H., & Francey, S. 1991, *Friendly Kids, Friendly Classrooms*, Pearson Education, Melbourne.
26. Wells, J., Barlow, J. & Stewart-Brown, S. 2002, 'A systematic review of universal approaches to mental health promotion in schools', Health Services Research Unit, Oxford.
27. Garaigardobil, M., Magento, C. & Etxeberria, J. 1996, 'Effects of a co-operative game program on socio-affective relations and group cooperation capacity', *European Journal of Psychological Assessment*, 12: pp. 141–152.
28. O'Malley, M., Katz, K., Renshaw, T. & Furlong, M. 2012, 'Gauging the system: Trends in school climate measurement and intervention', in *The Handbook of School Violence and School Safety: International Research and Practice* (2nd edn), S. Jimerson, A. Nickerson, M. Mayer & M. Furlong (eds), Routledge, New York, pp. 317–329.
29. Collie, R.J., Shapka, J.D., & Perry, N.E., 2012, 'School Climate and Social–Emotional Learning: Predicting Teacher Stress, Job Satisfaction, and Teaching Efficacy', *Journal of Educational Psychology*, 104, (4), 1189–1204 0022-0663/12 DOI: 10.1037/a0029356.
30. Oberle, E. & Schonert-Reichl, K.A., 2016, 'Stress contagion in the classroom? The link between classroom teacher burnout and morning cortisol in elementary school students', *Social Science & Medicine*, 159: pp. 30–37.
31. Garbacz, S.A., Swanger-Gagne, M.S. & Sheridan, S.M. 2015, 'The role of school-family partnership programs for promoting student SEL', in *Handbook of Social and Emotional Learning. Research and Practice*, Durlak, J.A., Domitrovich, C.E., Weissberg, R.P., & Gullota, T.P. 2015, The Guilford Press, New York.
32. Greenberg, M., et al. 2003, 'Enhancing school-based prevention and youth development through coordinated social, emotional, and academic learning', *American Psychologist*, vol. 58, pp. 466–474.

33. Greenberg, M.T., Domitrovich, C. & Bumbarger, B. 2001, 'Preventing mental disorders in school-age children: a review of the effectiveness of prevention programs', Center for Mental Health Services (CMHS), Substance Abuse Mental Health Services Administration, US Department of Health and Human Services.
34. 'Effective school health promotion: Towards health promoting schools', 1996, The National Health and Medical Research Council's Health Advancement Committee.
35. Weissberg, R.P. & O'Brien, M.U. 2004, 'What works in school-based social and emotional learning programs for positive youth development', *The Annals of the American Academy of Political and Social Science*, vol. 591, pp. 86–97.
36. Wells, J., Barlow, J. & Stewart-Brown S. 2003, 'A systematic review of the universal approaches to mental health promotion in schools', *Health Education*, vol. 103, no. 4, pp. 197–220.
37. CPPRG, 1999, 'Initial impact of the fast track prevention trial for conduct problems: 11 classroom effects', *Journal of Consulting and Clinical Psychology*, vol. 67, pp. 648–657.
38. O'Shaughnessy, T.E., et al. 2002, 'Students with or at risk for emotional-behavioral difficulties', in *Interventions for children with or at risk for emotional and behavioral disorders*, Lane, K.L., Gresham, F.M. & O'Shaughnessy, T.E. (eds), Allyn & Bacon, Boston.
39. Severson, H.H. & Walker, H.M. 2002, 'Proactive approaches for identifying children at risk for sociobehavioral problems' in *Interventions for children with or at risk for emotional and behavioral disorders*, K.L. Lane, F.M. Gresham & T.E. O'Shaughnessy (eds), Allyn & Bacon, Boston.
40. Reivich, K. 2005, 'Optimism lecture' in *Authentic Happiness Coaching*, University of Pennsylvania.
41. Andrews, G., Szabó, M. & Burns, J. 2001, 'Avertable Risk Factors for Depression', beyondblue, the Australian National Depression Initiative.
42. Beck, A.T. 1979, *Cognitive Therapy and the Emotional Disorders*, Penguin Books, New York.
43. Ellis, A. & Harper, R. 2008, *A New Guide to Rational Living* (3rd edn), Wilshire Book Company.
44. Seligman, M.E.P. 1995, *The Optimistic Child*, Random House, Sydney, www.unsdsn.org/happiness.
45. Hattie, J. 2009, 'Visible Learning: A Synthesis of Over 800 Meta-analyses Relating to Achievement', Routledge, London. Direct quote, 20 words.
46. Marzano, R.J., Pickering, D.J., & Pollock, J.E. 2001, 'Classroom instruction that works: Research-based strategies for increasing student achievement', Alexandria, VA: Association for Supervision and Curriculum Development.
47. Johnson, D. & Johnson, R. 2009, 'An Educational Psychology Success Story: Social Interdependence Theory & Cooperative Learning', Educational Researcher, 38; 365. http://er.aera.net
48. Roseth, C.J., Johnson, D.W. & Johnson, R.T. 2008, 'Promoting early adolescents' achievement and peer relationships: The effects of cooperative, competitive and individualistic goal structures', *Psychological Bulletin*, vol. 134, no. 2, pp. 223–246.
49. McGrath, H. & Noble, T. 2010, *HITS and HOTS, Teaching + Thinking + Social Skills*, Pearson Education, Melbourne.
50. McCarthy, F.E. 2009, 'Circle Time Solutions. Creating Caring School Communities', Report for the NSW Department of Education and Training.
51. Roffey, S. 2014, *Circle Time for Student Wellbeing*, Sage Publications, London.
52. Marzano, R.J. 2007, *The Art & Science of Teaching: A Comprehensive Framework for Effective Instruction*, Association for Supervision and Curriculum Development, Alexandria, Virginia.
53. Dweck, C.S. 2006, *Mindset, The New Psychology of Success*, Random House, New York.
54. Stanley, M. & McGrath, H. 2006, 'Buddy systems: Peer support in action', in *Bullying Solutions. Evidence-based approaches for Australian schools*, H. McGrath & T. Noble (eds), Pearson Education, Sydney.
55. McGrath, H. & Noble, T. 2011b, 'Report of the Evaluation of the Impact of Training Teachers in Bushfire-affected Schools to Use the Bounce Back Classroom Resilience Program in their Classrooms', Victorian Department of Education and Early Childhood.
56. Rickard, N.S., 2014, 'Editorial for Music and Wellbeing Special Issue', *Psychology of Well-Being: Theory, Research and Practice*, 4:26, www.psywb.com/content/4/1/26.

CHAPTER 2

The Bounce Back! curriculum

IN THIS CHAPTER

- A detailed summary of the 10 *Bounce Back!* Curriculum Units for Years F–2, Years 3–4 and Years 5–6: Core values, Social values, People bouncing back, Courage, Looking on the bright side, Emotions, Relationships, Humour, Being safe, and Success plus a summary of an extra unit: Elasticity (available digitally)

INTRODUCTION

There are three levels in the *Bounce Back!* program:

1 Years F–2, which is suitable for students in the first three years of primary schooling, i.e. students aged approximately five to seven

2 Years 3–4, which is suitable for middle primary students, i.e. students aged approximately eight to 10

3 Years 5–6, which is suitable for upper primary students, i.e. students aged approximately 11 to 12.

Each year level includes:

- a **Handbook**, which outlines the theory, rationale and evidence-based research that underpins *Bounce Back!* and how to implement and sustain the program
- **Curriculum Units** based on evidence-informed research in Positive Psychology/Positive Education, social and educational psychology and Social and Emotional Learning (SEL).

Curriculum Units

The 10 **Bounce Back! Curriculum Units** are:

1. Core values
2. Social values
3. People bouncing back
4. Courage
5. Looking on the bright side
6. Emotions
7. Relationships
8. Humour
9. Being safe
10. Success (STAR! for Years F–2, CHAMP! for Years 3–4 and WINNERS! for Years 5–6).

There is also an extra Science unit, called Elasticity, which is available digitally.

Unit 1: Core values and Unit 2: Social values

> No act of kindness, no matter how small, is ever wasted. (Aesop)

Our values are at the heart of who we are and what we do. When students' behaviour is guided by prosocial values such as being friendly and inclusive, respectful and supportive of others, compassionate and kind they are more likely to develop positive and satisfying relationships with their teachers and their peers. When students' behaviour is guided by core values such as honesty, fairness, responsibility and acceptance of difference they act with integrity. Students acting according to these social and core values are more likely to experience better mental and physical health, improved learning outcomes and more successful relationships as adults[1-3].

✦ What are values?

Values are the relatively stable, pervasive and enduring beliefs that each person holds about what is right and wrong and what's most important in life. They form the basis of how we see ourselves as individuals, how we see others and how we interpret the world in general. Our values form the 'moral map' that guides our behaviour and choices.

In education there is increasing interest in values as well as the concept of character, and the strategies that schools can adopt to develop students' values or character. The different disciplines of Positive Education, social and emotional learning and character education all focus on the importance of 'good character' and the core values that underpin the concept. The terms 'character', 'character strengths', 'values', 'virtues' and 'ethical understanding' as behavioural expectations are often used interchangeably in the literature which can be confusing. In **Bounce Back!** the terminology has been simplified by consistently using the term 'core values' for a student's beliefs about right and wrong and what's important in life, and the term 'social values' for the values that underpin the way students treat others. **Bounce Back!** uses the term 'character strengths' for personal strengths such as courage.

✦ Teaching values

When damaging riots occurred across the UK in 2011, a call went out for character building in schools. David Cameron, the British prime minister at the time, claimed that the riots were caused by people 'showing indifference to right and wrong' and indicated that schools could be part of the solution to counter the 'slow-motion moral collapse'[3]. The positive impact of **Bounce Back!** on student social and emotional wellbeing and character in schools in Scotland, UK, is cited in the government report on the UK riots as a possible solution. The panel proposed that 'building character should be a central part of every school's purpose'[4].

A major study on values/character was conducted by the United Kingdom Jubilee Centre for Character and Virtues involving 68 schools, 255 teachers and more than 10 000 students[3]. The study focused on diverse schools – including state and independent, faith and non-faith, large and small, rural and urban – and assessed students' measured capacity for moral reasoning. Its conclusion was that any kind of school can nurture good character with the right approach. The high performing schools had a strong commitment to developing the whole child, made 'moral teaching' a high priority, allocated class time to discuss moral issues and had at least one teacher who was knowledgeable and passionate about building student character. Ninety-one per cent of the high performing schools said they could rely on parents to develop good character in their children compared to 52 per cent of the teachers in the lowest performing schools. The study highlighted the important role of family–school partnerships in a social and emotional learning initiative.

Promoting specific core values across the whole school is the key feature of the highly successful model of School-wide Positive Behaviour Support (SWPBS), also called Positive Behaviour for Learning (PBL)[5,6]. It was also the key feature of the Australian Values Education Good Practice Schools Projects, which looked at different projects ranging from using values-focused pedagogies to education fostering intercultural understanding, social cohesion and inclusion[7].

In both studies the researchers found that students' prosocial behaviour and connectedness to school is significantly improved when a school's shared values are explicitly articulated, explicitly taught, modelled by staff and embedded in the mainstream life of the school. Teachers consciously create many opportunities for students to practise and be rewarded when they are observed putting their school's values into action. Typically, each SWPBS/PBL school chooses three to five core values that become whole-school behavioural expectations. An example is the value of 'respect' which can then become behavioural expectations such as 'respect yourself, respect others, respect property'.

'Being respectful to others' means treating others fairly, regardless of differences, and not putting others down. Respectful relationships can be defined as regular and ongoing social interactions in which each person feels valued, accepted, included, supported and physically and emotionally safe. It also means being treated with respect by teachers and peers, a factor essential to students' wellbeing, sense of safety and trust in relationships. Such relationships contribute to a positive school climate where students feel connected to their peers, teachers and school. The SWPBS guidelines highlight the importance of at least 80 per cent of the staff making a commitment to the school's chosen core values in order to ensure there is consistency in implementation from class to class[8]. To facilitate consistency across the school, it is suggested that each school develops an 'expectations matrix' of what their school's values mean in terms of student behaviour in all classes and non-classroom areas.

The Social values unit has a strong focus on kindness. Kindness counts – encouraging children to be kind to others has benefits for the giver, not just the recipient. In a study conducted in 19 classrooms in Vancouver, nine to 11 year olds were asked to perform three acts of kindness for anyone they wished (e.g. gave someone part of my lunch, gave mum a hug when she was stressed by her job, did the vacuuming) versus visit any three places they wished (e.g. visit grandma, the mall etc.) per week over the course of four weeks. Students in both conditions improved in wellbeing but the students who performed kind acts experienced significantly better peer acceptance than students who simply visited places[9]. The children's acts of kindness were often performed at home but appeared to have a spin-off effect in increasing the children's sense of wellbeing which in turn increased their popularity at school. Increasing peer acceptance is related to a variety of important academic and social outcomes, including being less likely to be bullied. This research highlights the importance of intentionally building into the curriculum the prosocial activities that are in the two 'values' units both regularly and purposefully.

Unit 1: Core values and Unit 2: Social values teach the following universal values through literature, media stories, video clips, drama and role-plays, writing, drawing and speaking activities and opportunities for students to engage in classroom and school community activities that provide service to others. Many of the activities promote ethical and intercultural understanding. Through this rich range of age/year-level activities both 'values' units will help teachers support a whole-school approach to Positive Education/positive behaviour management, create a positive school climate and enhance student wellbeing.

Bounce Back! core values

- **Acceptance of differences:** recognise the right of others to be different; do not exclude or mistreat others because they are different; act on the inclusive belief that diversity is to be celebrated and other people are fundamentally good.
- **Honesty:** tell the truth, play by the rules and own up to things you have done.
- **Fairness:** focus on equity and address injustices.
- **Responsibility:** act in ways that honour promises and commitments; look after the wellbeing of those less able.

Bounce Back! social values

- **Kindness and Compassion:** care about the wellbeing of others and offer/show support where needed.
- **Cooperation:** work together to achieve a shared goal; cooperation also includes cooperating for world peace and for the protection of our environment.
- **Respect for others:** act towards others in ways that respect their rights; for example, to have dignity, to have feelings considered, to be safe and to be treated fairly.
- **Self-respect:** accept one's self and develop a well-grounded sense of one's own character and behaviour.
- **Friendliness and inclusion:** act towards others in an inclusive and kind way; actively reach out to others in friendship.

Unit 3: People bouncing back

Our greatest glory is not in 'never falling', but in rising every time we fall. (Confucius)

This unit introduces the concept of human resilience, or the capacity of people to 'bounce back' after experiencing difficulties or challenges. In Years F–2, students are introduced to the BOUNCE! acronym:

- **B**ad feelings always go away again.
- **O**ther people can help you feel better if you talk to them.
- **U**nhelpful thinking makes you feel more upset. Think again.
- **N**obody's perfect – not you and not others.
- **C**oncentrate on the things that are still good when things go wrong.
- **E**verybody has unhappy times sometimes, not just you.

In Years 3–4 and Years 5–6, students are introduced to the BOUNCE BACK! acronym:

- **B**ad times don't last. Things always get better. Stay optimistic.
- **O**ther people can help if you talk to them. Get a reality check.
- **U**nhelpful thinking makes you feel more upset. Think again.
- **N**obody is perfect – not you and not others.
- **C**oncentrate on the positives (no matter how small) and use laughter.
- **E**verybody experiences sadness, hurt, failure, rejection and setbacks sometimes, not just you. They are a normal part of life. Try not to personalise them.
- **B**lame fairly. How much of what happened was due to you, to others and to bad luck or circumstances?
- **A**ccept what can't be changed (but try to change what you can change first).
- **C**atastrophising exaggerates your worries. Don't believe the worst possible picture.
- **K**eep things in perspective. It's only part of your life.

The coping statements in the acronyms are underpinned by key Cognitive Behaviour Therapy (CBT) principles. The acronyms help students learn the statements by heart and recall them when they experience a setback which will help them be more resilient. In this unit there is also a focus on the ways in which nature bounces back (e.g. bush regeneration, skin repair, the immune system) and how people can 'bounce back' after hardship or academic or social difficulties.

Teaching students coping skills makes it more likely that they will be able to respond effectively and adaptively to challenges and times of adversity, manage emotional distress and have optimal levels of wellbeing. Coping skills provide them with the thinking skills, behaviours and attitudes for making their lives less distressing, happier and more productive overall.

Unit 4: Courage

Courage is resilience to fear, mastery of fear, not absence of fear. (Mark Twain)

The focus of this unit is on:

- understanding that if there is no fear, there is no courage
- understanding the differences between everyday courage, heroism (acting bravely to help someone else in danger), thrill-seeking, professional risk-taking and foolhardiness

- recognising that everyday courage can be either physical (e.g. learning to snorkel), psychological (e.g. sorting out a disagreement with a friend) or moral (e.g. supporting someone who is being treated unfairly despite the risk of losing friends or being criticised)
- understanding that fear is relative – what makes one person scared or nervous may not make another person scared or nervous
- developing the skills and perceptions that lead to being more courageous in many areas of one's life (e.g. public speaking).

Courage is not the absence of fear or distress but the capacity to act despite the fear. The courageous person faces the fearful situation and tries to resolve it, despite the discomfort produced by their fearful or anxious thoughts, feelings and/or physical reactions.

Courage is needed to persist and deal with hardships or setbacks, and to tackle a difficult and threatening task. It is a 'voluntary' action and there is always a risk attached that may lead to undesirable consequences such as not succeeding, feeling foolish or being bullied too. Courage and being brave in a difficult situation is defined as a 'character strength' in the VIA character strengths framework from the VIA Institute on Character[10] and in the Jubilee Centre 2015 report on character and virtues: 'Character Education in UK Schools'[3].

In ancient times, Aristotle believed that a person develops courage by doing courageous acts. Rachman[11], an early researcher in courage, investigated the courage of army bomb disposal experts. He identified that the main factor that helped them to be courageous was their confidence in their training. This suggests that teachers can play an important role in encouraging students to tackle something that is difficult or anxiety-provoking for them (e.g. giving a class talk) by teaching them the relevant skills (e.g. for public speaking) and then starting small and providing safe settings for them to gain confidence. Also, helping students to self-reflect on their courageous behaviour helps them develop a courageous or growth mindset which will encourage future acts of courage[12].

Unit 5: Looking on the bright side

It is better to light a candle than to curse the darkness. (Chinese proverb)

This unit focuses on skills and strategies associated with optimistic thinking:

- **Open-mindedness and flexibility when solving problems:** having confidence in one's ability to solve problems and to take positive actions.
- **Positive tracking:** looking for and commenting on the positives that you encounter in your own life (however small) and in the actions of other people.
- **Positive conversion:** finding small positive aspects, opportunities and learning experiences in negative events in your life and the mistakes you make.
- **An optimistic explanatory style**[13,14]**:** explaining and interpreting setbacks and difficult times in your life in a way that makes it more likely that you can cope well with them and move on from them. This involves:
  - seeing bad times as temporary ('just now') rather than permanent ('always')
  - perceiving that most setbacks and difficult times are 'temporary' ('things will get better'), they happen to other people too ('not just me') and are limited to the immediate incident not the whole of your life ('just this').
- **A sense of hope:** hopefulness has been shown to contribute to success and wellbeing[15]. It involves expecting things to work out, being forward-looking and proactive, and having the confidence to persevere when faced with adversity[19].
  - A capacity for hope where you are forward looking and hope things will work out is defined as a 'character strength' in the VIA character strengths framework (see pages 43–44).
  - Hope contributes energy to goal-seeking and achievement. Hopefulness is important to the achievement of all types of goals such as learning goals, social goals, physical goals and performance goals.

- **Gratitude and appreciation:** In *Bounce Back!* students learn about two types of gratitude:
  - **gratitude towards people:** appreciating and feeling grateful for what another person has done for you, e.g. by being kind, helping you and saying thank you.
  - **gratitude for the good things in your life:** feeling grateful for the good things in your day, in your life and in your past.

In a 2008 study by Froh[16], young adolescents (aged 11–14) took part in an educational curriculum intervention in which they were asked to undertake a daily routine for two weeks, in which they identified five things in their life for which they were grateful. These participants, in comparison to a similar group of same-age adolescents who did not participate in the intervention, were assessed three weeks after the intervention as being happier, more optimistic and more satisfied with their school, family, community, friends and themselves. They also gave more emotional support to other people in their life. There was also evidence that the gratitude intervention was linked to enhanced psychological and social functioning up to six months later[17].

The activities in this unit also help to build class optimism. Optimistic thinking has been described by American Psychologist, C. Peterson[18], as 'the "velcro" construct of resilience, to which everything else sticks'. A student who thinks optimistically tends to look on the bright side of situations and hopes for the best, even when things are not looking good. Being optimistic can empower students to persevere and help them to get on top of challenges and manage life's difficulties. Conversely, pessimism involves expecting failure, anticipating bad outcomes, or a tendency to take a gloomy view of things.

Optimistic thinking is also a contributing factor to getting along well with others and having good physical health. In contrast, pessimism, especially a pessimistic explanatory style[20,21] is linked to a sense of hopelessness and despair and, sometimes, depression (see pages 46–48, for more information about explanatory style).

Unit 6: Emotions

Joy is not in things, it is in us. (Richard Wagner)

This unit focuses on teaching students to:

- understand that very few events are good or bad in themselves and that how you think about something strongly influences how you feel about it
- recognise, enjoy and recall their own positive emotions such as happiness, pride, contentment, curiosity, surprise and excitement and the events that promote these positive feelings
- boost and enhance positive feelings by sharing them with others
- recognise and manage their unpleasant emotions such as anger, sadness, worry, disappointment and embarrassment and understand that these emotions can give us warnings about things that might need to be changed or addressed
- understand that they have choices about how they manage their emotions and the actions they take
- recognise the feelings and intentions of others and respond with empathy
- use positive self-talk and low-key emotional language
- develop a capacity to be more 'mindful'.

The best predictor of a child becoming a satisfied and happy adult, according to the British Cohort Study, is not their academic achievement but their emotional health in childhood[22]. A great deal of research under the Positive Psychology umbrella has shown that people who frequently experience and express positive emotions are more resilient[23], more resourceful[24], more socially connected[25] and are more likely to function at optimal levels[25,26]. Fredrickson's 'broaden and build' model[27] is helpful to understand the key role of positive emotions for optimal functioning. The model proposes that even brief experiences of positive emotions such as interest, joy, security, gratitude, hopefulness and amusement can broaden both your thoughts and actions, and over time these positive emotions build a greater capacity for developing positive relationships and greater confidence. People who are generally happier are also more resilient and recover more quickly from adversity than those who are less happy.

Correctly recognising and naming their emotions helps students to understand and manage their lives and their relationships more effectively and with less stress. This unit incorporates activities that help young people understand how their thoughts affect their feelings and their behaviour. An important message is that their perception or interpretation of an event helps to determine how they feel, not just the event per se. If they are over-aroused and interpret an event in a negative, hopeless or threatening light, then they are more likely to experience strong unpleasant emotions such as anger or despair. Strong unpleasant emotions may make it more difficult for them to be resilient and 'bounce back'. If they stay calm and find a helpful way to interpret a situation, then they are better able to cope and to problem solve.

Poor management of strong emotions such as anxiety, anger, fear and sadness narrows a person's range of thoughts and limits action choices. They are more likely to act impulsively with anger and be more vulnerable to substance abuse and other acts of self-harm. Learning how to express emotions in a positive and assertive way helps people feel more in control when things are difficult. This unit encourages young people to reflect on what makes them happy, proud and satisfied, a theme that is picked up again in Unit 10: Success.

Positive emotions are also contagious and build a positive class and school climate. As well as explicitly teaching students about emotions, the ***Bounce Back!*** program promotes positive emotions in the classroom. For example:

- feelings of belonging are promoted through relational strategies such as Circle Time and cooperative learning
- feelings of excitement and enjoyment in learning are generated through educational games
- feelings of optimism about academic success are promoted through learning skills for setting realistic goals, framing success in terms of student effort and persistence, encouraging positive thinking and challenging unhelpful thinking
- feelings of satisfaction and pride are promoted by students identifying and recognising their different strengths and valuing and celebrating different learning products.

✦ Mindfulness

Mindfulness in education is rapidly increasing in popularity as educators observe the benefits of mindfulness strategies for their students. Mindfulness involves two skills: the first is learning to relax quickly and consciously, i.e. using self-regulation; the second is paying attention to the present moment without judgement. In contrast, when people are on 'autopilot' they are usually less aware of what is happening, so they may miss the details (and often the positives) in their life and also miss opportunities to grow or challenge themselves.

A review of 14 studies integrating mindfulness training in schools found the following student improvements: social skills, academic skills, emotional regulation, self-esteem, positive mood, academic skills and better memory and attention. Students also showed less anxiety, stress and fatigue[28].

Unit 7: Relationships

> In order to have friends, you must first be one. (Elbert Hubbard)

This unit focuses on skills and attitudes that help students to:

- develop skills for making and keeping friends
- develop skills for getting along well with others
- develop skills for managing disagreements
- self-reflect about their current levels of skills in these areas.

Having a friend is an important source of wellbeing for students, as it is for all of us. Although many students would like to be popular and/or well accepted by all their peers, their relationships with their friends are more important[29].

Friendships can provide students with closeness, a sense of connection and safety, affirmation and, when needed, social and practical support. Friendships also provide a context in which students can practise and refine their social skills and develop empathy and moral reasoning[30–32].

Students who have poor relationships with their peers are more likely to use drugs in adolescence, misbehave, report anxiety/depressive symptoms, and drop out before finishing secondary school[33–36].

In a major longitudinal study Caprara and colleagues found that teacher ratings of prosocial behaviour in Year 3 were better predictors of Year 8 academic achievement than academic achievement in Year 3[37,38]. A meta-analysis of 148 studies involving 17 000 students conducted in 11 different countries concluded that positive peer relationships explained 33–40 per cent of variation in academic achievement[39].

Social skills are not only 'relationship builders' but are also 'academic enablers'[38,40]. The Relationships unit explicitly teaches students social skills by providing guidelines on the 'dos and don'ts' of skills like negotiating, respectfully disagreeing, playing fairly, being a good winner and loser, having an interesting conversation and managing conflict well. Students practise these social skills through the activities and relationship-building teaching strategies, like cooperative learning, Circle Time and educational games. These social skills create efficient classrooms that also help students to benefit from academic instruction[38]. Displays of prosocial behaviour patterns and restraint from disruptive and antisocial forms of behaviour have been consistently and positively related to peer acceptance, achievement motivation and academic success[41].

Unit 8: Humour

> A person without a sense of humour is like a wagon without springs. It's jolted by every pebble on the road. (Henry Ward Beecher)

The focus of this unit is on:

- activities that develop an understanding of the processes and styles of humour
- activities that highlight how humour can be used to help cope with hard times and when supporting others
- activities to help students to differentiate between humour that helps and humour that harms, stereotypes, trivialises or denies
- opportunities for students to participate with classmates in humorous activities through Giggle Gym sessions and brief daily humorous activities that can be used as a stress break in class.

Laughter has been shown to relax and calm the body, reduce anxiety and stress, and create a more positive mood[41,42]. 'Finding the humorous side' can sometimes be an effective strategy for being resilient, and can help students cope with a difficult situation. In their review of research, Banas et al.[43], identified that the use of positive humour in education has the capacity to create a more relaxed and engaging learning environment for students. Teachers who make learning 'fun' tend to be liked and respected by students (especially boys)[44] and are more likely to be rated by their students as interesting, motivating, thought-provoking and having created a low-anxiety learning environment[45]. Shared laughter helps all of us to connect and bond. Research consistently demonstrates that laughing results in beneficial physiological changes in our bodies that act to improve our health and help us fight illness[46-48]. This understanding underpins the therapeutic use of humour in medical contexts.

The activities in the 'Humour' unit enable teachers to engage in amusing and fun activities with their students. Incorporating aspects of the unit into classroom activities helps students feel more connected with each other and with their teacher and helps them stay engaged and on task. Laughter and humour hold students' attention and create positive emotions, thereby helping them to be more receptive and attentive to what they are learning. Cognitively, humour usually involves the perception of incongruity or paradox in a playful context. However, humour can also be demeaning and hurtful when it reinforces sexual, racial or cultural stereotypes, or is at the expense of another person through cynical or sarcastic comments.

Unit 9: Being safe

> When someone is cruel or acts like a bully, you don't stoop to their level. No, our motto is, when they go low, we go high. (Michelle Obama)

The focus of this unit is on:

- understanding terms such as 'bullying', 'cyber bullying' and 'cyber harassment' and discriminating between bullying behaviour and other kinds of anti-social behaviour
- understanding the difference between asking for support, acting responsibly to support someone else and 'dobbing' or telling on someone

- skills for being confident and assertive; this should not lead students to believe that if they are bullied it is their fault
- skills and attitudes that help students respond adaptively to being bullied or put down, for example:
  - accepting that if you have 'self-respect', then you 'self-protect'
  - asking for support
  - verbal and non-verbal assertiveness
- skills for understanding and managing negative peer pressure
- skills for discouraging bullying and offering bystander support
- understanding the impact of bullying not only on the person being mistreated but also on bystanders, and recognising the link between bullying and other aspects of society such as historical incidents of oppression and persecution, racial vilification and sledging in sport
- providing opportunities for students to initiate and implement student-owned and student-directed approaches to prevent bullying.

Bullying occurs at some level in all primary and secondary schools[49] and all students can potentially become involved in bullying others or being bullied. Many students report occasionally taking part in some form of bullying and most students are teased or experience some form of peer harassment during their years at school[50]. One in five students (20 per cent) report being regularly bullied in 2015 compared to 27 per cent in 2007[51]. Increasingly, students are both bullied and cyberbullied[52,53]. Cyberbullying is more likely to occur outside school hours and off the school site, but the effects are felt in school hours because of the breakdown of relationships when school resumes.

All Departments of Education across Australia advocate that schools have a whole-school anti-bullying policy and a whole-school approach to the prevention and management of bullying incidents. Given the complex nature of bullying, the multi-component nature of **Bounce Back!** is consistent with recommended guidelines on anti-bullying initiatives[54]. A meta-analysis of 30 well-designed evaluations of anti-bullying interventions identified a multi-component approach as having the greatest impact and reducing bullying incidents by an average of 20 to 23 per cent[55,56].

As a whole-school SEL program, the **Bounce Back!** curriculum includes recommended multi-components of an effective anti-bullying program. This includes a focus on developing a positive school climate and explicitly teaching prosocial values with clear behavioural expectations and effective behaviour management strategies, as well as teaching social and emotional skills and coping skills to enhance student wellbeing and resilience. Unit 9: Being safe also provides an explicit anti-bullying curriculum such as child-friendly definitions of what is bullying and what isn't bullying, and ways to support classmates and other students who are being bullied. One of the most significant strategies in the meta-analyses for reducing school bullying was high levels of playground supervision. Unit 9: Being safe also provides guidelines for student-owned initiatives to share responsibility in anti-bullying initiatives, including making the playground safe for everyone.

Unit 10: Success (STAR!, CHAMP!, WINNERS!)

An aim in life is the only fortune worth finding.
(Robert Louis Stevenson)

The focus of the unit is on activities that:

- teach students how to identify their own relative strengths and limitations; strengths can be ability based (e.g. identified by Gardner in his Multiple Intelligences Theory[57]) or character based; a strengths-based approach is strongly advocated in Positive Psychology and Positive Education[61,62]
- help students to understand that strengths can be developed and limitations can also be improved through effort
- teach students to use self-knowledge of their strengths to help them succeed across many areas of their life, with a particular emphasis on collecting evidence for conclusions about oneself, not just hoping or making unwarranted, unrealistic and deflated or inflated assumptions
- teach students about a growth mindset; a 'growth mindset' involves believing that effort rather than ability is the most important ingredient in being successful and leads to persevering and working hard, rather than giving up easily when faced with setbacks and obstacles[59,60]

- develop skills of self-discipline and self-management (e.g. grit, willpower, effort, time management and organisational skills)
- teach the skills and processes of achieving goals (e.g. setting goals, identifying different pathways to achieving the goal, making a plan with achievable steps, taking sensible risks, persisting in the face of obstacles, solving problems and being resourceful when things are challenging or when something goes wrong)
- challenge students to use their initiative and be resourceful, and hence understand the real-life 'rocky up-and-down' process of goal achievement
- help students understand the concept of 'psychological flow'[58], a positive outcome that occurs when they are using their strengths and skills and are immersed in an activity that offers them a challenge and fully absorbs their attention in a positive way
- encourage meaningful participation. Meaningful participation in school and community-based activities helps students gain a sense of purpose – a critical component of student wellbeing. Activities that are most likely to create a sense of 'purpose' for students are those that are worthwhile and that affect other people, not just themselves. This can involve, for example, an older student working with younger students to teach wellbeing themes, school-based projects such as anti-bullying campaigns and community projects such as reciprocal learning projects in a nearby retirement village, where students teach digital skills and residents teach card games.

✦ The Success acronyms

Unit 10 is based on a core acronym for each of the three different year levels:

- STAR! in Years F–2
- CHAMP! in Years 3–4
- WINNERS! in Years 5–6.

Each acronym reinforces age-appropriate key messages for success. Being successful includes knowing one's strengths and limitations and using that self-awareness to set goals, monitor progress and achieve in different areas deemed important by oneself and others. Achieving one's goals is linked to being hopeful or optimistic that success is achievable. With hope, you are more likely to find solutions to problems or different pathways to achieve one's goals[15].

Extra unit: Elasticity eBook

The Elasticity unit (available digitally) introduces the scientific concept of physical resilience or 'bouncing back'. When something is resilient, it is elastic and capable of returning to its original shape after being stretched, squashed or bent. The Elasticity unit can serve as an introduction to Unit 3: People bouncing back. The main focus is on:

- investigating and experimenting with elastic forces (e.g. rubber bands, bouncing balls)
- stretching (e.g. elasticised fabrics, skin).

REFERENCES

1. Engels, R.C., Finkenauer, C., Meeus, W. & Dekovic, M. 2001, 'Parental attachment and adolescents' emotional adjustment: The associations with social skills and relational competence', *Journal of Counselling Psychology*, 48(4): pp. 428–439.
2. Rhodes, J.E., Grossman, J.B. & Resch, N.L. 2000, 'Agents of change: Pathways through which mentoring relationships influence adolescents' academic adjustment', *Child Development*, 71(6): pp. 1662–1671.
3. Arthur, J., Kristjansson, K., Walker, D., Sanderse, W. & Jones, C. 2015, 'Character Education in UK Schools, Research Report', The Jubilee Centre for Character & Virtues, University of Birmingham.
4. 'After the Riots 2012, The Final Report of the Riots Communities and Victims Panel', UK Government, http://riotspanel.independent.gov.uk/wp-content/uploads/2012/03/Riots-Panel-Final-Report1.pdf
5. Sugai, G., Horner, R., & Lewis, T. 2009, 'School-wide positive behaviour support implementers' blueprint and self-assessment', Eugene, OR: OSEP TA-Center on Positive Behavioral Interventions and Supports.
6. Bradshaw, C., Koth, C., Thornton, L. & Leaf, P. 2009, 'Altering school climate through school-wide positive behavioral interventions and supports: Findings from a group-randomized effectiveness trial', Prevention Science, 10: pp. 100–115.
7. Lovat, T. & Toomey, R. 2007, 'Values education and quality teaching: The Double Helix effect', David Barlow, Sydney.
8. www.pbis.org/school/swpbis-for-beginners
9. Layous, K., Nelson, S.K. Oberle, E., Schonert-Reichl, K.A. & Lyubormirsky, S. 2012, 'Kindness Counts: Prompting Prosocial Behaviour in Preadolescents Boosts Peer Acceptance and Wellbeing', PLOS, open access: http://dx.doi.org/10.1371/journal.pone.0051380
10. www.viacharacter.org
11. Rachman, S.J. 1990, *Fear and Courage* (2nd edn), W.H. Freeman and Company, New York.
12. Hannah, S.T., Sweeney, P.J. & Lester, P.B. 2007, 'Toward a courageous mindset: The subjective act and experience of courage', *The Journal of Positive Psychology*, vol. 2, no. 2, pp. 129–135.
13. Seligman, M.E.P. 1995, *The Optimistic Child*, Random House, Sydney.
14. Gillham, J.E., Shatte, A.J., Reivich, K. & Seligman, M.E.P. 2001, 'Optimism, Pessimism, and Explanatory Style', in *Optimism and Pessimism: Implications for theory, research and practice*, E.C. Chang, American Psychological Association, Washington.
15. Lopez, S.J., et al. 2009, 'Measuring and promoting hope in schoolchildren', in *Promoting Wellness in Children and Youth: Handbook of Positive Psychology in the Schools*, R. Gilman, E.S Huebner, M. Furlong (eds), Lawrence Erlbaum, Mahwah, New Jersey.
16. Froh, J.J., Sefick, W.J., Emmons, R. 2008, 'Counting blessings in early adolescents. An experimental study of gratitude and subjective wellbeing', *Journal of School Psychology*, 46: pp. 213–233
17. Froh, J.J., Bono, G. & Emmons, R.A. 2010, 'Being grateful is beyond good manners: Gratitude and motivation to contribute to society among early adolescents', *Motivation and Emotion*, 34, pp. 144–157.
18. Peterson, C. 2000, 'The future of optimism', *American Psychologist*, vol. 55, no. 1, pp. 44–55.
19. Carver, C.S., Scheier, M.E. 1999, 'Optimism', in *Coping. The Psychology of What Works*, C.R. Snyder (ed), Oxford University Press, New York, pp. 182–204.
20. Andrews, G., Szabó, M., Burns J. 2001, 'Avertable Risk Factors for Depression', beyondblue, the Australian National Depression Initiative.
21. Andrews, G., Szabo, M., Burns, J. 2002, 'Preventing major depression in young people', *British Journal of Psychiatry*, no. 181, pp. 460–462.
22. Layard, R. & Hagell, A. 2015, 'Healthy Young Minds: Transforming the Mental Health of Children', in *World Happiness Report 2017*, J.H. Helliwell, R. Layard, J. Sachs (eds), Sustainable Development Solutions Network, New York, www.unsdsn.org/happiness.
23. Fredrickson, B. & Tugade M. 2004, 'Resilient individuals use positive emotions to bounce back from negative emotional experiences', *Journal of Personality and Social Psychology*, 86 (2): pp. 320–333.
24. Lyubomirsky, S., Diener, E. & King, C. 2005, 'The Benefits of Frequent Positive Affect: Does Happiness Lead to Success?', *Psychological Bulletin*, 131(6): pp. 803–855.
25. Mauss, I.B., Shallcross, A.J., Troy, A.S., John, O.P., Ferrer, E., Wilhelm, F.H., et al. 2011, 'Don't hide your happiness! Positive emotion dissociation, social connectedness, and psychological functioning', *Journal of Personality and Social Psychology*, 100(4), pp. 738–748.
26. Fredrickson, B.L., Losada, M.F. 2005, 'Positive affect and the complex dynamics of human flourishing', *American Psychologist*, 60(7), pp. 678–686.
27. Fredrickson, B. 2013, 'Positive Emotions Broaden & Build', *Advances in Experimental Social Psychology*, 47: pp. 1–53.
28. Meiklejohn, J., Phillips, C., Freedman, M.L., Griffin, M.L., Biegel, G., Roach, A. & Saltzman, A. 2012, 'Integrating mindfulness training into K-12 education: Fostering the resilience of teachers and students', *Mindfulness*, 3(4): pp. 291–307.
29. La Greca, A. & Harrison, H. 2005, 'Adolescent peer relations, friendships, and romantic relationships: Do they predict social anxiety and depression?', *Journal of Clinical Child & Adolescent Psychology*, 34(1): pp. 49–61.
30. Hodges, E.V.E., Boivin, M., Vitaro, F. & Bukowski, W.M. 1999, 'The power of friendship: Protection against an escalating cycle of peer victimization', *Developmental Psychology*, 35(1): pp. 94–101, http://dx.doi.org/10.1037/0012-1649.35.1.94
31. McGrath, H. & Noble, T. 2010, 'Supporting positive pupil relationships: Research to practice', *Educational & Child Psychology*, 27(1): pp. 79–90.
32. Schonert-Reichl, K.A. 1999, 'Moral reasoning during early adolescence: Links with peer acceptance, friendship, and social behaviors', *Journal of Early Adolescence*, 19: pp. 249–279.
33. Bond, L., et al. 2000, 'Improving the Lives of Young Victorians in Our Community – A Survey of Risk and Protective Factors', Centre for Adolescent Health (available from www.dhs.vic.gov.au/commcare), Melbourne.
34. Doll, B. & Hess, R.S. 2001, 'Through a New Lens: Contemporary Psychological Perspectives on School Completion and Dropping Out', *School Psychology Quarterly*, 16 (4): pp. 351–56.
35. Marcus, R.F. & Sanders-Reio, J. 2001, 'The influence of attachment on school completion', *School Psychology Quarterly*, 16: pp. 427–44.
36. Barclay, J.R. & Doll, B. 2001, 'Early prospective studies of the high school dropout', *School Psychology Quarterly*, 16(4): pp. 357–369.

37. Caprara, G.V., Barbaranelli, C., Pastorelli, C., Bandura, A. & Zimbardo, P.G. 2000, 'Prosocial foundations of children's academic achievement', *Psychological Science*, 11 (4): pp. 302–306.
38. Gresham, F.M. 2016, 'Social skills assessment and intervention for children and youth', *Cambridge Journal of Education*, 46:3, pp. 319–332: DOI:10.1080/0305764X.2016.1195788
39. Roseth, C.J., Johnson, D.W. & Johnson, R.T. 2008, 'Promoting early adolescents' achievement and peer relationships: The effects of cooperative, competitive and individualistic goal structures', *Psychological Bulletin*, 134(2): pp. 223–246.
40. Wentzel, K.R. 2009, 'Peers and academic functioning at school', in *Handbook of peer interactions, relationships, and groups*, K.H. Rubin, W.M. Bukowski, B. Laursen (eds), Guilford Press, New York, pp. 531–547.
41. Colom, G., Alcover, C., Sanchez-Curto, & C. Zarate-Osuna, J. 2011, 'Study of the effect of positive humour as a variable that reduces stress. Relationship of humour with personality and performance variables', *Psychology in Spain*, 2011, 15(1): pp. 9–21.
42. Martin, R.A. 2006, *The Psychology of Humor*, Academic Press, NY.
43. Banas, J.A., Dunbar, N., Rodriguez, D., & Liu, S. 2011, 'A review of humor in education settings: Four decades of research', *Communication Education*, 60 (1): pp. 115–144.
44. Keddie, A. & Churchill, R. 2004, 'Power, control and authority: issues at the centre of boys' relationships with their teachers', *Queensland Journal of Teacher Education*, 19(1): pp. 13–27.
45. Makewa, L.N., Role, E. & Genga, J.A., 2011, 'Teachers' Use of Humor in Teaching and Students' Rating of Their Effectiveness', *International Journal of Education*, 3 (2).
46. Lefcourt, H.M. 2001, *Humor: The Psychology of Living Buoyantly*, Plenum Publishers, New York.
47. Martin, R.A. 2001, 'Humor, laughter and physical health: Methodological issues and research findings', *Psychological Bulletin*, vol. 127, pp. 504–519.
48. Rodriguez, T. 2016, 'Laugh lots, live longer', *Scientific American Mind*, 27(5): 17.
49. Elias, M. 2003, 'Academic and social-emotional learning', *International Academy of Education*, I: 5–3 1.
50. Espelage, D.L. & Swearer, S.M. 2003, 'Research on school bullying and victimization: What have we learned and where do we go from here?', *School Psychology Review*, 32(2): pp. 365–383.
51. Rigby, K. & Johnson, K. 2016, 'The Prevalence and Effectiveness of Anti-Bullying Strategies employed in Australian Schools', University of South Australia, Adelaide, available at: www.unisa.edu.au/ Anti-bullying eport-FINAL.pdf
52. Cross, D., et al. 2009, 'Australian Covert Bullying Prevalence Study (ACBPS)', Child Health Promotion Research Centre, Edith Cowan University, Perth, https://docs.education.gov.au/system/files/doc/other/australian_covert_bullying_prevalence_study_executive_summary.pdf
53. Smith, P.K., et al. 2008, 'Cyberbullying: Its nature and impact in secondary school pupils', *Journal of Child Psychology and Psychiatry*, vol. 49, no. 4, pp. 376–385.
54. Bradshaw, C. 2015, 'Translating Research to Practice in Bullying Prevention', *American Psychologist*, 70(4): pp. 322–332.
55. Ttofi, M.M. & Farrington, D.P. 2011, 'Effectiveness of school-based programs to reduce bullying: A systematic meta-analytic review', *Journal of Experimental Criminology*, 7, pp. 27–56. http://dx.doi.org/10.1007/s11292-010-9109-1
56. Farrington, D.P., & Ttofi, M.M. 2009, 'School-based programs to reduce bullying and victimization (Campbell Systematic Reviews No. 6)', Campbell Corporation, Oslo, Norway, http://dx.doi.org/10.4073/csr.2009.6.
57. McGrath, H. & Noble, T. 2005, *Eight ways at once. Book One: Multiple Intelligences + Bloom's Revised Taxonomy = 200 differentiated classroom strategies*, Pearson Education, Sydney.
58. Shernoff, D.J. & Csikszentmihalyi, M.P. 2009, 'Flow in schools: Cultivating engaged learners and optimal learning environments', in *Promoting Wellness in Children and Youth: Handbook of Positive Psychology in the Schools*, Gilman, R., Huebner, E.S. & Furlong, M. (eds), Lawrence Erlbaum, Mahwah, New Jersey, pp. 131–146.
59. Dweck, C.S., Walton, G.M. & Cohen, G.L. 2015, 'Academic Tenacity. Mindsets and Skills that Promote Long-Term Learning', Bill & Melinda Gates Foundation, https://ed.stanford.edu/sites/default/files/manual/dweck-walton-cohen-2014.pdf
60. Dweck, C.S. 2006, *Mindset. The New Psychology of Success*, Random House, New York.
61. White, M. & Waters, L.E. 2015, 'Strengths-based approaches in the classroom and staffroom', in M.A. White, A.S. Murray (eds), *Evidence-Based Approaches in Positive Education*, Positive Education, DOI 10.1007/978-94-017-9667-5_6.
62. Seligman, M. 2009, 'Positive psychology and positive education workshop notes', in Mind & its Potential Conference, Sydney.

Wellbeing and resilience

IN THIS CHAPTER

- Definitions of student wellbeing, teacher wellbeing, mental health, mental fitness, resilience, and social and emotional learning
- A focus on student wellbeing at the heart of educational policy – the Australian Curriculum's general capabilities are addressed in the 10 **Bounce Back! Curriculum Units**
- The protective environmental factors as well as personal and social and emotional skills that support student wellbeing and academic success
- Approaches to differentiating the **Bounce Back!** curriculum for diverse learners, such as those who are gifted, English language learners or those who have experienced trauma

INTRODUCTION

Student wellbeing is inextricably linked to student learning. Students with optimal levels of wellbeing and resilience are more likely to have higher academic achievement and complete their schooling, have better mental and physical health, be more resistant to stress and are more likely to engage in a socially responsible lifestyle[1-3]. Students who are actively engaged in learning are more likely to be strongly connected to their school, their teachers and their peers and are more likely to exhibit positive behaviour at school. There is a bi-directional relationship between factors that contribute to student wellbeing, student engagement and academic engagement. For example, school connectedness contributes to student academic outcomes, but student academic outcomes also enhance school connectedness.

Students with low levels of wellbeing are more likely to disengage from learning, drop out of school, have a higher risk of unemployment and poverty and have low levels of participation in their community. Studies in 2005 indicated that they could also expect to earn approximately AUD$500 000 less in their working life than someone who completes school[4]. The psychological, social and physical impacts of an individual's level of wellbeing and resilience are evident both in the short and long term.

Promoting wellbeing using a whole-school approach is viewed as an integral part of a school effectiveness strategy[5]. It offers a significant return on the resources and time invested by schools[6]. A whole school approach to student wellbeing also increases students' attendance at school[7], enhances their engagement with classroom activities, and their readiness to learn, improves their educational outcomes and enables them to be benefit from high quality teaching[5]. The academic success that follows is then linked to higher levels of wellbeing in adulthood[8,9]. Students' social relationships with their peers along with and the acquisition of effective social and emotional competencies are also significant predictors of student wellbeing and students' academic performances[10,11]. A whole school approach to wellbeing enables students and the school community to thrive and prosper.

What is student wellbeing?

Bounce Back! defines student wellbeing according to the Australian Government's 'Scoping Study into Approaches to Student Wellbeing':

> Optimal student wellbeing is a sustainable emotional state characterised by (predominantly) positive mood and attitude, positive relationships with other students and teachers, resilience, self-optimisation (knowing and using strengths), and a high level of satisfaction with learning experiences at school[12,13].

A logical starting point for educating student wellbeing is to work from a robust and evidence-based definition of student wellbeing that effectively has the power to guide a school's policy and its practices. Naturally a child's family, home and community all significantly impact on a young person's wellbeing. However, our definition takes an educational perspective and focuses on the actions that schools and school systems can adopt to help children and young people flourish within a school context.

What is teacher wellbeing?

Teacher wellbeing is the overall level of satisfaction that a teacher feels about their work, experiences and relationships within the school. Teachers who have a high level of psychological wellbeing are more likely to work productively and creatively and have lower levels of absenteeism and health problems.

'Optimal' teacher wellbeing is an ongoing and predominantly positive emotional state within and about the workplace that is characterised by:

- acting resiliently in the face of challenges, changes and stressful situations
- feeling safe, valued, supported and connected
- having a sense of optimism
- having positive relationships with students, colleagues and the school community
- feeling satisfied with workplace tasks and with the availability of opportunities for meaningful contribution
- having high levels of self-respect.

Teaching **Bounce Back!** has been found to have a significant impact on improving teacher wellbeing[14] and on teachers' perceptions of an increase in their own professional and personal resilience[15].

What is mental health?

Mental health is defined by the World Health Organization (WHO) as 'a state of wellbeing in which an individual realizes his or her own potential, can cope with the normal stresses of life, can work productively and fruitfully, and is able to make a contribution to her or his community'[16].

The positive dimension of mental health is stressed in WHO's definition of health as contained in its constitution: 'Health is a state of complete physical, mental and social wellbeing and not merely the absence of disease or infirmity'[16].

What is mental fitness?

Nearly everyone understands how physical fitness can improve an individual's physical health and wellbeing, but what about 'mental fitness'? The term mental fitness is used by many schools instead of 'mental health' or 'wellbeing' because it is seen as a more student-friendly term. In her work in Positive Education, Paula Robinson[17] has found the term 'mental fitness' to be more acceptable to some secondary school students, especially boys, than wellbeing. The construct of mental fitness is employed by ReachOut, a not-for-profit organisation that provides practical tools and support to help young people. The Orb online game is designed to teach key messages about improving mental health and wellbeing to secondary school students. In the ReachOut Orb Teacher Resource[18] mental fitness is explained:

> People who are mentally fit have a greater capacity for positive mood, self-awareness, the skills for coping with challenges and accessing opportunities, good relationships with others and success in achieving their goals[18].

What is resilience?

There are many different definitions of resilience but they all refer to the capacity of the individual to overcome odds and demonstrate the personal strengths needed to cope with hardship or adversity. Benard[19] suggests resilience is a set of qualities or protective mechanisms that give rise to successful adaptation despite high-risk factors during childhood.

The *Bounce Back!* program defines resilience as the ability to cope and 'bounce back' after encountering negative events, challenges, difficult situations or adversity and to return to almost the same level of emotional wellbeing. It is also the capacity to respond adaptively to difficult circumstances and still thrive. Children and young people need to be both socially and academically resilient to flourish in today's world.

'Bouncing back' is a concrete concept and is easily learnt, even by very young children. However, telling children to 'bounce back' should not convey that it is easy to do, nor should it minimise the effort, sadness and pain that it sometimes takes to overcome a serious setback or great adversity.

✦ Resilience is dealing with challenges, changes and adversity

Students and young people can also apply the attitudes and skills of 'bouncing back' to challenges such as not giving up on a difficult task, adapting to a step family, resolving a fall-out with a friend, coping with not getting into a sporting team or a school performance or moving to a new house or school. Being resilient also involves being prepared to seek out new experiences and opportunities and take reasonable risks. Risk-taking may involve some setbacks and rejections but it also has the potential to create more opportunities for successes and wellbeing.

What is Social and Emotional Learning?

Social and Emotional Learning (SEL) involves teaching and encouraging students to develop social and emotional competencies through explicit instruction and student-centred learning approaches that help them engage in the learning process and develop analytical, communication and collaborative skills[3]. Students learn SEL skills most effectively when they are explicitly taught, modelled, practised and applied in diverse situations. This increases the likelihood that students will learn to use these skills on a daily basis. SEL programming also enhances students' social and emotional competence by establishing positive class and school climates which are safe, caring, cooperative, well managed and participatory[2,3]. A systematic schoolwide approach to SEL programming also involves partnerships with families.

Bounce Back! adopts the five SEL domains advocated by CASEL (Collaborative for Academic, Social and Emotional Learning) for organising the SEL skills taught in the program (see the table on pages 30–31). These five domains are: self-awareness, self-management, social awareness, relationship skills and responsible decision making.

Student wellbeing at the heart of educational policy

Across the globe, federal, state and local school policies have been established to foster the social, emotional and academic growth of young people. Although different terms are used, most agree on the core purposes of education. Most countries want their students to attain mastery of the academic curriculum and to become confident and resilient individuals who are also responsible local and global citizens[3,20]. One example of an educational policy that drives the education agenda is the National Declaration on the Educational Goals for Young Australians[21]. These goals highlight the vital role that schools play in promoting the intellectual, physical, social, emotional, moral, spiritual and aesthetic development and wellbeing of children and young people.

At the heart of this policy is the educators' responsibility for the development of successful learners, confident individuals and active and informed citizens as defined below:

- **Successful learners** not only have the essential skills of literacy and numeracy, but are also creative and resourceful individuals with a capacity to think critically, to analyse information and to solve problems. They also have the capacity to learn and plan, to collaborate, to communicate ideas and to work independently.

- **Confident and creative individuals** are able to make rational and informed decisions, to be optimistic and have a sense of wellbeing, to accept responsibility for their own lives and to demonstrate respect for others.

- **Active and informed citizens** act with moral and ethical integrity and develop into responsible local and global citizens.

✦ Australian Curriculum general capabilities

The National Declaration on Educational Goals for Young Australians provides the direction and underpins the development of the Australian Curriculum. The Australian Curriculum's general capabilities[22] are expected to be embedded in all curriculum areas to all students. These capabilities are not only traditional literacy and numeracy skills, but also skills related to social and emotional learning (see the diagram below).

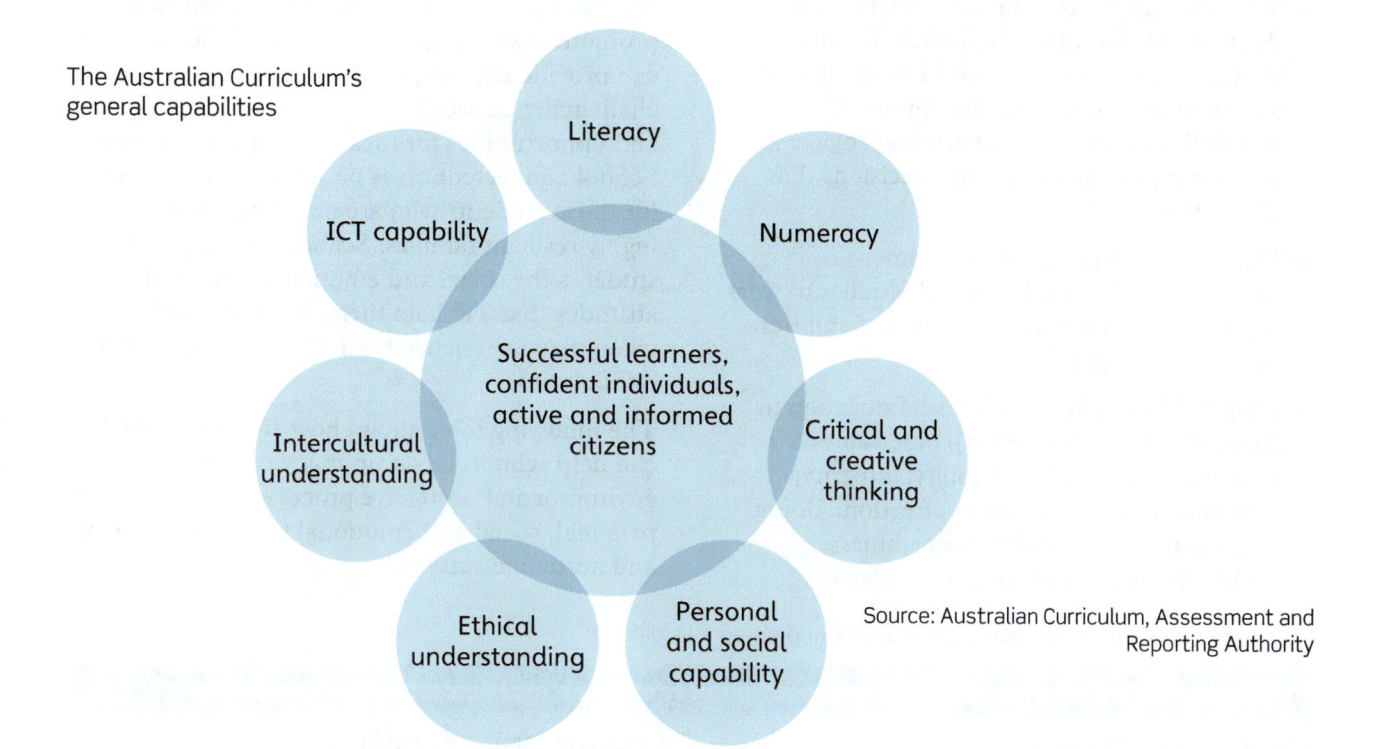

The Australian Curriculum's general capabilities

- Literacy
- Numeracy
- ICT capability
- Intercultural understanding
- Ethical understanding
- Personal and social capability
- Critical and creative thinking

Successful learners, confident individuals, active and informed citizens

Source: Australian Curriculum, Assessment and Reporting Authority

The following table identifies how the general capabilities are addressed in the *Bounce Back!* **Curriculum Units**.

Australian Curriculum general capabilities	Bounce Back! Curriculum Units
Literacy	All units include a range of books, films, poems and many literacy activities.
Numeracy	Most units feature numeracy activities.
Information and Communication Technology (ICT) Capability	All units feature ICT activities.
Critical and Creative Thinking	All units include higher order thinking tools and activities.
Personal and Social Capability	All units encourage self-management, self-awareness, self-knowledge, social awareness and social management, and use teaching strategies that build social capabilities. The following units also explicitly teach personal and social capabilities: Unit 1: Core values, Unit 2: Social values, Unit 3: People bouncing back, Unit 5: Looking on the bright side, Unit 6: Emotions, and Unit 7: Relationships.
Ethical Understanding	All units feature ethical understanding.
Intercultural Understanding	All units explore interacting and empathising with others, particularly through class discussions.

Chapter 3 Wellbeing and resilience

Student wellbeing also underpins other national Australian educational frameworks, such as:

- National Safe Schools Framework[23] (2011): all Australian schools are safe, supportive and respectful teaching and learning communities that promote student wellbeing
- The National Youth Strategy[24] (2010): the Australian Government's vision is for all young people to grow up safe, healthy, happy and resilient and to have the opportunities and skills they need to learn, work, engage in community life and influence decisions that affect them
- Family-School Partnerships Framework[25] (2008): a guide for schools and families to work together to enhance the wellbeing of children and young people
- National Framework for Values Education in Australian Schools[26] (2005): nine values for schools – respect; responsibility; integrity; care and compassion; fair go; freedom; doing your best; honesty and trustworthiness; understanding, tolerance and inclusion.

Protective processes that promote student wellbeing and resilience

Most young people spend six or more hours a day at school. Apart from families, schools are the most important socialising agents that provide access to a positive environment that promotes wellbeing and resilience. Schools can provide key people who show they care, a challenging curriculum, support for learning and opportunities for meaningful participation. School connectedness is particularly important for those students who are not connected to highly resilient families. Schools can also teach students the social and emotional skills and attitudes that will help them 'bounce back' when they experience hardship, frustrations and difficult times.

The following table shows how **Bounce Back!** can help schools to set up many of these environmental protective processes and teach the personal, social and emotional skills for wellbeing and academic success.

Key components of protective environments and personal skills

Environments that promote student wellbeing, resilience and academic success	
School connectedness • A sense of belonging to a good school • Meaningful participation and contribution • Opportunities for strengths to be affirmed • Opportunities for taking initiative • Supportive and inclusive school culture • Physical and psychological safety at school • Strong school rules about bullying and violence **Peer connectedness** • Intentional development of peer relationships • Use of teaching strategies that connect students and build positive school culture • Cooperative learning activities • Circle Time • Peer support strategies • Older students working with younger students **Teacher connectedness** • Intentional development of teacher-student relationships • Teacher warmth and availability • High expectations, academic support and differentiated curriculum • Cooperative and prosocial classroom culture • Positive behaviour management • Clear and consistent boundaries	**Positive family–school links** • Strong teacher–family connections **Family connectedness** • Expression of warmth and affection with at least one family member • Good communication and shared activities • Positive approach to solving family problems • Family loyalty, affirmation and support • Children having responsibilties at home • Prosocial and shared family values **One caring adult outside the family** • Availability and interest in the child • Expresses unconditional positive regard **Community-connectedness** • Awareness of and access to support services • Involvement in community service • Involvement in prosocial clubs and teams • Awareness of community norms against anti-social behaviour • Strong cultural identity and pride **Spiritual and religious involvement** • Participation in spiritual and religious communities

(Continued)

Personal, social and emotional skills and attitudes for student wellbeing and academic success

Self-awareness
- Identifying and regulating own emotions and thoughts*
- Accurate self-perception*
- Recognising own strengths and limitations*
- Well-grounded self-confidence*
- Optimistic thinking*
- Self-efficacy*
- Having a sense of meaning, purpose and future
- Self-reflection skills

Self-management skills
- Coping resiliently with difficult and challenging situations*
- Using helpful and rational thinking skills and attitudes
- Normalising instead of personalising
- Regulating one's emotions to handle stress and control impulses*
- Self-motivation*
- Self-discipline*
- Skills for setting and working towards personal and academic goals*
- Organisational skills*
- Growth mindset: holding a belief that effort will pay off*
- Grit: persisting in overcoming obstacles*
- Using humour appropriately
- Acting with courage
- Skills for adaptive distancing from distressing and unalterable situations
- Age-appropriate independence

Social awareness
- Taking the perspective of others (i.e. understanding their point of view or argument)*
- Empathising with others*
- Appreciating diversity*
- Showing respect for others*
- Prosocial values such as kindness and compassion
- Understanding social and ethical norms for behaviour*
- Awareness of family, school and community resources and supports*

Relationship skills
- Having a belief that relationships matter
- Social skills for establishing and maintaining healthy and rewarding relationships with diverse individuals and groups*
- Friendship skills*
- Conflict management skills*
- Resisting inappropriate social pressure*
- Seeking and offering help when needed*

Responsible decision making
- Consideration for the wellbeing of oneself and others*
- Analysing and evaluating situations*
- Identifying and solving problems in academic and social situations*
- Ethical responsibility (i.e. acting in an ethically responsible way by making constructive choices about personal behaviour and social interactions based on ethical standards, safety concerns and social norms)*

*Social-emotional learning skills also endorsed by CASEL
© McGrath, H. & Noble, T. 2017, **Bounce Back!** Pearson

✦ Environments that promote student wellbeing and resilience

School connectedness

School connectedness means the extent to which students feel they belong to a school that accepts, protects and cares about them, affirms them as people with positive qualities, and provides them with meaningful and satisfying learning experiences. School, above all other social institutions, provides unique opportunities for young people to form relationships and meet and work with peers and caring professional adults on a daily basis. School can offer young people hope and pathways for their future. Being connected to school is linked to increased student engagement and participation in school[5,27], higher levels of academic achievement[6,28,29], greater likelihood of completing school[30], increases in positive behaviour and less disruptive or anti-social behaviour[3,31-34]. School connectedness is also linked to lower rates of health risk behaviour and mental health problems[29,30,32].

Peer connectedness

For most young people, one of the major reasons for going to school is their desire to connect socially and emotionally with their peers. They look forward to seeing their friends, and enjoy belonging to both a friendship group and the larger peer group. Schools can create the kind of social structures that enhance the development of such relationships and foster a sense of acceptance, belonging and fitting in. Such structures are included in the **Bounce Back! Curriculum Units** and include the use of cooperative learning groups, Circle Time, class meetings, classroom committees and peer support groups.

A range of cooperative learning strategies, cooperative thinking tools and educational games are outlined in Teaching strategies and resources. Each **Curriculum Unit** incorporates many engaging learning activities which enable students to connect with each other and develop their social skills. Unit 1: Core values, Unit 2: Social values and Unit 7: Relationships also explicitly teach prosocial values and specific social and emotional skills. In addition, all the **Bounce Back! Curriculum Units** include learning activities that facilitate students getting to know each other through the sharing of perceptions and experiences related to the topics covered.

Teacher connectedness

Promoting positive relationships at school has been identified by many researchers as a core component for improving student wellbeing and engagement in learning. The quality of teaching and the teacher–student relationship, above all else, makes the most significant difference to student learning outcomes[35,36]. Feeling connected to their teachers helps students not only to be more motivated and to experience more successful learning outcomes, but also to become more resilient[14,19] and to stay at school rather than drop out. However, a number of research studies have suggested that students today do not feel closely connected to many of their teachers, especially in secondary schools[37,38]. Often a students' perceived low-level connection with their teachers comes as a surprise to the teacher.

Schools can empower teachers to establish positive and close relationships with their students in a number of ways. They can:

- limit the number of teachers that students come into contact with
- make time for teachers to get to know their students well through Positive Education initiatives
- make sure teachers have time to meet with those students who need more academic support or personal development
- provide opportunities for professional development in areas such as differentiating the curriculum, personal development, resilience and student counselling
- 'power up' their student wellbeing and support services.

Teachers can also take up the challenges of becoming more connected to their students and creating a prosocial and resilient classroom culture. They can do this by modelling resilient attitudes and skills, establishing a collaborative classroom climate, communicating warmth and positive expectations, adopting classroom practices that affirm student strengths, using positive behaviour strategies, respecting and acknowledging the value of individual differences, and by taking the time to get to know their students as people, not just as students.

As they teach the **Bounce Back!** program, teachers are very likely to gain a deeper understanding of the core components of resilience and become more resilient themselves[14,39]. Becoming more resilient enables most teachers to more effectively model resilience skills and attitudes, and to become more skilled at counselling students by referring to their common understandings from the BOUNCE BACK! acronyms (see page 61).

In addition, all **Bounce Back! Curriculum Units** contain classroom-friendly learning activities that can directly and indirectly create stronger teacher–student connectedness through sharing experiences and feelings.

Positive family-school links

Students are more likely to become more resilient, learn more effectively and complete school when their family and the school work together to give the same messages[40-42]. **Bounce Back! Information for families** includes information about the **Curriculum Units** to build better family understanding and support for the **Bounce Back!** messages. The information can be included in school newsletters, websites or emails home.

Family connectedness

A high level of family connectedness is one of the most important protective environmental resources[43-46]. Young people who feel they are supported by their families, have parents or carers who set and enforce rules in their homes, and feel respected for their individuality while belonging to a cohesive and stable family are likely to be resilient[46] All families face challenges at different times. In some families those challenges relate to the typical developmental stages of their children, or their relationship with a partner. In others they relate to death, illness, marital separation, financial hardship, job loss, mental illness, alcohol and substance abuse or other kinds of adversity.

Family connectedness is the extent to which young people feel a sense of involvement and acceptance in their family, and the degree to which they feel close to other members of their family. It also relates to the extent to which families communicate effectively with each other, spend time with each other in shared activities, express and enact loyalty and commitment to each other, solve family problems and pull together in the face of adversity. All families have strengths that can be accessed in difficult times. Of course, many families need additional support and care, but a useful starting point is to help a family in need to understand and develop the strengths they already have and then help them to learn more of the skills that underpin resilience.

One caring adult outside the family

Research into resilience has identified that having one adult in their life who is not a parent, but who is accessible and caring towards them and believes in them, is a highly significant protective factor for young people[19]. The adult may be a part of the extended family, such as an older sibling, a grandparent, an uncle or aunt, or a cousin. They may be a family friend, a youth worker, a sporting coach or a teacher. Benard[19] talks about the 'turnaround teacher' who can give young people the courage and confidence to cope in difficult circumstances. Caring about a young person means seeing the possibilities in them, acting compassionately towards them and being concerned for their wellbeing. It means looking beyond their often negative and challenging words and actions and seeing their underlying feelings of anger, pain, fear, insecurity and confusion[19]. Caring also means being a sympathetic confidante for their distress and worries by carefully listening to and believing their story, and by showing interest, respect and empathy[47].

Community connectedness

Community connectedness means positive participation in the life of the wider local community and willingness to access community resources. Schools, churches, youth clubs, sports clubs and other community institutions can provide an infrastructure for young people's connection with their community. Opportunities for positive youth community involvement, such as participation in sports teams, art and drama groups and membership of prosocial youth groups, has been identified as one of the most prevalent protective factors in enhancing youth wellbeing[44]. The other two major protective factors in this study were core values and family connectedness.

It is worth noting that informal rather than formal community connections often are more powerful. When asked who helped them to succeed against the odds, resilient young people in a longitudinal study by Werner and Smith[48] overwhelmingly gave credit to members of their extended family (grandparents, siblings, aunts or uncles), neighbours and teachers, and mentors in voluntary community associations with youth groups. Young people sought support from these informal community networks and valued this kind of support more often than the services of formal community organisations, mental health professionals and social workers.

Being connected to people in one's community has been shown to correlate strongly with self-confidence, having a feeling of control over one's life, not being involved with anti-social groups, and having higher educational aspirations and achievement[49]. However, it is not clear how much this correlation reflects the fact that those young people who are likely to seek access to the community in the first place are already more resilient and are also more likely to have high levels of family support, high ability and high socio-economic status.

Schools are in an excellent position to help young people connect with their local community. This focus can work in different ways. Some schools become involved in community service projects while others collaborate with community agencies and programs to meet students' needs through the collaboration of school-based health, family and welfare professionals. Other schools provide community education programs or after-school care, or invite the community to make use of school facilities, such as the gym, after hours.

Spirituality and religious life

> I think that the very purpose in life is to seek happiness. ...Whether one believes in religion or not...we are all seeking something better in life. So, I think, the very motion of our life is toward happiness. (Tenzin Gyatso, the Dalai Lama, 1998)

Spirituality refers to the human tendency to search for meaning in life through self-transcendence or the need to relate to something greater than oneself. Religion refers to a spiritual search that is connected to formal religious institutions. People with spiritual faith report higher levels of happiness and life satisfaction[50], are more likely to be physically healthier and live longer[51] and are more likely to retain or recover emotional wellbeing after suffering divorce, unemployment, serious illness or bereavement than people without such faith[52,53].

Many explanations can be offered for the connection between spiritual involvement and resilience:

- Communities with shared spiritual values usually provide social support and connection for members, as well as a sense of belonging and affirmation. Many religions offer unconditional love and acceptance.

- For many people, a spiritual faith provides them with a sense of purpose, and satisfies a basic human need of wanting our lives to have some kind of meaning[50]. Seligman[54] has argued that the loss of meaning, as well as the loss of a sense of purpose, is contributing to today's high levels of depression among young people.

- Many religions offer people a sense of hope, often through prayer, when facing adversity, as well as answers to some of life's deepest questions[50].

- The principles and beliefs associated with many religions encourage an acceptance of, and stoicism in the face of, things that can't be changed.

- Some religions encourage the practice of deep self-reflection and the facing of truth and pain with courage.

Bounce Back! does not directly address spirituality. Those schools with religious affiliations will already have faith-focused learning experiences and strategies in place. However, the values addressed in the Core values and Social values units have been derived from those that underpin most religions, whether they be, for example, Christian, Buddhist, Muslim or Jewish. These values focus on integrity and self-respect, fairness and justice, support, care for others, compassion, acceptance of differences, cooperation, friendliness and respect for the rights of others. Of course, these prosocial core values are not held only by people with religious beliefs. Many people who are not affiliated with any religion, and would consider themselves to be agnostic or atheist, also endorse and try to live by these values.

Differentiating the Bounce Back! curriculum

Today's classrooms are more diverse, more inclusive and more plugged into technology than ever before and are more likely to include students from a wide range of different religious and cultural backgrounds, experiences, personalities, abilities, social and emotional skills and levels of wellbeing[55]. Creating and maintaining an inclusive culture where every student feels welcomed as a learner and a valued peer is essential to maximising the outcomes of all learners in the classroom. The *Bounce Back!* curriculum is designed to create an inclusive culture where all children are welcomed, included and respected and where diversity is celebrated. Many children have extra challenges because of their learning needs or their backgrounds and these children will particularly benefit from *Bounce Back!* topics that help them become more resilient and cope better with setbacks.

In the differentiated classroom, teachers can modify the curriculum content, the learning strategies and/or the learning products to meet the diverse needs of the different students in their classrooms. Differentiation, rather than a 'one size fits all' approach increases the likelihood that all students will be engaged and succeed in learning.

The developmental structure of the *Bounce Back!* curriculum incorporates the same curriculum topics from Foundation to Year 6, sequenced in age-appropriate topics. This means that teachers can readily access topics from different year levels which may be more appropriate for their student cohort. For example, a class with a high number of English language learners might find the lessons in a younger level more accessible for some of their students. Gifted learners might be challenged by lessons for older students. Students with an autism spectrum diagnosis may need more repetition and practice of the skills.

Bounce Back! can be differentiated by:

- integrating the lessons with current curriculum areas such as English or literacy, Science, etc.
- the choice of literature and follow-up activities that can be language-based, inquiry-project based, art-based, drama-based, music-based etc.
- the selection of teaching strategies from the diverse range provided in the program
- the selection of different thinking tools that can be used with a topic
- the length of time spent on each unit to suit the learning speed of the students in a particular class
- using a variety of learning products and assessment tools that can provide formative and summative assessment of what students have learnt. Assessing students' existing skill levels at the start of a unit (e.g. resilience, specific social skills, growth mindset, etc.) enables the teacher to tailor the content and activities in the lessons to meet students' diverse learning needs. The assessment can be carried out informally through a Circle Time discussion or by using other *Bounce Back!* activities such as introductory postbox surveys.

✦ Differentiating Bounce Back! for gifted learners

Learner strengths and limitations

No student is gifted in all areas. *Bounce Back!* provides opportunities for students to identify both their strengths and limitations using their ability strengths (multiple intelligences framework; see pages 42–43) and their character strengths (Unit 10: Success). Understanding each student's areas of relative strength enables teachers to provide opportunities for extension, enrichment and complexity in that student's area(s) of strength as well as stretch them in areas where they show limitations.

Social and emotional challenges

Gifted students can have high energy, creativity, intensity and high aspirations which may create a mismatch with their classroom/school environment where the pace of learning is too slow for them. They may also have difficulties in finding compatible friends and experience pressures 'to be like everyone else'. Such factors can create risks to a gifted student's social and emotional development so they can particularly benefit from *Bounce Back!* topics.

Thinking skills

Bounce Back! provides many opportunities for students to enhance their critical, creative, ethical and empathic thinking skills as they engage with the curriculum. Cooperative thinking tools are outlined in Teaching strategies and resources and are incorporated in the **Curriculum Units**. They provide effective scaffolding to structure and challenge students' thinking. These cooperative thinking tools also help students to develop important social and emotional skills such as considering others' viewpoints, respectfully disagreeing and being an effective listener.

Working with other students

Gifted students benefit from working with similar peers who have strengths in the same ability areas. Student action teams can work together and across year levels on 'big picture' projects such as enhancing schoolwide wellbeing or an anti-bullying campaign. Some students with high levels of empathy and advanced social skills would also enjoy working with younger students on aspects of the program.

✦ Differentiating Bounce Back! for students who have experienced trauma

Incidence and effects of trauma on learning

Statistics vary, but anywhere from a quarter to a half of primary-aged children are likely to have experienced at least one traumatic event[56]. Many will have experienced multiple events including abuse and neglect. For some high-risk groups, such as students living in Out of Home Care (OOHC) or students of refugee background, the percentage who have experienced trauma is almost 100 per cent[56].

There is more and more research into the effects of trauma on the developing brain, with conclusive evidence that ongoing childhood trauma can lead to difficulties in areas such as memory, concentration, motor coordination, language development, cognitive development and, notably, difficulties with emotional regulation[57,58]. It is possible to look at the age and neurological developmental stage at which trauma occurred and potentially see the resulting difficulties, e.g. a two-year-old child that is in the process of acquiring language at the time they experience significant trauma is more likely to have difficulty with speech and language later on in childhood than a 10-year-old child who experiences the same trauma[57].

Recovery through social and emotional learning

The three most important evidence-based directions that teachers can focus on to promote recovery after complex (ongoing) trauma are:

1 creating a sense of safety
2 building positive relationships and a sense of belonging
3 teaching the skills needed for emotional regulation[59,60].

It is important to recognise that students who have experienced trauma are likely to take longer to feel safe and to trust others, so it will also take them longer to build positive connections and friendships than their classmates. Similarly, these students will find it a lot more challenging to recognise, express and regulate emotions than other students.

Many of the activities in *Bounce Back!* (e.g. Circle Time) help to build a safe space for these children to express their emotions and to build connections with their peers and their teachers. The use of children's literature can also provide a safe way to explore some of the key themes of resilience without having to explore specific traumatic issues. Complex trauma is highly correlated with learning difficulties, so using activities of various modalities (e.g. drawing, songs, picture books) can be helpful for these learners.

When to seek professional help

Working with young people who have experienced significant trauma can be very complex and extremely challenging. It may be useful to speak with your school counsellor or another specialist for advice about how to safely navigate working with these students.

✦ Differentiating Bounce Back! for English language learners (EAL/D)

Culturally inclusive

The Core values, Social values and Relationships units, plus the focus on relationship-building teaching strategies (e.g. cooperative learning and Circle Time), help classmates to be respectful towards and supportive of each other and facilitates *Bounce Back!* classrooms as culturally inclusive.

Language instruction

The use of quality children's literature in **Bounce Back!** is designed to promote substantive classroom discussion of key resilience messages. Such discussions can enhance vocabulary development and communicative language skills. Picture books also offer a focus on visual literacy. Follow-up literacy activities can be readily adapted to meet the diverse needs of English language learners. Most **Curriculum Units** contain a range of engaging activities and educational games that scaffold language development including sentence completions, memory cards, cross-offs, mystery square and reader's theatre.

Strengths in different areas

Earlier research using multiple intelligences as a framework for curriculum differentiation found that English language learners became more engaged in learning and achieved more academically when given opportunities to demonstrate their learning through non-academic products such as a role-play or skit, drawings or flow charts, and so on[61]. **Bounce Back!** offers diverse options for children to demonstrate what they have learnt and understood.

Scaffolds for thinking

The diverse range of thinking tools in the program provides scaffolds for critical, creative, ethical and empathic thinking. These benefit all students but particularly English language learners who may not have the language to engage in substantive discussion without the visual scaffolding and question prompts provided by the thinking tools (see Teaching strategies and resources).

Working with students from refugee backgrounds

Students who have come from refugee backgrounds are likely to be both English language learners and to have also experienced trauma. For these young people, there is often a great deal of complexity in both their academic/learning needs and their social and emotional wellbeing. A classroom environment of safety and a sense of belonging will be the first steps towards recovery. Many of the activities in **Bounce Back!** help build positive peer relationships and a sense of connection and safety in a classroom. Focusing on the visual features in the picture books in each unit, as well as drawing and music activities, may help with both their language understanding and their recovery.

It is important to be sensitive to working with potentially triggering topics such as grief, loss or war when teaching refugee students. Refer to the guidelines on safe discussions in the Teaching strategies and resources chapter. It may also be useful to speak with your School Counsellor or another specialist for advice about how to safely navigate working with these students.

REFERENCES

1. Collaborative for Academic, Social and Emotional Learning, 2010 [cited 18/1/10], available from www.casel.org
2. Zins, J.E., et al. (eds) 2004, *Building Academic Success on Social and Emotional Learning: What Does the Research Say?*, Teachers College Press, New York.
3. Durlak, J.A., Domitrovich, C.E., Weissberg, R.P., & Gullota, T.P. 2015, *Handbook of Social and Emotional Learning. Research and Practice*, The Guilford Press, New York.
4. 'Better outcomes for disengaged young people: Initial scoping, analysis and policy review', 2005, Department of Premier and Cabinet, DESCS SA Government.
5. Brooks, F. 2014, 'The Link Between Pupil Health And Wellbeing and Attainment: A Briefing for Head Teachers, Governors and Staff in Education Settings', Public Health England, Department of Health (DH) Public Health England.
6. Banerjee, R., Weare, K. & Farr W. 2014, 'Working with "social and emotional aspects of learning" (SEAL): Associations with school ethos, pupil social experiences, attendance and attainment', *British Educational Research Journal*, 40, 4, pp. 718–742.
7. Challen, A., Noden, P., West, A. & Machin, S. 2011, 'UK Resilience Programme Evaluation: Final Report', DfE: http://eprints.lse.ac.uk/51617/1/West_etal_UK-resilience-programme-evaluation-final-report_2011.pdf.
8. Brooks, F. 2013, 'Chapter 7: Life stage: School Years', in *Chief Medical Officer's Annual Report 2012: Our Children Deserve Better: Prevention Pays*, Davies, S.V., Department of Health.
9. Gutman, L. & Vorhaus, J. 2012, *The Impact of Pupil Behaviour and Wellbeing on Educational Outcomes*, DfE, London.
10. Duckworth, A & Seligman, M. 2005, *Self discipline outdoes IQ in predicting academic performance.*
11. Flook, L., Repetti, R. & Ullman, J. 2005, 'Classroom Social Experiences as Predictors of Academic Performance', *Developmental Psychology*, 41, pp. 319–327.
12. Noble, T., McGrath, H.L., Roffey, S. & Rowling, L. 2008, 'Scoping Study into Approaches to Student Wellbeing: A Report to the Department of Education', Employment and Workplace Relations.
13. 'NSSF: National Safe Schools Framework', 2011, Ministerial Council for Education, Early Childhood Development and Youth Affairs: https://docs.education.gov.au/system/files/doc/other/national_safe_schools_framework.pdf
14. Axford, S., Schepens, R. & Blyth, K. 2011, 'Did introducing the Bounce Back! Programme have an impact on resilience, connectedness and wellbeing of children and teachers in 16 primary schools in Perth and Kinross, Scotland?', *Educational Psychology*, 12 (1): pp. 2–5.
15. McGrath, H. & Anders, E. 2000, 'The Bounce Back! Program', in *Turning the tide in schools drug education project*, Victorian Department of Education.
16. World Health Organization Definitions of Health and Mental Health: www.who.int/features/factfiles/mental_health/en/
17. Robinson, P., Oades, L.G. & Caputi, P. 2015, 'Conceptualising and measuring mental fitness: A Delphi study', *International Journal of Wellbeing*, 5(1): pp. 53–73.
18. ReachOut Orb Teacher Resource 2015, Years 9 and 10: Australian HPE and NSW PDHPE Curriculums: https://www.tes.com/teaching-resource/reachout-orb-11309950
19. Benard, B. 2004, *Resiliency: What We Have Learned*, WestEd, San Francisco.
20. Noble, T. & McGrath, H. 2015, 'PROSPER: A New Framework for Positive Education', in *Psychology of Wellbeing*, www.springer.com/-/0/AU7CNS2GmRg70md7zMEi
21. www.curriculum.edu.au/verve/_resources/National_Declaration_on_the_Educational_Goals_for_Young_Australians.pdf
22. www.australiancurriculum.edu.au/generalcapabilities/overview/introduction
23. https://studentwellbeinghub.edu.au/educators/national-safe-schools-framework#
24. http://www.youthpolicy.org/national/Australia_2010_National_Youth_Strategy.pdf
25. www.familyschool.org.au/files/3013/8451/8364/Familyschool_partnerships_framework.pdf
26. http://www.curriculum.edu.au/verve/_resources/Framework_PDF_version_for_the_web.pdf
27. Osterman, K. 2000, 'Students' need for belonging in the school community', *Review of Educational Research*, vol. 70, no. 3, pp. 323–367.
28. Lee, V.E., et al. 1999, *Social Support, Academic Press, and Student Achievement: A View From the Middle Grades in Chicago*, Chicago Annenberg Challenge, Chicago.
29. Catalano, R.F., et al. June 2003, 'The importance of bonding to school for healthy development: Findings from the Social Development Research Group', in Wingspread Conference on School Connectedness, Racine, Wisconsin.
30. Bond, L., et al. 2007, 'Social and school connectedness in early secondary school as predictors of late teenage substance use, mental health, and academic outcomes', *Journal of Adolescent Health*, vol. 40, no. 357, pp. 9–18.
31. Marzano, R.J., Marzano, J.S. & Pickering, D. 2003, 'Classroom Management that Works: Research-based Strategies for Every Teacher', Association for Supervision and Curriculum Development, Alexandria, Virginia.
32. Lonczak, H.S., et al. 2002, 'The Effects of the Seattle Social Development Project: Behavior, pregnancy, birth, and sexually transmitted disease outcomes by age 21', archives of *Pediatric Adolescent Health*, vol. 156, pp. 438–447.
33. Wilson, D. & Elliott, D. June 2003, 'The interface of school climate and school connectedness: An exploratory review and study', in Wingspread Conference on School Connectedness, Racine, Wisconsin.
34. Durlak, J. A., Weissberg, R. P., Dymnicki, A. B., Taylor, R. D. & Schellinger, K. B. 2011, The Impact of Enhancing Students' Social and Emotional Learning: A Meta-Analysis of School-Based Universal Interventions, *Child Development*, 82, 1, pp. 405-432.
35. Hattie, J. 2009, *Visible Learning: A Synthesis of Over 800 Meta-analyses Relating to Achievement*, Routledge, London.
36. Rowe, K. 2001, 'Keynote Address', in Educating Boys in the Middle Years of Schooling Symposium, St Ignatius School, Riverview.
37. Trent, F. 2001, 'Aliens in the classroom or: the classroom as an alien place?' in 'Association of Independent Schools, NSW Sex, Drugs & Rock 'n Roll Conference', New South Wales.
38. Fuller, A., McGraw, K. & Goodyear, M. 1998, *The Mind of Youth Resilience: A Connect Project*, Victorian Department of Education, Victoria.
39. McGrath, H. & Anders, E. 2000, 'The Bounce Back! Program' in *Turning the tide in schools drug education project*, Victorian Department of Education.
40. Black, R. 2007, 'Crossing the bridge: overcoming entrenched disadvantage through student-centred learning' [cited 16/6/08], available from www.educationfoundation.org.au
41. Redding, S., et al. 2004, *The Effects of Comprehensive Parent Engagement on Student Learning Outcomes*, www.adi.org/solidfoundation/resources/Harvard.pdf.

42. Reschly, A.L. & Christenson, S.L. 2009, 'Parents as essential partners for fostering students' learning outcomes' in *Handbook of Positive Psychology in Schools*, Gilman, R., Huebner, E.S. & Furlong, M. (eds), Routledge, New York.
43. Suldo, S. 2009, 'Parent-child relationships' in *Handbook of Positive Psychology in Schools*, Gilman, R., Huebner, E.S. & Furlong, M. (eds), Routledge, New York.
44. Bond, L., et al. 2000, *Improving the Lives of Young Victorians in Our Community – A Survey of Risk and Protective Factors*, Centre for Adolescent Health, available from www.dhs.vic.gov.au/commcar, Melbourne.
45. Masten, A.S., et al. 1999, 'Competence in the context of adversity: Pathways to resilience and maladaptation from childhood to late adolescence', *Development & Psychopathology*, vol. 11, no. 1, Winter, pp. 143–169.
46. Werner, E.E. 1993, 'Risk, resilience and recovery: Perspectives from the Kauai longitudinal study', *Development and Psychopathology*, vol. 5, pp. 503–515.
47. Benard, B. & Slade, S. 2009, 'Listening to students: Moving from resilience research to youth development practice and school connectedness' in *Handbook of Positive Psychology in Schools*, Gilman, R., Huebner, E.S. & Furlong, M. (eds), Routledge, New York.
48. Werner, E.E. & Smith, R.S. 1993, *Overcoming the Odds: High Risk Children from Birth to Adulthood*, Cornell University Press, Ithaca, New York.
49. Larson, R.W. 2000, 'Toward a psychology of positive youth development', *American Psychologist*, vol. 55, no. 1, pp. 170–183.
50. Myers, D.G. 2000, 'The funds, friends and faith of happy people', *American Psychologist*, vol. 55, no. 1, pp. 56–67.
51. George, L., K., et al. 2000, 'Spirituality and health: What we know, what we need to know', *Journal of Social and Clinical Psychology*, vol. 19, no. 1, pp. 102–116.
52. McIntosh, D.N., Silver, R.C. & Wortman, C.B. 1993, 'Religion's role in adjustment to a negative life event: Coping with the loss of a child', *Journal of Personality and Social Psychology*, vol. 65, pp. 812–821.
53. Ellison, C.G. 1991, 'Religious involvement and subjective wellbeing', *Journal of Health and Social Behaviour*, vol. 32, pp. 80–99.
54. Seligman, M.E.P. 2002, *Authentic Happiness*, Free Press, New York.
55. Tomlinson, C.A. 2014, *The Differentiated Classroom: Responding to the needs of all learners*. 2nd edn, ASCD, Alexandria, Virginia.
56. Saunders, B.E. and Adams, Z.W. 2014, 'Epidemiology of Traumatic Experiences in Childhood', *Child and Adolescent Psychiatric Clinics of North America*, 23(2): pp. 167–184.
57. Perry, B. 2009, 'Examining child maltreatment through a neurodevelopmental lens: Clinical applications of the neurosequential model of therapeutics', *Journal of Loss and Trauma*, 14: pp. 240–255.
58. Porges, S.W. 2011, *The Polyvagal Theory: Neurophysiological Foundations of Emotions, Attachment, Communication, and Self-regulation*, WW Norton, New York.
59. Bath, H 2015, 'The three pillars of trauma-wise care: Healing in the other 23 hours', *Reclaiming Children and Youth*, 23 (4), pp. 5–11.
60. Blaustein, M.E. & Kinniburgh, K.M. 2010, *Treating Traumatic Stress in Children and Adolescents: How to Foster Resilience through Attachment, Self-Regulation, and Competency*, Guildford Press, New York.
61. Noble, T. 2004, 'Integrating the Revised Bloom's Taxonomy with Multiple Intelligences: A planning tool for curriculum differentiation,' *Teachers College Record*, 106(1), pp. 193–211.

CHAPTER 4

Social, emotional and coping skills for wellbeing and resilience

IN THIS CHAPTER

- A review of the personal coping skills, qualities and attitudes that underpin **Bounce Back!**
- Differentiating between everyday stressors such as a change in routine and major stressors such as family trauma
- The correlation between CASEL's five social competencies based on Social and Emotional Learning (self-awareness skills, self-management skills, social awareness skills, relationship skills and responsible decision-making) and the **Bounce Back! Curriculum Units**

INTRODUCTION

Student wellbeing and resilience are complex concepts. Resilience is the possession of personal skills and protective factors that help students cope in difficult times. This chapter looks at the social and emotional coping skills that can help young people develop a sense of wellbeing in which they are mostly positive, happy and resilient, have good relationships with family and friends, and are satisfied with their learning experiences at school.

We cannot protect young people from the stress of difficult life events, but we can help them develop the personal skills and assets necessary to cope with these events.

The five core competencies identified by the Collaborative for Academic, Social and Emotional Learning (CASEL)[1] as categories of school-based Social and Emotional Learning (SEL) skills (see pages 5–6) all contribute to wellbeing and resilience and are taught in the **Bounce Back! Curriculum Units** (see page 81). This chapter expands on the details and evidence base for those skills so that they can be taught well.

Everyday and major stressors

Learning social and emotional coping skills can help students manage everyday stressors as well as major stressors. Everyday stressors are the typical situations and challenges that most students face as they proceed through developmental stages. They include changes in routine, social disappointments and the challenges involved in starting school, changing school or advancing from one year level to another as well as academic challenges. Whether these everyday events are stressful or not will depend in part on the student's personal coping skills and their home and school environment. Major stressors or risk factors are events such as family trauma or severe bullying. At these times, young people will typically need extra support to access and employ resilient attitudes and skills. Examples of everyday and major stressors are outlined in the table below.

Everyday and major stressors and risk factors

Everyday stressors	Major stressors
Pre-school (1–4 years) • Birth of sibling • Adjustment to childcare • Transition to pre-school • Separation from attachment figures **Primary school (5–12 years)** • Transition to school • Competition with peers • Peer relationships • Peer teasing • Peer pressure (e.g. to follow a fad or do something they don't want to do) • Sibling pressures • Homework • Poor academic outcomes • Teacher conflicts • Disappointments connected with sport or other extracurricular activities • Fear of oral class presentations • Worry about tests • Time pressures (balancing schoolwork demands and extracurricular or home demands) • Child–parent conflicts • Early puberty **Adolescence (13–18 years)** • Hormonal changes • Growth changes • Physical appearance • Peer pressure • Heightened sexuality • Issues of independence and freedom • Relationship issues • Increased responsibility for self in school • Career and university choices • Transition to work • Managing school and part-time work • Gender role issues	**Death** • Parent • Sibling • Close relative • Close friend • Favourite pet **Serious illness or disability** • Self • Parent • Sibling • Close relative • Close friend **Other extraordinary trauma** • War • Natural disasters; e.g. fire, flood, drought, cyclones • Legal problems • Sexual and/or physical abuse and/or neglect • Robbery or assault • Road trauma, either witnessing or being involved **Family issues** • Divorce • Remarriage • Job loss, job start • Witnessing abuse/violence • Mental illness • Alcohol/drug abuse • Criminal and civil law issues, trials and being jailed **Change** • Standard of living • School • Residence • Number of people living in home • Parental contact (e.g. parent working long hours/shift work or loss of contact) **Being bullied** • Physical • Verbal • Social exclusion • Cyberbullying

Social, emotional and coping skills: Self-awareness

This section provides more information on the self-awareness skills of:

- strengths
- optimistic thinking
- self-efficacy
- self-respect
- a sense of meaning and purpose
- a growth mindset for academic and social resilience.

✦ Recognising strengths and limitations

A converging message from both the Positive Education movement and CASEL is that a strengths-based approach is important for the promotion of student wellbeing and academic engagement. Researchers from CASEL explain that:

> …there is no good alternative to a strengths-based approach to working with children. It involves a) establishing positive relationships with children based on their assets and their potential contributions as resources to their schools and b) finding naturally occurring contexts in which they can enact positive roles for which they must learn skills to be successful.[2]

A 'strength' has been defined as a way of behaving, thinking or feeling for which an individual has a natural capacity. Strengths can help students achieve optimal functioning while pursuing valued outcomes[3-5]. Wood[5] describes 'personal strengths' as the characteristics of a person that allow them to perform well or at their personal best. Most students find using their strengths in their schoolwork is far more enjoyable and productive than working on their weaknesses, especially for those students whose strengths are not in the traditional academic domains[6].

When students work with their strengths they tend to learn more readily, perform at a higher level, are more motivated and confident, and have a stronger sense of satisfaction, mastery and competence. Opportunities to identify and sometimes work with their strengths are especially important for students who are not academically strong[6]. Students who are given feedback on their strengths are significantly more likely to feel highly engaged and to be more productive than those who only receive feedback on their weaknesses. Results for the strengths-based feedback groups (compared to control groups with no feedback) included increases in year-point average, attendance and self-confidence[7,8].

Bounce Back! Unit 10: Success incorporates two models for identifying and engaging students' strengths. One is Gardner's Multiple Intelligences Theory for intellectual strengths (or abilities)[9] and the other is Peterson and Seligman's Values in Action (VIA) framework for character strengths[10].

Bounce Back! uses three approaches for engaging students' strengths:

1. **Identifying a student's strength.** Unit 10: Success provides age-appropriate tools for students to identify their ability and character strengths so they have an opportunity to develop a deeper understanding of their relative strengths and limitations.

2. **Building up a strength** is the process of identifying a strength that still requires more work, such as a student's language skills (intellectual strength) or a student's skills at persevering or being brave (character strengths).

3. **Building upon a strength** is the process of creating opportunities for students to use and develop their intellectual or character strengths, e.g. extending a student's artistic ability (intellectual) or their leadership skills (character).

Intellectual strengths and abilities

Howard Gardner's Multiple Intelligences Theory (MI)[9] has been widely adopted in schools since its first publication over 30 years ago[11,12]. The model identifies eight intelligences.

Gardner's eight intelligences

• Verbal–linguistic	• Musical
• Logical–mathematical	• Interpersonal
• Visual–spatial	• Intrapersonal
• Bodily–kinaesthetic	• Naturalist

MI theory's main claim is that it is more productive to describe a student's cognitive ability in terms of several relatively independent but interacting intelligences than a single 'general' intelligence. With MI theory the question changes from 'how smart is this student?' to 'how is this student smart?'

In other words, 'what are the relative strengths of this student across all eight intelligences?' It is important that supporters of the MI framework don't fall into the erroneous trap of labelling students by their MI strength. It is also important not to erroneously link the MI framework with the now debunked concept of 'learning styles, for which there is no scientific evidence whatsoever'[13].

Gardner[12] defines 'intelligence' as a bio-psychological potential to process particular types of information, to solve problems or create products that are valued in at least one culture or community. Each student has an 'intelligence profile' that is a description of their relative strengths and weaknesses across the eight intelligences. According to Moran[14] what makes the MI approach so powerful is how the different intelligences interact and combine to achieve a purpose. Rich and challenging learning tasks do not isolate one intelligence but rather combine intelligences to achieve a purposeful learning outcome.

A differentiated curriculum based on Gardner's MI Theory has the potential to build a positive educational community in which students value and celebrate student differences and which supports students who struggle with learning to achieve more academic success[15-18]. An evaluation of outcomes in 41 schools that had been using MI theory for curriculum differentiation for at least three years found significant benefits of the MI approach in terms of improvements in student engagement and learning, student behaviour, and parent participation[15]. This evaluation found that students with learning difficulties greatly benefited as indicated by their increased effort and motivation in learning, and their improved learning outcomes when offered different entry points into the curriculum and different ways to demonstrate their understanding of the curriculum.

Another well-known framework for differentiation is Bloom's taxonomy which provides a hierarchy of thinking skills from simple recognition and recall to high order critical and creative (design) thinking. ***Bounce Back!*** draws on the MI framework (across eight intelligences) and Bloom's taxonomy of six levels of thinking to provide activities that extend and enrich the curriculum. The MI/Bloom Matrix in *Eight Ways at Once* has been widely used in Australian schools for curriculum differentiation[16,17]. Teachers' use of the matrix in two primary schools over 18 months was shown to have increased their sense of professional competency in effectively catering for diverse students' learning needs and also developed their competencies in helping their students set goals and make meaningful choices about their learning tasks and products[16-18].

Character strengths

A focus on character strengths has become very popular in Positive Psychology/Positive Education. The Values in Action (VIA) framework (see the table below) developed by Peterson and Seligman[10] incorporates 24 character strengths organised in six categories called virtues.

Values in Action framework for character strengths

Wisdom and knowledge	**Justice**
• Creativity • Curiosity • Judgment (critical thinking) • Love of learning • Perspective (wisdom)	• Teamwork (citizenship, social responsibility, loyalty) • Fairness • Leadership
Courage	**Temperance**
• Bravery (valour) • Perseverance (persistence, industriousness) • Honesty (authenticity, integrity) • Zest (vitality, enthusiasm, vigour, energy)	• Forgiveness • Humility • Prudence • Self-regulation (self-control)
Humanity	**Transcendence**
• Love • Kindness • Social intelligence	• Appreciation of beauty and excellence (awe, wonder) • Gratitude • Hope (optimism) • Humour (playfulness) • Spirituality (faith, purpose)

Source: http://www.viacharacter.org/www/Character-Strengths/VIA-Classification

An individual's strongest strengths (the top 3 to 5) are considered 'signature strengths'. Signature strengths are seen to be so central to a person's psychological identity that suppressing or ignoring them would seem unnatural and very difficult. The five character strengths for adults that appear to be most highly related to life satisfaction are: hope, zest, gratitude, curiosity and love[19]. An energising staff-building activity is to ask all staff to complete the adult survey (on the VIA Institute on Character website) and then share how they have used one of their signature strengths at school. There is also a survey available for 10 to 17 year olds. The table below suggests 10 ways of 'spotting' your own strengths.

The potential benefits of using this framework across a whole F–12 school is described by White and Waters[20,21]. In their study, character strengths have been embedded in English Literature classes, in the primary curriculum, in sports coaching, in training students for school leadership positions and in counselling students. The authors demonstrate how students from the beginning of school are developing their knowledge of how to identify, explore, further develop and apply their character strengths. They argue that the combination of these different initiatives under the umbrella of Positive Education has contributed to 'a cultural tipping point where the strengths initiatives across the school are fusing to create a strengths-based culture'[21] (p. 6–7).

Other examples of the VIA framework used in education include Proctor's examination of the 'Strengths gym'[22]. Adolescents who participated in exercises in the program that were based on character strengths experienced a significant increase in life satisfaction and positive affect from baseline to post test. The Strath-Haven Positive Psychology program also used the VIA character strengths framework in their Language and Arts classes[23]. Pre-test to post-test comparisons showed that the students in these classes reported greater enjoyment and engagement in school compared to students in a control group. Teachers also reported that the program improved students' strengths related to learning such as curiosity, love of learning and creativity. Parents and teachers reported improvements in students' social skills. Quinlan[24] also describes a six-session classroom-based strengths intervention with nine to 12 year olds. Students reported higher levels of positive affect, classroom engagement, autonomy and satisfaction of relatedness needs, class cohesion and strengths use.

Ten ways to spot your own strengths

Childhood memories
What do you remember doing as a child that you still do now – but most likely much better? Strengths often have deep roots from our earlier lives.

Energy
What activities give you an energetic buzz when you are doing them? These activities are very likely calling on your strengths.

Authenticity
When do you feel most like the 'real you'? The chances are that you will be using your strengths in some way.

Ease
What activities do you excel at and come naturally to you – sometimes, it seems, without even trying? These will likely be your strengths.

Attention
Where do you naturally pay attention? You're more likely to focus on things that are playing to your strengths.

Rapid learning
What are the things that you have picked up quickly, learning them almost effortlessly? Rapid learning often indicates an underlying strength.

Motivation
What motivates you? When you find activities that you do simply for the love of doing them, you are likely to be working from your strengths.

Voice
Monitor your tone of voice. When you notice a shift in passion, energy and engagement, you're probably talking about a strength.

Words and phrases
Listen to the words you use. When you're saying: 'I love to …' or 'It's just great when …', the chances are that it's a strength to which you are referring.

To do list
Notice the things that never make it on to your 'To do' list. Things that always seem to get done often reveal an underlying strength that means we never need to be asked twice.

Source: Adapted from: Linley, A. (2008), *Average to A+: Realising Strengths in Yourself and Others. (Strengthening the World)*. CAPP Press, Warwick, UK.

Experiencing 'psychological flow' by using one's strengths

Students experience 'psychological flow' when they are so immersed in an activity that hours pass like minutes, their mind is totally focused and they are completely absorbed in what they are doing. Athletes call it 'being in the zone'. The state of flow occurs when students encounter a challenging task that tests their skills but they also have the skills and strengths or capacities to meet the challenge. So both the challenge and the skills really stretch them. If the challenge exceeds their skills they become anxious; if their skills exceed the challenge of the task, they are likely to be bored. Csikszentmihalyi[25] investigated the phenomenon of flow by interviewing thousands of people from many different walks of life, including large cohorts of teenagers. He concluded that flow is a universal experience that has the following characteristics:

- clarity of goals and immediate feedback on progress, e.g. in a competitive game students know what they need to achieve and whether they are winning or losing
- complete concentration on the activity at this present time
- actions and awareness are merged, e.g. a student is immersed in an art project and the process of painting becomes almost automatic
- losing self-consciousness is a common experience but after each flow experience, self-confidence is strengthened
- sense of control over the task or activity and not worrying about failure
- time passes more quickly than expected
- activities are intrinsically rewarding.

Activities that lead to a flow experience depend on the individual, and may include sport, dancing, involvement in the creative arts and other hobbies. Other activities that can lead to a flow experience include socialising, studying, reading and working. In fact, most daily activities can lead to flow as long as the task is sufficiently complex to activate the 'high challenge–high skill' criterion. Providing opportunities for students to identify and use their strengths in challenging tasks is much more likely to create optimal learning experiences than using passive teacher-controlled tasks such as passively watching a film, completing worksheets or listening to 'lectures'.

Strengths and flow in Bounce Back!

Students are encouraged to identify and use their character strengths in Unit 10: Success and in the activities in the **Curriculum Units**. These provide age-appropriate opportunities to 'build up' or 'build upon' their different strengths. Flow is also addressed in Unit 10: Success.

✦ Optimistic thinking

Optimism can play a vital role in helping students cope with setbacks or new situations. Optimism is a general belief that good rather than bad things will generally occur in life. It's a tendency to expect positive outcomes, to look on the bright side of things and to think optimistically about the future (within the bounds of reality). Conversely, pessimism involves expecting failure, anticipating bad outcomes and a tendency to take a gloomy view of things.

As mentioned in Chapter 2 (pages 18–19), **Bounce Back!** incorporates two perspectives for developing optimistic thinking. One perspective is from the 'expectancy' perspective, where optimism is defined as having a disposition or tendency to expect things to work out, to be forward looking and proactive and to have the confidence to persevere when faced with adversity[26]. The other perspective is based on an individual's 'explanatory style', i.e. how you explain the cause of events to yourself [27,28].

Optimistic thinking has been linked to:

- maintaining high levels of wellbeing during stress
- taking risks in the belief that there is a good chance that a positive outcome will be achieved
- persevering when things become difficult or after failure
- the use of adaptive strategies such as effective problem solving, obtaining social support and looking for any positives in stressful situations
- feeling confident and presenting in a confident way
- being successful in academic, athletic and vocational endeavours
- being popular
- having good health, engaging in health-promoting behaviour
- living longer and being more physically healthy.

Chapter 4 Social, emotional and coping skills for wellbeing and resilience

People who tend towards pessimism often feel down and helpless. Everything seems overwhelming and too hard to fix. They tend to look on the worst side of things and to feel a sense of hopelessness and despair. Pessimism is linked to:

- a greater risk of being depressed
- maladaptive strategies such as avoiding or denying problems, or giving up without even trying
- failing because the individual hasn't persisted or taken risks
- not doing as well in academic, athletic and vocational endeavours as their strengths would predict
- being socially isolated
- getting sick more often and being more vulnerable to infection.

Reivich[29] indicates that our optimism or pessimism becomes a habit by the end of primary school – and like any habit, the longer we practise it, the harder it is to change. It is important to teach children from an early age to think optimistically.

Good expectations

Building up an expectation that good things can happen is linked to feeling confident and in control of your life and having a sense of personal competence or mastery. Mastery is usually attained through the successful achievement of goals over time and hence the positive expectation that you can repeat the process. Conveying positive but realistic expectations to students and encouraging them to persevere can also help them develop optimistic thinking. Persevering and being successful, especially when a task is challenging, promotes optimism and self-efficacy. Helping students find the positive features of difficult situations, however small, also enhances optimism. Another term for this is 'positive tracking'.

Explanatory style

Explaining why bad things happen:
Our 'explanatory style' is the way we explain to ourselves why events happen to us[27,28]. This determines how optimistic or how helpless/pessimistic we become when we encounter everyday setbacks as well as momentous defeats. The pessimistic explanatory style for negative events leads to having little sense of control and a loss of hope. On the other hand, the optimistic explanatory style leads to a stronger sense of power over one's life and a belief that the future can be bright even if the present seems bleak.

There are three dimensions to our explanatory style for adversity: personal, permanent and pervasive as outlined in the following table.

Pessimistic and optimistic explanatory styles when bad things happen

	Pessimistic explanatory style	**Optimistic explanatory style**
1. Personal How much we think a negative situation has happened because of our personal attributes	**Because of me** Negative events happen mostly because of one's own defects, stupidity, unworthiness or because one is jinxed and attracts bad luck.	**Not just me** Negative events have many different causes, including circumstances outside one's control, bad luck and the behaviour of other people.
2. Permanent How permanent we think a negative situation will be	**Always** The situation will be ongoing and long-lasting.	**Not always** A negative event is probably not going to last very long or is a 'one-off'.
3. Pervasive How much we think this one negative situation pervades other parts of our life	**Everything** A negative event spoils everything.	**Not everything** A negative event is specific and affects one relevant part of life.

The following table compares two students who are both feeling socially isolated a month after starting at a new school. One uses a pessimistic explanatory style for why they are having difficulties making friends, while the other uses an optimistic explanatory style.

Explaining why good things happen:
Explanatory style for explaining good events is just the opposite of bad events. There are again three dimensions, as outlined in the table at the bottom of this page: 'Pessimistic and optimistic explanatory styles when good things happen'.

Explanatory styles for a negative event: feeling isolated at a new school

Pessimistic explanatory style	Optimistic explanatory style
Because of me Everyone has a friend except me. Nobody likes me because I'm not cool and not good at sport.	**Not just me** I wish I had a friend at my new school. But I remember when my cousin started at a new school – she found it hard to make friends, too. Mum is going to ask the teacher to help me get to know people in my new class.
Always I'm never going to make friends.	**Not always** It's hard being new at school but soon things will get better.
Everything I hate it that we moved. I don't like my teacher or my new school or the kids in my class. Everything is going wrong!	**Not everything** I haven't made any friends at school yet. But I've made friends with the kids next door so that's good, and I'm having a good time with my new netball team.

Pessimistic and optimistic explanatory styles when good things happen

	Pessimistic explanatory style	Optimistic explanatory style
1. Personal How much we think a good event has happened because of our characteristics and behaviour	**Not just me** The good event is not related to my personal characteristics, hard work or effort. Success instead might be due to good luck, accidental circumstances or favourable treatment.	**Because of me** The good event happened mostly because of my abilities, hard work and effort. It is okay to enjoy and take credit for a good event.
2. Permanent How long we think the benefits of a good event will last	**Temporary** A good event is likely to be short-lived or it is a 'one-off'.	**Ongoing** The good situation is likely to be ongoing and long-lasting.
3. Pervasive How much we think the good event will affect other parts of our life	**Just this** A good event is specific and affects just one relevant part of life. There is no carry-over effect.	**Other things** A good event can have a positive effect on many parts of our lives.

The following table shows an example of two students who both do well reading to the class. One uses a pessimistic explanatory style for why they did well and the other uses an optimistic explanatory style.

Explanatory styles for a positive event: doing well at reading

Pessimistic explanatory style	Optimistic explanatory style
Not just me I wasn't the only kid who read well. Other kids read well, too. The teacher gave me an easy book to read.	**Because of me** I read well in class today because I have been doing lots of reading at home to get better.
Temporary Sometimes I make lots of mistakes when I read in class. I'll probably read badly next time.	**Ongoing** I'm getting better and better at reading because I've worked hard to improve.
Just this I read well today but my other schoolwork isn't very good.	**Other things too** I really like reading in class. My schoolwork is really improving and so is my goal-shooting at netball.

Optimistic thinking in Bounce Back!

The BOUNCE BACK! acronym in Unit 3: People bouncing back contains statements to build students' optimism and challenge negative thinking and a pessimistic explanatory style for events. It focuses on:

- understanding that bad events are temporary
- understanding that one bad event doesn't have to spoil your whole life
- not personalising bad events and normalising instead, i.e. accepting that some things which happen to us happen to nearly everyone – they're pretty normal
- not over-emphasising your own faults and blaming yourself completely
- identifying the bit you might be responsible for and what you can learn from your own actions or mistakes so you can avoid doing the same thing again
- learning from other people's contributions to what happened so you get a better idea of what to look out for next time
- accepting that there are some random factors over which we don't have control. These factors usually are described as 'bad luck', 'random' or 'unfortunate circumstances'.

Optimistic thinking is also taught in Unit 5: Looking on the bright side with a focus on explanatory style, positive tracking, and appreciation and gratitude.

A cautionary note

Being overly optimistic can be counter-productive if it is unrealistic. Constant striving for control over events without the human or material resources to achieve a goal, or without seeing real obstacles, can lead to a sense of helplessness and depression. We all face objective limits to what we can change or achieve no matter how hard we try.

Teacher optimism about student academic achievement

Teachers' optimism about their ability to make a difference in their students' lives in their own classrooms correlates with higher student performance and greater academic success[30]. Such optimism can be contagious. One study identified that teachers' shared or collective optimism in expecting their students to perform well academically was more important in influencing their academic achievement than the students' socio-economic status, other demographic data and previous achievement history[30]. Another study found that when the teachers collectively raised their expectations of their students, made their students aware of this and challenged them academically, they were consistently rewarded by improved student learning; students' confidence in their learning increased and their behaviour improved[27].

Teachers may not feel empowered to make a difference at the system level of whole-school change, but working with their students in their own classrooms is working in their circle of influence. Reflecting on the kinds of teaching practices that foster student wellbeing and resilience in the classroom means not only reviewing 'what' is taught, but also 'how' it is taught.

♦ Self-efficacy

Explanatory style is also linked to self-efficacy. Young people who habitually blame themselves whenever things go wrong and don't give themselves credit for the good things that happen in their life are more likely to have low self-efficacy. Self-efficacy is having confidence in your ability to solve a particular problem or perform a specific task.

Those who don't overly blame themselves when things go wrong feel less guilt or shame when bad events happen because they also take into account the behaviour of others or adverse circumstances. They are less likely to feel disempowered when they encounter a setback, and when good things happen in their lives their self-confidence increases. They tend to 'pat themselves on the back' privately whenever anything they do, however small, is successful. They feel empowered because they believe that their own efforts have made the difference.

Greater self-efficacy in an area of one's life leads to greater effort and persistence in the face of setbacks in that area. A student with high self-efficacy in relation to a task will also set higher goals, be less afraid of making a mistake or failing and will look for new strategies when old ones fail, i.e. be more optimistic. But if self-efficacy is low for a task or situation, a student might avoid the task altogether or give up easily when problems arise.

Self-efficacy in Bounce Back!

The **Bounce Back!** coping statements in Unit 3: People bouncing back aim to increase young people's self-efficacy by encouraging them to understand the links between how they think about events and outcomes, and how they feel and act. Unit 10: Success aims to increase students' self-knowledge and self-management by learning skills in planning goals, monitoring progress and evaluating performance. The focus is on developing a growth mindset for success that focuses on effort, not ability[31].

♦ Self-respect

The construct of self-respect encapsulates the social, emotional and coping skills associated with self-awareness and self-management. In many ways self-respect can be seen as an outcome indicator of teaching the social, emotional and coping skills in the **Bounce Back!** program.

We define self-respect as an attitude of self-acceptance and approval for one's own character and conduct. According to Dillon[32] (p. 226):

> Individuals who are blessed with a confident respect for themselves have something that is vital to living a satisfying, meaningful, flourishing life, while those condemned to live without it or with damaged or fragile self-respect are thereby condemned to live constricted, frustrating lives cut off from possibilities for self-realisation, self-fulfilment and happiness.

The construct of self-respect is a more useful construct for educators and parents or carers than the construct of self-esteem. As far back as 1996, Professor Roy Baumeister, formerly a strong advocate of the self-esteem movement concluded:

> It is ... with considerable personal disappointment that I must report that the enthusiastic claims of the self-esteem movement mostly range from fantasy to hogwash. The effects of self-esteem are small, limited, and not all good ... And most of the time self-esteem makes surprisingly little difference[33] (p.14).

An analysis of 200 research studies that focused on the impact of enhancing self-esteem found there was no convincing evidence that enhancing self-esteem improves student learning or achievement, reduces anti-social behaviour or prevents or reduces substance abuse[34].

The difference between self-esteem and self-respect is important. Self-esteem is an evaluation of one's 'worth' as a person and ranges from low to high. Self-esteem focuses more on successes, what one can do, what one looks like and/or what one has. Therefore, self-esteem fluctuates because it is usually highly dependent on feedback from others.

To respect something, on the other hand, is to accept it. So self-respect can be viewed as an attitude of self-acceptance. Self-respect is not contingent on success because there are always setbacks and failures to deal with; nor is it reliant on comparisons with others because there are always people who are better than us. With self-respect individuals accept themselves because of who they are, not because of what they can or cannot do.

Young people can be taught to behave in ways that develop and also demonstrate their self-respect. Students with self-respect are more likely to behave in the following ways.

Self-awareness

- They focus more on their strengths than their limitations and do not over-focus on comparing themselves with others.
- They understand that it's okay to be different, to act differently or to have a different viewpoint. They see themselves as neither inferior nor superior to other people.
- They continually work on developing evidence-based self-knowledge (such as an understanding of their ability strengths and character strengths) by looking for evidence rather than just using 'wishful thinking'.

Self-management

- They respond to challenges and difficult times in their life by acting with courage and resilience. Resilience means coping and 'bouncing back' when something has gone wrong or things don't turn out as desired.
- They adopt a positive approach to life. This means focusing on things that go well in their everyday life, expressing gratitude to people who support them and being grateful for the good things in their life.
- They accept themselves (and other people in their life) as imperfect. They continue to be self-accepting even when they make mistakes or errors of judgment, or they don't do as well as they had hoped.
- They understand that it is always pleasant to receive positive feedback from others but not to become dependent on it. They use their own judgment as well.
- They enjoy their own achievements but avoid being arrogant about them. They remember to balance pride with humility and acknowledge the successes of other people as well.
- They trust their own judgment and have faith in themselves. They try to make sound decisions about what is best for them but also listen to, and incorporate advice and wisdom from people they trust.
- They consider the views and ideas of other people but are not automatically swayed by them. They weigh up what is said to them or about them by others and then make up their own mind rather than thinking, 'if someone else says it, then it must be true'.

Self-control

- They have a growth mindset and show grit. They work hard and acknowledge their efforts and persistence, even when they are not successful in what they were trying to achieve.
- They remind themselves that everyone has self-doubts occasionally and try not to let theirs get in the way of what they want to achieve.

Self-protect

- They make good choices and act in ways that protect their health, wellbeing, safety and reputation.
- They acknowledge their right to be treated respectfully and fairly and not to be mistreated by others. If it becomes necessary, they take non-aggressive and appropriate steps to protect this right. They don't let others put them down and they don't put themselves down either.

Respect for others

- They work towards having a set of clear moral values to guide their life and their decisions, e.g. honesty, compassion, acceptance of differences, inclusion and respect for others.
- They avoid deliberately hurting or belittling others and try not to get caught up in situations where others are doing so.
- They are prepared to stand up for what is right. They try to put their values into practice and not let themselves down when they are put to the test.
- They extend compassion and support towards others and try to help others in trouble.

Self-respect in Bounce Back!

All units incorporate some of the social, emotional and coping skills associated with the development of self-respect. For example, self-respect and respect for others are important values introduced in the Unit 2: Social values. Students who self-protect have self-respect because they take steps to change the situation if they mistreated in some way (also see Unit 9: Being safe). There is a focus on self-awareness and self-control in Unit 10: Success, where students are assisted to identify their strengths, set goals and develop a growth mindset and grit. There is also a focus on several of the self-respect characteristics and skills in Unit 3: People bouncing back.

✦ A sense of meaning and purpose

Finding purpose and meaning in one's life is one of the key elements of wellbeing. Purpose is seen as a reliable marker of flourishing[35], thriving[36], psychological wellbeing[37], resilience[38,39] and life satisfaction[40-42]. In contrast, a lack of purpose appears to contribute to poor mental health and higher psychological distress in both young people[43] and adults[44].

The terms 'meaning' and' purpose' are often used interchangeably in research literature. Purpose has been defined as 'a stable and generalised intention to accomplish something that is at once meaningful to the self and of consequence to the world beyond the self'[45]. Therefore, purpose indicates engagement in a meaningful activity that has some positive impact on others and thinking about how to extend that activity into the future[14]. Purpose has three main components: a long-term intention or goal, an action plan and commitment, and a beyond-the-self motivation[46]. The kinds of activities that are most likely to create a sense of meaning and purpose for students are those that have an impact on other people, not just themselves. According to Seligman, 'a meaningful life is one that joins with something larger than we are – and the larger that something is, the more meaning our lives have'[47]. He states that life is given meaning when we use our signature strengths every day 'to forward knowledge, power or goodness'.

Having a sense of meaning and purpose is quite an abstract concept for primary-aged children, and is more likely to grow in importance as they develop and mature. Research at the Stanford Youth Purpose Project[14,50] found that only about a quarter of young people aged 12 to 22 have a sense of purpose in how they can contribute to the big picture and are actually engaged in relevant activities to achieve a greater sense of purpose. However, young people who form and sustain a sense of purpose show exceptional initiative in seeking opportunities and building a support network to help them achieve their particular purpose[14,48].

A sense of purpose also fuels academic tenacity and better academic outcomes. One study encouraged secondary school students to write in their Science lessons every three or four weeks over a school term a brief essay describing how the content they had studied could apply to their lives[49]. Students in the intervention group expressed more interest in Science at the end of the term and earned higher Science grades than students in the control group. Importantly students' grades only improved if the students themselves came up with the reasons why the schoolwork was relevant and not when their teachers simply told them why the material should be relevant to their lives.

Sense of purpose in Bounce Back!

How does **Bounce Back!** help primary school students develop a sense of purpose? One way is to encourage students to self-reflect on the relevance to their lives of the key messages in **Bounce Back!** Encouraging students to have a deep self-awareness of their personal and ability strengths will help them identify purposeful goals as they grow and mature. Another way is to create opportunities for students to participate in student action teams[50] that benefit their class or school community based on **Bounce Back!** key messages such as 'Making our school safe for everyone' campaign or a 'Schoolwide Wellbeing' campaign.

A student action team is a group of students who identify and tackle a school or community issue: they research the issue, make plans and proposals about it, and take action on it[50]. They demonstrate a sense of purpose by committing time, energy, resources and knowledge to achieving their goal. Schools that have implemented student action teams indicate a substantial positive change in areas such as knowledge, skills, attitude and connectedness, and students who took part specifically identified their increased level of engagement at school[50].

Other school initiatives built into **Bounce Back!** that can foster a sense of purpose include:

- older children working with younger children to teach key messages
- classroom committees
- fundraising initiatives
- presentations to families on **Bounce Back!** topics.

Many other ideas for 'purposeful' age-appropriate projects are included in Unit 10: Success. All these activities provide real-life, purposeful, problem-solving contributions that illustrate how a student or group of students can and do intentionally and purposefully contribute to their school or local community.

✦ A 'growth mindset' for academic and social resilience

Low resilience has a negative impact on students' academic and social outcomes. Low academic resilience is linked to students developing a fixed mindset where they perceive their intelligence or ability is fixed and unchangeable. In contrast, high academic resilience is linked to a 'growth' mindset where students believe that with effort and hard work they can learn and master new material.

Academic mindset: Dweck and Blackwell have investigated the impact of a growth mindset on student learning outcomes for more than 20 years[51]. They have found that students with a growth mindset achieved increases in Mathematics grades over Year 7 and Year 8. In contrast, students with equal measured ability who had a fixed mindset (i.e. they viewed their intelligence/ability as fixed and unchangeable) did not achieve this level of improvement. The impact of a growth mindset was apparent for students at all levels of ability. Their research also demonstrated that students with a growth mindset used more complex thinking strategies and meta-cognitive strategies (i.e. self-monitoring of their learning), which led to deeper processing and understanding of the curriculum. The table below outlines the differences between a fixed and growth mindset.

Give more 'process praise' than 'person praise'

Teacher and family feedback on student performance influences the development of a growth or fixed mindset. Telling students 'you did well on that test, you must be really smart' leads to a fixed mindset, whereas telling students 'you did well on that test, you must have worked really hard' focuses their attention on effort and builds a growth mindset.

Giving children 'process praise' rather than 'person praise' is more likely to motivate them, to develop a 'growth mindset' and help them to be resilient and succeed in the face of challenge.

'Process praise' is a specific form of positive feedback that highlights the processes a student used to succeed in achieving an outcome. Examples of such processes include: effort, willpower, organisation, persistence, problem solving, research, determination. The example shown in the table on the opposite page differentiates feedback that promotes a 'fixed mindset' from that which promotes 'a growth mindset'.

Growth mindset versus fixed mindset

	How a student with a 'fixed mindset' thinks	How a student with a 'growth mindset' thinks
Basic assumption	My basic abilities are fixed traits that can't be changed.	My basic abilities can be improved with motivation, effort and strategy.
Likely main goal	My main focus is to demonstrate my ability.	My main focus is to learn new things, increase my skills and knowledge and improve my 'personal bests'.
View of failure or poor performance	Disappointment or failure shows that I have low ability.	Disappointments or failures indicate that I didn't put in enough effort and/or I didn't use a good strategy.
Most likely response after performing poorly	I'll ignore the feedback I received because it is a threat to my view of myself. There is no point putting in more effort.	Feedback is an opportunity to learn how to do better. I'll work harder and persist despite this setback.
Likely response to new challenges	I'll avoid new challenges so that I can continue to look good.	I'll have a go at this new challenge to see how far I can go.

Person praise vs process praise

Scenario	Person praise: feedback that promotes a 'fixed mindset'	Process praise: feedback that promotes a 'growth mindset'
A student has spent a lot of time writing and illustrating a story for younger students at the school.	Great job. You are so clever!	You have put such **a lot of effort** into making your story interesting and **you didn't give up** until you got it right.

A growth versus fixed mindset impacts students in the following areas:

- **Goals:** They are eager to set goals to learn and grow (growth); or care more about looking smart or at least not looking stupid (fixed).

- **Self-reflections/Explanations for a setback:** A setback indicates that they need to work harder and alter their strategies (growth); or signals that they lack natural talent. For example, 'I need to work harder' (growth) as opposed to 'I am not smart' (fixed).

- **Learning strategies in face of setbacks:** A setback may lead to a change in strategy, such as asking for help, or thinking: 'I need to learn my six times table first' (growth); as opposed to becoming defensive: 'Times tables are stupid' (fixed).

- **Social mindset:** Similarly, students' mindsets can influence their social resilience. Yeager[52,53] found that students who were bullied or excluded by their peers and who had a 'fixed mindset' about their personality saw the bullying situation as unchangeable, concluding that they must be unlikeable and those who were being mean to them must be nasty people. These students not only reacted more negatively in the short term to this social adversity but also showed high levels of stress, worsening health and lower grades over the school year. However, other students who were also bullied or excluded but who had 'a growth mindset' in regard to their personality and the social behaviour of the other students, were more likely to ask for support and problem solve. They were also significantly less likely to endorse aggressive vengeful responses and reported fewer negative emotions such as shame or hatred.

- **The power of 'not yet':** Part of helping students develop a growth mindset is helping them to understand that they are a 'work-in-progress' and can accomplish their goals and improve with time and effort. That is where the power of 'yet' comes in. By adding the word 'yet' to their vocabulary, they can achieve more grit[53] (see page 56). For example, if they are not able to play a challenging musical piece or solve a difficult Maths problem, adding the word 'yet' to those statements makes them more optimistic and more likely to persevere:

  - I can't play that tricky musical piece ... yet.
  - I can't solve that Maths problem ... yet.
  - I can't negotiate well ... yet.

Although attempts to teach students to adopt a 'growth mindset' have been successful, Yeager[53] has warned that such training needs to be customised for different student populations. For example, Blackwell[51] improved secondary school students' growth mindset by teaching them that greater effort in learning could strengthen their brains. However, Yeager[53] found that university students frequently put forth great effort but used very poor strategies when faced with obstacles and did not ask for help. Teaching these students to focus on *effort + strategy + help from others* significantly improved their results and course completion.

Growth mindset in Bounce Back!

The idea that effort pays off in terms of learning, as well as the importance of having a growth mindset rather than a fixed mindset about their abilities, is taught in Unit 10: Success and also links to helpful and optimistic thinking taught in the Unit 3: People bouncing back and Unit 5: Looking on the bright side. The importance of effort is a focus in all units.

Research on learning and the brain

Research on neuroplasticity (the malleability of the brain) over recent years aligns with the notion of a growth mindset. It is now understood that learning causes substantial changes in the human brain[54]. Learning causes the cells of the brain to develop new connections, and existing connections become stronger. Studies in neurophysiology, neuroanatomy and brain imaging have all shown that when people learn and practise new skills, the areas of the brain responsible for those skills become larger and denser with neural tissue and that other areas of the brain are activated when the individual performs related tasks. Thus, our brains have the capacity to develop throughout life, but only in response to the stimulation of challenge and learning. Teaching students about malleability of the brain, in other words 'the harder they work the smarter they will become', providing challenging material that stretches them, and motivating them to apply effort and take an active role in their learning contributes to a growth mindset and higher achievement[53].

Social, emotional and coping skills: Self-management

Self-management skills include coping and self-discipline skills. Coping skills help students to be resilient when faced with a difficult or challenging situation. These coping skills include the capacity for helpful and rational thinking, normalising instead of personalising, adaptive distancing for difficult situations and being able to regulate emotions in stressful situations. Self-management skills also include skills associated with being motivated and self-disciplined to work towards and persevere in achieving both personal and academic goals. It includes having a growth mindset and recognising that effort and hard work will pay off and displaying grit and persistence when faced with obstacles. Sometimes it requires courage or a sense of humour to put things in perspective.

This section provides more information about the self-management skills of:

- helpful and rational thinking
- normalising
- adaptive distancing
- grit.

◆ Helpful and rational thinking

Helpful and rational thinking derives from the original Cognitive Behaviour Therapy (CBT) model, which was developed by Aaron Beck[55]. CBT is based on the understanding that how you think affects how you feel, which in turn influences how you behave. In particular, rational thinking is drawn from the Rational Emotive Therapy (RET) model developed by Albert Ellis[56-60] from the original CBT model. CBT is based on the assumption that strong feelings such as anxiety, depression and anger are exaggerated and, in some cases, caused by our own thoughts and beliefs. CBT is a practical, action-oriented approach to coping with problems and enhancing personal growth. It has become recognised throughout the world as a highly successful form of treatment for depression, anxiety and anger. Distortions in our thinking play a key role in causing and maintaining low coping skills. What we think about a negative event can exaggerate our emotional and behavioural reactions.

The CBT model emphasises the use of tactics to help people change their thinking, feelings and behaviour. These tactics are all based on the assumption that unhelpful thinking can be identified and helpful thinking can be substituted:

1. Challenge unhelpful and irrational beliefs such as:

    - unrealistic expectations of self or others (*I must be perfect and never make any mistakes*)
    - the belief that you can't help the feelings you have (*there is nothing I can do about how I feel*)
    - catastrophising (*if something CAN go wrong, then it definitely WILL go wrong; the worst outcome is inevitable so I had better try to cope with it in advance; it is the end of the world if something negative happens*)
    - mind-reading (*I can guess what they're thinking about me*)
    - overgeneralising (*if something bad has happened to me once, it will happen again*).

2. Use 'reality-checking' by talking to other people in order to understand how others see the situation and by checking the 'evidence' and facts that supposedly support conclusions.

3. Accept those things that cannot be changed because they are not under one's control.

Helpful thinking has the following features:

- It is evidence-based and encourages checking facts and/or cross-checking with others to get a second opinion.

- It involves being open-minded and flexible in your thinking and looking for other ways to solve a problem when blocked.
- It acknowledges that how you think affects how you feel and how you behave, and that negative emotions, though powerful, can be managed.
- It doesn't involve irrational generalising from 'once' to 'all the time'.
- It doesn't involve trying to read someone's mind.
- It involves considering alternative explanations rather than jumping to conclusions.
- It results in self-soothing and a stronger sense of self-confidence in dealing with problems.

Helpful and rational thinking in Bounce Back!

Unit 3: People bouncing back explicitly teaches helpful and rational thinking skills.

✦ Normalising

Normalising, instead of personalising, is an indirect aspect of optimism. Normalising involves recognising that many life challenges also happen to lots of other people, are typical of a set of circumstances or are a stage of development. In contrast, personalising involves the belief that something that is relatively normal happens only to you, not others, in other words it happens *because* you are who you are. If we personalise, we say: 'that happened to me because I am me, so there is nothing I can do about it because it will undoubtedly happen again because I will always be me'.

When we personalise, we automatically think, 'What's wrong with me?' or 'Why me?' If we normalise, we automatically think, 'What's wrong here?' and ask, 'Is this an out-of-the-ordinary event or the kind of thing that happens quite frequently to other people?' In normalising, we say: 'That happened to me because it is one of those things that happen to many people in their lifetime, not just me. If others can deal with it, so can I.' Over time, people who personalise everyday difficulties develop a pessimistic explanatory style and a negative self-perception where they think they are jinxed, doomed or inadequate.

Young people need to be shown how to normalise many of the changes in their behaviour, roles and relationships that are due to 'everyday' developmental stressors. Challenges to our wellbeing can occur at any time due to illness, accidents, loss or trauma, but there are also everyday stressors at different developmental stages when everyone is likely to experience some anxiety and uncertainty. Many of these are listed in the 'Everyday and major stressors' chart on page 41. Young people need to understand that others are also likely to experience the same kinds of feelings and it is normal at these turning points to experience some anxiety. Sharing their concerns with others helps with this 'normative' process.

It is also important that those working with young people clearly understand the developmental stages and characteristics of each stage of childhood development. Without this understanding, there is a risk of overreacting or under-reacting to young people's problematic symptoms.

Normalising in Bounce Back!

Unit 3: People bouncing back focuses on explicitly teaching the skill of 'normalising' encapsulated in the 'E' message in the acronym:

Years F–2: **E**verybody has unhappy times sometimes, not just you.

Years 3–6: **E**verybody experiences sadness, hurt, failure, rejection and setbacks sometimes, not just you. They are a normal part of life. Try not to personalise them.

✦ Adaptive distancing

Adaptive distancing involves emotionally detaching yourself from parental, school or community dysfunctions. It means realising that you are not the cause of, and cannot control, the dysfunction of others. Such distancing helps students to provide a protective buffer[61]. Being able to 'adaptively distance' yourself from distressing and unalterable situations can mean:

- not blaming yourself for things that you aren't responsible for, such as your parents' difficulties
- accepting that there are some things that can't be easily changed, such as having a sibling with a chronic illness or an alcoholic parent
- finding a therapeutic place where you can go when things are at their worst, such as a spot where you feel better able to think clearly

- engaging in a challenging mental distraction such as working on a non-emotional task or project or making plans or lists
- thought stopping, where you 'blink' to get rid of distressing thoughts and focus instead on a memory of a special and happy time
- moving temporarily away from the people who are part of the difficult situation; for example, going to another room when your siblings are arguing. Adaptive distancing is not the same as using substances such as drugs and alcohol, which merely offer the illusion that there is no situation to be dealt with or accommodated.

Adaptive distancing in Bounce Back!

Adaptive distancing is addressed in Unit 3: People bouncing back and Unit 5: Looking on the bright side.

✦ Grit

Grit, like growth mindset, is about persevering and not giving up when faced with challenges or obstacles. Grit is a term coined by psychologist Angela Duckworth. She defines it as:

> a willingness to sustain interest and maintain effort towards achieving a relatively long-term goal or outcome such as finishing a big project or training to get into a sports team or drama group[62].

It is the combination of *effort* (hard work), *willpower* (self-discipline) and *persistence* (not giving up when faced with an obstacle).

A study by Duckworth and Seligman[63] found that Year 8 students' capacity for self-control or 'grit' (assessed by teachers, parents and self-report) was a better predictor of their academic achievement including their performance on standardised tests, than the students' IQ scores. In fact, grit/self-control was seen as a better predictor of academic success overall than their IQ score. Their self-control also predicted fewer absences from school, more time spent studying, and less time watching television.

Grit in Bounce Back!

The idea that grit pays off in terms of learning and in achieving your goals is taught in Unit 10: Success.

Social, emotional and coping skills: Social awareness

Developing students' capacity for social awareness involves helping them empathise with and take the perspective of others. It also involves developing a moral compass that underpins the values in Unit 1: Core values and Unit 2: Social values, such as appreciating diversity in people of different races and cultures, showing respect, kindness and compassion for others, and understanding social and ethical norms of behaviour. Students also need to recognise the support they can access from their family, school and community.

The following section provides more information about empathy that underpins all values and is essential for developing strong and positive relationships.

✦ Empathy

Empathy underpins social and emotional learning and moral development. Students who 'share' or 'understand' someone else's distress that is a result of their own anti-social behaviour are more likely to stop and avoid doing it again. High levels of empathy are linked to prosocial behaviour, while low levels of empathy are linked to anti-social behaviour including bullying, aggression and criminal activities. Being able to empathise is part of being resilient. Empathy has three components: cognitive, affective and action.

1 **Cognitive component**
   - The cognitive component involves reading someone's expressions and behaviour to identify on an intellectual level how the person is feeling. Drawing on one's own experiences can enhance this.
   - It could also involve 'putting yourself in someone else's shoes' to try to understand their perspective or point of view.

2 **Affective (emotional) component**
   - This is the capacity to emotionally experience the feelings of another. Affective empathy can also be defined as experiencing a vicarious emotional response to the perceived emotional experience of another. This could be a real person or a fictional character. The empathic person 'mirrors' the emotions and behaviour of another person as though they were experiencing it themselves rather than simply witnessing it.

3 **Action component**
   - The action component could also be termed 'empathic concern' and involves responding to the perceived distress of another with words or actions of kindness or support.

Having well-developed empathic skills can help students to:

- engage in more prosocial behaviours and avoid anti-social behaviours such as bullying; they use their empathy and prosocial values to guide their attitudes and behaviour towards other people (e.g. how will that person feel if I steal their pen/say something nasty?)
- be less likely to tolerate bullying behaviour on the part of others; they are also more likely to refuse to take part in bullying and more likely to act to prevent it or extend their support to the student being mistreated
- be less judgmental and more accepting, show more kindness and support and therefore have more positive relationships
- handle conflict more effectively, as they are more likely to try to see both sides of a situation
- develop a capacity for ethical thinking. As students encounter more sophisticated issues and ideas, they need to recognise that there are legitimate viewpoints apart from their own. Good thinkers can hold two opposing ideas in their mind at once. They can also clearly state the view they don't agree with as well as the one they do agree with.
- develop a sense of social justice and concern for others in the broader community
- not personalise other people's behaviour; if they can see why a person may be behaving towards them in a particular way, they are less likely to see that behaviour as a direct personal attack
- have better friendships and support networks; students who show that they are trying to understand another's point of view and feelings are more likely to be liked and sought out, and others are more likely to respond to them by showing them the same sensitivity and concern.

Social awareness skills in Bounce Back!

Empathy for others underpins all the core values in Unit 1: Core values and Unit 2: Social values such as appreciating diversity, showing respect for others, showing kindness and compassion and understanding social and ethical norms of behaviour.

Empathy is also critical to developing the social and emotional skills discussed in Unit 7: Relationships. Learning to take the other perspective in a conflict situation is also taught in this unit.

Social, emotional and coping skills: Social management and relationship skills

The starting point for teaching students the social skills that underpin good relationships with classmates, peers, family and friends is having a belief that relationships matter. See Chapter 2 for more information about the research that underpins relationships skills.

Relationships skills in Bounce Back!

Unit 7: Relationships teaches social skills for establishing and maintaining healthy and rewarding relationships with diverse individuals and groups, friendship skills and conflict-management skills. Unit 9: Being safe addresses the relationship skills of resisting inappropriate social pressure and seeking and offering help when needed.

Social, emotional and coping skills: Responsible decision making

Responsible decision making involves developing the ability to make constructive choices about one's own behaviour and one's social interactions based on ethical standards, safety concerns and social norms. These skills and understandings can be taught by helping students to identify problems and predict, analyse and evaluate possible outcomes in academic and social situations where they consider the wellbeing of themselves and others.

Responsible decision making in Bounce Back!

Learning about being responsible is explicitly taught in Unit 1: Core values, Unit 2: Social values and Unit 9: Being safe. The cooperative thinking skills used in all units encourage skills of critical, creative, ethical and empathic understanding. Unit 7: Relationships draws on the social norms based on social awareness.

REFERENCES

1. Collaborative for Academic, Social and Emotional Learning, 2007 [cited 18/1/10], available from www.casel.org.
2. Elias, J.E., et al. 2003, 'Implementation, sustainability, and scaling up of social-emotional and academic innovations in public schools', *School Psychology Review*, vol. 32.
3. Govindji, R., & Linley, P. 2007, 'Strengths use, self-concordance and well-being: Implications for strengths coaching and coaching psychologists', *International Coaching Psychology Review*, 2: pp. 143–153.
4. Linley, A. & Harrington, S. 2006, 'Playing to your strengths', *The Psychologist*, 19: pp. 86–89.
5. Wood, A.M., Linley, A.P., Maltby, J., Kashdan, T.B. & Hurling, R. 2011, 'Using personal and psychological strengths leads to increases in wellbeing over time: A longitudinal study and the development of the strengths use questionnaire', *Personality and Individual Differences*, 50: pp. 15–19.
6. Noble, T. 2004, 'Integrating the Revised Bloom's Taxonomy with Multiple Intelligences: A planning tool for curriculum differentiation', *Teachers College Record*, vol. 106, no. 1, pp. 193–211.
7. Harter, J.K. 1998, 'Gage Park High School research study' cited in Daly, A.J. & Chrispeels, J. 2005, 'From problem to possibility: Leadership for implementing and deepening the process of effective schools', *Journal for Effective Schools*, vol. 4, no. 1, pp. 7–25.
8. Williamson, J. 2002, 'Assessing student strengths: Academic performance and persistence of first-time college students' cited in Daly, A.J. & Chrispeels, J. 2005, 'From problem to possibility: Leadership for implementing and deepening the process of effective schools', *Journal for Effective Schools*, vol. 4, no. 1, pp. 7–25.
9. Gardner, H. 1999, *Intelligence Reframed: Multiple Intelligences in the Twenty-First Century*, Basic Books, New York.
10. Peterson, C. & Seligman, M. 2004, *Character Strengths*, Oxford University Press, New York.
11. Gardner, H. 1983, *Frames of mind*, Basic Books, New York.
12. Gardner, H. 2006, *Multiple intelligences: New horizons*, Basic Books, New York.
13. Willingham, D.T., Hughes, E.M. & Dobolyi, D.G. 2015, 'The scientific status of learning styles theories', *Teaching of Psychology*, 42(3), pp. 266–271.
14. Moran, S. 2011, 'Measuring Multiple Intelligences and Moral Sensitivities in Education', *Moral Development and Citizenship Education*, 5: pp. 121–133.
15. Kornhaber, M., Fierros, E. & Veenema, S. 2003, *Multiple Intelligences: Best ideas from research and practice*, Allyn & Bacon.
16. McGrath, H. and T. Noble, 2005a, *Eight ways at once. Book One: Multiple Intelligences + Bloom's Revised Taxonomy = 200 differentiated classroom strategies*, Pearson Education, Sydney.
17. McGrath, H. and T. Noble, 2005b, *Eight ways at once. Book Two: Units of Work Based Multiple Intelligences + Bloom's Revised Taxonomy*, Pearson Education, Sydney.
18. Noble, T. 2004, 'Integrating the Revised Bloom's Taxonomy with Multiple Intelligences: A planning tool for curriculum differentiation', *Teachers College Record*, 106(1), pp. 193–211.
19. Park, N., Peterson, C. & Seligman, M.E.P. 2004, 'Strengths of character and wellbeing', *Journal of Social & Clinical Psychology*, vol. 23, pp. 603–619.
20. White, M. & Waters, L.E. 2015, 'Strengths-based approaches in the classroom and staffroom', in *Evidence-Based Approaches in Positive Education*, M.A. White, A.S. Murray (eds), Positive Education, DOI 10.1007/978-94-017-9667-5_6.
21. White, M. & Waters, L.E. 2014, 'A case study of "The Good School": Examples of the use of Peterson's strengths-based approach with students', *The Journal of Positive Psychology*, DOI: 10.1080/17439760.2014.920408.
22. Proctor, C., Tsukayama, E., Wood, A.M., Maltby, J., Eades, J.F., & Linley, P.A. 2011, 'Strengths gym: The impact of a character strengths-based intervention on the life satisfaction and well-being of adolescents', *The Journal of Positive Psychology*, 6: pp. 377–388.
23. Seligman, M.E.P, Ernst, R.M., Gillham, J., Reivich, K. & Linkins, M. 2009, 'Positive education: positive psychology and classroom interventions', *Oxford Review of Education*, 35 (3): pp. 293–311.
24. Quinlan, D.M., Swain, N., Cameron, C. & Vella-Brodrick, D.A. 2014, 'How "other people matter" in a classroom-based strengths intervention: Exploring interpersonal strategies and classroom outcomes', *The Journal of Positive Psychology*, http://dx.doi.org/10.1080/17439760.2014.920407.
25. Csikszentmihalyi, M., Rathunde, K. & Whalen, S. 1993, *Talented Teenagers*, Cambridge University Press, Cambridge, United Kingdom.
26. Carver, C.S. & Scheier, M.E. 1999, *'Optimism' in Coping. The Psychology of What Works*, Snyder C.R. (ed), Oxford University Press, New York, pp. 182–204.
27. Seligman, M.E.P. 1995, *The Optimistic Child*, Random House, Sydney.
28. Seligman, M.E.P. 1992, *Learned Optimism*, Random House, Sydney.
29. Reivich, K. 2005, 'Optimism lecture' in Authentic Happiness Coaching, University of Pennsylvania.
30. Peterson, C. 2000, 'The future of optimism', *American Psychologist*, vol. 55, no. 1, pp. 44–55.
31. Dweck, C.S. 2006, *Mindset. The New Psychology of Success*, Random House, New York.
32. Dillon, R.S. 1997, 'Self-Respect: Moral, Emotional and Political', *Ethics*, 107(2): pp. 226-249.
33. Baumeister, R. 1996, 'Should Schools Try to Boost Self-Esteem Beware the Dark Side', *American Educator*, vol. 20, Summer.
34. Baumeister, R.F., Campbell, J.D., Krueger, J.I. & Vohs, K.D. 2005, 'Exploding the Self-esteem Myth', *Scientific American*, 292, pp. 84–91.
35. Seligman, M.E. 2011, *Flourish: A visionary new understanding of happiness and wellbeing*, Simon & Schuster, NY.
36. Bundick, M.J., Yeager, D.Y., King, P. & Damon, W. 2009, 'Thriving across the life span', in *Handbook of lifespan human development*, W.F. Overton & R.M. Lerner (eds), Wiley, New York.
37. Keyes, C.L.M., Shmotkin, D. & Ryff, C.D. 2002, 'Optimizing well-being: The empirical encounter of two traditions,' *Journal of Personality and Social Psychology*, 82: pp. 1007–1022.
38. Benard, B. 1991, 'Fostering resiliency in kids: Protective factors in the family, school and community', Western Regional Center for Drug Free Schools and Communities, Far West Laboratory, San Francisco.
39. Masten, A.S. & Reed, M.G. 2002, 'Resilience in development', in *The handbook of positive psychology*, C.R. Snyder & S.J. Lopez (eds), Oxford University Press, New York, pp. 74–88.

40. Mauss, I.B., Shallcross, A.J., Troy, A.S., John, O.P., Ferrer, E., Wilhelm, F.H., et al. 2011, 'Don't hide your happiness! Positive emotion dissociation, social connectedness, and psychological functioning', *Journal of Personality and Social Psychology*, 100(4), pp. 738–748.
41. Bronk, K.C., Hill, P.L., Lapsley, D.K., Talib, T.L. & Finch, H. 2009, 'Purpose, hope, and life satisfaction in three age groups', *Journal of Positive Psychology*, 4(6): pp. 500-510.
42. Bronk, K.C., Finch, W.H. & Talib, T. 2010, 'The prevalence of a purpose in life among high ability adolescents', *High Ability Studies*, 21(2): pp. 133-145.
43. Shek, D.T. 1993, 'The Chinese purpose-in-life test and psychological well-being in Chinese college students', International Forum for Logotherapy, 16: pp. 35–42.
44. Debats, D.L. 1998, 'Measurement of personal meaning: The psychometric properties of the life regard index', in *The human quest for meaning: A handbook of psychological research and clinical applications*, P.T.P. Wong & P.S. Fry (eds), Lawrence Earlbaum, Mahwah, NJ, pp. 237–259.
45. Damon, W., Menon, J. & Bronk, K.C. 2003, 'The development of purpose during adolescence', *Applied Developmental Science*, 7(3):119-128, p. 121.
46. Damon, W. 2008, *The Path to Purpose. How Young People Find Their Calling in Life*, Simon & Schuster, NY.
47. Seligman, M.E.P. 2002, *Authentic Happiness*, Free Press, New York, p. 260.
48. Malin, H., Reilly, T. S., Quinn, B., & Moran, S. 2014, 'Adolescent purpose development: Exploring empathy, discovering roles, shifting priorities, and creating pathways', *Journal of Research on Adolescence*, 24, pp. 186–199. doi:10.1111/jora.12051.
49. Hulleman, C.S. & Harackiewicz, J.M. 2009, 'Promoting interest and performance in high school science classes', *Science*, 326, pp. 1410–1412.
50. Holdsworth, R., Cahill, S. & Smith, G. 2003, 'Student action teams. An evaluation of implementation and impact', Parkville: Faculty of Education, University of Melbourne.
51. Blackwell, L.S., Trzesniewski, K.H. & Dweck, C.S. 2007, 'Implicit Theories of Intelligence Predict Achievement Across an Adolescent Transition: A Longitudinal Study and an Intervention', *Child Development*, 78(1): pp. 246–263.
52. Yeager, J., Fisher, S. & Shearon, D. 2011, *Smart Strengths: Building Character, Resilience and Relationships in Youth*, Kravis Publishing, New York.
53. Yeager, D.S. & Dweck, C.S. 2012, 'Mindsets that promote resilience: When students believe that personal characteristics can be developed', *Educational Psychologist*, 47(4): pp. 302–314.
54. Dweck, C.S., Walton, G.M. & Cohen, G.L. 2015, 'Academic Tenacity. Mindsets and Skills that Promote Long-Term Learning', Bill & Melinda Gates Foundation, https://ed.stanford.edu/sites/default/files/manual/dweck-walton-cohen-2014.pdf
55. Beck, A.T. 1979, *Cognitive Therapy and the Emotional Disorders*, Penguin Books, New York.
56. Burns, D. 1980, *Feeling Good: The New Mood Therapy*, Avon Books, New York.
57. Clark, D. & Beck, A. 1999, *Scientific Foundations of Cognitive Theory of Depression*, John Wiley, New York.
58. Ellis, A. 1988, *How to Stubbornly Refuse to Make Yourself Miserable about Anything. Yes, Anything!*, Pan Macmillan, Sydney.
59. Ellis, A., et al. 1997, *Stress Counselling: A Rational Emotive Behaviour Approach*, Cassell, London.
60. Ellis, A. & Dryden, W. 1987, *The Practice of Rational Emotive Therapy*, Springer, New York.
61. Benard, B. 2004, *Resiliency: What we have learned*, WestEd, San Francisco.
62. Duckworth, A. 2011, 'The significance of self-control', Proceedings of the National Academy of Sciences, 108(7), pp. 2639–2640.
63. Duckworth, A. & Seligman, M. 2005, 'Self-discipline outdoes IQ in predicting academic performance in adolescents', *Psychological Science*, 16(12), pp. 939–944.

CHAPTER 5

Teaching the BOUNCE BACK! acronym

IN THIS CHAPTER

- Guidelines for teaching the BOUNCE! and BOUNCE BACK! acronyms
- The principles in the BOUNCE! and BOUNCE BACK! acronyms and their key messages
- Advice for using the BOUNCE BACK! acronym as critical question prompts in many curriculum areas
- Ten myths and realities about resilience
- When to refer a student for professional help

INTRODUCTION

The BOUNCE BACK! acronym acts as a kind of 'coathanger' for the program. This chapter provides guidelines for teaching the acronym, and explains the key principles that underpin each statement. The main focus of the **Bounce Back!** program is to help students understand the coping statements so they can apply and use them in difficult times. The BOUNCE BACK! and BOUNCE! acronyms are available as Blackline Masters (BLMs) and as digital tools for use on an Interactive Whiteboard (IWB) – see Unit 3: People bouncing back.

Guidelines for teaching the acronyms

The coping statements that form the BOUNCE BACK! acronym should be learnt so they can be used by students when needed. The following ideas will help students understand and learn the acronym.

- Check for understanding and unpack new or unfamiliar vocabulary in the acronyms as needed.
- Repeat and revisit the acronym over each year level so that students master and easily recall the coping statements at times of difficulty.
- Involve parents and carers in the program, which will provide opportunities for the acronym to be reinforced and discussed at home as well as at school. Ideas for involving families are covered in the *Bounce Back!* **Curriculum Units** and **Information for families** that can be used for newsletters, the school website or sent home.
- Three levels of delivery are outlined below. More class time can be spent on Levels 1 and 2 and less time at Level 3.
    - Level 1: Students focus on the statements and what they mean.
    - Level 2: Students focus on the ideas and concepts as applied to others such as family, friends, puppet or cartoon characters, people in the news, books and films, and so on. This allows the concepts to be 'one step removed'.
    - Level 3: Students focus on the ideas and concepts as applied to themselves.
- Provide a classroom climate of safety and trust during all discussions and activities (see Teaching strategies and resources for advice about how to achieve this).
- Encourage students to refer to the coping statements in the acronym when they are trying to support friends and classmates.
- Refer to the coping statements when managing a playground or classroom problem or situation.
- Wherever possible, link the program to other areas of the curriculum, e.g. Humanities and Social Sciences, Science, Technology, English, Health and Physical Education, Personal Development, Religious Education or protective behaviours programs.

The key principles in BOUNCE! and BOUNCE BACK!

The BOUNCE! (Years F–2) and BOUNCE BACK! (Years 3–4 and Years 5–6) acronyms are based on the key *Bounce Back!* principles, based on Cognitive Behavior Therapy (CBT), which underpin the coping statements. Although BOUNCE! consists of simpler versions of the first six BOUNCE BACK! statements for lower primary students, it is still important to talk to children in Years F–2 about 'bouncing back'.

The BOUNCE! acronym is:

- **B**ad feelings always go away again.
- **O**ther people can help you feel better if you talk to them.
- **U**nhelpful thinking makes you feel more upset. Think again.
- **N**obody is perfect – not you and not others.
- **C**oncentrate on the things that are still good when things go wrong.
- **E**verybody has unhappy times sometimes, not just you.

The BOUNCE BACK! acronym is:

- **B**ad times don't last. Things always get better. Stay optimistic.
- **O**ther people can help if you talk to them. Get a reality check.
- **U**nhelpful thinking makes you feel more upset. Think again.
- **N**obody is perfect – not you and not others.
- **C**oncentrate on the positives (no matter how small) and use laughter.
- **E**verybody experiences sadness, hurt, failure, rejection and setbacks sometimes, not just you. They are a normal part of life. Try not to personalise them.
- **B**lame fairly. How much of what happened was due to you, to others and to bad luck or circumstances?
- **A**ccept what can't be changed (but try to change what you can change first).
- **C**atastrophising exaggerates your worries. Don't believe the worst possible picture.
- **K**eep things in perspective. It's only part of your life.

Chapter 5 Teaching the BOUNCE BACK! acronym

✦ Bad times don't last. Things always get better. Stay optimistic.

In BOUNCE! (Years F–2), this statement is: *Bad feelings always go away again.*

The key messages are:

- Bad times and unpleasant feelings are (nearly) always temporary. Things in your life will get better so don't give up. It is important to stay optimistic and hopeful.
- Sometimes it takes a while for a difficult situation to improve, but it does always improve.
- Sometimes the situation may not improve (e.g. if someone is dying), but your feelings about it will improve if you work on them.
- When things are really bad, just try to get through one day at a time.

✦ Other people can help if you talk to them. Get a reality check.

In BOUNCE! (Years F–2), this statement is: *Other people can help you feel better if you talk to them.*

The key messages are:

- Nothing is so awful that you can't talk about it to someone you trust. Things will be easier if you share your worries but it takes courage to do so.
- Everyone needs someone to talk to now and then. Talking to someone about what is troubling you is a sign of strength, not weakness.
- Talking about what is worrying you with someone you trust means they can give you support. If you don't talk to them, they won't know that you need help.
- Talking to other people allows you to 'cross-check' your ideas and perceptions with them. In this way, you can see if they see the situation in the same way you do.
- If you talk to someone you trust you can get a 'reality check' because they will tell you if they think you are not being realistic. Maybe you are getting the facts wrong or you don't have all the facts you need. Maybe you are seeing things in a distorted way.

✦ Unhelpful thinking makes you feel more upset. Think again.

In BOUNCE! (Years F–2), this statement is the same: *Unhelpful thinking makes you feel more upset. Think again.*

The key messages are:

- Our thoughts strongly influence our feelings and actions. Changing how we think helps us to manage how we feel.
- Unhelpful thinking involves thinking things such as:
  - 'Everybody *must* like me.' (There is no-one who is liked by everybody.)
  - 'I must never make a mistake.' (Everyone needs to make mistakes to learn things.)
  - 'I must never lose.' (Everyone has to lose sometimes.)
  - 'Bad things always happens to me.' (They don't, but you are probably only noticing the bad things that happen to you and not noticing the good things that also happen to you.)
- Don't mistake your feelings for facts. Just because you feel self-conscious doesn't mean people are looking at you. Sometimes you need to do a 'reality check'.
- Use low-key words for your feelings and they will stay more easily under control. For example, say to yourself: 'I am annoyed' rather than 'I am furious', or 'It is unpleasant and I don't like it' rather than 'It is a disaster and I can't stand it'.

✦ Nobody is perfect – not you and not others.

In BOUNCE! (Years F–2), this statement is the same: *Nobody is perfect – not you and not others.*

The key messages are:

- There is no such thing as a perfect person. We all have flaws. Perfection is not an option but improvement and striving for high standards are options.
- You're not perfect so don't be too hard on yourself when something doesn't turn out as well as you had hoped. Judge yourself by effort and be kind to yourself.

- Others (including parents, teachers, brothers, sisters and friends) are not perfect so don't have unreasonable expectations of them.
- Mistakes are part of learning. We all have to make mistakes to get better at things.

✦ Concentrate on the positives (no matter how small) and use laughter.

In BOUNCE! (Years F–2), this statement is: *Concentrate on the things that are still good when things go wrong.*

The key messages are:

- Finding something positive in a difficult situation, no matter how small, helps you to hang on and feel a bit more hopeful.
- Feeling more hopeful helps you to feel better and cope better.
- Finding something funny in a difficult situation, even if it is only a small thing, will help you feel better able to cope. Laugher helps to relieve stress and worry.

✦ Everybody experiences sadness, hurt, failure, rejection and setbacks sometimes, not just you. They are a normal part of life. Try not to personalise them.

In BOUNCE! (Years F–2), this statement is: *Everybody has unhappy times sometimes, not just you.*

The key messages are:

- Bad things happen to everyone, even though you may think they happen only to you.
- Courage is needed when you feel sad or disappointed or when you fail at something.
- 'Personalising' is thinking that when something bad happens it only happens to you. People who say 'I'm a jinx' or 'Bad things always happen to me' are personalising.
- Normalising is more helpful and realistic. This means accepting that bad things, such as rejection or failure or frustrations, happen to everyone now and again, not just you. Sometimes they seem to happen all at once! It's normal!

✦ Blame fairly. How much of what happened was due to you, to others and to bad luck or circumstances?

The key messages are:

- Don't just blame yourself when bad things happen – consider how much of what happened was due to your own behaviour, how much was due to other people and how much was due to bad luck or circumstances (such as being in the wrong place at the wrong time or random events).
- When something bad happens, try to do a pie chart showing:
  - How much is down to me?
  - How much is down to others?
  - How much is down to bad luck and circumstances?

✦ Accept what can't be changed (but try to change what you can change first).

The key messages are:

- You can try to change the things over which you have some control. For example, if you are worried about schoolwork there are lots of things you can do to improve your skills, such as asking your family or teacher for help, making a plan and practising the skills. If you have had a disagreement with a friend, you can try to talk with them about what is troubling you.
- Some things you are worrying about may be other people's worries, like Mum's or a friend's, not yours. It is not helpful to worry about things that you have no control over or cannot change.
- Accepting what you can't change also means accepting other people for what they are, even if they don't measure up to what you would like. This does not mean you always like what they do, but you accept that they are who they are. You can't change them, but if you accept them, they might be better able to change themselves.

- **✦ Catastrophising exaggerates your worries. Don't believe the worst possible picture.**

The key messages are:

- Catastrophising means thinking about the worst possible thing that could happen and believing that it will happen. For example:
  - 'If I don't do well in this test or project, the whole term will be ruined.'
  - 'If I go to drama classes, I'll probably make a fool of myself.'
- Catastrophising makes you feel worried and miserable. You probably won't feel like doing anything because you expect the worst.

- **✦ Keep things in perspective. It's only part of your life.**

The key messages are:

- If you don't keep things in perspective, you get upset over very little things and make mountains out of molehills. You forget about the good bits and see only the bad bits.
- When something happens, some ways to help keep things in perspective are to ask yourself:
  - 'Does this really matter? Am I getting upset over very little?'
  - 'On a scale from 1 to 10, how important is this to me really?'
  - 'How much of my life has this really affected?'
  - 'How many parts of my life are still exactly the same and still as good as they were?'
  - 'Is it really the end of the world?'

How to use the BOUNCE BACK! acronym

The BOUNCE BACK! acronyms can be used in a variety of ways.

- Use the acronym as the basis for on-the-spot counselling and behaviour management.
- Display the acronym as a poster in the classroom so that students, teachers and support staff can regularly refer to it, both privately and in class discussions. This is also a good visual reminder for family helpers.
- Make a copy for teachers on yard duty so they can refer to coping statements in response to playground incidents.
- Place an enlarged copy of the acronym somewhere in the staffroom so that teachers and support staff can work on their own coping skills and become more positive models.
- Create a new visual of the poster each year so that it doesn't become 'stale' and get ignored. Involve students in making posters using different fonts and graphics.
- Consider having the acronym in the school diary (if there is one) and on the school website or newsletter.
- Display posters made by students of the various acronyms (e.g. BOUNCE!, BOUNCE BACK!, STAR!, CHAMP!, WINNERS!) in classrooms and corridors.
- Ensure that parents and carers are also aware of the acronym and its coping messages. Provide them with copies of the acronym and ask them to continue the conversation at home.
- It is also very important that school counsellors, social workers, psychologists and speech pathologists are aware of the *Bounce Back!* program.

Using the BOUNCE BACK! critical question prompts

Use the BOUNCE BACK! prompts (see Teaching strategies and resources) to continually link the program to the mainstream content of the classroom. These questions can be used in discussions on books, films, news items, biographies, historical events and global issues, and also with events that happen on a day-to-day basis.

For example, if you were discussing a news story about someone saving a child from a burning house, you could ask: 'Who was the bravest person here? How do we know that? What might have helped them to be brave?' If you were discussing a story that you were reading to the class, you might ask: 'Where was this character using optimistic thinking? What evidence do we have that they were still able to stay hopeful? How did the main character make their plan to try to achieve their goal? What problems did they have to deal with along the way? In what ways did they persist?'

Ten myths and realities about resilience

The construct of resilience has become very popular. When a construct is popularised, there is a risk of it becoming over-simplified. The following section outlines some of the myths and realities related to the term 'resilience'. The realities draw on the resilience research literature. The complexity of the construct highlights the complexity of helping young people to become more resilient.

Myth 1: The best way to prevent problems for young people is to focus on what 'causes' the problems (the risk factors) and on the group of young people who seem to have the most risk characteristics.

Reality: The majority of 'high risk' children and adolescents do not develop anticipated problem behaviours, such as abuse of illicit drugs. There is not a simple direct correlation between the risk factors in young people's lives and their problems. Also, it is not easy for teachers to prevent or change risk factors. A more effective approach is a holistic one that teaches the social and emotional skills that help young people cope more successfully with the risk factors in their lives. However, this does not deny the need to create safe environments in which children and adolescents do not suffer abuse, neglect, bullying, violence and poverty.

Myth 2: Young people will never be able to escape the cycles of violence, poverty or failure that have characterised the lives of their parents, family or community members.

Reality: Fundamental to the concept of resilience is the capacity to 'bounce back' in the face of adversity. This capacity may be linked to a positive change in a person's environment and/ or the learning of new coping skills. All people have the capacity for positive change and for the development of personal coping skills. For some young people from difficult home environments, school and peer connectedness as well as finding a teacher who cares can play a crucial role in helping them develop some resilience to cope with the complexities of their lives. For others, learning personal skills, such as how to set and work towards goals, can give them a sense of purpose and future. This can help them to distance themselves from events in their lives that are distressing and cannot be changed. A combination of many processes provides more protection than one or two.

Myth 3: Resilience is an inborn characteristic. You either have it or you don't.

Reality: It is evident from research that some children are genetically predisposed to be less resilient and some to be more resilient. The Australian Temperament Project[1] has demonstrated that some characteristics that are present at birth are still present in the teen years. Some of these characteristics are:

- being bored easily
- not adapting easily to new situations
- having intense emotional reactions to situations
- being hard to calm down and comfort
- being shy.

Some young people inherit a genetic predisposition towards anxiety, depression or forms of mental illness, even though these may not always be apparent in early life. Others are born with cognitive and/or behavioural disabilities (such as dyslexia, attention deficit disorder, autism and learning difficulties) that make it harder for them to cope and develop protective resources. Some young children suffer from long-term damage to their developing brain and are more at risk of anxiety and depression as adults as a result of early abuse and neglect. Each risk factor creates an extra challenge for parents, teachers and others as they try to support and care for such young people.

Although children are born with differing predispositions to becoming resilient, it does not mean that any one outcome is 'inevitable'. Even with predispositions and disabilities, children can become more resilient if they are in protective environments and if they are taught resilience skills and attitudes. Resilience is best viewed as a developmental process rather than a fixed trait. Young people who may be predisposed towards being less resilient may be even more in need of programs such as **Bounce Back!** than their peers.

Myth 4: A resilient person will demonstrate resilient behaviours in all situations.

Reality: People can readily demonstrate some resilient capabilities in one context but not in another. For example, a student may be uncooperative and unfriendly at school, but different when they are playing with cousins. A teacher may demonstrate high self-confidence when teaching students but less self-confidence in speaking to a group of parents. In both these examples, the different social contexts provide different levels of threat for the individual. Speaking publicly to a group of parents can be more threatening for teachers than talking to a group of students because they have had less opportunity to practise these skills.

When the social context or environmental circumstances change, our resilience can also change. Skills learned in one context do not always apply in other situations because the new context may contain more threats or new/different circumstances. Resilience is a dynamic process that is highly influenced by not only the individual's personal coping skills and sense of wellbeing, but also their current social context.

Myth 5: Resilience can easily be observed in the behaviour of young people.

Reality: The multi-faceted nature of wellbeing and resilience, with their social, emotional and cognitive components, sometimes makes it difficult to 'see'. Some students can appear resilient, confident and 'cocky', but under stress or threat they go to pieces and make poor choices. Others can seem fragile and non-adaptive, but cope well in very stressful circumstances.

Myth 6: All professionals working with young people agree on what resilience is and how it is best developed.

Reality: The concept of resilience has multiple meanings within and across different professional groups. For professionals working in the context of community/social welfare, the main focus in the development of resilience will most likely be enhancing protective environmental factors such as an individual's or a family's access to community support agencies and building family strengths.

For professionals in psychology and counselling, the main focus will most likely be using counselling research to teach personal coping skills that can create resilience.

For teachers, the main focus will most likely be on enhancing both school-related protective factors and teaching social, emotional and coping skills for wellbeing and resilience at a whole-class level. Teachers at the same school can also hold different views on whether a particular student is resilient or not. One teacher may see acting-out, defiant behaviour as not coping, whereas another teacher may see the same behaviour as indicative of this student demonstrating resilient behaviour given their tough life.

The concept of a resilient person is socially constructed. Planning and implementing a wellbeing program that builds resilience requires an understanding of both the environmental protective factors and the personal coping skills and beliefs that are valued in a particular cultural and ethnic community.

Myth 7: You need to identify all the risk factors in a young person's life before you can help them to be more resilient.

Reality: A focus on only the risk factors runs the risk of negatively labelling young people and focusing on their problems rather than possible solutions. As one young survivor said: 'Abuse is what happened to me, not who I am'[1]. This person demonstrates 'survivor's pride', a term coined by Wolin and Wolin[2] to refer to the well-deserved feelings of accomplishment that result from withstanding the pressures of hardship. Survivors want their struggle to be recognised and honoured, not pitied, and they want to be seen as someone with strength, not as a victim.

A focus on problems can set up a cycle of failure. A cycle of failure leads to a sense of helplessness and a propensity to feel overwhelmed and to give up. It is more productive to engage in a talent search of a young person's strengths and reframe their ability to overcome some of their difficulties as proof of their adaptability, strength, intelligence, insight, creativity and tenacity. A focus on solutions can set up a cycle of positive actions. A positive cycle can engender a sense of empowerment and hope.

Myth 8: Resilience can easily be developed through simple social and educational interventions. A focus on one protective factor, such as improving social skills, will make a student resilient.

Reality: Resilience is multi-dimensional and reflects the social context of a student's life as well as their personal coping skills. Teaching only one set of skills, such as increasing social competence, will have limited long-term effects if some of the other factors in a student's environment don't change. A multi-factored approach that includes environmental protective processes as well as personal skills is more likely to help young people develop wellbeing and resilience than a one-dimensional program. The earlier a program teaches the personal skills, the more likely it will help students learn life skills that foster resilience and help them to flourish.

Myth 9: Resilience solves all problems; if a young person is resilient, then they can survive anything.

Reality: No-one is invulnerable. No-one completely escapes life's lessons and challenges. All of us have scars and every one of us has their breaking point. If the risk factors in a young person's life increase and their protective resources decrease, they can find themselves unable to cope either temporarily or for a longer period of time. Resilience is sometimes difficult to foster because of the multiple and complex interacting protective mechanisms and risk factors in children's lives.

Myth 10: Resilient children demonstrate the same kinds of personal coping skills at all ages.

Reality: Resilience is a developmental process; therefore, children will experience different everyday stressors and demonstrate different coping skills at different ages. Everyday stressors are the typical kinds of stressors that young people face as they proceed through the developmental stages. A typical everyday stressor for a pre-schooler may be separation from their parents when starting pre-school or school; for a primary school student it may be disappointments relating to sport or schoolwork or peer teasing; and for adolescents it may be maintaining part-time work as well as achieving at school. Any program designed to help young people successfully manage everyday stressors needs to be made age-appropriate and tailored to the students' cognitive, social and emotional, and physical developmental stage.

Indicators for referring a student for professional help

Teachers are the 'first-aid workers' in students' mental health and often feel concerned about the emotional or social wellbeing of an individual student but feel out of their depth in helping them. Under those circumstances it is best to refer the student for professional help. Here are some indicators:

- A student has no-one in their life they feel they can easily access and talk to.
- There is a pattern of ongoing depressed mood, even in very young children.
- There is a pattern of ongoing social and emotional withdrawal, especially if the student has previously been more socially outgoing.
- The student has been bullied or socially rejected over a long period of time.
- The student appears to have a very limited understanding of social interaction and has problems forming bonds with other students. This may be an indicator of an Autism Spectrum Disorder and specialist support may be needed.
- The student has a history of difficulties with angry outbursts or marked problems with controlling impulses.
- Many absences from school with 'indefinite' reasons (e.g. tiredness, felt unwell). These are often indicators of anxiety and/or depression (and sometimes of being bullied).
- Frequent visits to sick bay, sometimes (but not always) in a dramatic way or in an agitated emotional state. This might be an early indicator of generalised anxiety, obsessive-compulsive disorder (OCD) or depression.
- Talking about suicide. There is no discernible pattern as to who will attempt suicide. Some who talk about it don't do it, and others who talk about it may attempt to do so. It should always be taken seriously.
- Marked change in a previous pattern without reason (e.g. no longer submitting homework, not going out with friends any more, discontinuing sporting involvement).

REFERENCES

1. Vassallo, S. & Sanson, A. (eds), 2013, *The Australian Temperament Project: The first 30 years*, Australian Institute of Family Studies, Melbourne.
2. Wolin, S. & Wolin, S.J. 2010, 'Shaping a Brighter Future by Uncovering "Survivor's Pride"', accessed 2/2/10, www.projectresilience.com/article19.htm

CHAPTER 6

Implementation and maintenance of Bounce Back!

IN THIS CHAPTER

- Guidelines for successful implementation and maintenance of *Bounce Back!*
- The five stages of quality implementation: decision stage, planning and preparation, implementation, sustaining, and improving the program
- *Bounce Back!* assessment, and assessment tools to measure current and improved levels in student wellbeing and resilience
- Guidelines to refresh *Bounce Back!* with Appreciative Inquiry, a strengths-based approach to organisational change
- Advice for managing challenging teacher–student and parent–teacher relationships

INTRODUCTION

Bounce Back! can be implemented in a range of different ways to address each school's individual needs and characteristics. A focus on student wellbeing means that school leadership can coordinate the positive school and classroom practices that connect the whole-school community and develop all teachers' commitment to teaching a student wellbeing program.

Noble and McGrath conducted research with 10 schools that had been implementing *Bounce Back!* for between five and 12 years. In the findings, all the school leaders identified student wellbeing as a school priority[1]. A leadership focus on student wellbeing can integrate and unify different school initiatives such as anti-bullying initiatives, mental health initiatives, social skills training, peer support/buddy programs, positive behaviour management strategies such as Schoolwide Positive Behavior Support (SWPBS) or Positive Behavior for Learning (PBL) and restorative practices. It can also give coherence to diverse school initiatives and activities.

A focus on student wellbeing has the high probability of school community 'buy-in', given that many schools are grappling with discipline problems, bullying and lack of student engagement, to name just a few current concerns. Student wellbeing is at the heart of the Positive Education and Social and Emotional Learning (SEL) movements. A focus on student wellbeing provides a clear picture that the whole school community can articulate and 'carry in their heads and their hearts'[2] (p. 206).

Implementing Bounce Back!

✦ Implementation factors

The research with the 10 schools that had successfully implemented the **Bounce Back!** program identified a combination of school-based factors, school-system factors and program-specific factors as important to the implementation of the program.

The **school-based factors** most often mentioned as contributing to the program's successful and ongoing implementation were:

- making student wellbeing and social and emotional learning a top priority in the school and recognising that it underpins academic learning
- the provision of a high level of leadership support for the program
- adopting a whole-school approach which recognises that all aspects of the school community can have an impact on students' health and wellbeing, and that learning and wellbeing are inextricably linked. Given that young people spend much of their first 17 years in a school environment, school is not only the focal point of children's academic development but also their social and emotional development, since it is where they make friends and develop healthy relationships. Implementing **Bounce Back!** across the whole school means that:
    - there is a focus on both explicit teaching of the program and on embedding the understandings and concepts across the whole school environment (e.g. it is aligned with classroom and school norms, the school's values, the school's approach to behaviour management and with student structures such as buddy programs)
    - the program is taught across all year levels
    - teachers have opportunities for relevant professional learning to build expertise
    - teachers act as role-models for the program
    - families are partners in the development of their child's social and emotional learning
    - the content of the program is integrated with a range of different curriculum areas where appropriate.
- keeping families informed about the program and providing suggestions for ways in which they can be involved with further enhancement of their children's social and emotional learning (see **Bounce Back! Information for families**)
- providing opportunities for staff to undertake relevant professional learning
- assigning at least a weekly designated time for teaching the program
- supporting a key staff member to undertake actions to facilitate all teachers' implementation of the program and maintaining the profile within the school over time
- linking the program to other components of the school such as school values, behaviour management policy and the school's improvement plan.

The **school-system factors** most often mentioned as contributing to the program's successful and ongoing implementation were:

- the program aligned well with education policy guidelines, recommendations and important research outcomes
- regional school systems made student wellbeing and social and emotional learning a very clear school system priority.

The **program-specific factors** most often mentioned as contributing to the program's successful and ongoing implementation were:

- the program is user-friendly, easy to teach, flexible and adaptable
- the program is acceptable in terms of the time and commitment involved
- teachers feel confident about teaching the program, enjoy teaching it and believe it is important to teach
- a high level of successful student outcomes from the program were observed
- the multi-faceted approach in each unit enables links to be made with a range of curriculum areas and inquiry units (e.g. Health and Physical Education, English, Maths, Science, Humanities and Social Sciences, General Capabilities, etc.)
- the high-quality and engaging supplementary resources (books, poems, songs, films) and follow-up literature and language activities are easily integrated with aspects of the English curriculum
- the structure of the program and the consistency of key messages make it easy to achieve the intended outcomes.

Five stages for quality implementation of Bounce Back!

1. **Deciding to implement Bounce Back!**
   - Is your school 'SEL ready'? Do staff have a reasonable degree of knowledge about SEL and why it matters?
   - Is enhancing student wellbeing and resilience a priority for your school?
   - Does *Bounce Back!* 'fit' with your school's vision and values?
   - Will the program 'fit' with the way your teachers teach, e.g. use of children's literature and relationship building teaching strategies? How will they feel about giving time to teaching the program?
   - Is your leadership team supportive of implementing *Bounce Back!*?

2. **Planning and preparing for implementation**
   - Is appropriate professional learning available for your staff?
   - Is it feasible to establish a '*Bounce Back!* team' (or coordinator)? What will their responsibilities be?
   - How will your '*Bounce Back!* team' support the provision of resources that will help teachers implement the program?
   - Will one or two members of the leadership team (and/or the '*Bounce Back!* team') be available to coordinate the roll-out?

3. **Implementation**
   - How can implementation be monitored so there is reasonable consistency of delivery and time allocation for the program? For example, observing *Bounce Back!* lessons and checking teachers' programs.
   - How can helpful feedback and support be regularly provided to teachers and how will any obstacles be identified and addressed?
   - How can you encourage staff to share their skills, knowledge and resources in relation to teaching and using *Bounce Back!*?
   - How can you ensure reasonable fidelity and time commitment to the program by all staff?
   - How can the program be timetabled for consistency of time given to delivery, e.g. will all classes (or each year level) across the school have a *Bounce Back!* lesson at the same time?
   - What assessment tools will you use to assess progress before and during implementation (see tools for measuring wellbeing and resilience, available digitally)?

4. **Sustaining the program**
   - How and when can you assess the initial and ongoing impact of the program?
   - How will you keep families informed about the program in order to maintain their support and cooperation?
   - How will your '*Bounce Back!* team' assist staff to refresh the program in order to maintain their enthusiasm and commitment?
   - How will the leadership team/'*Bounce Back!* team' plan ahead for loss of key staff and the induction of new staff e.g. Will you develop an induction manual for new staff and/or appoint mentors?

5. **Improving the program**
   - How will you identify what's been working well and what can be improved? How often will you do this?
   - How can your staff be enabled to visit other schools that are implementing the program to explore and share ideas and resources?
   - What additional professional learning and resources would add value to the implementation of the program?

Source: Adapted from Durlak, J.A., et al. 2015[3]; Noble, T. & McGrath, H. 2017[1]

✦ Five stages for quality implementation of Bounce Back!

The five stages (see above) provide a framework for school leaders and student wellbeing teams to assess their school's readiness to implement *Bounce Back!* The evidence-based steps provide leadership support to facilitate the program's successful implementation and sustainability. It draws on feedback from schools over many years and further implementation research[3].

✦ Implementation tips

The key message shared by the wellbeing coordinators interviewed in the 10 schools that had implemented *Bounce Back!* for five to 12 years[1] was to make it as easy as possible for staff to teach the program.

Ways to support staff to implement the program are outlined on the following pages.

Dedicate weekly curriculum time

Many schools have a weekly **Bounce Back!** session (usually 45 minutes to one hour). During this session, some schools undertake a similar topic of the program for all classes. For example, all teachers focus on Unit 6: Emotions and take a similar theme, such as anger management. In other schools, each teacher chooses the topic for their **Bounce Back!** lesson and there isn't necessarily any commonality with other classes.

Map lessons to the scope and sequence charts

Ideally, all of the key points in each unit of **Bounce Back!** are covered in every class every year. This ensures that the key points are revisited many times and makes it more likely that students' wellbeing will increase and they will begin to think and act resiliently in both the short and long term. However, schools are very busy places and this may not always be feasible. Some schools alternate the units so that half are taught in one year and the rest in the next year. It is essential that all the teachers working at the same level collaboratively plan the activities and books that each class will use across the units. This saves students studying the same content for two or three years in a row.

Scope and sequence charts are available digitally to assist with planning.

Integrate Bounce Back! with a range of curriculum areas

Outlining the key learning areas addressed in each topic on your school's scope and sequence chart for the term makes it easy for teachers to write these outcomes into their program and see the curriculum links to the program.

Activities from **Bounce Back!** units can be included in English, Health and Physical Education, Personal Development, Humanities and Social Sciences, The Arts, Maths, Science, Technology and Religious Education lessons. **Bounce Back!** lessons can be linked with different curriculum outcomes. For example:

- You might start with the Bob Graham's book *Let's Get a Pup! Said Kate*. (English)
- You might then follow up with a Circle Time activity and discussion on the core value of compassion. (Health and Physical Education (Relationships), Personal Development/Pastoral Care)
- Students might prepare a fact sheet about looking after a puppy (English, Science) or role-play a scenario (The Arts).
- A cross-off word activity could be developed around the words in the book in the next literacy block session. (English)
- A small-group collaborative project on the work of the RSPCA or similar organisations might be a longer-term follow-up. (English, Humanities and Social Sciences, Technologies)
- In a school that has Religious Education, there could be a cross-reference to the story of the *Good Samaritan*.

Curriculum correlation charts are also available digitally to assist with planning.

Use Bounce Back! themes as a guide for selecting books

Some of the best books for teaching literacy are those that incorporate **Bounce Back!** themes such as courage, coping with adversity, relationships, conflict and emotions. Each **Curriculum Unit** begins with a list of resources (books, films/videos, poems, songs and websites) recommended in the program.

Give all students a Bounce Back! workbook or journal

It is a good idea for all students to have their own **Bounce Back!** workbook or journal in which they record their answers to activities, write **Bounce Back!** stories, keep a copy of their acronym and record their self-reflections on the class activities.

Consider school- and community-based projects

Promote school engagement through whole-school activities such as buddy programs, musical or dramatic performances, fundraising events and 'celebrating strength' days when every student showcases a talent.

Community service has several benefits. It allows students an opportunity to feel proud of their school and develops a sense of social justice and responsibility. It can also allow some less academic students to excel and all students to be connected to the larger community. Staff could consider:

- a community project for elderly people, such as performing, visiting or reading to people
- undertaking work with a local pre-school
- a schoolwide student wellbeing campaign.

Encourage staff to share and collaborate

Have staff meetings

Staff meetings provide opportunities for staff to showcase new literature and video clips, films, songs and poems that support the program. Encourage staff to share new ideas and tips at staff meetings and demonstrate how they taught a particular topic. Staff can also share their progress in implementation. Use the cooperative teaching strategies as a way to facilitate staff discussion on any topic but also model and practise the different cooperative learning strategies (see Teaching strategies and resources).

It is also very important that school counsellors, social workers, psychologists and speech pathologists are aware of the *Bounce Back!* program.

Use a glossary

Develop a *Bounce Back!* glossary to ensure that all staff (and students) are using the terms in the same way; for example, what does courage, resilience, optimistic, kindness, respect, loyalty, values and/or strengths mean?

Organise and share resources

Create digital folders or use stickers to label the different *Bounce Back!* resources by year level, based on your scope and sequence chart. For each term, organise and store the resources in tubs/containers in the staffroom or library or in folders on the intranet. Consider including appropriate books in your reading programs, including take-home reading.

Negotiate release time for collaborative team planning

Time for innovation is a perennial problem in schools. Translating a new program into classroom-friendly activities and checking that the new ideas mesh with curriculum outcomes takes considerable time. Often it is time that teachers simply don't have. Shared problem-solving can sometimes help with the issue of providing more time for new programming.

Give the program high visibility

Display the *Bounce Back!* posters and messages in the school. The school website and newsletter can be important marketing tools. Keep the school community informed about the implementation of *Bounce Back!* and involve students in ideas to promote the best things about your school.

Have regular assembly items with a *Bounce Back!* theme. Most families enjoy seeing their children presenting at assembly. Having the same theme such as courage across the whole school allows all year levels to provide short developmentally appropriate items such as a song, skit, role-play or poem on the theme.

Reinforce Bounce Back! at home

Prepare resources lists for home use and recommend books from the school or local library or films and video clips that reinforce key messages. Send home *Bounce Back!* tasks so that students talk about the program's key messages with their family.

Utilise *Bounce Back!* **Information for families** to reinforce the key messages for each **Curriculum Unit**.

Develop an induction manual and mentoring

Develop an induction manual for new staff that includes the school vision for the program, guidelines on how the school is implementing the program (e.g. scope and sequence charts) and a list of teachers who are happy to help or answer questions or to have visitors in their classroom. Arrange for each new staff member to be mentored for a term as they plan for and teach the program. Consider implementing peer coaching where teachers observe and give feedback on each other's *Bounce Back!* lessons.

Network with other Bounce Back! schools

Network with other schools using the program or create opportunities for teachers to visit classes implementing *Bounce Back!* in other schools to see the program in action. This could also be an opportunity to establish mentoring opportunities.

Bounce Back! assessment

✦ Formative assessment

In a *Bounce Back!* classroom assessment is ongoing. Assessment is today's way of understanding how to modify tomorrow's teaching. The topics provide teachers with day-to-day data on students' readiness for learning specific social and emotional learning skills, their strengths and interests and their approaches to learning. Some students may prefer to write down what they have learnt in a *Bounce Back!* journal, others present what they've learnt through a role-play or song and so on. Assessment doesn't just occur at the end of a unit in order to identify what students learnt (or didn't learn).

Formative assessment data will also emerge from Circle Time discussion, different group's responses to tasks, teacher–student interviews, *Bounce Back!* journal entries, student surveys such as the postbox surveys, teacher observation of students using the targeted social and emotional skills and a host of other ways. A pivotal goal is to help students to develop self-awareness and self-management of their own social and emotional learning skills, to develop positive relationships with classmates and to take responsibility for decision making. Effective decision making is influenced by encouraging students to continually analyse their own work relative to clearly articulated goals.

✦ Summative assessment

At benchmark points in learning *Bounce Back!* key messages (e.g. at the end of a unit) teachers can use summative assessment to formally record student growth. See the tools for measuring wellbeing and resilience below that enable students to demonstrate their skills and understanding. Assessment in *Bounce Back!* is always more about helping students apply and demonstrate what they know, understand and can do than cataloguing their mistakes.

✦ Assessment tools for measuring wellbeing and resilience

The *Bounce Back!* tools for measuring wellbeing and resilience provide a great range of options for schools on how to evaluate student progress as a result of implementing the program. Most of the tools can be used before and then during implementation of the program to document changes in student wellbeing and resilience.

For the classroom teacher

Resilient Behaviour Scale (F–6): This inventory can be used for teacher ratings of individual student wellbeing and resilience linked to the key concepts in each *Bounce Back!* unit.

Class Assessment Inventory (F–6): This inventory can be used as a formative or summative assessment of what your students have learnt about the *Bounce Back!* key concepts. As formative assessment it can provide feedback to teachers on what concepts are well understood by students and what concepts need to be revisited and taught again at the end of each unit. As summative assessment it helps to identify what students have successfully learnt.

Teacher's Observations of Classroom Connectedness (TOCC): This inventory measures teachers' perceptions of the level of class connectedness in their classroom. It assesses teachers' observations and perceptions of the emotional and social climate in their classroom. It can be used to identify:

- teacher observations of a negative social climate and low levels of class connectedness
- discrepancies between the students' perceptions as a class and their teacher's perceptions.

Teacher Assessment of Resilience Factors In their Classroom (TARFIC): This inventory measures the degree to which a teacher's current classroom practices foster student wellbeing and resilience. It contains the following nine categories:

- creating a safe classroom environment
- building confidence and self-respect
- supporting students
- teaching initiative, goal-setting and problem-solving skills
- developing optimistic and helpful thinking
- creating a prosocial classroom culture
- encouraging cooperation
- building relationships
- teaching the skills of conflict management.

The TARFIC can be completed by teachers to:

- reflect on their classroom practices, organisation and management to identify areas that need development in the interests of fostering wellbeing and resilience in students
- assess the level of changes teachers have made in their class by completing it again at a later stage

- remind themselves of the classroom protective factors that contribute to student resilience
- identify areas where the whole-school staff is doing well and areas where practices can be developed.

If teachers collate their results, the whole-staff findings can be used to identify school needs in regards to professional development or program planning.

For students (Years 3–6)

PEPS (Protective Environmental Processes Scale): This inventory is a student self-report on the environmental protective processes and resources in their life. There are different versions for Years 3–4 and Years 5–6. It can help teachers to identify students who have a comparatively low number of protective external processes and resources for developing resilience. If a student is identified as having fewer external resources than most, then the school can consider:

- setting up a relationship for that student with one caring adult, not necessarily a teacher
- helping the student feel more connected to school in a number of ways
- identifying students who do not feel connected to a teacher – this can then be addressed through actions by the teacher(s).

PRASE (Protective Resilient Attitudes and Skills Evaluation): This is a student self-report on how well students think and act resiliently. The items correspond to each of the 10 statements in the BOUNCE BACK! acronym. The PRASE quiz can help teachers to:

- identify non-resilient thinking that inhibits the development of resilience in an individual student – having this knowledge gives teachers an opportunity to focus on developing more resilient thinking in interactions and discussions with that student
- identify non-resilient thinking that may be relatively common across a whole class – this can be helpful in directing extra attention to reviewing and consolidating specific coping skills in the acronym
- ascertain progress (after re-administration at a later point) in student learning of the skills and attitudes taught through the BOUNCE BACK! acronym.

SPOCC (Students' Perceptions of Classroom Connectedness): This inventory is a report of students' perceptions of the level of classroom connectedness in their classroom and is an adaptation of the teacher version. It assesses students' perceptions of the emotional and social climate of their classroom and their sense of belonging. It can be used to:

- identify individual students who do not feel like they belong or do not feel connected to their classmates and/or their teacher or who do not feel safe in the classroom
- assess the perception by the whole class of the emotional and social class climate, by collating the frequency of the responses of all students in the class
- identify the areas that concern or disappoint many of the students in the class so they can be addressed
- ascertain, after re-administration, if there have been improvements in the class climate and class connectedness, as reflected by more positive perceptions by individual students and the class as a whole.

Assessing change

✦ Changes in individual students' resilient behaviour

It can be difficult in a school context to directly observe an increase in student wellbeing and resilience. A 'sleeper' effect often occurs with students learning social and personal skills; many students understand the new coping skills and attitudes but they can often lie 'dormant' until the student is:

- more mature
- more confident about using the skills or
- encounters a situation that urgently requires their use.

Nonetheless, there are some indicators of increases in individual student resilience, such as:

- making more references during student discussions or in other contexts to the statements used in the BOUNCE BACK! acronym

- demonstrating more effective coping behaviour under challenging conditions such as being embarrassed, making a mistake or losing a friendship
- achieving better learning outcomes
- demonstrating improved peer relations and higher levels of social acceptance
- in Years 3–6, having a higher overall score on the PRASE quiz (or higher scores on individual questions) when it is re-administered at a later date
- in Years 3–6, having a higher score on the SPOCC, indicating that the student perceives improvement in class connectedness.

✦ Changes in the bigger picture

Some of the assessment tools can be used to gauge the bigger picture of changes that are happening in the school. Documenting improvements is not only important to justify the inclusion and continuation of the **Bounce Back!** program, but can also provide a 'positive feedback loop' to sustain the ongoing implementation of the program.

Possible indicators that the program is having a positive effect on the bigger picture of student wellbeing, resilience and student behaviour across the school might be found in the following ways.

For Years 3–6:

- improved scores on SPOCC
- improved frequency of scores on specific items of SPOCC
- improved frequency of scores on PRASE
- improved frequency of scores on specific aspects of the PRASE.

These improvements may be detected for a class, a particular year level or across the school.

For all year levels:

- an increase in observations of classmates' acts of cooperation, kindness and support for each other, an increase in positive mood of a student or students, an increase in a student or students' positive relationships with classmates both in the classroom and in the playground and/or in behaviour or comments that reflect the statements in the BOUNCE or BOUNCE BACK! acronyms

- fewer student absences from school
- fewer sick-leave days taken by staff
- lower rates of playground disputes and misbehaviour reported by the teachers on yard duty
- lower rates of senior staff involvement with student misbehaviour
- lower rates of students being suspended from school
- reduction in the number of bullying incidents
- reduction in the number of students changing schools for unclear reasons
- increase in family involvement in school
- positive feedback from families about student behaviour at home
- improved learning outcomes because students are no longer distracted from learning.

Using Appreciative Inquiry to refresh Bounce Back!

Appreciative Inquiry (AI) is a collaborative, strengths-based approach to organisational change and development[4]. AI assumes that every organisation has things that give it life when it is most alive, effective, successful and connected in healthy ways to its community. AI has been used in many schools and school districts to help people identify what's best about their school or school district.

AI is based on the positive principle that the positive emotions and energy associated with identifying, celebrating and building on strengths enable people to transform their school and move it in new directions. By identifying what is positive in your school and connecting to this positive core heightens a school community's shared vision, energy and action for change. In contrast, traditional school change initiatives focus on analysing and solving problems that can lead to downward spirals of blame and negative energy.

The most common version of AI follows five stages, as shown on the following page.

The five stages of Appreciative Inquiry
1. Define Agree on the focus and scope of the inquiry. For example, how can we enhance student wellbeing in our school, or student engagement or student achievement? How can we enhance teacher wellbeing?
2. Discover This is a five-step stage: (i) individual, (ii) pairs, (iii) sharing in groups of four, (iv) analysing in groups of four, and (v) presenting to the whole staff group. Use generative questions (i.e. those that are most likely to lead to changed thinking and actions) to identify what has worked well in the past and what are the 'best features, assets and potentials' of the school that can be built on.
3. Dream Develop a shared vision of how the school could be, if everything in the 'Discover' step that could contribute to the defined focus (e.g. enhanced student wellbeing) was in place.
4. Design Draw up a plan of new actions to co-construct the vision, incorporating relevant information from the 'Discover' step.
5. Deliver Implement the actions and build in sustainability.

Source: Based on Cooperrider, D. L., Whitney, D. & Stavros, J. M. 2008, *Appreciative Inquiry handbook for leaders of change* (2nd edn), OH: Crown, Brunswick.

The following table outlines five stages of Appreciative Inquiry that could be implemented with the whole school to help refresh and re-energise staff's teaching of the ***Bounce Back!*** program.

An Appreciative Inquiry into the best ways to 'refresh' Bounce Back!		
Stage of inquiry	**Grouping**	**Steps**
1. Define	Whole staff group	Spend 10 minutes discussing and recording what 'Refreshing ***Bounce Back!***' means and why it is important to do this.
2. Discover What is the 'positive core' of your school and what can be learnt from your shared past?	Individual staff members	**Step 2.1: Individual reflections** Each participant reflects on a previous experience that stands out for them as a peak ***Bounce Back!*** experience, a time when they felt energised and satisfied because the program was making a difference and going well. This might have occurred when teaching a class, when observing children's behaviour or other types of feedback. Participants make notes on: • What was working so well and why? • What was happening that contributed? What actions were being taken? What structures were in place? • What key people made a difference and how? • How did <u>you</u> contribute and what strengths did you use to do so?
	Staff members in pairs	**Step 2.2: Sharing in pairs** One person tells their partner about the personal experience/situation/time they have just reflected on. They use prompting questions (see examples above) plus 'tell me more' prompts to stimulate further details and record notes. Then they swap roles.
	New groups of four staff members	**Step 2.3: Sharing in a group of four** Two pairs join up to make groups of four. Each person re-tells their partner's reflection to the other pair, i.e. four reflections are retold in total.

(Continued)

An Appreciative Inquiry into the best ways to 'refresh' Bounce Back!		
Stage of inquiry	**Grouping**	**Steps**
	Same groups of four as in step 2.3	**Step 2.4: Analysis of the four reflections** The group works together to identify the main 'themes' from their four reflections, focusing on: • What have we learnt from the past about the factors that make a significant difference to the success of **Bounce Back!**? These contribute to ideas for the future based on what has worked in the past. • What are the 'best things' about the school in terms of its assets and potential for successful improvement (e.g. its people, students, school community, commitment, resources, leadership, values, etc.)? These contribute to the school's 'positive core' that can now be built on when plans are made for 'refreshing' the program. Each person also has a specific role in this step: • One person is the group's note-taker. • One person will be spokesperson for step 2.5. • Two people work together to make a mind-map of the group's themes (to be placed around the room for the whole group before step 2.5 begins).
	Whole staff group	**Step 2.5: Whole-group feedback and summary** Each group's spokesperson summarises for the whole staff what was 'discovered' in their small group about: • what could make a positive difference when working towards refreshing **Bounce Back!** • the best features/assets/potential within the school and its past successes that could be harnessed to help achieve this. The facilitator creates a list of each group's themes and ideas and identifies commonalities to create a 'big picture'.
3. Dream Co-construct a vision of how the school could be if the implementation of the program were updated and enhanced.	Whole staff group	Staff co-construct a vision of how the school could be if all the things they can think of that could contribute to refreshing **Bounce Back!** were in place, based on these questions: • What changes and additions could enhance how the school looks, acts, thinks like, and feels? • What changes could be made to the physical layout and organisation of the school and classrooms? • What additional structures could be introduced? • What different teaching and learning processes could be added? • What additional resources could be made available and how?
4. Design Co-construct a plan for that vision to become reality.	Whole staff group	Staff then co-construct a plan by negotiating and identifying the best ways to turn the vision into reality. Decisions are made based on: • two small actions that could be taken immediately that would make a significant difference to achieving the vision • other actions that could be taken throughout the term/year • one 'bold' action that has the potential to be a 'game-changer' • ways in which each staff member could informally 'improvise' and make their own contributions to the changes.
5. Deliver Determine the best steps to turn actions into reality.	Whole staff group	Staff then make negotiated decisions about who will be involved in each of these 'actions' and how and when they will report back. They also: • select a date not too far away when they will collect follow-up data that can identify progress • decide what form this follow-up will take (e.g. surveys, whole-staff discussions, etc.) and when it will happen.

Advice for managing challenging situations

Teachers working in schools spend time each day engaged in what has been termed 'emotional labour'; in other words, dealing with families or students whose behaviour is challenging or requires support. Such interactions can be stressful and require good interpersonal skills as well as skills for managing the teacher's own feelings as well as the feelings of those involved. The following section provides some guidelines on how to develop teachers' skills to better manage such situations.

✦ Managing feelings

At times, negative feelings must be controlled because they could lead to an undesirable reaction by others or make a situation worse. To produce a positive outcome sometimes a teacher may need to mask how they are really feeling. This means being careful about what is said, adapting your tone of voice, controlling facial expressions and other indicators of your true feelings. This type of self-regulation may require thinking in a rational way that helps you to calm down. For example, teachers may be expected to:

- smile and be welcoming to all students and families, even those they may find difficult – this usually requires smiling and expressing warmth through choice of words and voice tone and/or engaging in conversation, etc.
- stay calm and in control when a difficult student behaviour needs to be managed
- give 'bad news' about a student's behaviour or learning to families in a positive, empathic and caring way
- stay calm and in control when verbally 'challenged' in a confronting way by a student or family member
- express warmth and concern to a distressed student or family member.

Useful social skills that help when managing difficult conversations and the feelings of others include:

- active listening
- respectful disagreeing
- empathic responding
- responding assertively
- positive tracking.

Active listening

This skill requires a teacher to take a more direct role in responding to what they have heard, rather than passively receiving the information. It involves listening and then giving a 'proof of listening' response. For example, the teacher could briefly summarise in their own words the main points of what the other person has just said and/or ask a question as a way to check that the teacher has properly understood.

Example: A student (Sarah) is describing to you how upset she was when another student (Lily) told several other people in class about her parents separating.

Sarah: 'Lily told at least three of the people in our class about what has happened. I'm so upset she shared my family's personal information.'

You: 'So Lily didn't respect your family's privacy. Have you told her how you feel?' (Summarise the issue and ask a relevant question to 'prove listening'.)

Respectful disagreeing

This skill involves identifying and stating the points of agreement (however small) before expressing points of disagreement.

Example: A parent is angry about what he believes to have been your unfair treatment of his son.

Parent: 'Ben wasn't the one who started the argument. Oliver took Ben's basketball without asking and then wouldn't give it back. What was Ben supposed to do – just put up with it and not do or say anything? It wasn't right that he wasn't allowed outside to play at recess.'

You: 'I agree that Oliver took Ben's basketball without permission and that Ben was very upset about that. But it wasn't okay for him to try to push Oliver over in the yard. Ben knows that such behaviour is unacceptable and there are better ways to deal with a situation like that.' (State points of agreement first before stating disagreement.)

Empathic responding

This skill involves attempting to see the world through the other person's framework and then to respond verbally and non-verbally in ways that let them know that you:

- understand their view of things
- understand and respect how they are feeling
- don't judge them.

Example: A parent has just told you how upset she was when another parent was rude to her.

Parent: 'Jess's dad was rude to me when he found out Ayesha got the main part in the school play. He said she didn't deserve the part.'

You: 'I think most people would feel upset if another parent had said that. It would have been a difficult situation for anyone to deal with.' (Express understanding and non-judgemental respect.)

Assertive responding

The skill of assertive responding requires teachers to be upfront about their views or about what they want to happen but not in an aggressive or demanding way. It usually requires one or more of the following components:

- the use of an I-statement rather than a you-statement (e.g. 'I think that plan would be unlikely to work' instead of 'Your plan is unworkable')
- the use of a 'broken record' tactic where they continue to restate their position in slightly different ways
- a statement of consequence (what will happen) rather than threats (what might happen)
- a refusal to be side-tracked ('That's not relevant at this point').

Example: A colleague is keen that you rearrange the shelves of a shared bookcase to suit her need to store large picture books. You would rather leave it as it is because if it were rearranged you wouldn't be able to store as many of your own books.

Colleague: 'This is the best way to make sure that what I need is easily accessible.'

You: 'But it wouldn't work for me as it means I wouldn't be able to put as many of my books in the bookcase.' (I-statement)

Colleague: 'But surely you could store some of them in the large cupboard at the back of the room?'

You: 'I don't want to have to do that as they are more readily accessed now. I'd prefer to leave things as they are.' (Refuse to be side-tracked. Use a broken-record statement.)

Colleague: 'Okay, I could put my books in the box over there.'

Positive tracking

This skill involves focusing on strengths and progress, highlighting the positive aspects of a situation and fostering hope. Sometimes it involves 'positively reframing' – this means converting mistakes or negative situations by identifying the small positive aspects. Care is needed to avoid being patronising.

Example: Alex (student) arrives at school and finds out there is a Maths test that she'd forgotten about. She is upset and tells you (teacher) about it. She wants to go home.

Alex: 'I've forgotten about the Maths test. I feel sick and want to go home.'

You: 'It would have been better if you'd remembered, but there's not much you can do about it now. You'll just have to give it your best shot. You've been doing really well in class with this topic. Even if you don't do as well as you would like, it's not the end of the world.' (Focus on the positives and reframe the situation in a way that fosters hope.)

REFERENCES

1. Noble, T. & McGrath, H. 2017, 'Making it real and making it last! Sustainability of teacher implementation of a whole school resilience program', in *Resilience in Education: Concepts, Contexts and Connections*, M. Wosnitza, F. Peixoto, S. Beltman, & C.F. Mansfield (eds.), Springer.
2. Senge, P. 1990, *The Fifth Discipline: The Art and Practice of the Learning Organisation*, Doubleday, New York.
3. Durlak, J.A., Domitrovich, C.E., Weissberg, R.P., & Gullota, T.P. 2015, *Handbook of Social and Emotional Learning, Research and Practice*, The Guilford Press, New York.
4. Cooperrider, D.L, Whitney, D. & Stavros, J.M. 2008, *AI handbook for leaders of change* (2nd ed.), Crown, Brunswick, OH.

Teaching strategies and resources

Circle Time

What is Circle Time?

Circle Time is a planned and structured framework for whole-class discussion. The whole class sits in a circle so they can see and hear each other, and everyone is included in the Circle Time activities and discussion. Being in a circle means the group is more engaged and distractions are less likely. Everyone has the opportunity to speak and be listened to. Circle Time works best on chairs, although some teachers have younger students sitting on the floor in a circle. Circle Time is used in every **Bounce Back!** Curriculum Unit. It builds classroom community, positive relationships and teaches Social and Emotional Learning (SEL) skills.

What happens in Circle Time?

A typical Circle Time discussion in **Bounce Back!** follows this format:

- a reminder of the Circle Time rules (see below)
- a reminder about the talking prompt that you are using (see page 82) – only the student who has the prompt can speak
- an introductory game (optional), energiser or simulation
- an activity that introduces the topic for Circle Time (often reading a relevant book)
- a whole-class discussion, with students participating in a variety of ways, for example:
  - every student may be invited to speak around the circle
  - selected students may be invited to speak
  - students may be asked to volunteer to make a comment or answer a question
  - students may be asked to discuss in pairs or threes and then one person in each pair is invited to explain what they agreed on
- a final activity that closes the circle, e.g. summarising the key messages from the class discussion or a sentence completion (e.g. One thing I learnt is … One thing that surprised me was … One thing that was new … I feel …)
- a follow-up group or individual activity after Circle Time (usually).

The Circle Time rules

When everyone is sitting in the circle, begin the session by stating the rules.

1. Everyone has a turn, and when one person is talking (i.e. the person who has the talking prompt), everyone else listens.
2. You may pass if you do not have anything to say (but the teacher may come back and ask you again when you have had a bit more time to think about what you want to say).
3. No put-downs are allowed during Circle Time.

An introductory game or energiser (optional)

This can be a name game, greeting or energiser. Each person takes a turn around the circle. For example, you could use:

- **silent greetings**: pass the smile, high-five, Mexican wave or handshake around the circle
- **spoken greetings**: go around the circle with everyone greeting the class using as many different greetings as possible, hi, hello, nice to see you, good morning, bonjour etc.
- **name games**: I am (name) and this is (name person on right) and this is (name person on the left).

Mixing students up in Circle Time

Students often sit in the circle next to their friends, so mixing them up to interact with different classmates helps to build class connectedness and maintain Circle Time energy. Some ideas for mixing them up include:

- personal categories; e.g. stand up and change places if you:
  - have blue eyes (brown eyes/green eyes)
  - have a sister (brother/pet)
  - can ride a bike (climb a tree/play a musical instrument/swim)
  - like olives (spaghetti/bananas/apple juice)
  - have a birthday in/have a name beginning with/like swimming (football/doing jigsaws) etc.
- given categories:
  - everyone in circle is numbered off, then even numbers change places
  - everyone receives a 'category card' (see page 88), one of the categories change places (e.g. everyone who is a country change places) – other categories include seasons, flowers, colours, alphabet, shapes, animals, months.

Talking prompts

Talking prompts remind students whose turn it is to speak, as only the person who holds the prompt is allowed to talk. The job of the other group members is to listen actively. Use different talking prompts, or work as a class to make an official 'class talking prompt'. Younger students love using small soft toys or other small toys. Older students like using wrap wristbands, soft balls or novelty balls. All ages like using a torch with cellophane over the light so it glows in a dim room. Use talking prompts in Circle Time and in cooperative group work if you feel that students are not having an equal say.

Closing the circle

The final activity in the Circle Time session might be summarising the key messages from the class discussion. This could be a sentence completion: 'One thing I learnt is …', 'One thing that surprised me was …', 'One thing that was new …', 'I feel …'

This reflection could be completed as a timed Think–ink–pair–share (see page 97).

Safe class discussions

It is essential to create a classroom climate of safety, so students feel that their self-disclosures and any differences in opinions, feelings, ideas or behaviour will be respected by their classmates. It is also important to help students learn about the kinds of personal information about themselves and others that are appropriate to share in class discussions. This climate of trust can only be built up over time and can easily be destroyed by insensitive comments or put-downs. **Bounce Back!** does not have a strong focus on students sharing deeply personal information about themselves or people they know.

There are two levels of personal disclosure in **Bounce Back!**

1. At the first level, students talk about their own ideas and opinions, give examples of concepts and processes, and talk about the concepts and ideas as applied to puppet characters, cartoon characters, book characters, people in the news and so on. For example:
   - Can you think of an example of a situation in which someone your age might feel worried?
   - Why was Henry so sad?
   - What do you think courage is?
   - What are some good ways for the puppet to respond here?

2. At the second level, students talk about the ideas and concepts as applied to themselves and, perhaps, other people they know, such as family or friends. For example:
   - Can you think of a time when someone you know achieved a goal they set for themselves? What did they do to achieve it?
   - What situations do you (or do students your age) find most scary?

Guidelines for helping students feel safe in class discussions

1 Teach the skills of 'listening well' and 'respectful disagreeing' before students start their discussion.

These skills need to be taught beforehand, and students need to be reminded to use them before each discussion-based activity or debrief. Consider using the following strategies.

- There are many activities in this resource that give students the chance to learn and practise the skill of listening, e.g. Think–ink–pair–share (see page 97) and Partner Retell (see page 95). There are also listening activities in Unit 7: Relationships.
- Use a talking prompt that is held by the person talking and is a signal for others not to interrupt.
- Use talking tokens. If the same students tend to dominate the discussion, give each student two talking tokens and ask them to place one in front of them when they speak. They then have to wait until other students have used their talking tokens until they can speak again.
- 'Respectful disagreeing' involves encouraging students to first re-state what the other person said that they agree with, before stating their different opinion. For example, 'I can see what Emma means about parachuting being dangerous because the parachute might fail (*this is the bit that I can agree with*), but I don't think it would be as dangerous as bungee jumping (*this is where I differ*).'

2 Have a strongly enforced 'no put-downs' rule in place at all times

Remind students about the rule before any discussion and remember to enforce it in a non-humiliating way. Don't forget to include non-verbal put-downs in this category. This rule also relates to the core value of accepting differences in people (see Unit 1: Core values) and not negatively judging others because they hold different values and ideas. There are more details on strategies for reducing put-downs in Unit 9: Being safe.

3 Paraphrase and clarify what students say when they make unclear comments

Often students make comments or ask questions that are not clear to other students or even perhaps to themselves. Initially, the language of feelings and relationships is not an easy one for many students. If this happens, re-state what they have said in a simpler or clearer way and check it with them.

4 Avoid tasks that require students to expose too much of their personal lives or feelings

Remember not to ask students to do or discuss anything you would not be comfortable doing or discussing yourself. However, perhaps you need to consider whether you are 'typical' before using yourself as the benchmark in this way. Do you think you are more disclosing or shyer than the norm?

5 Understand that some students find it difficult to self-disclose

The fact that a student finds it difficult to talk personally, even at a relatively superficial level, does not mean they are not interested in the topic, or that they are upset about it. They are probably still learning a lot even if they are not speaking much. Some students are just shyer than others, or they become more anxious when they are the centre of attention. Others fear peer disapproval. Here are some ideas to facilitate the inclusion of all students in the discussion.

- Remind students that having a different opinion is everyone's right. Even if they don't agree with what someone has said, they need to respect that person's right to a different opinion.
- Give students the right to 'pass' on any question, but encourage them to try to contribute to the discussion where they can, and not to 'pass' too often.
- Use puppets, which allow issues and feelings to be presented and discussed 'one step removed'.
- Gently try to include reluctant speakers in the discussion, but don't put them on the spot. For instance, ask a few students (by using their names) if there is anything they would like to add. Include in this group some of those students who have already spoken and those who haven't, so the focus isn't directly on the student who hasn't contributed.
- Structure some small-group or partner discussion tasks rather than always running whole-class discussions. Some students feel uncomfortable being the centre of attention in a whole-class discussion, but feel less threatened by open-ended discussions in a small group. Encourage the group to 'own' everything that is said within the group and report back about what 'we talked about' rather than focusing on individual opinions or stories. It can be distressing for a student to hear a group member say, while reporting to the class, 'Josh told us about …' This obviously depends a lot on the nature of the discussion. Also encourage everyone to sign any group product to enhance team interdependence and ownership.
- Provide students with less threatening alternatives when offering them opportunities to self-disclose. For example, instead of saying 'Tell us about a time when you finished a friendship' you could say 'Why do you think friendships sometimes end?'
- Invite students to describe a situation or likely emotions from the perspective of someone else or a character in a story or movie. The gap between describing the emotions felt by someone else and self-disclosing is not large, and they will probably feel more comfortable expressing their own emotions with more practice. For example, you can say:
    - 'Does anyone have any suggestions about how a new student of your age might feel about being different in this way?'
    - 'What sort of feelings would Fatima possibly have at this point in the story? Why might she feel that way?'
- Remind students that they can choose to self-disclose at a relatively superficial level by giving less detail, simplifying a story or leaving out specific information and so on. It is not dishonest to do so under these circumstances.

6 Remember that some students feel anxious about finding a space in the discussion, so find a way to 'let them in'

Some students feel anxious when they are competing for their turn to talk, and perhaps find themselves interrupted or 'talked over'. When there is a lull in the discussion, ask a general question such as, 'Does anybody else have something to add?' Then scan the room, making specific but brief eye contact with those students whom you perceive as having not said much so far, but not pressuring them.

7 Understand that some students may be tempted to disclose too much

Occasionally, some students are energised by the opportunity to talk about a personal issue and they blurt out more than they should. At the time they may not think through the consequences of revealing too much about themselves, classmates, friends or family. Afterwards they may feel uncomfortable. This doesn't happen very often, but it might.

Here are some suggestions to minimise this possibility.

- Have a 'no names' rule in place most of the time. Remind students at the start of a discussion to be cautious about giving identifying details about the people they mention, and stress the importance of protecting privacy. Instead they could say something like:
    - 'I knew someone who …'
    - 'I know of a situation where …'
    - 'A relative I know …'

- Before starting a class discussion, let students know that you will use 'protective interrupting' if you think they are saying something that is either too personal, only indirectly related to the topic, or too complicated to be discussed in a whole-class discussion. Before the discussion, say something like: 'Remember, sometimes it may be better to talk to me about some things that are worrying you after the lesson rather than discuss these things in class. If that happens, I will say something like, "Excuse me, Tom, can you and I talk about that later when we have more time?"'

Stress that you do not want anyone to feel that you have interrupted because you are not interested in what they are saying. Make a note about it and be sure to follow up later.

8 Always debrief students after any form of drama or role-play

Students can easily confuse how someone pretends to be in a role-play with how they really are. Using puppet drama can minimise this effect somewhat. You could also say something like: 'Welcome back, Briony and Sanjay (their real names), and goodbye, Jenny and Jake (their role-play names). Now, although we all know that this was just drama, sometimes our brains can mix up the actor with the role. Let's remember that Briony and Sanjay are not like Jenny and Jake, they were just acting like them. Sanjay, how did you feel about playing the role of Jake? How are you different from Jake? Briony, how did you feel about playing the role of Jenny? How are you different from Jenny?'

9 Ask all students to respect each other's confidentiality

Students need some expectation of confidentiality in discussions. You could say something like: 'Remember that anything that is said in this room should stay in this room.'

But you also need to point out to students that while you hope and expect that everyone will honour that rule, you cannot guarantee them confidentiality. Ask them to think about what might happen with any personal information they disclose, and remind them not to discuss anything about themselves or their family and friends they would not like others to talk about in out-of-class time.

10 Keep in mind that many boys are less practised at self-disclosure than girls

Asking boys to talk about their feelings about specific issues may run the risk of making some of them feel vulnerable and contradict their socialisation about not showing their feelings.

So it's reasonable to expect that some boys will sometimes feel uncomfortable with talking or writing about their feelings or openly declaring their fears, doubts, insecurities or affection to their classmates. They will often show that discomfort by being silly, misbehaving or cracking jokes. But don't make the mistake of thinking that they are not taking in what is being discussed, even if they appear to be dismissive and unengaged.

Boys are likely to have the same concerns about friendships, everyday courage and so on and the need for the relevant skills, but may have fewer opportunities to discuss or develop them in their peer life. You could say something like: 'We might talk about some slightly personal issues here, so please respect the importance of what we're talking about.'

11 Be aware of and show sensitivity to cultural differences

Western psychological therapeutic and counselling principles as well as Western educational principles and practices underpin the **Bounce Back!** program. Many of these principles are in accord with Eastern philosophies, such as some Buddhist principles. However, our society is so diverse in its ethnic and cultural make-up that sensitivity in choosing appropriate activities and adapting concepts may be needed in some classes, in order to take account of students' cultural differences in regard to language, values, background and experiences.

Literature prompts

Picture books and novels are used throughout **Bounce Back!** as a starting point or to reinforce key messages. Information on how and where to access the resources used in the **Bounce Back!** program is available.

The following questions can be used to guide student reading and reflection on texts. They can be used for discussion in a whole class, a cooperative pair or a group. They can be used with activities such as Partner Retell (see page 95) and Think–ink–pair–share (see page 97).

Prompts to help students understand the text

- What do you already know about this topic (e.g. courage)?
- What do you think this book might be about? (after showing the cover)
- Who are the characters/people/animals?
- What happens?
- Where is it set?
- When did _____ happen?
- How/Why did it happen?
- What happened in the beginning/middle/end?
- What does the cover/title tell us about the text?
- What does this picture tell you? How does it make you feel?
- What do you think might happen next? Why?

Prompts to help students to think critically about the text

- What is this story about? How do we know?
- Who is in the story? Who is missing from the story? Who should/could be there?
- Who tells the story? What might another character say if they were asked?
- Do you like the story? Why/Why not?
- How could we change the ending of the story?
- What if a character did something different? How might the story be different?
- What characters do you like? What characters don't you like? Why?
- What clues do the words or pictures give us about how the characters are feeling?
- What do you think the author wants the reader to think about?
- What does the author want us to believe about the world and the people in it? What suggests this to us? Does this 'fit' with what you believe about the world and about people? Why/Why not?
- What is the message/moral in the book? What is the author telling us? Do you agree with the author's message? What might you do differently now you have read this book?
- What might this character be thinking right now?
- Why did the story end in this way?
- What does the ending mean?
- How did the book make you feel? Is this a happy or sad book?
- In what ways is this book the same as/different to your favourite book?
- What if this book had no pictures?

Bounce Back! key message prompts

These questions help students to understand the key *Bounce Back!* concepts when using the recommended literature. They can be used with books, poems, songs, video clips and films in the program, or any other texts. Some questions will be more suitable for some resources than others.

- **Questions focusing on predicting likelihood**:
  How likely is it that what this person is worried about will happen?

- **Questions focusing on courage**:
  Who showed courage in this story? What fear did they get over? What risks did they take? Were they thoughtful or foolhardy risks?

- **Questions focusing on grit (perseverance), growth mindset (effort) and goal setting**:
  Where in the story did someone refuse to give up? What plans did the characters in the book make? Did anyone in this story learn from the mistakes they made? What problems or obstacles did they meet along the way? Did the person work hard? What did they want to achieve? What goal did they set? Did working hard help them to do well? What things could the character not do yet?

- **Questions focusing on 'Bad times don't last. Things always get better. Stay optimistic'**:
  When did the character find out that their bad times didn't last and things got better?

- **Questions focusing on 'Other people can help you feel better if you talk to them. Get a reality check'**:
  Who did the character speak to when they were feeling sad/when they were worried/when they had a problem? How did speaking to someone help them to feel better? Did anyone in this story jump to decisions without proof?

- **Questions focusing on 'Unhelpful thinking makes you feel more upset. Think again'**:
  What feelings did the different people in this story have? (Stress accurate naming of the feeling and its intensity, as described in Unit 6: Emotions.) Who was angry in the story? Was it helpful to be angry or not? What might have happened if they stayed calm and didn't get angry? Did anyone in this story change the way they were thinking so that their thinking was more helpful (i.e. helped them not to exaggerate, to look for facts and to find a solution)?

- **Questions focusing on 'Nobody is perfect – not you and not others'**:
  How was this character 'not perfect'? How were other characters not perfect? What mistakes did they make? Is anyone perfect? When have you made a mistake? Did your mistake help you to learn?

- **Questions focusing on 'Concentrate on the positives (no matter how small) and use laughter'**:
  Did anyone in the story find something good in the bad situation? Did anyone look on the bright side? Did anyone see anything funny in the situation that helped them to cope better?

- **Questions focusing on 'Everybody experiences sadness, hurt, failure, rejection and setbacks sometimes, not just you. They are a normal part of life. Try not to personalise them'**:
  What were the difficult or hard times in the story? Do these things happen to everyone? Do you know other people your age who have had this sort of setback too?

- **Questions on relationships**:
  Was this character a good friend? In what ways? How did the character's relationship with others affect the story's ending/outcomes? Where did conflict or problems happen and how were they dealt with?

- **Questions focusing on emotions and empathy**:
  How did this character feel? What words or pictures tell us how they felt? How did their feelings make them do what they did? Do you think this was a good thing to do? How would you feel if you were this character? Would you do what they did?

Organising students into pairs and groups

The best approach to organising students into groups or pairs is 'random grouping'. This means that students are allocated to groups and 'mixed up' rather than choosing who they will work with. If you do this for 90 per cent of the time, then you can allow students to select their own work partners the rest of the time (but tell them that 'free choice' grouping will be disbanded if everyone hasn't been invited into a group within two minutes).

Random grouping contributes to a more inclusive and positive classroom culture, characterised by a sense of connectedness as everyone gets to know and work with everyone else. Here are some ways of randomly organising pairs or groups of three for a class of 24.

Name cards or craft sticks

Write everyone's first name on a card or craft stick (or ask them to do this with their own name). The teacher pulls out three from a container (or two for each pair).

Numbering off

Number each student from 1 to 8. Students with the same number go in the same group. If you have more than 24 students, choose the extra one or two to be 'wild cards' who can choose any group to go to. If you have more than 26, make extra groups.

Category cards

Make eight sets of three cards for groups of 3 or four cards for groups of 4. Write a number from 1 to 3 on the back of each card in each set (to use for allocating roles). On the front of each card, paste or draw a picture or write a word related to a current theme. Students draw a card from a container and then find the other two students who have the same or a matching card. Sets could be made around:

- eight different animals (the **Animal Asks e-tool** could also be used and is referred to in the Curriculum Units)
- eight different forms of transport (e.g. car, ship, truck, bicycle, bus, tram, plane, rickshaw)
- eight countries (students form groups with other students who have a fact about the same country, e.g. the name of the country, its main river, capital city, famous monument, language spoken)
- eight postcards (or old birthday or Christmas cards) or pictures from magazines turned into three-piece jigsaws
- eight sets of number facts that all have the same answer, e.g. one set of three cards could all have an answer of 10 (e.g. 2×5, $5 + 5$, $8 + 2$)
- eight sets of playing cards that match on number, not suite
- eight sets of pictures or words that start with the same letter (e.g. cow, cup, cat, carrot) or the same letter combination (e.g. think, thank, throw).

Line-ups

Students line up in two lines either randomly or on the basis of a criterion such as the order of their name in the alphabet (first name or last name) or birthdays (month first, then day). Then the first four in the line form a group, and then the next four and so on.

You could also 'shuffle' two lines by asking the first two people in line one to go to the end of their line, and the last two in line two to come to the front of their line. Then make groups based on two people from each line. This mixes students up so close friends aren't together.

Class meetings and school committees

Class meetings

Class meetings can be conducted using a Circle Time format. However, separate classroom meetings can also be held. These are problem-solving meetings in which everyone discusses difficulties that have arisen in class or in the playground. For example, the teacher may ask the class: 'What can we do about students using put-downs or name calling?' Students may ask: 'How can we convince the teachers that we need an extra 15 minutes for our sports lesson?' Classroom meetings are excellent sessions to teach how meetings are run and to practise social skills, such as respectful disagreeing and listening. They can also help students to learn how to request permission through the chairperson to speak, wait for their turn, express their opinion, use 'I' messages, manage conflict and negotiate. Good problem-solving skills are developed and students can increase their sense of competence in this structured environment.

The structure of classroom meetings:

- Everyone sits in a circle.
- Roles: a rotating chairperson, a secretary who keeps minutes and gives everyone a copy, and a timekeeper. The teacher's role is mostly to accept and listen to different students' ideas and help the class reach solutions that everyone can accept. The teacher does not run the session but may still participate and, if appropriate, subtly facilitate participation by comments and questions.
- Length of meeting: 10–15 minute meetings work well for younger year levels, and up to 30 minutes for students in older year levels.
- Appropriate meeting times: holding the meeting just before recess, lunch or home time ensures there is a natural cut-off, even if it's in the middle of a hot discussion. If this happens, the teacher can say: 'We will begin the next meeting with this problem'. However, meetings held directly after recess or lunchtime can reduce negative playground incidents, as students are able to problem-solve directly after any incidents.

Setting up class and school committees

Student participation in class, year level or school committees can foster a sense of responsibility for self and others, and can increase their commitment and connectedness to the school. Through committee participation, students can practise social-emotional skills such as cooperation, listening, respectful disagreeing, negotiation, conflict resolution, showing initiative, setting goals and monitoring progress. On class committees, students usually work with only two or three other students. Ideally, each committee:

- has the necessary combined skills to perform its tasks
- has some idea of good goal-setting skills
- has a limited life so that membership can be rotated (e.g. each term or for five to six weeks)
- does not get too 'bossy'
- can co-opt another classmate to assist the committee temporarily if necessary
- keeps records along the way and writes a final report at the end of its tenure of their achievements.

Some suggestions for small class committees are:

- birthday celebrations committee (includes the teacher's birthday too!)
- classroom meetings committee: plans, announces, chairs, takes minutes and reports on class meetings
- classroom liaison committee: plans ways to get to know and socialise with other classes
- display committee: designs and maintains classroom displays and collections
- Giggle gym committee (see page 250): this group finds and displays and finds funny cartoons, jokes, songs, poems and stories, and organises fun and humorous games for the class to play
- zoo-keeping committee: advises on suitable classroom animals and ensures they are well cared for.

Teaching strategies used in Years 3-4

Animal asks

A student's name is randomly chosen and this child chooses one of eight animals. Each animal corresponds to a question number (1–8) to be answered. Sometimes the prepared questions are specific to a topic; sometimes they are generic. The student answers the question and then randomly chooses another student to answer the question again or to summarise the first answer. An **Animal Asks e-tool** is available for the IWB where students select an animal and the teacher reads out a corresponding question they have prepared.

Before or after?

The aim of this game is to be the first team of three or four students to guess the mystery word from a list of words that everyone has seen. The game reinforces alphabetical ordering of words.

1. Each team has a turn at selecting one of the words on the list and asking a person (e.g. the teacher) for information about that word, e.g. 'We would like some information about the word "bounce".'
2. The person then gives feedback on whether the team's selected word is before or after their mystery word in the alphabet, e.g. 'Your word "bounce" is before my mystery word in the alphabet.'
3. If the word the team has asked for information about is the person's mystery word, then that person wins the round!
4. Each team is allowed only one guess (at any time) when they think they know the mystery word. No person in the group can make a guess unless everyone in the group agrees.
5. If the guess is wrong, the person says, 'I'm sorry, but your guess is incorrect and you are now out of this round.' The game continues with the other teams.
6. The first team to guess the word wins the game.

Pair vs pair version for a games round robin

Before or after? can be played as part of a cooperative games round robin (see page 98). One pair decides on its mystery word from the list and the other pair tries to work it out. Each pair's score is the number of words they need to get information about before their guess is correct, so the lowest score wins. Some units have a **Before or After? e-game** version available.

Bingo strips

Make a list of 15 words to be used in the game and revise them with students. Make one Bingo strip (i.e. five squares joined to each other in a row) for each student, with each strip containing a different combination of five words from the list. Make a separate card for each of the 15 words and place them in a container. Draw out one word at a time. Students cross off any matching word they have on their strip. The first student to cross off all five squares on their strip calls out 'Bingo!' and wins.

BRAIN

This strategy uses the acronym BRAIN:

    Beautify it in some way.

    Replace or reorganise some parts of it.

    Add or remove parts of it.

    Increase or decrease parts of it.

    Name it differently.

Students work in groups of five (because there are five statements in the BRAIN acronym) and each person is responsible for leading a discussion from one of the five perspectives allocated to them from the BRAIN statements. Then students make an improvement plan (e.g. for the classroom, a backpack or the playground). This strategy is supported by a **BRAIN e-tool**.

Bundling

Each student has four strips of paper. They write one different word (e.g. four feelings words) or a theme-related fact on each strip (e.g. mistakes help you learn). Each student then teams up with two other students. They sort their strips into different categories (i.e. bundles) and then label their bundle (e.g. pleasant feelings). Each group reports to the class.

Circuit brainstorm

1. On six large sheets of paper, write six theme-related questions that are open-ended. In Unit 7: Relationships a good question would be, 'What is one thing that a good friend does?' One good question for a Circuit brainstorm (Unit 9: Being safe) could be, 'Write one example of how you could support someone who is being bullied.'
2. Set up six stations around the room and place a different question at each.
3. Organise students into groups of four and number them off from one to four. Each number represents one of the following roles: writer, time-checker, sheepdog (who moves them on) and reporter.
4. Groups can only move to the next station on the teacher's signal. At each station the group writes (in a different coloured pen) a response to the question that is different from any other response already written.
5. When all groups get back to the sheet they started with, the reporter from each group reads out the six responses to the question that they first started with (their 'home station').

Collective classroom research

Put up a large poster or set aside a large area of the bulletin board. Tell students that everyone will be researching the question asked, e.g. 'What are the health benefits of having pets?' All students then bring their answers research material for the designated question.

Keep a ring binder full of empty plastic document sleeves for students to insert any printed or drawn material. Remind students to acknowledge the source of their information correctly. Students then pin their information on the board.

Cooperative number-off

1. Students number off in their group from one to three.
2. The teacher asks a question and the group decides on their negotiated answer. Every person in the group must be clear about what the group's answer is.
3. The teacher calls a number (one, two or three) and only the student in each group with that number gives their group's answer, either orally or by writing it down.

Cross-offs

In this word game, students cross off categories of things to find the secret message. The secret message is a key teaching message for each *Bounce Back!* unit. Some units include a **Cross-offs e-game** version.

Cut-up sentences

This is a good activity to consolidate key messages. Write six short, theme-related sentences. Cut each sentence into individual words and place all the pieces of each cut-up sentence into a separate envelope. Make enough sets for each pair of students to have one set of all six sentences. Some units have an **e-game** version available.

Four corners

This activity is good for stimulating discussion.

1 Find four squares of different coloured paper (e.g. red/blue/green/yellow). Stick a different coloured square on the wall near each corner of the room.

2 Prepare a number of theme-related questions about personal preferences and experiences. Each should have four choices to select from. For example:

'Which thing would you find the scariest? The red corner is going to the dentist, the blue corner is riding a horse, the green corner is staying at a friend's house for the first time, and the yellow corner is being lost in a crowd.'

3 Ask students to go to the corner that best represents what they think. When they get there, they should discuss why they chose that corner. If there are more than three or four students in one corner, they should break into two groups.

Freeze frame and rewind

This is a drama activity that helps students to understand issues or to empathise with people in particular situations. It can also be used with puppet plays.

1 Give groups a scenario to act out, e.g. a conflict situation or a scene from a story, or they could retell or make up a simple story.

2 At a vital point in the story, ask the actors to stop and freeze. This gives the participants and the audience time to reflect on what has happened, think about the effect of what the actors said or did had on the other characters in the story, and anticipate what might happen next. Ask students in the audience about their feelings, their actions and so on.

3 'Rewind' allows students to rewind a scene and do it with a different ending.

Good genie/Bad genie

This strategy helps students to understand that there are two ways of thinking about the same situation: a helpful, positive way and an unhelpful, negative way. It can be used as a puppet play or drama in conjunction with the freeze frame strategy. It can be a small-group role-play with two or three actors plus a good genie and a bad genie.

The group role-plays a scenario with the good genie and bad genie giving conflicting advice. The good genie whispers positive messages to the main character about choices they can make (e.g. 'Be brave because …', 'Be honest because …', 'Be strong because …'). The bad genie whispers negative messages (e.g. 'Give up because …', 'Tell a lie because …', 'Just walk away and don't do anything because …').

Costumes can help students to see and understand clearly the roles of the good and bad genie. The good genie wears a sparkly, gold or white turban and the bad genie wears black. If using this strategy with puppets, make puppets to look like a good genie and bad genie.

Inquiry-based learning

Inquiry-based learning is a student-centred or active learning approach that starts with asking students questions to raise their curiosity about a topic, then building on this to develop their information processing and problem-solving skills. The essence of inquiry-based learning is that students participate in the planning, development and evaluation of their projects and activities. The focus is on 'how they know' rather than on 'what they know'. For example:

1 **Tuning in: Posing questions**
   - What do I want to know about this topic?
   - What do I need to know?
   - What do I know already? How do I know this?

2 **Finding out: Finding resources**
   - What kinds of resources might help?
   - Where do I find them?
   - How do I know that the information is correct?

3 **Sorting out or interpreting the information**
   - Does this information help me to answer my question?
   - How does this relate to or match what else I know?
   - What parts are different to my answer?
   - Does it raise new questions?

4 **Reporting findings**
   - What is the main point? What is the main thing to report about this topic?
   - Who is my audience?
   - How does this connect to other things we are learning?
   - How will I present my findings? (e.g. slide show, demonstration, role-play, puppet show, class talk, poster)

Inside–outside circle

1. Students form two concentric circles (facing each other) so each student has a partner.
2. The teacher poses a question or issue.
3. One person in each pair answers and then they swap and the other person answers.
4. On a signal, the outer (or inner) circle moves two or three spaces and the process is repeated with a new partner and a new question.
5. Step 4 is repeated two or three more times.

Lightning writing

This strategy gets students quickly engaged in writing down all the things they can think of on a topic in a short time frame of one or two minutes.

1. Tell students they have only one minute to write down all the things (words and phrases) they can think of on the topic, e.g. 'Write down what you think of when I say the word "success"' or 'What do you think is meant by "bouncing back"?'
2. At the end of the specified time, ask different students to share their answers as a springboard for further teaching. You could give the students sheets of paper already printed with an interesting border or graphics, plus the heading 'Lightning writing' with a lightning bolt.

Memory cards

This is a good activity to consolidate vocabulary. The memory cards are mixed up and placed face down. Students take turns to turn over one card and try to find its pair. The winner is the student who matches the most pairs. There is an **e-game** version available in some Curriculum Units.

Movers and shakers

This is a personal survey in which students give their responses by making specific movements rather than verbal answers.

1 Prepare about six Yes/No questions/statements and attach some movement options to each. For example:
   - Pretend to bounce a ball with your right hand if you play in a netball or basketball team.
   - Put your left hand on your hip if you have ever had a friend who has moved to another school.
   - Put your hands over your eyes if you have a night light on when you are sleeping.
2 Ask the whole class to stand up, leaving space to stand and move without bumping others.
3 Ask each question.

Multiply and Merge

1 Give each student four strips of paper. On each strip they write one simple response to a simple question, e.g. What are the four best ways to be a good friend to someone?
2 Each student then pairs up with another student and they negotiate to decide on the pair's best four of the eight responses they started with.
3 Each pair then joins with another pair and all four negotiate to decide on their best four of the eight responses they started with.
4 Each group of four reports on their final best four responses.

Musical stop and share

Music is played while students mill around the room. When the music stops, they pair up with the person nearest to them and discuss a theme-related question asked by the teacher, e.g. for Unit 10: Success (CHAMP), 'How do you make sure that you remember to take your lunch with you each day?'

Mystery square

This game can be used in a cooperative games round robin (see pages 98–100 for more games ideas).

Make up a 4 × 4 (or 5 × 5) mystery square grid of 16 or 25 words. Each pair has a copy of the grid. The aim of the game is to use as few questions as possible to guess the word in the other pair's chosen mystery word. The pair who has picked the word to be guessed can only give the following answers to the other pair when they ask each question: 'Yes', 'No', 'I can't answer that' or 'Can you please ask that in another way?' An answer of 'I can't answer that' or 'Can you please ask that in another way?' isn't counted in the total of questions asked. An incorrect guess is counted as a question. Students cannot ask location-based questions, such as 'Is it in the top three rows?' or 'Is it in the second column?'

1 Each pair goes to a quiet place and works out which word they will pick for the other pair to guess. They also plan good questions to ask when it is their turn to try to guess the other pair's mystery square word.
2 The first pair has a round of asking questions while the second pair gives answers and keeps count of the questions asked and incorrect guesses. When they have correctly guessed the mystery word, they swap roles with the second pair.

Each pair has two rounds of trying to guess the other pair's word. They keep a record of the total number of questions they had to ask across those two rounds. The winning pair (if the game is part of a round robin) is the pair that has asked the fewest questions in total across their two rounds.

PACE

PACE stands for the four steps of this strategy:

Predict what will happen.

Argue for your prediction.

Check by testing, surveying or researching.

Explain any differences between what you predicted and what you found.

1. Organise students into groups of three and allocate one of the following roles to each student: writer, reporter and time-checker. Pose a theme-related survey question, e.g. What will be the most common response given by the people in our class to the question 'What kind of celebration makes you feel happiest?'

2. Each group of three then negotiates to decide on their prediction of the result (the most popular class response) and why they think that. They write their prediction on an A3 sheet of paper and post it on the wall or write it on the board.

3. All students in the class (and maybe students in another class of the same year level) individually and privately write their answer to the question on a piece of paper, fold it up and post it in the survey box. The most popular class result is identified and each group writes a report on what they found out, whether or not they were correct in their prediction and possible explanations for their accuracy or inaccuracy.

Partner Retell

Students work in pairs and interview each other about a given topic (e.g. on the value of responsibility: 'What chores do you do at home and how often? What do think of those chores? How do you make sure you do them?') Then they pair up with another pair and take turns at summarising and sharing what their partner said in the previous interview sessions. Alternatively, they report what their partners said in a whole-class context. Remind students that they need to listen especially well because they will be retelling what their partner said.

Pairs rally, pairs compare

1. Organise students into pairs. Each pair has one sheet of paper and one pen. They take turns at writing one response to the topic question or task (e.g. Write down all the ideas you can both think of that students your age can do to help save our planet). They then pass the paper to their partner to write one response (without talking). They keep writing and passing until they run out of ideas or the time is up (e.g. three minutes).

2. Each pair then joins with another pair. One pair reads their responses and the other group ticks any responses on their sheet of paper that are the same. The other pair reads out any new ideas from their list that the first pair did not mention.

3. The two pairs then write their ideas as a combined list with no duplications.

Paper plate quiz and People pie

These are some different ways to conduct whole-class surveys for Yes/No questions.

1. Prepare a paper plate for each student. One side has a smiley face with a big 'Yes', the other side has a frowning face with a big 'No'. You could also have different colours, e.g. smiley face yellow, frowning face blue. A craft stick could be added for a handle. Students could also make the actual plate.

2. Everyone sits in a circle with their paper plate.

Teaching strategies and resources

3 Ask the whole class a question that requires a Yes or No answer, for example: 'Do you have a pet?' 'Have you ever grazed your knee and it got better?' The students show the Yes or No side of their plate in response. Alternatively, they could just raise their hand in response to a simple Yes/No question.

4 For 'People pie', the students then move into a single circle, with all the Yes people sitting together and all the No people sitting together.

5 The teacher stands in the centre of the circle with a long piece of wool and passes it to the people at the ends of the Yes section to make a visual pie graph. Count the number of people in each of the two categories.

Some variations are:

- Students can predict how many will answer 'Yes' and 'No' before they respond.
- Students can use class data to draw up their own pie graphs after the activity.
- Students write a report of the findings and make their own drawing of a pie chart that represents the data.
- Students could predict how many people will answer 'yes' and 'no' before the survey using the PACE strategy on page 95.

People scavenger hunt

Each student has a chart headed 'Find someone who. . .', with a list of categories on it, e.g. has a cat/likes olives, etc. They talk to classmates to find someone different for each category and write each person's name against that category.

Postbox survey

1 Prepare a sheet of six numbered simple theme-related survey questions for each student. Each student individually writes their answers to the six survey questions on their sheet and cuts them into six strips.

2 Make six postboxes or folders numbered one to six and place them around the room as far apart as possible. Each student posts their six answers into the corresponding numbered postboxes.

3 Form groups of four. Each group takes one box and sorts the answers into at least three different categories, records the numbers of answers in each category and selects one good example of a response in that category. Note that sometimes the categories will be easy for students to work out (e.g. if the question just asked students to reply 'Yes', 'No' or 'Unsure'). Sometimes they will have to work out their own simple categories (e.g. the question asked students to name their favourite board game and categories might be 'Word games', 'Number games' and 'Memory games').

4 Each group reports their results to the class. This data then serves as the basis for class discussion on any issues raised in the anonymous Postbox survey. Students can also write a report on the results of the whole class.

Quick quotes

Print a head-and-shoulders photo of each student and enlarge it. Display all photos on a bulletin board and ask students to cut out white paper to make a big speech bubble coming out of their mouth. Students stick their written answers to different questions. For example: 'What is one good way to calm down when you feel angry?' Jack says: 'I think that the best way to calm down if you feel angry is to play with your dog or jump on a trampoline.' Display students' responses to a specific question for several days, then ask them to take them down and repeat the process with another theme-related question.

Reader's theatre

Adapt a simple text such as a picture book for Reader's theatre. Choose and type out simple lines of dialogue in the text for students to read. The teacher can be the narrator and the students can take it in turns to read their assigned script. Give students their assigned script beforehand, demonstrate how the dialogue can be read, and then give them time to practise reading their lines with expression.

Reflections

In a whole-class context, students take turns to select and answer a reflective question about the topic. There is an **e-tool** version available in some Curriculum Units.

Round table

Students work in a small group at a table, looking for things in a specified category (e.g. in a magazine or on printed sheets) or grouping things into specific categories.

Example A: Each group has a sheet of A3 paper. Each student cuts out and pastes onto the sheet a picture of someone feeling happy. In the next round, and with another A3 sheet of paper, they repeat the process with someone looking sad.

Example B: Groups of three sit around a table. Each student has one A3 sheet, labelled with a different category (e.g. Happy, Sad, Angry). There is a set of pictures and glue sticks in the middle of the table. Each student finds a picture that fits the category on their sheet, pastes the picture on the sheet and passes the sheet clockwise to the next person.

The students keep pasting and passing until all their pictures are used.

Secret word

Students work out the secret letter in each clue. They then form a word from all the letters. The secret word completes an important *Bounce Back!* message. There is an **e-game** version available in some Curriculum Units.

Smiley ball

This is a good way to get students to answer questions:

1. Draw a smiley face on a medium-sized plastic ball.
2. Organise students in a circle on the floor (to roll the ball) or in chairs (to throw the ball).
3. Say a student's name, roll the ball to them and then ask them a question. They answer and then roll the ball back to you.
4. Keep going with the other students, repeating the question or asking different questions.
5. Ask students to put their hands behind their back when they have had a turn.

TEAM coaching

Students complete and score an individual quiz with 6–10 factual questions based on simple (but important) content, such as unit spelling words. Then, in groups of four, they pool their quiz scores to get a total group score, identify where errors were made and set a goal for an improved group score for the second quiz (to be taken individually in ten minutes' time and based on the same or similar material). They then work in their group to help each other to re-learn the material and identify good ways to understand and remember it. Students then take the second individual quiz (which can be the same as or similar to the first quiz), correct their answers and work out their score. They return to their groups, pool their scores and work out their second total group score and their group's overall improvement.

Think–ink–pair–share (TIPS)

Each student takes time to reflect on their answer to a question posed by the teacher and write down a few key words before they share their thoughts with a partner. (TIPS was adapted from Lyman, F., 1981, *The Responsive Classroom Discussion: The Inclusion of All Students*, Mainstreaming Digest, University of Maryland, College Park, MD.)

Throw the dice

Prepare a sheet of six questions. Make one copy for each group of four students. Give each group one dice and one question sheet. Each student has a turn to throw the dice and answer the theme-related question that corresponds to the number thrown. If a student throws a number that is the same as they have already thrown, they should have another throw. However, if a student throws a number that someone else has already thrown, they can answer the same question. If the same question keeps coming up, they can throw again. You can give students the sheet of questions the day before the activity so that they can think about their responses to all of them or discuss them with family and friends. This is especially important for socially anxious or shy students.

Whisper game

This is a listening activity.

1. Write a different, theme-related word on each of eight cards. Create four identical sets of the eight cards. Three sets will be used by each of three teams of students. One set will be used by the teacher.
2. Divide the class into three equal teams. Each team sits on the floor or in a line of chairs behind each other, facing the back of the room. The first player in each team faces the teacher.
3. Place one set of well-shuffled cards at the back wall end of each of the three teams.
4. Select one card from your set and hold it up (or write it on the board) so that each of the front players (who are the only players facing you) can see it easily. They whisper the word down their line and the last player in their team has to pick out the same card from the pile in front of them, run to the teacher and give them the card they think is correct. The player who arrives first with the correct card earns three points for their team, the player who is second earns two points and the player who is third earns gets one point.
5. Repeat this process with the player who delivered the card to the teacher then becoming the first player in each team who starts the 'whisper'.

Cooperative games round robin

A round robin is a great way to develop the skills students need to be able to cooperate with each other. Before or after? (see page 90), Memory cards (see page 93) and Mystery square (see page 94) are excellent games to use as part of a cooperative games round robin. See Unit 7: Relationships for further game suggestions. Other suitable games are described on the following pages.

Big words, small words

Each pair plays against another pair to try to be the pair that can earn the highest score by finding small words made from letters in a larger word. There are two rounds (each with a different word to work with). Each round lasts four minutes. Two-letter words earn two points, three-letter words earn three points and so on. The teacher provides the big word for each round. Rules are negotiated in class (e.g. do plurals count?).

Bingo for pairs

Make a list of 25 words to be used in the game. Make approximately six sets of these words (for a class of 24) and place each set in a separate container (i.e. one set for each group of four which contains two competing pairs). Ask each pair of students to make one Bingo 'strip' (eight joined squares in a row) and write in any eight of the words from the list. The four players take it in turns to draw out one of the words from their container and read it out. Each pair crosses off that word if they have it. The first pair to cross off all eight cells on their Bingo strip calls out 'Bingo!' and wins that round. Pairs play three games against the other pair and record who wins. Remind students to keep the 'drawn' words separate so that answers can be checked if necessary.

Card challenge

The aim of the game is to be the pair that scores the most points. Each pair is dealt three playing cards from a standard deck of cards from which the Jack, Queen and King have been removed. They work cooperatively to make a three-digit number by putting the numbers on their cards together in any way they like, e.g. 4, 6 and 5 could be either 465, 456, 654, 645, 564 or 546. Each pair tells the other pair what their chosen combination is. One pair rolls a dice. If the number rolled is an 'even' number, then the pair with the highest number wins that round. If the number rolled is an odd number, the pair with the lowest number wins that round. The winning pair is the one with the most 'wins' after ten rounds.

Four Kings

Pairs play against pairs. The pair with the lowest combined scoring hands at the end of the game wins. For this game, all Kings are worth zero, all Aces are worth one, Queens and Jacks are worth ten, and other cards are scored at their face value.

1. One person from each group of four (two pairs) takes it in turns to be the dealer for each round. The dealer deals four cards to each player and places the rest of the pack face down in the middle to become the draw pack.

2. Going clockwise from the left of the dealer, each player draws a card from the draw pack in turn, and then throws out one of their own cards face up on the discarded pile. Alternatively, they can choose to pick up the top card on the discard pile instead of one from the draw pack.

3. When all the cards in the draw pack have been used up, each player adds up the value of their four cards and combines the total with that of their partner. The pair with the lowest score wins. Play three rounds.

Greedy pig

Students play in pairs against two other pairs and try to obtain the highest total score. Each pair has a turn to throw a dice and add the numbers they throw. They can retire from playing in that round whenever they want to. However, if a six is thrown before they 'retire', they lose all of their score for that round. The first players in each team have a go and then, in the second round, their partners have a turn. The winning pair is the one with the highest total after six rounds (i.e. each player in each pair plays three times).

Multiplication challenge

Students play in pairs against another pair. Each group of two pairs will need one deck of cards. Before you start, write on the board Ace = 1, Jack = 10, Queen = 11, King = 12. The cards are dealt out evenly so that each pair has half the pack. Each pair places their stack face down in front of them. Both pairs turn over their top card at the same time. They multiply the two top cards and whoever shouts out the correct answer first puts the cards in their pair's winning pile. When all the original stack has been played, they count how many cards they have won. This game could also be used with another mathematical process such as addition, subtraction or division.

Speedy Gonzales

Each pair competes against another pair to try to complete the task in the fastest time. They play between four and eight rounds (each with a different focus) and average out their times. Ideas for rounds:

- sort a list of words (or words on cards) into alphabetical order
- sort playing cards into the correct order (i.e. Ace–King) with the left hand only
- sort cards containing fractions and decimals into ascending order
- sort a list of words (or words on cards) into nouns, adjectives and verbs

- list as many words that they can think of containing a specific letter combination (e.g. 'cl', 'ee', 'rst', 'thr') in four minutes
- list as many words that they can think of that have 'm' as the third letter in four minutes. For other combinations, one pair draws a letter card from a pile and the other pair throws the dice to select the location of the letter in the word (e.g. 'K' as the second letter)
- list as many words that they can think of in four minutes that include the two letters that are drawn out of a container.

Ten circles

This is a variation of the game Hangman, in which each pair tries to guess a word that the other pair has selected. State whether they need to select a five-letter, six-letter, seven-letter or eight-letter word. The selecting pair draws the number of dashes to indicate each letter in the word they have selected. The guessing pair has ten coloured counters (or a sheet on which they have drawn ten circles). The guessing pair suggests one letter at a time and the other pair writes that letter on the correct dash(es). If it isn't in the word, they take one of the other pair's counters (or cross off one of their circles). When the guessing pair finally works out what the word is, they swap over with the other pair and become the selecting pair. Each pair's round score is the number of counters/circles they have left after identifying the word. Their final score is the total number after three rounds (i.e. each pair guesses three times).

Word detective

This game involves guessing a word after analysing feedback. One pair chooses a word in which no letter is repeated, and then they say, 'We are thinking of a four-letter word (or three- or five- letter word)'. The other pair writes down what they guess the word to be and receives the following written information under their guess:

- A tick (or green line) means the letter is correct and in the correct position.
- A dot (or orange line) means the letter is correct but in the wrong position.
- A cross (or red line) means the letter is not correct.

For example, if the chosen word was 'back' and the other pair guessed the word 'cart' they would receive this feedback:

C A R T
· ✓ ✗ ✗

The aim of the game is to use as few feedback words as possible in order to work out what the word is. Each pair plays two rounds against another pair. The final score for each pair is their total number of words used in the two rounds when they were trying to guess the word. The lowest total score wins the overall game.

Yes/No

Each pair of students has five tokens. Each pair has two three-minute rounds (alternating) during which they ask the other pair any questions they can think of to try to get them to say 'yes' or 'no'. Saying yes includes nodding, saying 'yeah' or similar. Likewise, saying no includes shaking the head, saying 'nuh', etc. Players are not allowed to repeat a phrase that they have already used in their response to a question, and they are not allowed to not respond, lie or use non-answer words or phrases such as 'I don't know', 'perhaps' or 'maybe'.

When one pair succeeds in getting a member of the other pair to say 'yes' or 'no', they receive a token from the other pair. If one pair breaks one of the rules, they must give one of their tokens to the other pair. The winner is the pair with most tokens after the four three-minute rounds. Allow pairs to engage in strategic planning before the rounds start.

Note: Please refer to McGrath, H. & Noble, T., 2010, *Hits and Hots + Teaching + Thinking + Social Skills* for more information on some of these strategies.

Classroom resources

The following resources are used to support the Curriculum Units.

Bounce-backers

The bounce-backer comes back after being tipped over and becomes a great visual prompt for young students to remember that when they get knocked down or are feeling sad/low, they can 'bounce back'.

Materials needed:

- a hollow plastic playpen ball already cut in half. These can be bought cheaply in packs of 50 from discount shops or early childhood shops
- one craft stick for the body (extra craft sticks for the arms and legs are optional)
- thick paper or cardboard to make a circle for the face, or a photo of each student
- modelling clay, play dough or plaster-of-Paris
- markers, scissors, sticky tape and glue to share

Steps:

1. Students fill the half-ball with play dough or modelling clay.
2. They stick the craft stick in the middle, draw a face on the cardboard circle (or add their own photo – just their face or their whole body) and then paste it onto the craft stick.
3. They can make arms and legs from craft sticks and then draw and cut out clothes for the bounce-backer. Or print out photos of each student in school uniform for them to paste on their bounce-backer.

Variations and follow-ups:

- A teacher or older peer buddy can fill the half-ball with plaster-of-Paris and, when half set, insert the craft stick.
- An alternative is to stick a small wooden skewer in the centre of the ball with the pointy end up. When the plaster has set, they stick a table tennis ball or a small polystyrene ball (available from craft shops) onto the skewer. Then they draw eyes and mouth or use googly eyes.
- Add a costume to the bounce-backer. Draw a circle with a 21 cm diameter onto light card. Draw lines to divide the circle into thirds. Cut one of the lines to the centre of the circle. Draw and colour/paint the costume for the bounce-backer in one of the sections of the circle next to the cut line. Then make the circle into a cone shape by overlapping the paper until only the costume part of the cone can be seen.
- Talk about the motion of the bounce-backer. The bounce-backer comes back after being tipped over as its centre of gravity shifts. Comparisons can be made with seesaws.

Bounce Back! journal

It is recommended that every student has their own journal in which to record key learnings, reflections and ideas, and lists of books to read. Worksheets can be kept there too. For younger children this could be a scrapbook, while for older children a digital folio or exercise book is recommended.

Class books and digital class books

Class books can be made in shapes that reflect the contents (e.g. a heart shape for a book on feelings or families). Cut out cardboard to make the shaped covers. Then cut out a page for each student who is contributing to the book in exactly the same shape and size.

Digital photos of each student's page can be made and the photos inserted into slides to make a digital class book.

Teaching strategies and resources

Cube pattern

This cube pattern can be enlarged and made into a dice (e.g. a feelings dice) or suspended on a string as a cube to display information (e.g. six positive things in my life).

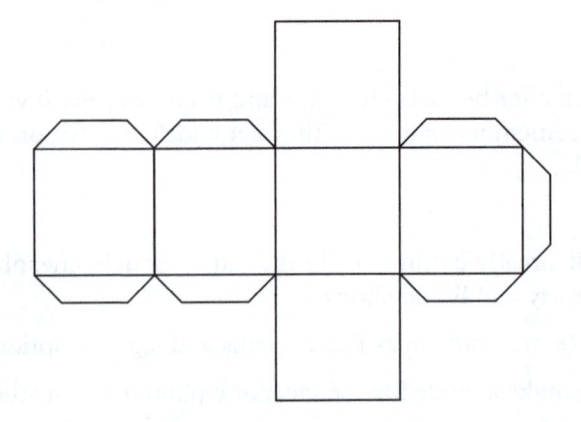

Digital stories

Students use digital software to make a personal and positive story about themselves (e.g. about an event in their life that has a clear beginning and end, and shows them using their strengths, such as learning to ride a bike and persisting and not giving up). Their story could also be about what they like to do, what they want to do in the future etc. Students start by writing an initial script of approximately 75 to 100 words. Then they plan a storyboard to tell their story, discuss their script with someone else and then revise the script. They select content, select and sequence images (photos, drawings, video clips), use voiceover to tell their story, create transition and colour effects, and add music or sound effects.

Digital book trailers

A digital book trailer promotes a book, just like film trailers promote films. Students write a short script about what they want people to know about the book, and then use digital software to create a presentation that promotes it. They create content by inserting text and images (from the book or other sources), a voiceover, transition and colour effects, music, mood-setting scenery and special effects. The following suggestions are adapted from Chris Cheng (Cheng, C., *Trailers*, http://www.chrischeng.com/wp-content/uploads/2012/11/making-book-trailers.pdf)

- Try to capture your audience's attention with the very first slide.
- Aim to get people interested and excited about the book.
- Keep the book trailer short (no more than 90 seconds).
- Don't fill any slide with too much information or detail.
- Limit the number of fonts and template styles that you use.
- Make sure that you include the book cover, the names of the author and illustrator and publication details.

Flip book

Materials needed:

- two A4 sheets of the same coloured paper or thin card
- three sheets of white A4 paper
- markers or crayons
- coloured wool
- a hole puncher to share with other members of the class

Steps:

1. Fold the three sheets of white paper in half and cut along the fold to make six half sheets.
2. Place them together to make a book of six pages. These sheets of paper make the bottom half of the A4 book.
3. Use two A4 sheets of same-coloured paper to make the front and back cover of the book.
4. Use a hole puncher to make two holes in the top half and two holes in the bottom half of the book (the six half pages and two covers).
5. Use wool to tie the covers and pages together.
6. On the top half of the book (inside back cover), students write the main statement (e.g. 'I feel happy when …'). On each of the six sheets of the book they write and illustrate six endings that complete the main statement (e.g. Mum or Dad reads me a story, I visit my cousins, I ride my bike).

Fridge magnet frame

The fridge magnet is designed to serve as a memory jogger for key messages for the BOUNCE BACK! and CHAMP acronyms or a prompt for goals students have set themselves.

Materials needed:

- ruler
- coloured paper (for inserts)
- a piece of thick cardboard (150 cm × 100 cm) for the base of the frame
- paint and paintbrush/markers
- very small flat magnets (available at hardware stores and some newsagents or toy shops)
- marker pen
- PVA glue and scissors to share

Steps:

1. Measure and draw a frame 1 cm from the edge of the cardboard.
2. Draw a second frame 1 cm inside the first frame
3. Use a marker pen to draw a picture that extends into the outer frame (see illustration).
4. Cut out the inside rectangle.
5. Glue a small magnet to each of the four corners.
6. Write the message on the coloured paper and insert it behind the frame.

Lift-up flaps and circles

Lift-up flaps and circles offer students a chance to invite classmates to interact with their work. They write a question on the front of the flap or circle (e.g. What animals cooperate with each other?). The answer is found when you lift up the flap to see what is written underneath (e.g. meerkats).

Little flaps can be attached to a very large sheet of cardboard (including flaps by different students) or to a bulletin board. To make a little flap, fold a small piece of card in two (like a place card or a small birthday card) and paste it onto cardboard, or attach it with a drawing pin (in the bottom part) to a bulletin board.

Big flaps sit on a bench or desk.

Materials needed:

- an empty shoe box with lid
- plastic document sleeves
- coloured cardboard
- a handle to lift up the top, e.g. a champagne cork attached with a screw and washer underneath (optional).

The question is written on a piece of cardboard, placed in the plastic sleeve and taped to the outside of the lid of the box. The lid sits on the box. The answer is written on another piece of card, placed in a plastic sleeve and attached to the inside bottom of the box. Add a handle to the lid. Using masking tape, attach the lid to the box at the opposite end to the handle.

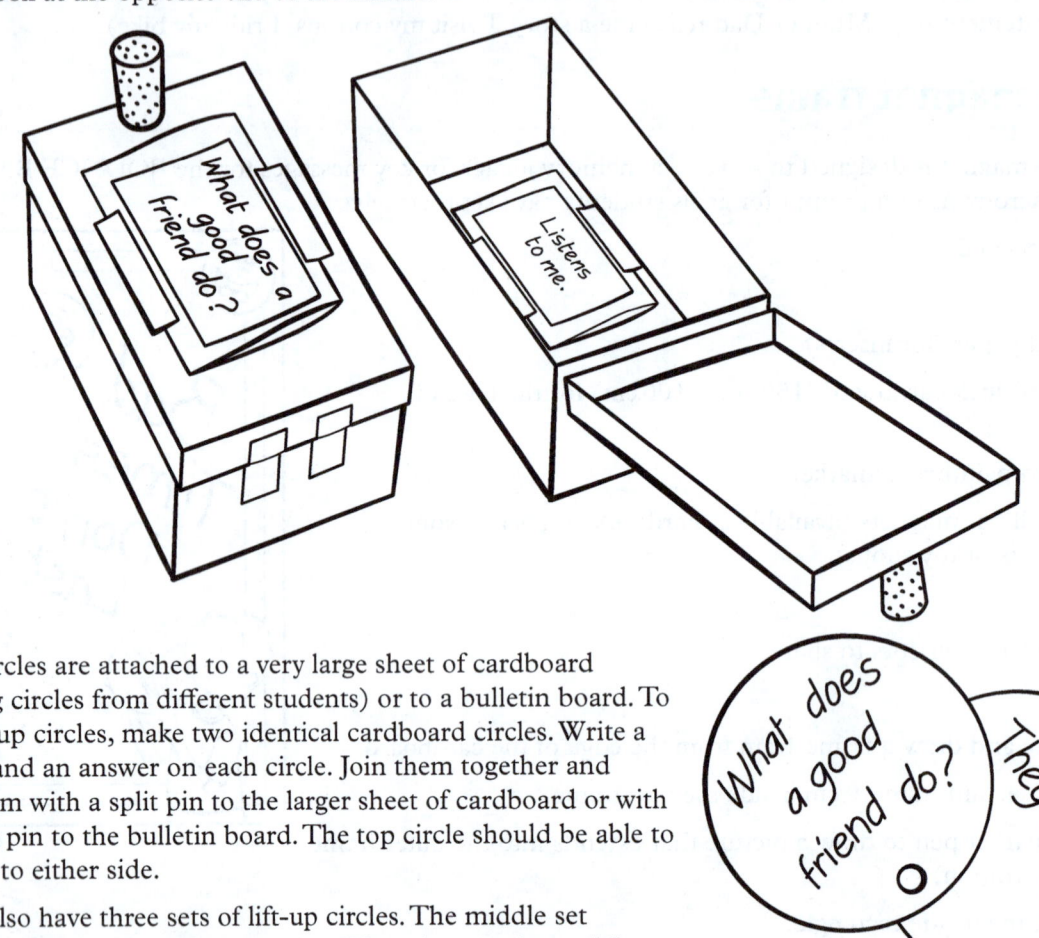

Lift-up circles are attached to a very large sheet of cardboard (including circles from different students) or to a bulletin board. To make lift-up circles, make two identical cardboard circles. Write a question and an answer on each circle. Join them together and attach them with a split pin to the larger sheet of cardboard or with a drawing pin to the bulletin board. The top circle should be able to be swung to either side.

You can also have three sets of lift-up circles. The middle set contains a single circle with a question. The other two have different answers, one correct and one incorrect. On the bottom of the correct answer is a smiley face and the words: 'Well done! You are correct!' On the bottom of the wrong answer is a frowning face and the words: 'Sorry, you are wrong. Try again.'

Flaps can also be made with a question on one slide and the answer on the next slide, using digital software.

Students could work in groups of three to research a specific area of a topic such as 'Friendship'. Each group researches a different aspect of friendship. They present their project as a class flap display using all forms of flaps and lift-up circles. For example, 'Lift up the lid to find out how to be a good friend.'

Mobiles

A mobile is a sculpture with parts that move. Mobiles have two parts – the structure or base you hang things from, and the things you hang.

Bases can be made from skewers, a cork with two skewers inserted through it, bits of wood (cane, bamboo, driftwood, thin dowel, balsa wood), fine wire, cardboard, cardboard cylinders, drinking straws, string or fishing line.

Things to hang can be drawings, cards or cardboard shapes, things made of paper, small boxes, tissue, papier-mâché items, small toys and objects such as balls, wooden people (from craft shops), paper cut-out people, or small stones.

Puppets and masks

There are references to using puppets throughout the ten Curriculum Units. Following is a list of many kinds of puppets. Masks can also be used instead of puppets.

✦ Masks and stick puppets

Glue pictures of faces from magazines onto cardboard and add a craft stick to hold it with. Use just the eyes, the mouth or include the whole face. Cut out small eye-holes. Similarly, you could make paper plate masks to hold. Cut out eye-holes and add wool for hair.

✦ Finger puppets and hand strappers

Version 1: Use felt finger covers as illustrated.

Version 2: Make hand strappers by making a long paper watch with an animal shape or person's face in the position where the watch face would be. Strap them over the back of the hand and use fingers as legs.

Version 3: Cut out a circle on stiff card with two holes in the base for fingers. Students draw on the card or paste their drawings on the card as illustrated.

Version 1   Version 3

✦ Balloon puppets

Add a balloon to a cardboard cylinder. Thread the string that ties the end of the balloon through the cylinder and tape to the side. Add a face and other features.

✦ Paper bag puppets

Draw a face and hair on a paper bag. Stuff the bag with crumpled paper. Attach to a stick with a rubber band.

✦ Glove puppets

Use a woollen or rubber glove. Staple an image onto the top of the glove. Or make the glove into an animal by stitching on fabric ears (e.g. furry fabric) and buttons for eyes. On a rubber glove you can draw features with a permanent pen. Add buttons for eyes.

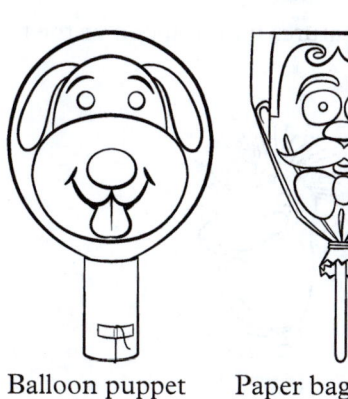

Balloon puppet   Paper bag puppet

Teaching strategies and resources

✦ Paper plate puppets
Cut a paper plate in half. Add a craft stick to use as handle. Then add wool, string etc. for hair, and draw in the face.

✦ Paper spring puppets
Draw a body and then make legs and arms out of paper springs. To make the springs, students cut out two long strips of paper. Paste the paper at right angles to each other and then fold one on top of the other until all the paper is folded into a spring. Glue to the body of the puppet. Paste a long stick or craft sticks to the back of the puppet.

✦ Self-photo puppets
Use photos of students' faces and glue them onto cardboard. Make a cardboard body. Add craft sticks or a wire coat-hanger (straightened and then doubled) for a handle.

✦ Shadow puppets
Draw the shape of an animal or person on cardboard. Cut it out and make large eye-holes. Straighten out a wire coat-hanger to make a long handle. Tape the puppet to the end of the handle. Wrap masking tape on the other end. Make a screen with a bed sheet hung over a rope. Put a light source such as a lamp between the puppet and the sheet.

✦ Soft toy/animal puppets
Use students' old soft toys or animals as puppets. Make a hole in the base and insert dowelling to serve as a handle.

✦ Sock puppets
Cut a cardboard rectangle about 7 cm × 20 cm and fold it in half to form the inside of the mouth. Place the cardboard inside the sock and glue in place. Decorate the sock.

✦ Split pin puppets on strings
Cut the shape of the character or animal from cardboard. Join legs, arms and head to the body with split pins. Add string to the head, arms and legs so that different parts of the puppet can move.

✦ Wooden spoon/Craft sticks puppets
Draw features on the spoon or the top of a craft stick.

Sock puppet    Split pin puppet    Wooden spoon puppet

Responsibility Pie Charts (RPC)

A Responsibility Pie Chart (RPC) is a concrete way to understand that many negative situations occur because of a combination of the following three factors.

- **Own actions**: How much did my own behaviour contribute to the situation? *(me)*
- **The actions of others**: How much did the behaviour of others contribute to the situation? *(others)*
- **Random unpredictable factors**: How much did bad luck or circumstances (e.g. weather, timing, coincidences, lack of knowledge, illness) contribute to the situation? *(bad luck/circumstances)*

Students can individually make the simple RPC – a moveable device that allows them to change the amounts of responsibility they attribute to each of the three factors as they think about the situation. When using the RPC, it is possible for students to attribute no responsibility to 'bad luck/circumstances' and no responsibility to 'others', but there must always be at least 10 per cent responsibility attributed to their own actions ('me').

Some students allocate too much responsibility to their own actions or characteristics. Point this out when you are working with them. Some allocate too much blame to external factors. They need to be made aware that they are not seeing their own behaviour accurately.

Alternatively, the teacher can make an RPC to use when talking one-on-one with a student. Try to avoid the use of the words 'blame' and 'fault' and instead use terms such as:

- How much was … responsible for what happened?
- How much was what happened due to …?
- How much did this happen because of …?
- How much does … explain what happened?

This is also a good peer buddy activity.

Instructions for drawing and using a simple RPC

- Draw a circle on a piece of paper.
- Students think about their situation and identify the details of the three factors: their own actions, the actions of other people and bad luck.
- Then they allocate what they see as an honest percentage of responsibility due to each of the three categories, i.e. 'Me', 'Others' and 'Bad luck', and draw these on the circle to complete a RPC.
- Look at the RPCs with the students and help them re-think the percentages in case they misjudged them.
- Help the students identify what they can learn from each of the three categories so that the negative situation is less likely to happen again.

Instructions for making a moveable RPC

Materials needed:

- **BLM Templates for Making a Moveable Responsibility Pie Chart**
- one A4 piece of heavy yellow cardboard
- one A4 sheet of red cardboard
- one A4 sheet of blue cardboard
- a split pin with 0.75 cm ends.

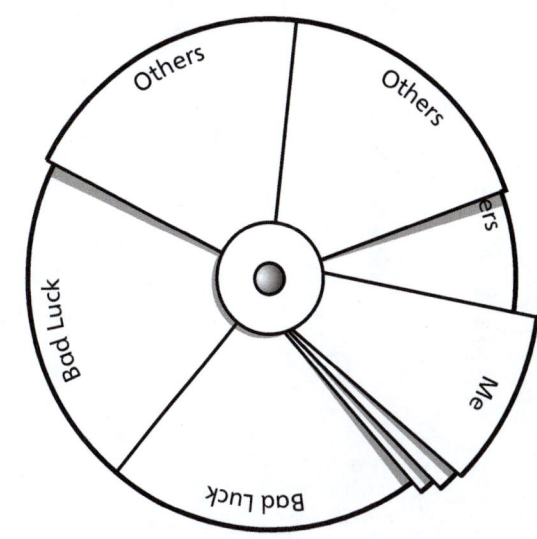

Steps:

1. To make the base: cut out the circle from sheet A (Bad luck) on the heavy yellow cardboard.
2. To make the second layer: photocopy two copies of sheet B (Others) on blue cardboard. Cut out the five segments.
3. To make the top layer: photocopy two copies of sheet C (Me) on red cardboard. Cut out the ten segments.
4. Assemble the device with the yellow base at the bottom, followed by the light blue layer (five segments) and then the red layer on the top (ten segments). Insert the split pin through the middle.

Wax-resistant badges

Materials needed:

- wax crayons
- white card
- dark-coloured poster paint
- paintbrush
- scissors
- double-sided tape
- safety pins

Steps:

1. Students draw a shape for the badge with wax crayons, e.g. a pot and sunflowers for 'Looking on the bright side', a funny face for 'Humour', a medal for 'CHAMP' or 'Everyday courage'. They colour the drawing in bright colours.
2. Paint over the wax drawing with the poster paint.
3. When the paint is dry, the crayon will shine through.
4. Cut out around the drawing to form the badge.
5. Turn the badge over.
6. Use a piece of double-sided tape to attach the safety pin.

Core values

KEY MESSAGES

Values are easy to say and sometimes hard to do.
A value is a belief that you have about how you should behave. Nobody is perfect, but you can try to put your values into practice. Do what you believe are the 'right things', even though you may not always succeed.

It is important to be honest.
Being honest means:

- telling the truth
- not stealing or cheating
- giving things back when they belong to someone else
- 'owning up' when you have done the wrong thing.

It also means telling people information that they need to know but being tactful or aware of others' feelings.

It is important to be fair to other people.
Being fair means:

- being honest
- following the rules
- returning favours and kindnesses
- helping others to get a fair deal.

This includes helping others to be included in groups and games and not to be bullied. It also means understanding that everyone in our community needs to be treated fairly. This includes people from different backgrounds. Being fair also means applying the same rules to everyone and not being prejudiced or treating others differently.

It is important to be responsible.
Being responsible means not letting people down, and doing what you said you would do without having to be told all the time to do so. It also means:

- doing your chores
- trying to be on time so that you don't upset other people's plans
- being sensible
- helping those who need it.

It is okay to be different.
Everyone is different and that's okay. If you feel okay about differences in people, you:

- get to know people who are different to you
- include them in games and conversation
- see that it is a good thing for people to be different in lots of ways.

It is not kind to tease or exclude people who are different to you. You need to learn to just put up with those differences you may not like.

Learning objectives
In this unit, students will further develop their understanding of the:

- importance of having values
- values of honesty, fairness, responsibility and accepting difference.

Resources list

A complete list of resources including references for core and additional books, films, video clips, poems, songs and websites is available.

Being honest

Resources

◆ Books

The Boy Who Cried Wolf

This well-known Aesop's fable tells the story of the young shepherd who, feeling bored and wanting to play a practical joke, cries 'Wolf!' when no wolf is there. When a wolf really does attack his sheep, no-one comes to help him.

The Great White Man-Eating Shark

In this picture book, Norvin makes and wears a dorsal fin so he looks like a great white shark. Nobody dares to go swimming so Norvin has the bay to himself, until a real shark comes along.

Ricky Sticky Fingers

Ricky has developed the bad habit of stealing from others when he wants something. Then he lies to cover up what he has done. He realises stealing is wrong and stops doing it after someone has apparently stolen his bike and he finds out what it feels like to have something stolen.

Circle Time or classroom discussion

Read a book to start discussions about being honest.

Discussion questions

- In what way was the character in the book dishonest?
- What happened when the character was dishonest?
- How did the character feel when people found out they had been untruthful?
- What do we mean by 'being trustworthy'? Why is it good to be trustworthy?
- What would happen if we couldn't trust people to be honest with us? For example, what would it be like if we couldn't trust our teacher, our doctor, our dentist, our parents, the bus driver, the shop assistant etc.?

Organise an Inside–outside circle (see page 93). Students then take turns discussing with their different partners the following questions using the 'no names' rule:

- Has someone ever told you a lie? How did you feel?
- Has someone ever stolen something from you or your family? How did you feel?
- Has someone borrowed something from you and not given it back? How did you feel?
- How would your family feel if you told them a lie?
- What would you do if you heard your friend telling a lie?
- Would you want to be friends with someone you knew was stealing? Why/Why not?
- How would you feel if you behaved dishonestly? Why?
- Who is the first to be suspected when something dishonest has happened? (Someone who has been dishonest before.)

- Why can it be hard to have enough courage to own up?
- What do you think about someone who does own up? Are they courageous or silly?

Bring students back to the circle, then ask for some examples of what they talked about for each question (again using the 'no names' rule).

Activity

Fable writing

Discuss the concept and features of a 'fable' with students. A fable is a short fictional story that usually features animals (or other things from nature, e.g. trees) that have been given human qualities (e.g the ability to speak) and which teach a specific moral lesson. Aesop is the most well-known of the fable authors. Ask if anyone can name another fable. Examples include *The Hare and the Tortoise*, *The Ant and the Grasshopper* and *The Lion and the Mouse*.

Students write their own version of *The Boy Who Cried Wolf* or draw an illustration for an imaginative text about honesty.

Drama

Good genie/Bad genie

Use this strategy (see page 92) with students using puppets to act out situations in which one character is tempted to be dishonest. You will need three puppets (see pages 105–106 for ideas). One puppet acts as the dishonest voice saying 'Do it', a second puppet acts as the honest voice saying 'Don't do it because…', and the third puppet is in the middle of the honest/dishonest puppets. You could use situations such as:

- being tempted to take money from someone's school bag
- being confronted with something you did, like damaging something, and being tempted to lie about it
- being tempted to keep something that someone else has lent you
- lying about something to seem cool to your friends.

Cheating

Resources

✦ Books

Honest Ashley

Ashley's homework was due in the next day but she hadn't got around to doing it. She was faced with the temptation to cheat after her friend told Ashley that her sister was doing the homework for her. However, Ashley didn't want to cheat so she woke up early to get it done instead.

I Repeat, Don't Cheat!

Jessica's best friend Lizzie copies Jessica's homework and sometimes cheats in games. When Jessica agrees to help Lizzie write a poem as part of their schoolwork, she is shocked that Lizzie takes all the credit for it in class. Jessica discusses her problem with her teacher.

Help Me Be Good: Cheating

This book focuses on not cheating in games, and encourages children to not let a strong desire to win become more important than the fun of the game. It also highlights the importance of being a good loser and why the rules of a game matter.

✦ Video clip

ABC's *Behind the News* has many news segments on cheating in sport, such as 'Sport Cheating', 'Sport Doping' and 'Tennis Doping'.

Circle Time or classroom discussion

Read one of the books or show a video clip. Cheating goes against the values of being honest and being fair. To demonstrate this, begin the Circle Time with a brief simulation in which you ham it up and 'cheat' while playing Snap with one of the students (e.g. always look at your next card before you play it). Make it clear to the students that you are deliberately cheating to make a point. Stress the 'no names' rule when discussing cheating.

Discussion questions

- When I pretended to be looking at my next card, what was I doing?
- What are some of the ways in which people can cheat?
- Why do people cheat? (They want to win, they want to impress others.)
- Do you feel as good about winning if you have cheated to win?
- How do you feel about someone when you know they have cheated? Do you want to be their friend?
- In what ways can people cheat in sporting activities, such as the Olympic Games?
- What thoughts and feelings do you have about people who cheat in sport?

Activities

- In pairs, students make posters that say 'Cheating spoils things'.
- In groups, students create an information report or news bulletin about why it's important not to cheat in games or sport.
- Students pair up to write an imaginative text, create a small skit or make a cartoon strip about a child who cheats in a board game. They then re-do with a 'non-cheating' outcome.

Being tactful

Resources

✦ Books

Being Frank

Frank always tries to be honest, but sometimes he's too honest – he tells his teacher that her breath smells and the school principal that his hair looks like a weasel. Grandpa Ernest helps Frank learn about the importance of being tactful.

Lucy the Good

Lucy van Loon is a girl with a strong sense of fairness and justice, who often ends up impulsively saying and doing what she thinks is right. When she has to share her bedroom with her Tante (Aunt) Bep who is visiting from Holland, things don't go very well at first.

Circle Time or classroom discussion

Read one of the books to the class, then discuss the issues of honesty and being tactful using the discussion questions.

Discussion questions

- What did the character say to be tactful?
- What do people mean when they say 'Honesty is the best policy'?
- Is it always good to be completely honest about what you think of people? Could you see problems with telling someone exactly what you are thinking?

Talk about being tactful, which is the art of being honest in a kind way when it is necessary, or sometimes not saying anything at all if you don't need to. Give an example from one of the books.

- Tell us about a time when your feelings have been hurt by the thoughtless comment of another, even if it was true.

Emphasise that before people say something to another person they should always ask themself:

- Is what I am going to say true?
- Do I need to say it?
- Is it going to hurt someone's feelings?
- How can I be kind while still being honest?

If the thing they're going to say isn't true or necessary, then hurting someone's feelings is tactless and unkind. There are other, kinder ways to respond that don't involve being completely dishonest, or another option is just saying nothing.

- What are 'little white lies'? Is it okay to tell white lies? (Lies you tell to prevent another person being upset and having their feelings hurt.)
- How can you be tactful when asked directly what you think and your answer would hurt the person's feelings? (Find some good part to comment on, or make a non-specific comment e.g. 'It's cool' or 'That's interesting'.)
- Why do you think the author of *Being Frank* named the two key characters 'Frank' and 'Ernest'?

Activity

▶ Students draw a three-frame comic strip with speech and thought bubbles titled: 'This is being tactful' or 'This is not being tactful'.

Drama

How to be tactful

Use Freeze frame and rewind (see page 92). Write the following scenarios on cards and place them in a container. In pairs, students take turns at pulling out a card and acting out the scenario.

- Your classmate has bought a new jumper and says, 'What do you think of my new jumper?' You don't like it but the colour is nice.
- Someone younger says, 'Do you like the drawing I did?' and you think it's not very good.
- Your teammate shoots for goal in basketball and misses. You feel like telling them that they are a bad thrower, but you don't want to hurt their feelings.
- Your parent says, 'I spent two hours making dinner. I hope you like it.' Unfortunately, you don't like it very much.
- A family member shows you their new cap and says, 'What do you think?' You think it is very uncool even though it looks okay on them.

- Your friend gets a very short haircut and says to you, 'It's really terrible, isn't it?'
- You go and see a cousin, friend or family member perform in a school concert. They don't sing very well and forget some of their lines. After the concert, they ask you what you thought of it.
- Someone proudly shows you their new dog, a little dog that doesn't stop barking and jumping, and says, 'Isn't he cute?'

Being fair

Resources

✦ Books

Farmer Duck

A duck lives with a very lazy farmer who makes the duck do all the work on the farm. The duck's animal friends become increasingly upset over this unfairness, and they find a way to drive the lazy farmer away and run the farm as a cooperative group of animals without him.

Refugees

Two wild ducks become refugees when their swamp is drained. Their journey in search of a new place to live exposes them to danger, rejection and violence before they are given a new home. The human parallels are obvious.

✦ Poem

Colin

Circle Time or classroom discussion

Start by reading the poem *Colin* or one of the books listed. Talk about being fair and stress that sometimes people think differently about what they think is 'fair'.

Discussion questions

- What was unfair in the story/poem?
- How did the character's behaviour backfire on them?
- What do we mean by 'being fair'? (Making sure everyone gets a reasonable deal – not necessarily a completely equal deal, applying rules consistently, not cheating, looking at a situation from both people's point of view, finding all the relevant facts, including others, and treating people equally.)
- What if our class had no rules? What might happen? Would that be fair?
- Why do people sometimes disagree about whether something is fair? (They have different opinions, they might not be looking at it from both points of view, they may not have thought carefully enough about it, they may be in different positions e.g. a teacher compared to a student or a parent compared to a child.)
- What rules in our class or in our school do you think are fair and why?

Activities

▶ Students write their own version of the poem *Colin*.

'In' group versus 'out' group

Conduct an 'In' group versus 'out' group simulation. This simulation will take most of the day. At the end of the activity follow up with the questions. Select a category that will divide the students into roughly two groups, even if the size is a little uneven. You could use categories such as:

- a family member drives you to school most days or you make your own way
- you have been at this school since the first year of primary school
- your name is in the first/second half of the alphabet.

Work out who is in each category. Tell the class that everyone is to take part in a 'class play'. Before recess, tell students (e.g. those with names starting with the first half of the alphabet) that they are in the 'out' group and all the others are in the 'in' group and tell them they are the 'cool' group. Make sure that the 'out' group gets unfair treatment/gets rejected (e.g. they go out for recess last, they sit at the back of the class, they're not readily acknowledged when their hand is up, they're put into groups whereas the 'in' group can choose who they work with etc.). Then after recess repeat the procedure with the roles reversed – the 'in' group becomes the 'out' group. Before the lunch break, debrief the simulation with discussion questions such as:

- Were the people in the 'out', or 'uncool', group really less important or less valuable?
- Did they deserve to be treated like that?
- Hayley, you were in the 'out' group in the morning, weren't you? Is Hayley really someone whom we would reject and treat unfairly and unkindly? (No, she was playing a part in our whole class role-play.)

Students can then take it in turns to say how it felt when they were in the 'in' and the 'out' group. Make the point that people are often considered to be uncool (i.e. in the 'out' group) for no good reason, just like today, and that it isn't fair or kind. Ask the following questions:

- Why do some people get less of a fair deal? (They don't have a chance to speak for themselves, the people with the 'social power' are not being kind.)
- What is prejudice? (Some people believe that other people are less 'worthy' just because they are different in some way.)
- Have you seen 'in' groups and 'out' groups in the playground? (Emphasise the 'no names' rule.)
- Why do students sometimes say 'You can't play in our game'?
- Is anyone really the 'boss' of a game?
- Should one student be allowed to say to another student that they can't join in a game, conversation or activity?
- Should the teacher insist that students include another student in a game?
- What if you brought something to play with? Should you be able to say who can or can't play with it?
- When you are picking other students to have a turn in a classroom activity, should you be fair and give everyone a turn, not just pick your friends all the time?
- Could we make a rule that no-one can say 'no' if someone else wants to join their game or conversation? What would be fair? What would be kind? Would these rules work for us? Would we have some 'exceptions'? (e.g. can girls say 'no' to boys and vice versa? Can you say no if the game has been going on for a while and it can't be interrupted?)

Class or school rules analysis

Make an A4 copy of up to six class or school rules or norms. In groups of four, students use the Cooperative number-off strategy (see page 91) where each group decides if each rule is fair (or not) and why it is (or isn't) a fair rule. Call on each group at random to share their answer and their reasons with the class.

Game

▶ Play the **Is This Fair? e-activity** as a whole class. In pairs, students then write their own quiz questions and quiz another pair.

Social justice

Resources

✦ Books

For Every Child

This book features 14 rights from the United Nations Convention on the Rights of the Child, and retold in simple, evocative text. Each right is illustrated by a different illustrator.

Lost and Found Cat: The True Story of Kunkush's Incredible Journey

A family has to flee from war-torn Iraq, but they don't want to abandon their beloved cat, Kunkush. They hide him on the boat to Greece, but he becomes lost and his broken-hearted family has to continue without him. Incredibly, the cat is eventually reunited with his family.

Circle Time or classroom discussion

Read one of the books. Discuss with students that social justice reflects the values of being fair and being kind and is about helping others in our community get a fair deal. See also Unit 2: Social values.

Discussion questions

- Tell us about a time when you or somebody else was not treated fairly. (e.g. someone pushed in front of you, someone was teased or left out.)
- Are there any groups of people around the world who are not treated fairly?
- Can you think of examples of people in our community who sometimes don't get a 'fair go'? (Aboriginal and Torres Strait Islanders, homeless people, the elderly, refugees, people with disabilities.)
- Who can tell of a time when their family has given money or support to a charity that tries to make the lives of some people more fair?
- Do you know of any organsiations that help people? Do you know what they do? (World Vision, Salvation Army, The Smith Family, RSPCA, Red Cross.)

Activities

▶ Model how to structure a letter. Students write letters of appreciation to say thank you to people or organisations who have assisted with a school fundraiser or for the work a charity does e.g. the RSPCA or the Red Cross.

▶ Invite speakers from relevant organisations to talk about their work.

▶ Read **BLM John Flynn** with students and have them answer the questions. This could be a take-home task.

▶ Students do an Inquiry-based investigation (see page 92) on a social justice organisation that works with children. In groups of three, students investigate one organisation and then present their conclusions to the class using a slide presentation.

Fundraising

Discuss ways you could make a difference as a class to an unfair situation, even in a small way, e.g. raise money to sponsor a child overseas (World Vision), raise money to sponsor a child to stay in school (The Smith Family), raise money to provide breakfasts for students who come to school without eating because of lack of food and/or care (the Red Cross). With students, organise a fundraiser (e.g. cake stall, coin trail, recycled goods market) at school for an organisation of their choice.

Being responsible

Resources

✦ Books

A Year on Our Farm

This book is an exploration of a year on an Australian farm seen through the eyes of three children who help their parents with many farm jobs. Illustrations show the changing seasons, and the different activities and responsibilities that the children carry out.

The Firekeeper's Son

This story is set in nineteenth-century Korea. Every night, when Sang-hee's father sees that the ocean is clear of enemies, he climbs the mountain to light a fire to let the palace know all is well. When Sang-hee's father breaks his ankle, Sang-hee takes over this great responsibility.

Horton Hears a Who!

When Horton hears a cry for help from a speck of dust, he is determined to protect the minute creatures who live on it. The other animals don't believe such tiny creatures actually exist, but Horton follows through on his promise to help save the Whos in Whoville.

✦ Film

Horton Hears a Who!

> **Teacher reflection**
> As a child, what responsibilities did you have? How do you think those responsibilities help you now with your sense of responsibility and wellbeing? Can you share this with your students?

Circle Time or classroom discussion

Read one of the books listed or watch the film.

Discussion questions

- What does being responsible mean? (Refer to the Key messages, page 109.)
- What did the character do that showed they were being responsible?

Organise the class into an Inside–outside circle (see page 93) so each student has a partner. Ask them to take turns sharing with a different partner one example of how a child their age can act responsibly in each of the following situations:

- at home (Put your things away, make your bed etc.)
- looking after a pet (Remember to feed them.)

- looking after your belongings (Don't leave your bike outside in the rain.)
- in the classroom (Do what the teacher asks, don't use put-downs.)
- in the playground (Include others in games, put your rubbish in the bins, don't fight.)
- with friends (Be loyal.)
- at the beach or at the park (Swim between the flags, take turns on the play equipment.)
- playing a team sport (Follow the rules of the game, help your team.)
- at school (Be on time.)

Stress that being responsible also means that you do what you said you would do, e.g. if it's your job to feed the dog, you remember to do it and you do it properly.

Ask all students to form a circle and ask different students to share examples of being responsible in relation to these different situations:

- What do we mean when we say that someone is reliable?
- What chores can your family rely on you to do at home?
- Tell us about a time when you behaved responsibly.
- What does being punctual mean? Why is it important to be on time?
- What do you do with your rubbish if you are being responsible?
- How does a responsible person behave in the sun?
- What is the responsible thing to do if you know that someone is being bullied?
- What can we all do to take some responsibility for caring for our environment? (Recycle plastic bags etc.)
- How is being sensible being responsible? Give some examples.

Activities

▶ All students contribute one page to a 'Being Responsible' class book (see page 101) on one thing they will work on to be more responsible.

Students' home responsibilities

Use the People pie strategy (see page 95) with a selection of the following questions. How many students:

- make their bed in the morning?
- help to set the table for dinner (or clear away)?
- pack their own schoolbag?
- make their school lunch?
- put their toys and games away before bedtime?
- help take care of a family pet or younger sibling?

Collect the class data and then students can draw a pie chart on the selected home chores that they nominated.

Take-home task

Interview a family member

Students interview a family member, such as a parent, grandparent or older relative, about the chores they were responsible for when they were the same age as students. Make a class comparison chart followed by report writing.

It's okay to be different

Resources

✦ Books

We're All Wonders

A story based on August Pullman – an ordinary boy with an extraordinary face. Just like all children, August wants to be included. But because of his severe facial disfigurement, he is often excluded. This book can link to difference, kindness, including others and empathy.

Something Else

Something Else tries very hard to look and act like everyone else, but is never able to belong. One day Something (who is also very different) knocks on his door, and Something Else responds unkindly, before eventually learning an important lesson about accepting differences.

We Belong Together: A Book About Adoption and Families

A simple colourful book that explores adoption and the many different ways of being a family, e.g. multicultural families, one-parent families, families with two parents of the same gender, adoptive families and the traditional nuclear family.

✦ Song

'It's Not Easy Being Green'

Circle Time or classroom discussion

Read and discuss one or more of the resources listed. Talk about what it means to accept others who are different. It is saying that differences are okay and we will try to live with differences we are not used to. We will look for and find the good things about those differences.

Discussion questions

- In what ways can people be different?
- How do people behave if they think it is okay for people to be different from them? (Talk about how difference means 'just as good'. It doesn't mean 'not as good as'.)
- What are some of the good things about many people with differences living and working together?
- Share one way in which you think you are different from everyone else in the class.

Activities

- Create a 'We are all different' display and ask students to bring photos and items that emphasise the ways in which they are different. Students can use lift-up flaps with 'This is one way in which (person's name) is different' written on the flap (see page 103). Underneath they write what the difference is.

- Conduct a class survey to highlight differences in students' Saturday morning routines. Then ask, 'Is any way of spending Saturday morning better or worse, or are they just different?'

- Students use a Venn diagram to compare themselves with a partner: How are they alike? How are they different? Some examples might be: favourite food, television show, ice-cream flavour etc.

- Organise a cooking activity for students where they work with adults from different cultures to cook foods from those cultures. The different foods can be shared at lunchtime.

- Visit a museum that has a display of cultural diversity (e.g. an immigration museum) as part of an inquiry unit.

Comparing similarities and differences in opinions

Students decide individually on their responses to the statements below (agree/disagree) and then compare them with a partner:

- An apple is better to eat than an orange.
- A horse is better to own than a dog.
- Playing basketball is more fun than playing computer games.
- You can learn more from books than from TV or films.
- Blue is a nicer colour than yellow.
- Games make better presents than clothes.

Debrief as a class, highlighting that differences in opinion are good.

Four corners differences

Ask students to think about the sports or games they like to play. Label each corner of the classroom (or draw a large diagram of the classroom on the board) with the name of a different sport or game. Ask students to go to the corner that best represents the sport or game they prefer to play, pair up with someone else in that corner and share why they both like that sport (see page 92).

People pie

Use the People pie strategy (see page 95) to conduct in-class surveys about differences. Follow up with class graphs. Some ideas are:

- Are you left-handed or right-handed?
- Do you suffer from allergies or not?
- Were you born in Australia or another country?
- Do you have a step-parent or not?
- Do you like football or not?
- Do you prefer to read a book or play on the computer?

Postbox on differences

Use the Postbox strategy (see page 96) using the following questions:

- What country/countries did your family originally come from?
- What is your favourite sport/game to play?
- How many people live in your house?
- What is your favourite TV program/movie/food/drink?
- How many pets have you had in your lifetime?

Celebrating cultural diversity

Using the cultural diversity of your classroom as a starting point, discuss with students the ways in which all cultures are different but also the same. For example, most cultures:

- make bread a staple part of their diet, although they have different kinds of bread
- have a hot drink, such as tea or coffee, for social rituals
- have festivals and celebrations
- play ball games.

You could use these as a basis for an inquiry unit on celebrating different cultures. This bread discussion can be followed by a cooking activity or a visit to a bakery to see the different styles of bread and pastries. Many bakeries now have a selection of breads from different cultures.

Game

I like ice cream

This is a variation on the traditional game of 'I went shopping and I bought …'

Select a theme that can be connected to differences regarding preferences or characteristics, e.g. how are we different in what we like to eat, are good at, like to do at home for fun, like to read etc.

Students sit in a circle. A ball is needed so that can be rolled from one student to another. Start the round by stating something that you really like (e.g. 'I like ice cream'). Roll the ball to a selected student. They then repeat what you have said and add one thing that they like ('Mr Adams likes ice cream and I like chocolate'). The next student in turn states what they love and so on ('Mr Adams likes ice cream, Shani likes chocolate and I like smoothies'). Each student must offer a new response.

Embed it

Take digital photos of students behaving in accordance with specific values and make a bulletin board display or slide show display to demonstrate values in action. Label the photos, e.g. 'Bella acted responsibly when she put her rubbish in the bin.'

Consolidation

Activities

▶ Students complete **BLM Cross-offs** individually or in pairs (see page 91). The secret message is: 'Try to do what you think is right.'

Cut-up sentences

Write out the sentences below, then cut them into individual words and place each cut-up sentence into an envelope (see page 92). Make enough sets for each pair of students to have one set of the six sentences. Each pair reconstructs the six sentences. You can also use the **Cut-up Sentences e-activity**.

- We can all try to be fair.
- People trust those who are honest.
- It is okay to be different.
- Being responsible means doing what you said you would do.
- Being responsible is not letting others down.
- Being fair means not cheating.

Values awards

Ask students to self-assess on the values, using **BLM My Core Values Report Card**. Give individual students a **Bounce Back! award** (see page 123), badges (see page 108) etc. as acknowledgement of their efforts to use specific values.

Which value made the difference?

Students use **BLM Which Value Made the Difference?** to suggest what happened in the middle of the story that led to a positive outcome. They write in the value as well. The value answers are: 1. responsibility, 2. it's okay to be different, 3. honesty.

Values in action

Using four sheets of paper, write one value (e.g. being honest, being fair, being responsible, it's okay to be different) on the top of each page. In groups, students do a Circuit brainstorm and write one example of what they can do to demonstrate that value in action (see page 91). It doesn't matter if they get some of them mixed up, as there is a bit of overlap in some cases.

Key vocabulary

Use the Whisper game, Mystery square or the TEAM coaching strategy to assist students to learn vocabulary and spelling related to values to a reasonable level of mastery (see pages 98, 94 and 97). Examples:

different/difference

honesty/honest

dishonesty/dishonest

fair/fairness

unfair/unfairness

just/justice/unjust

cheat/cheating

tact/tactful/tactless

true/truth/truthful

Reflections

Use the **Reflections e-tool** with the class, which asks these questions:
- What do we mean when we say that someone is reliable?
- Why is it important to be on time or punctual?
- Why is it important to have rules in games?
- Why do people get upset when someone breaks a promise to them?
- Give one example of how you are different from one of your friends.
- What is one job you are responsible for doing at home?
- What does it mean when we say that someone is trustworthy?
- Why is it important not to cheat in a game?
- What is an example of doing the right thing?
- What is one job you are responsible for doing in class?

These questions can also be used with Musical stop and share or Inside–outside circle (see pages 94 and 93).

▶ Make 'core values' cards and place them in a box face down. Students randomly choose a card with a core value on it (e.g. being honest, being fair, being responsible, It's okay to be different etc.) and give an example of a behaviour that goes with it.

Games

Play one of these games with the whole class or in groups.

- **Before or After? e-game** (see page 90)
- **Memory Cards e-game** (see page 93) – students match synonyms and antonyms. The words are:

    different – same

    fair – unfair

    hard – easy

    honest – dishonest

    just – unjust

    late – early

    like – unlike

    responsible – irresponsible

    right – wrong

    sensible – silly

    tactful – tactless

    truth – lie

- Bingo strips (see page 90) or Bingo for pairs (see page 98) using some of the key words in the unit.
- Big words, small words using words such as: honesty, fairness, trustworthy, dishonest, truthful, responsible (see page 98). The **Timer e-tool** can be used.

Bounce Back! award

Present the **Bounce Back! award** to students who have best demonstrated the values in this unit.

Unit 1 Core values 123

UNIT 2

Social values

KEY MESSAGES

Social values are beliefs about how you should behave towards other people.
Having strong social values means that you try to treat other people well. When you treat others well, they are more likely to treat you well too.

It is important to be kind.
Being kind means supporting and caring about other people by:
- helping them when they need it
- being thoughtful and generous
- giving encouragement
- listening when they have a problem
- being patient with them when they find it hard to do something.

It is important to be friendly and include others.
Being friendly means being kind and welcoming to others. It is friendly to include others even if they are not your friends or they are people who are hard for you to like. This means:
- looking in their eyes and smiling
- saying hello and talking to them
- finding something funny to laugh about together
- being kind to them
- inviting them to join in games and conversations.

Learn when it is appropriate to speak to strangers and when it is not. Don't speak to adult strangers until you are sure they are safe and unless a trusted adult is present.

It is important to cooperate.
Cooperating means working together with a partner or as a team to achieve something that you both want. Cooperation also means:
- sharing
- listening
- encouraging
- everyone having a say
- doing your share of the work
- making decisions that are fair to everyone.

When you don't fully agree about something, you need to negotiate. This means finding solutions or answers to problems so that everyone gets some of what they want.

It is important to treat other people with respect.
Respecting other people means treating others as you want them to treat you. It means you have to stop and think about the feelings and rights of others. Respect involves:
- being polite and using good manners
- not insulting or hurting others
- looking after shared property or the property of others
- asking permission to use things that belong to someone else
- speaking in a polite tone of voice.

It is important to respect yourself.
Self-respect is when you:
- like and accept yourself
- feel proud of your behaviour and the way you treat other people.
- believe that you matter too and should be treated well by others.
- self-protect, i.e. you take care of yourself and keep yourself from harm.
- speak up when someone doesn't treat you well.

> **? Learning objectives**
> In this unit, students will further develop their understanding of the:
> - importance of treating others as they would like to be treated
> - values of kindness, cooperation, friendliness, inclusion, and respect for self and others.

Resources list

A complete list of resources including references for core and additional books, films, video clips, poems, songs and websites is available.

It's important to be kind

Resources

♦ Books

Have You Filled a Bucket Today?

Children are told they carry an invisible 'bucket' that holds their feelings about themselves. When their bucket is full, they feel happy; when it's empty, they feel sad. Showing kindness and appreciation to others can help children fill their own bucket, and others' buckets too.

Kindness Is Cooler, Mrs Ruler

Mrs Ruler teaches her students to look for ways of showing kindness to their family members, their community and each other. She challenges them to perform 100 acts of kindness, and the whole class quickly catches on.

♦ Song

'Fill Your Bucket'

Circle Time or classroom discussion

Use one of the resources and follow up with discussion questions.

Discussion questions

- What is kindness? (Kindness means caring about the wellbeing and feelings of other people, not just our own. When we are being kind, we also offer care and support when someone else needs it.)

- How were the characters kind?

- How did the characters support others?

- What do kind people do? (Kind people continue to be kind even when other people are not. They don't expect anything in return for being kind to someone. They show kindness to other people because they want to help make someone else's life a little better.)

- How might we feel when we show kindness to someone else? (When we are kind to others, it helps us to feel happy and satisfied/proud of the way we treat other people.)

Share with students an example of a time in your own life when you needed some support and someone cared enough and was kind enough to offer it to you.

Using the 'Think–ink–pair–share' strategy (see page 97), ask students to take turns to talk about when they have needed support or help and someone has been kind to them. Discuss what giving support means. Follow up by making a chart on the board listing circumstances in which people might need support and how support might be given to them. For example:

- offering help with learning something
- listening to someone who has a problem they need to talk about
- wishing good luck to someone who has to do something difficult or scary

- being kind and helpful if someone is unwell
- standing up for somebody e.g. someone who is being bullied or teased
- encouraging others when they are finding something hard to do
- letting a teacher know when a classmate needs their help.

Students can then take turns around the circle to talk about one time when they have been kind to someone else.

Activities

▶ Explore the features of diary writing (e.g. first person, recording of events and feelings, etc.). Students can keep a Kindness diary where they record acts of kindness received and performed for a week. The school diary could be used.

▶ Students prepare a report on a book, film or TV program that features kindness and present it to the class.

▶ Students prepare questions for an interview with a classmate on how they have been kind, using questions beginning with *who, what, when, where, why* and *how*.

▶ Students complete **BLM How Could You Support Someone?** and share their answers as a class.

▶ Students complete **BLM Kindness Challenge** and share their answers as a class.

Bucket-filling

Each student has a folder with a picture of a bucket on the cover, a toy bucket or their own digital 'bucket' on the computer. Encourage students to perform acts of kindness, write about them and then place them in their own 'bucket'.

Our family is kind and supports us

Resources

✦ Book

Families, Families, Families!

Fun illustrations of all kinds of mothers, fathers, brothers, sisters and grandparents are used to demonstrate and celebrate all kinds of traditional and non-traditional families.

✦ Songs

'The Family Song'

'We Are Family'

Circle Time or classroom discussion

Sing the songs or read the book. Discuss with students the ways family members support and help each other.

Discussion question

■ How do our family members support us and each other?

Provide students with some 'starters', such as who in your family:

- plays games with you?
- makes nice things for you to eat?

- makes sure you have everything you need before you go to school?
- cuddles you or sits with you when you are feeling a sad, worried or unwell?
- takes you to the park or to the beach?
- takes you shopping?
- watches your favourite TV show with you?
- makes sure you are included in family discussions?
- takes you to activities and watches you play (e.g. sport)?

Activities

Lift-up flaps

Students make lift-up flaps and circles (see page 103) about people in their family who are kind to them and support them. The wording on the outside is 'Guess who …?' (e.g. 'drives me to swimming on Monday'). The answer is underneath (e.g. 'My Grandpa').

Mobile

Students make a mobile using cards, on which family members' names and how they support them are written (see page 105).

Family support calculations

In pairs, each student works out how many people in their family supports them each week. Start with Monday and work through each day of the week. Students also write down how these people support them.

Our teachers are kind and support us

Resources

✦ Book

Teacher (People Who Help Us)

This nonfiction book is based on a real teacher and follows him through a typical school day: what he does and why, and the people he encounters.

Circle Time or classroom discussion

Read the book and talk about how teachers care for and support students at school.

Discussion questions

- How did the teacher in the book care for and support his students?
- How do teachers care for and support students? (Listen to them when they felt sad, show them how to do something, teach them new things, take care of them when they hurt themselves, show them where to go when they are lost.)
- Can you remember a time when a teacher helped you?

Using **BLM People Hunt: Teachers Help All of Us**, students ask six different classmates about how teachers help all of us. They then return to the circle and each student shares one of the answers from their 'people hunt'.

Activities

- Students contribute illustrations and sentences to a class poster or class book (see page 101) entitled 'How teachers care for their students'.
- Explore the features of letters and emails (e.g. address, date, subject line, greeting, closing etc.). Students write a letter or email thanking a teacher at their school for an act of kindness.
- Students write a haiku poem about how teachers show kindness and support. A haiku uses a few words to create a picture in the reader's mind. It is written in three lines, with five syllables in the first line, seven syllables in the second line, and five syllables in the third line. This is a good activity to do as part of a spelling lesson.

Embed it

Teacher kindness challenges

- Send positive notes home to families about students.
- Tell your class three things you appreciate about them.
- Eat lunch with your students.
- Make time to play a special game or a Giggle gym activity (see page 250).
- Find time to catch and praise each student's behaviour.
- Bring a treat for the staffroom.
- Thank a colleague.
- Praise a colleague.

Being kind and supporting people we don't know very well

Resources

✦ Books

Somebody Loves You, Mr Hatch

Mr Hatch is a solitary man until he receives a surprise valentine message. This makes him so happy he starts to do kind things for everyone. When the postman tells him that the valentine was incorrectly delivered, Mr Hatch withdraws, but the neighbours show they do care for him.

Lily and the Paper Man

Lily sees a man selling newspapers. Initially, she is a bit scared of him, but when the colder weather arrives she notices that the man doesn't have enough clothes to keep warm. She organises clothing donations and even gives him the special quilt made by her grandma.

Amelia Ellicott's Garden

Amelia Ellicott lives in a formerly grand mansion with large grounds. She is very isolated from the community until a terrible storm wrecks much of her garden. Her neighbours come to help her, and this is the start of cooperation and friendliness between them.

Circle Time or classroom discussion

Begin the circle with everyone sending a non-verbal greeting around the circle (e.g. a smile and a high five). Read one of the books to the class.

Discussion questions

- How did the kindness shown in the story change someone's life?
- What effect did the kind acts have and why?
- Can being kind to someone who is lonely help them to feel happier?
- How does a warm greeting from someone make you feel?
- What would it be like if you didn't have much contact with people?

Activities

- Students make a card, a drawing or write a poem or short imaginative text for someone their family knows (an elderly neighbour, grandparent etc.) who lives by themselves to let them know you are thinking of them.
- In pairs, students prepare questions to ask someone they don't know very well (this could even be for a new school buddy).

Take-home task

Encourage students to tell their families about the work that their class has been doing on how to be kind to people who may be living on their own and might be lonely. Students ask if a family member could mail or take their card, drawing or story to someone (e.g. family member, family friend, neighbour, someone in an aged-care facility) to cheer them up.

Being kind to animals

Resources

✦ Books

How to Heal a Broken Wing

A young boy notices an injured pigeon with a broken wing on a busy footpath in the city. He takes the bird home to look after her, and with his mother's help she survives. They release her back into the wild.

Stellaluna

Stellaluna, a baby fruit bat, is attacked one night by an owl and falls into a bird nest. The mother bird only knows how to take care of birds so this means eating bugs, not being nocturnal and not sleeping upside down. Stellaluna does her best to adapt until reunited with her mother.

Jeremy

A tiny kookaburra, only a few days old, falls out of his nest and is carried home by a cat. The cat's family name him 'Jeremy' and take care of him. He grows stronger, until the time comes when he must fly back home.

Circle Time or classroom discussion

Read one of the books to start a discussion.

Discussion questions

- How was kindness shown in the book?
- Who can share one way you or a family member has been kind and caring to an animal that needed help?

Talk about how vets offer support and care for animals. Explain that sometimes the best way to be kind to an animal is to take it to a vet who can offer medical help.

- Has anyone ever seen one animal help another animal?
- Can different sorts of pets live together in the same house and be kind to each other?

Activities

- Students work with a partner to make a T-chart listing the ways in which animals care for people in one column, and the ways in which people care for animals in the other.
- Students undertake an inquiry-based learning project (see page 92) about how vets and veterinary nurses help families look after their pets (e.g. vaccinations, identity chips, fur clipping, treating injuries etc.).
- Using the Big words, small words strategy, students make as many small words as they can from the word 'veterinarian' (see page 98).
- Students write a brochure on how to care for a pet or animal.

Family pet survey

Students work as a class to develop five survey questions about families and pets and how they support each other. They then each ask three students in Years 3–6 who have a pet to complete the survey, and collate their responses as a class. This can work well as an activity supervised by older buddies.

Examples of questions:

- What kind of pet do you have at home?
- What type of animal do you think makes the best pet and why?
- How does your pet support and care for you?
- How do people in your family show support and care for your pet?
- Do you think having a pet has helped to make you a kinder person?

It's important to be friendly

Resources

✦ Books

Rose Meets Mr Wintergarten

Rose Summers and her family move next door to an unwelcoming mansion surrounded by fences. The neighbour, Mr Wintergarten, is not what they expect, and he reacts positively to the warmth of Rose's approach when she reaches out to him.

The Invisible Boy

Brian seems to be 'invisible'. None of the other kids in his class seems to notice him or include him in their group, or in their games and birthday parties. When a new boy arrives in the class, Brian is the first to welcome him and they successfully work together on a project.

My Two Blankets

A young girl escapes from her war-torn country and relocates to a safer country. She struggles with adapting to her new home but is supported by the kindness of a new friend. The girl concludes that she has two 'blankets' – her original language and culture, and her new life and language.

Circle Time or classroom discussion

Read one of the books to the class, then follow up with the discussion questions.

Discussion questions
- Where was friendliness shown in the books?
- What do we mean by a friendly person?
- What does a friendly class look like?
- What does a friendly school look like?
- How do you know when a person or place is friendly?

Then use the Bundling strategy (see page 91) and ask students to write three ways to be friendly. Make a chart on the board from their replies. Explain that friendliness is similar to but not the same as being a good friend. Stress that friendliness is different depending on whether or not you know the person.

Extending friendliness to people we know well and like usually means showing interest in them, including them in our games and conversation, and being kind to them. Friendliness to people we do not know very well usually means smiling and looking into their eyes, greeting and acknowledging them, talking to them, sharing a laugh and being helpful.

Repeatedly make the point that students should keep themselves safe by not being friendly towards any unknown adults or older children – particularly those who make them feel unsafe.

Activities

- Students make a list with a partner of the friendly things they could do, for instance for a classmate who is away sick for a while (e.g. write a get-well card), or for someone who seems lonely or is new to the class (e.g. invite them to join in a game).
- Use the Multiply and Merge strategy (see page 94) for students to decide on the four best ideas for making their school a more friendly place.
- Students work in groups of three to take turns using a digital camera to contribute to making a photographic class collage or slide show of 'Our class being friendly'.
- Complete the **Friendly or Not? e-activity** with the class.

Friendliness checklist

From the bundling activity and Circle Time discussion, the class creates a checklist that can be used to assess the level of friendliness in the classroom or in the playground. Display the checklist in the classroom as a reminder.

Students can also use the friendliness checklist to observe friendliness or lack of friendliness in the playground for a day and then, as a class, put together a list of what they found and write a report.

You light up my life!

Students make a string of cut-out light bulbs or lanterns and on each one they write one of the aspects of being friendly or an act of friendliness they have seen or experienced. Students can use one of the lines in the acronym LIGHTS as a prompt, because being friendly causes people to 'light up'.

Laugh with them

Include them

Greet them

Help them

Talk to them

Smile and connect with your eyes

Making a friendly flower

Students make a friendly flower by creating and colouring in a simplified flower drawing similar to a 'sunshine wheel'. Create a master drawing and photocopy it, or have students draw one large circle around a smaller, central circle, with lines drawn from the edge of the small circle to the large circle to form petals. The drawing should look similar to a wheel with spokes. Students colour in their flowers using different colours, such as a red centre and pink petals or a green centre and blue petals.

On each petal, students write one of the aspects or acts of friendliness they have seen or experienced, such as:

- spending time together
- showing interest
- smiling
- greeting
- eyes connecting
- talking
- laughing
- helping
- including.

When completed, cut around the edge of the large circle, attach a straw or stick to the back of the flower and display the class collection of friendly flowers in a vase.

Friendliness badges

Students make friendly wax-resistant badges (see page 108). They can be given to students at the end of each day or week for acts of friendliness. The recipient can wear the badge for a week.

Class friendly box

Make a class friendly box from a shoebox with a slot cut into the top of the lid. Leave friendly cards, decorated by students using drawing software, near the box. Students write a friendly comment and the person's name, and insert the card into the box. Read them out during a Circle Time each week or fortnight.

Class friendliness chain

Students take a pre-cut strip of paper, write down a friendly act they have received and from whom, and then loop it into a link to the class friendliness chain.

'My name is ____

____ [insert name] was friendly to me.

What they did or said that was friendly: ____'

Embed it

Superfriendly Week

Declare one week Superfriendly Week. Students are asked to engage in as many acts of friendliness as they can think of. These can be written down and posted in a Superfriendly postbox. Write the friendly actions on cardboard hearts attached to a string around a small branch of a tree in a pot of sand.

It's important to cooperate

Resources

♦ Books

Piggybook

Members of Mrs Piggott's family do not cooperate, and eventually she gets so tired of doing all the work that she leaves. After she leaves, Mr Piggott and the two boys get messier and messier until eventually all three turn into pigs!

Four Feet, Two Sandals

Two ten-year-old girls in a refugee camp each find one sandal from a pair in a collection of donated clothing. They decide that it is better to share the pair rather than each of them only wearing one shoe.

♦ Poem

I Have No Trouble Sharing

Circle Time or classroom discussion

Before Circle Time, ask students to pack up chairs, clean up rubbish or put away equipment (or similar tasks that require them to cooperate).

Discussion questions

- What does the proverb 'Many hands make light work' mean? How did it apply to what you just did?

- Tell us about a time when something was completed in a faster time and in a better way because everyone helped.

Discuss why things happen more successfully when people cooperate (the load is shared, enthusiasm is contagious; a sense of teamwork develops when people work together; it makes a big task seem less daunting or easier).

Read to the class and discuss one of the resources. Alternatively, use Lightning writing (see page 93) and ask students to write what they know about cooperation.

- What does cooperation mean?

Ask students for other words that are about cooperation and make a list on the board.

- How did the characters show cooperation?

- What was the good thing that came out of that cooperation? Give an example of how people you know cooperate. (Stress that cooperation is more than just being together or doing something together. Cooperation means everyone is working towards the same goal and all are contributing part of the work and trying to sort out problems together. Teamwork can also be used as a word describing cooperation.)

- What are the good things that happen when we cooperate with others? (We achieve more, we understand others better, we make better friends, we get closer to people, we learn to trust other people.)

- What skills do we need to use so that we cooperate well?

Explain that when people cooperate well, they:

- work together
- share materials
- share ideas
- take turns
- share the work
- listen to each other
- help each other
- encourage each other
- use good manners
- don't use put-downs
- sort out disagreements in a friendly way
- let the other person have a fair go.

> **Teacher reflection**
> How important is cooperation in your workplace? Can you think of two examples where cooperation enhanced the outcomes for all concerned?
>
> Are there any situations where more cooperation might be useful? How does collegial collaboration/cooperation (or lack of it) affect your school's climate? How might staff use cooperative learning strategies in staff meetings?

Activities

- Students work with a partner to make a class poster using the cooperative acronym TEAM (Together Everyone Achieves More, page 97). They include the skills needed for cooperating well.

- Students work with a partner to divide an A3 page into three columns and list ways they can cooperate at home, at school and with friends.

- Students make a shield-shaped wax-resistant badge (see page 108) with the message: 'We cooperate'. They wear their badge every time they undertake a cooperative activity.

- Take photos and make a slide show display of students undertaking cooperative activities and underneath write either 'We cooperate because we care about each other' or 'We did this together'. The latter label can also be placed on finished products and signed by all who cooperated together.

- In groups of three, students undertake and write a report on how they collaborated on a cooking activity, such as making sandwiches, fruit kebabs or faces, gingerbread people, pikelets or biscuits.

- In pairs, students estimate how far a box of straws would stretch if all the straws were placed end to end. Then they test their prediction.

- With access to a collection of small items, students form pairs and collaborate to investigate:
  - how many things can you find that are 1 cm long?
  - how many things can you fit on a 15 cm circle without any of the things touching?

- In pairs, students collaborate to write a sentence that includes an adjective, a verb, an adverb, an apostrophe and a plural in a grammar lesson.

- Students complete an inquiry-based project on how insects and animals cooperate with each other (e.g. ants, bees, meerkats). **BLM Meerkats** can be a good starting point.

- Students work with a partner to see how many small words they can make out of the big word 'cooperation' within ten minutes (see page 98). Use the **Timer e-tool**.

Humming songs

Divide the number of students in the class by four. For each group, prepare sets of four cards that have the same song written on them. For each set choose one simple song that is easily hummed (e.g. 'Rock A-Bye Baby', 'Row, Row, Row Your Boat', 'Twinkle Twinkle Little Star'; 'Happy Birthday', 'Jingle Bells', 'Yellow Submarine', 'We're Going to the Zoo', 'The Wheels on the Bus'). Put all of the cards into a container and ask each student to draw one. Explain that the aim is to find the other three people in their group by humming (lips must be closed!) their song until they find the others with the same song. They cannot show their card to anyone or act out the name of the song. Each time they are able to form a group within the time limit (try five minutes) each student gets one point. Then mix up the cards and repeat. Students see how many points they can earn over five rounds. Use the **Timer e-tool**.

Blends cooperation

Each group of three needs a large sheet of paper to paste things on and old magazines to cut pictures from. Give students 20 minutes to find as many pictures as they can that begin with the blend you have nominated (e.g. 'bl'), and then cut them out, paste them on their named sheet and write the words underneath. Have one cutter, one counter and one person doing the pasting.

Don't let the right know what the left is doing!

Students work with a partner to tie both sets of shoelaces, with one student using only their right hand and one student using only their left hand. Then they practise with their partner walking, hopping, skipping etc. with their arms crossed over and joined together behind their backs.

Games

Memory tray

Set up a tray of 20–30 items (or use 20–30 pictures). Show this to the whole class. Students work in pairs to help each other remember what is on the tray (the best strategy is to categorise the items). They cannot write anything down at this point. After students have studied the items for 2–3 minutes (depending on age) silently, the tray is removed and each pair is asked to discuss and write down the items they can remember. Each pair combines their two scores.

Slap, slap, clap, clap, click, click

This is played in a group of six. The aim is to practise the sequence until it can be done quickly and accurately. Students sit in a circle and chant and perform the following:

- slap (slap the right knee)
- slap (slap the left knee)
- clap, clap (clap twice)
- click (click the right finger)
- click (click the left finger).

The first four start. Then after the first two slaps, the second four start, like a song sung in 'rounds'. Can the group keep doing this for two minutes with no mistakes?

The Leaning Tower of Pisa

Use teams of six. The six members of each team must stand very close to each other. The teacher or leader calls out one of these instructions:

- lean left
- lean right
- lean forwards
- lean backwards without falling or raising either foot fully off the ground.

Each team has three 'lives' (i.e. they can make three mistakes before they are out of the game).

Cooperative ball pass

Six tennis balls or similar are needed. Students play in a group of six. They chant one, two, three, and on 'three' they all pass their ball to the person on their left and receive the ball being passed to them on the right. Try to go faster and faster.

Names and actions

This game has some similarity to the game of 'I went shopping', with each previous choice being added and copied. Organise students into pairs and before they sit down ask them to agree on a simple action (using only the upper body) that they will both do together when it is their turn. Then students sit in a circle next to their partner.

The teacher begins, for example, by saying 'I'm Ms Bryant and this is my action'. She then waves her right arm into the air and lowers it. Everyone says 'Ms Bryant' and then they all do Ms Bryant's action. The pair of students on the teacher's left then say their names and do their action, e.g. 'We are Cooper and Milos and this is our action' and then they clap their hands once. All of the students in the circle then say 'Cooper and Milos' and clap once, and then say 'Ms Bryant' and wave their right arm. This process continues until each pair has given their names and shown their action and the entire group has repeated it all.

Variations: instead of sitting, students can stand in the circle and use an action that involves the whole body, or they can have their own 'sound' (e.g. a roar, a giggle, a yahoo, a kookaburra laugh).

Take-home task

Students interview a family member about situations where cooperation was essential and many hands made light work (e.g. moving house, renovating the house, school working bee).

Embed it

After students work on a group task or one of the cooperative games and activities, they can use **BLM Cooperation Rubric** to give feedback to themselves and each other.

It's important to respect others

Resources

✦ Books

Manners

A collection of funny comic-book-style pictures about a variety of 'bad manners' and the promotion of the message that good manners matter.

My Mouth Is a Volcano

All of Louis' thoughts are so important to him that he interrupts others when they are busy or talking. The book focuses on ways to teach children the value of respecting others by listening and waiting for their turn to speak.

Circle Time or classroom discussion

Use the Bundling strategy (see page 91) and ask students to write three examples of good manners. Read and discuss one of the books.

Students can take it in turns to give one example of good manners that their families or teachers have taught them to use. Emphasise how all these 'good manners' show respect, consideration and thoughtfulness for other people.

Discussion questions

- How did the character show no respect for others?
- How did the character show respect to others?
- What do we mean by respect for others?
- How do people show respect and consideration to others?

Explain that respect for others usually means:

- appreciating what others can do well
- showing courtesy and good manners to others
- protecting and caring for shared property and the property of others
- thinking about how others might see things differently and accepting that this is okay
- acknowledging the rights of others
- avoiding insulting, injuring or interfering with others
- treating others in a way that allows them to maintain their pride and not be made to look foolish or ridiculous.

- Why are good manners a form of respect for others? (Good manners are simple social skills that respect the rights of other people.)
- What are considered to be good manners in your family?

Draw out examples from other cultures, e.g. some Aboriginal and Torres Strait Islander communities believe that it is good manners for children to look down at the floor when an adult is telling them off, and in many Asian cultures it is respectful (good manners) to help people 'save face' (i.e. not be embarrassed in front of others).

- How could we respect the right of others to 'save face' if:
    - they fell over in front of the class?
    - someone else was saying nasty, funny things about them and everybody else was laughing at them?
    - they made a mistake when they gave an answer?

Activities

Yes, please, or No, thank you?

This activity reminds children of the importance of using good manners in terms of saying 'Yes, please' or 'No, thank you'.

Ask students to shout out their answers as a group to the following questions.

- Would you like to swim with a school of baby dolphins? *Yes, please!*
  Would you like the baby dolphins to swim so fast that you get left behind? *No, thank you.*
- Would you like to visit the zoo and visit all of the animals? *Yes, please!*
  Would you like the monkeys to throw things at you? *No, thank you.*
- Would you like to have a picnic in a park with your friends? *Yes, please!*
  Would you like a nearby dog to run off with your sandwiches? *No, thank you.*
- Would you like to go to see a circus? *Yes, please!*
  Would you like one of the clowns to squirt water at you? *No, thank you.*

Play it again a few days later and ask students to suggest some new (and appropriate) 'paired questions' beforehand.

Class book

Make a class book of good manners (see page 101). In pairs, students write one page for good manners in the following situations:

- visiting someone's house
- going to a party
- working in a group
- eating dinner at a friend's house
- talking on the phone
- eating in a food hall or restaurant
- going to the movies or a show
- playing in a team
- sharing computers
- using email
- when coughing or sneezing.

Class quiz

Students complete **BLM A Good Manners Quiz** or prepare their own in groups of four. On cards, students write the question: 'What would you do if …?' and on the inside, they record their answer. Mix the cards together and have a class quiz.

Self-respect is important too

Resources

✦ Book
A Bad Case of Stripes

Camilla loves lima beans but never eats them because the other girls hate them. She develops a bad case of stripes, but when other children call out other 'patterns' (e.g. polka dots) that's what she gets covered in. Camilla finds out the cure is 'being herself', and eating lima beans.

✦ Song
'Respect Song'

Circle Time or classroom discussion

Use the resources to introduce the concept of self-respect (see page 124). Explain that you have self-respect when you:

- like and accept yourself
- are kind to yourself and don't put yourself down when you make a mistake
- know what your strengths are but you never boast
- believe you matter and should be treated well by others
- take care of yourself and protect yourself from harm
- don't compare yourself with others – you don't think you are either better or worse than anyone else
- feel proud of the respectful and kind way in which you treat other people.

Discussion questions

■ How does someone behave if they have self-respect? (They respect their own ideas and views, they treat others with respect, they accept it is okay to be different, they are honest, they have good values, they are positive, they try to be brave and resilient, they balance pride with being humble rather than bragging, they self-protect, they expect others to treat them with respect, they know their strengths, they have confidence in themselves and their own views.)

- How do we know that Camilla from the book hasn't yet developed enough 'self-respect'? (She doesn't have confidence in herself or her own views and ideas, she doesn't accept that it is okay to be different.)
- How do you think someone who has self-respect behaves?
- What do you think people with self-respect are likely to do to keep themselves safe:
    - at the beach?
    - on a bushwalk?
    - walking to and from school (road safety, stranger danger)?
    - at home?
    - if someone sends them nasty emails or text messages?
    - if someone tries to hurt them in the playground?
    - if someone keeps telling others not to play with them?

Activity

Students work in pairs to write a simple imaginative text about a character who doesn't have self-respect. Have students consider some of the problems that this could bring (e.g. in terms of health, safety, confidence, not knowing what they are good at, making unhelpful and discouraging comparisons, not standing up for themselves etc.).

Consolidation

Embed it

Keep classroom diaries and constantly changing photographic records of students putting social values such as cooperation, respect, kindness and inclusion into practice. Make labelled displays, or take digital photos of students behaving in accordance with specific social values and make a bulletin board or slide show display.

Activities

- Make social value cards, which students randomly choose from a pile. They then give an example of a behaviour that goes with it.
- Do Big words, small words (see page 98) using one of the social values words e.g. cooperation, respectful, kindness, friendly, manners and including.

Cut-up sentences

Write out the sentences below, then cut them into individual words and place each cut-up sentence into an envelope (see page 92). Make enough sets for each pair of students to have one set of the six sentences. Each student pair reconstructs the six sentences. The **Cut-up Sentences e-activity** can also be used with the whole class.

- Cooperation means working together.
- When we cooperate, we do our share.
- When we work together and cooperate, everyone achieves more.
- Be friendly and try to include other people.
- Using good manners shows respect.
- Kind people help and support others.

Values awards

Ask students to self-assess on social values using **BLM My Social Values Report Card**. Give individual students a **Bounce Back! award** (see page 141), an 'Honesty award', a 'Cooperation award' etc. or badge (see page 108) as acknowledgement of their efforts to use specific values.

Values in action

Use the Circuit brainstorm strategy (see page 91) and write one social value on the top of individual sheets of paper (see page 91). Each group writes one example of what they can do to demonstrate that value in action. It doesn't matter if some of them are mixed up, as there is a bit of overlap in some cases.

Key vocabulary

Use the Whisper game, Mystery square or the TEAM coaching strategy to assist students to learn vocabulary and spelling related to values to a reasonable level of mastery (see pages 98, 94 and 97). Examples include:

accept

apology/apologise

care/caring/carer

cooperate/cooperation/cooperating

encourage/encouragement/encouraging

fair/fairness/unfair

friend/friendly/friendliness

help/helpful/helpfulness

include/including

kind/kindness

listen/listening

manners

negotiate/negotiation

polite

respect/respectful/self-respect

share/sharing

solve/solutions

support/supporting

thought/thoughtful/thoughtfulness

Reflections

Use the **Reflections e-tool** with the class which asks these questions:

- What do we mean when we say that someone is kind?
- How do you feel when someone in your group does not do their share of the work?
- What is one example of good manners that you have used when visiting a friend's home?
- What is one job you do in your home to cooperate with your family?
- What is one way you have been kind to someone recently?

- Where or when would you use this good manner?
    - saying 'excuse me'
    - saying 'please'
    - saying 'thank you'
    - letting people know what time you will arrive
    - writing a thank-you note

These questions can also be used with Musical stop and share or Inside–outside circle strategies (see pages 94 and 93).

Games

▶ Play the **Memory Cards e-game** with the whole class or in groups (see page 93). Students match nouns to verbs or adjectives. The words are:

apology – apologise

cooperation – cooperate

encouragement – encourage

helpfulness – help

kindness – kind

fairness – fair

friend – friendly

negotiation – negotiate

thought – thoughtful

carer – caring

respect – respectful

share – sharing

support – supporting

▶ Play a game of Bingo strips (see page 90) or Bingo for pairs (see page 98) using some of the words listed above.

Bounce Back! award

Present the **Bounce Back! award** to students who have best demonstrated the values in this unit.

UNIT 3

People bouncing back

KEY MESSAGES

People can bounce back, just like balls bounce back.
A ball is pushed out of shape when it hits the ground. Then it bounces back to almost the same shape. When you have difficult or unhappy times in your life, you can bounce back too.

The BOUNCE BACK! acronym is the basis of this unit. You can learn the BOUNCE BACK! statements off by heart so that when you have any setbacks you can remember the statements to help you cope better. (See Handbook Chapter 5: Teaching the BOUNCE BACK! acronym, which explains the key concepts that underpin the acronym.)

Bad times don't last. Things always get better. Stay optimistic.
Bad times and unhappy feelings (nearly) always last for a short time. Things get better, even if it takes a little while. When things are difficult, just focus on getting through one day at a time. (See also Unit 5: Looking on the bright side.)

Other people can help if you talk to them. Get a reality check.
Nothing is so bad that you can't talk about it to someone you trust. Talking to someone you trust when you feel unhappy or worried will help you to bounce back and feel supported. It also gives you a reality check, which is evidence, new facts or other opinions that help you to see if you are being realistic. It takes courage to talk to someone about your troubles.

Unhelpful thinking makes you feel more upset. Think again.
Helpful thinking is sensible thinking, and it can make you feel better, calmer and more hopeful about things. Helpful thinking is based on evidence and real facts. Unhelpful thinking isn't based on what's real. It makes you feel more upset and less hopeful about things. Examples of unhelpful thinking are:

- jumping to conclusions without proof
- guessing what someone else is thinking (rather than asking them)
- seeing only one side of a situation
- exaggerating the facts or your feelings
- thinking that because something has happened once it will keep happening.

'I-can't-stand-it-itis' is also unhelpful thinking – it's when you tell yourself that you 'couldn't stand it' if something you didn't like happened or if you miss out on something. Stop and think again to change your unhelpful thinking into helpful thinking so you can feel better and make better decisions in your life. (See also Unit 6: Emotions.)

Nobody is perfect – not you and not others.
Everyone makes mistakes and gets things wrong sometimes – that's normal. There is no such thing as a perfect person. We are all just doing our best. We all have strengths and weaknesses. If you always try to be perfect, you will be too hard on yourself when you make a mistake or a poor decision, and you will lose self-confidence. If you want other people to be perfect, you will be too critical of and unfairly angry with them. This can hurt your relationships with family and friends.

Concentrate on the positives (no matter how small) and use laughter.
Look for the positives (the good bits) in a worrying or unhappy situation, even though they may be small. Ask yourself: 'Is there anything slightly funny about what's happening?' Use laughter in a helpful way to feel less stressed and more hopeful. This won't make your problems go away, but you will feel a bit better and more hopeful about solving your problems. (See also Unit 5: Looking on the bright side and Unit 8: Humour.)

Everybody experiences sadness, hurt, failure, rejection and setbacks sometimes, not just you. They are a normal part of life. Try not to personalise them.
It is normal to sometimes have some sad, painful and worrying times in your life. They happen to everyone now and then, not just you. Normalise them (see them as normal and happening to lots of other people) and don't personalise them (don't see them as happening just to you).

Blame fairly. How much of what happened was due to you, to others and to bad luck or circumstances?

Upsetting things usually happen because of three things – what you did, what other people did, and bad luck or circumstances. Try to be responsible and fairly work out how much the bad thing that has happened was due to these three things. Don't let yourself off the hook when you should take some responsibility for what happened, but don't 'overblame' yourself either.

Accept what can't be changed (but try to change what you can first).

There are some things in our life that we don't like much and we wish they were different. Do your best to try to change things you don't like (e.g. you might try some problem-solving if it is a friendship problem). But sometimes we can't do much to change things because they aren't in our control (e.g. moving to a new school or to a new house). Sometimes you just have to accept that this new situation is just the way it is, and find a way to put up with it. Finding something useful to do can help take your mind off it for a while (e.g. keeping busy playing music, enjoying nature, spending time with friends). But if it is a bad or unsafe situation that you can't change or is out of your control, speak to a teacher or another trusted adult.

Catastrophising exaggerates your worries. Don't believe the worst possible picture.

Catastrophising means thinking about the worst thing that could happen and then thinking that it will happen and getting upset about it now. Don't panic and make yourself miserable over something that may never happen. Do a reality check. Panicking over something that hasn't yet happened (but possibly could happen) is like seeing the weather forecast which says 'a chance of rain' and having your umbrella up all day 'just in case'. (See also Unit 6: Emotions.)

Keep things in perspective. It's only part of your life.

When you feel unhappy or worried about something, try to keep things in perspective. Remind yourself that things could be worse and this is not the end of the world. An upsetting situation usually affects only one part of your life, and doesn't have to spoil everything else. You may have a problem with a friend, but your family life is probably still fine, your pets are still fun and your basketball team is still playing well. Seeing the difference between a minor worry and a serious worry will also help you keep things in perspective.

> **Learning objectives**
> In this unit, students will further develop their:
> - understanding that changes in life are normal
> - knowledge of how to manage challenges, setbacks and difficult times.

Resources list

A complete list of resources including references for core and additional books, films, video clips, poems, songs and websites is available.

Life has ups and downs but you can bounce back

Resources

✦ Books

Lizzy's Ups and Downs: NOT an Ordinary School Day

Lizzy shares the good and bad parts of her day and how she felt about each (e.g. embarrassed, silly, jealous, happy and frustrated). The book emphasises that ups and downs are normal.

Sunday Chutney

Sunday Chutney's family has to move a lot because of her father's job, so Sunday is always the new kid at school. She copes well by accepting the inevitable changes and by looking for the positives.

✦ Poems

Monday Blues

The Wrong Start

✦ Song

'Bounce Back'

✦ Video clip

Boundin'

This clip features a dancing sheep who loses his confidence after being sheared. It encapsulates the BOUNCE BACK! messages.

Circle Time or classroom discussion

Before the discussion, ask students to complete individually **BLM People Bouncing Back: What Do You Think?** Read each statement and ask students to tick in the column labelled 'first time' to indicate whether they agree or disagree. Ask them to paste the quiz in their journal (or collect it). Ask them to complete it again at the end of the unit, using the 'second time' column.

Begin the session by showing how a rubber ball can be squashed out of shape but then bounces back. Use the resources to start class discussions.

Discussion questions

- In the resource, what is an example of an 'up' part of a day?
- In the resource, what is an example of a 'down' part of a day?

Explain this can also be called a setback.

- Can people be 'squashed' or experience a setback and still bounce back? (Yes, but sometimes it takes time and hard work to bounce back.)

Discuss the resources in terms of the following:

- It is normal to have ups and downs in our life.
- For most of us life is pretty good, but it can be challenging and difficult at times.
- Sometimes your unhelpful thinking makes you feel more upset. By changing your unhelpful thinking to helpful thinking, you feel better and cope better with the setback.
- You can bounce back from difficult times if you try.

Then explain the BOUNCE BACK! acronym using the **BOUNCE BACK! e-tool** and giving students the **BLM BOUNCE BACK! poster**. The acronym tells us how to bounce back and cope with setbacks and how to make our lives even better. Unpack any new or unfamiliar vocabulary. It is important that students are regularly exposed to the acronym and learn the statements. By doing this they are more likely to remember them for the rest of their lives. See Key messages (page 142) and Unit 5: Looking on the bright side for more information.

Activities

- Each student makes a puppet with paper springs (see page 106) or a badge with the message 'I bounce back' (see page 108).
- Use the **Missing Words: BOUNCE BACK! e-activity** with the whole class.
- Show the video of the song 'Bounce Back'. Consider teaching the song to the class.

Matching colours and feelings

Analyse the use of colours in the illustrations in *Sunday Chutney* to highlight Sunday's 'positive' and 'negative' perceptions. Ask students to draw a positive and negative event and use appropriate colours.

Make a bounce-backer

Every student will enjoy having their own bounce-backer with their photo or drawing on it (see page 101). It can be a useful prompt to remind students when they are struggling with a learning or social problem that they can 'bounce back'. Discuss what makes the bounce-backer bounce back. Gravity gives it the energy to bounce back. What happens if there is no weight in the bottom of the bounce-backer? What happens if the head is too heavy? Make the link between how the bounce-backer bounces back and returns to where it started, even after being pushed over, and how we can 'bounce back' after we have had an experience that 'knocks us over'.

> **Teacher reflection**
> What BOUNCE BACK! statement would you find most helpful to consider when you have a setback? Consider making your own desktop bounce-backer including a photo of yourself. It can serve as a useful visual prompt for you too, and it will encourage students to use their own bounce-backer as a prompt for coping. When you have a setback, show the class how you try to push it over (gently) but can't because it always 'bounces back'.

Backpack bouncer

Students can make a BOUNCE BACK! bouncer to attach to their backpack, such as a small 'doll', or a picture of a person with a T-shirt that says 'I bounce back', or they can draw a picture. It can be enclosed in a plastic luggage tag or laminated.

Take-home task

Encourage students to take the BOUNCE BACK! statements home and talk to their families about what the statements mean and how the BOUNCE BACK! statements can help everyone to bounce back when they make a mistake or feel unhappy. Students can make a BOUNCE BACK! fridge magnet frame to take home to teach the whole family the coping statements (see page 103).

Embed it

Using the BOUNCE BACK! acronym

The BOUNCE BACK! acronym can become the language of resilience across the school. Challenge students' unhelpful thinking. Use teachable moments to reinforce the BOUNCE BACK! statements when students experience setbacks to help them get through them. Use the literature prompts on page 86 to discuss classroom situations, books, videos, media events etc. Choose books that help to reinforce the BOUNCE BACK! messages.

Teachers on yard duty take a BOUNCE BACK! card containing the acronym as a focus for discussing playground issues that arise.

Bounce Back! journal

Many of the activities in this unit incorporate self-reflection questions. The students can record their reflections in response to the different exercises in a journal (see page 101). Students can also be encouraged to record reflections on how well they bounced back from various difficulties in their lives. Some possible questions:

- What do I remember about how I bounced back last time?
- What didn't work last time and what were the results of that?
- What did I learn when I bounced back?
- What have I learned from watching how others bounce back with a problem or setback?
- What is an example of helpful thinking that I used when I made a mistake?

Bouncing back from injury or being ill
Resources

◆ Books

Banjo Bounces Back
Banjo the horse loves playing 'hoofball' but one day he has a fall and has to stop playing for six weeks. He becomes bored, unfit and gloomy so decides to quit hoofball. When his friend Bella is admitted to 'horspital', Banjo realises that has let himself, the team and Bella down.

Sometimes You Barf
In this humorous story, Nancy vomits at school and is very embarrassed. The key message is that everybody barfs (vomits) occasionally – even animals – and it's a normal part of everyday life.

Circle Time or classroom discussion

Begin Circle Time by using the Movers and shakers strategy (see page 94): after each action ask students to do a thumbs up if they bounced back and got well again.

- Nod your head if you have ever had a broken bone.

- Rub your knee if you have ever grazed your knee.
- Pretend to sneeze if you have ever had a cold.
- Cover your ear if you have ever had an ear infection.
- Rub your eyes if you have ever gone to sleep after 10 pm.
- Rub your tummy if you have ever had a tummy ache.
- Pat your throat if you have ever had a sore throat.
- Cover your mouth if you have ever vomited.
- Touch your teeth if you have ever had a toothache.
- Wave your arms if you have ever been in hospital.
- Jump on the spot if you are allergic to something.

Read one of the books to start discussions about bouncing back.

Discussion questions

- What did the character bounce back from?
- How did the character bounce back?
- Why do we get better again?

Make a list on the board, for example:

- Our skin and bones can bounce back.
- Our immune system helps us to fight diseases and bounce back.
- Doctors and dentists help us to bounce back with their treatment and medications.
- Sleep helps our body to repair itself.
- Exercise and good food make us healthy and fit enough to be able to bounce back.
- Love and care from others like our family helps us to stay hopeful and get well again.

Activities

- Students write and draw about what helps them to bounce back when they are sick or injured.
- Use the People pie strategy (see page 95) on specific illnesses and injuries, e.g. 'Have you ever broken a bone?', 'Have you had a cold?' or 'Have you ever grazed your knee?'
- Make a class book (see page 101) about one way in which students have bounced back (e.g. 'I bounced back when I was sick/injured with ____ because … ').

Animals and plants can bounce back too

Resources

◆ Books

The Good Luck Cat

Woogie, a much-loved cat, survives, even after using up all of her 'nine lives'.

Tarra and Bella: The Elephant and Dog Who Became Best Friends

In this photographic real-life story, Tarra retires from the circus to become the first resident of the Elephant Sanctuary in Tennessee. She wasn't interested in becoming friends with any other elephants who moved in, but she and a stray dog named Bella became inseparable friends.

Fire

This book is told through the eyes of a cockatoo, who sees a raging bushfire that engulfs homes and land. After the fire, people demonstrate courage and kindness and new life grows.

Circle Time and classroom discussion

Read to the class and discuss one of the books. Ask students to swap seats if they have a dog. Then ask to swap if they have a cat, a bird, a rabbit or a fish. Use the People pie strategy (see page 95) to ascertain how many students have a pet and what kind. Ask some students to give some examples of ways in which an animal can become ill or injure itself.

Discussion questions

- How do animals bounce back after injury or illness? (Immune system, veterinary treatment, medication, love and care of their owners, being healthy to start with.)
- Has anyone seen a pet in a hospital or a place that cares for others?
- How can pets and animals help people to bounce back? (Physical benefits of owning a pet include improved health and wellbeing; social benefits include help with loneliness, encouraging regular routines with feeding and exercise.)
- How do plants bounce back when they have been hurt or neglected? (They can get better when given water, sunlight, being moved to a better place e.g. out of wind or shade, and being given new soil.)

Activities

- Students read **BLM Bush Regeneration** and then answer the questions.
- As a class, draw up two pie graphs: one on the number of students who have a pet, and the second on the different kind of pets owned by students in the class.

Book talk

Read *Fire,* then follow up with discussion on how communities of people support each other and bounce back after bushfires, and how animals and the bush bounce back. Refer to the image in the book of the firefighter giving water to a koala who was burned in a bushfire. This image is based on a photograph that was taken during the severe bushfires in Victoria in 2009. Follow up with an inquiry unit on how communities and the bush bounce back after bushfires.

Sick animal research

In groups, students research one of the following: WIRES (an organisation that helps injured animals), the RSPCA, how the zoo cares for sick animals, how vets care for sick animals, how farmers look after sick farm animals, how animals in bushfire or flood-affected areas are cared for. Each group presents their research to the class as a slide presentation or a poster.

Take-home task

Interview a pet owner

Students work in groups of three to develop questions to interview someone who has had a sick or injured animal that recovered. Make a class list of questions that all students then take home to use. Provide follow-up time in class for students to share their findings on how the animals bounced back.

Losing someone or a pet you love

Resources

✦ Books

The Sound of the Sea

This story focuses on the emotional journey of a young boy, Sam, who is still grieving over his mother's death. Sam's grandfather takes him to the rock pools at the beach, something he used to do with his mother. Sam realises that their shared memories can help him move forward.

The Tenth Good Thing About Barney

This is the story of a young boy's grief over the death of his beloved cat and how he learns to find the positive things in a sad situation.

✦ Video clips

Sesame Street: Expressing Emotions

This clip features children talking about how it helps to talk with others about their feelings when they have lost someone close to them.

Sesame Street: Memory Box

Elmo's cousin Jessie shows Elmo her memory box, a place where she keeps things that remind her of her dad.

> **Teacher reflection**
> Consider a time when you have experienced loss and grief. Helping students deal with death is a difficult but inevitable part of being a teacher. It may be a student's loss of a much loved pet, a family member or friend. Children aged eight to ten years old understand the finality of death but may think it happens to others, not to them or their family. Although children tend to grieve for shorter periods, their grief is no less intense than adults' grief. If a child is grieving, it may lead to the development of challenging behaviour, which may occur several weeks or months later.
>
> In discussion, use the terms 'death' and 'dying' rather than 'passed on', 'no longer with us' etc., which are confusing for children. Children are naturally curious, so encourage questions, but don't worry about having all the answers. What's more important is being available and responding in ways that show you care.

Circle Time or classroom discussion

Use the resources to start a class discussion about unpleasant feelings such as sadness, loss and grief.

Discussion questions

- How did the character show his/her feelings about the loss?
- How did the character learn to deal with these feelings?

Ask students to raise their hand if a family member such as a grandparent or aunt died before they were born.

- Who was it and why would you have liked to have met them?

Ask students to raise their hand if they have lost a loved pet.

- What pet have you lost and why did you love them?

Make the point that it is natural to feel sadness when we lose someone we love or a special pet, and we might always feel a little sad when we think about them. But after a while, our sadness won't be so big and overpowering. Use the **BOUNCE BACK! e-tool** and link this to the coping statements: ***B****ad times don't last. Things always get better. Stay optimistic* and ***E****veryone experiences sadness, hurt, failure, rejection and setbacks sometimes, not just you.* Even though we sometimes lose those we love, they are still with us in our hearts and we can think about how much we still love them by remembering happy times.

Also explain to the class that their friendship to a classmate who has experienced loss is very important. Help them to think about what students could say to their classmate, e.g. 'I'm so sorry about your pet. I know you will miss him very much.'

- How could we support a classmate who is sad and grieving? (Offer to play with them, send a card or drawing, help them with their schoolwork.)

Link to the coping statement: ***O****ther people can help you if you talk to them. Get a reality check.*

In the circle, follow up with a sentence completion activity: 'I miss ____. One good memory I have is ____. I am thankful for ____.' Give students the right to pass.

Activities

▶ Students write out their responses to the Circle Time open sentences and put them in a class memory box.

▶ Students write a message or draw a picture for someone who has recently experienced loss.

Other people can help if you talk to them – get a reality check

Resources

✦ Books

A Terrible Thing Happened

A terrible thing (we never actually find out what) happened to a young bear. For a long time, he feels sad and worried and has bad feelings because of the terrible thing. Eventually, he talks to his teacher about it and gradually he starts to feel less distressed.

Fire

See page 148. This book can also be used to focus on how people can help and offer support in times of adversity.

Onion Tears

Nam-Huong lives with her aunt and uncle and doesn't speak to anyone. She is mocked for her muteness, but the other children are unaware of her tragic story of loss. Finally, the kindness of her teacher enables Nam-Huong to tell her story.

Circle Time or classroom discussion

Begin the lesson with an Inside–outside circle (see page 93) where students share with a different partner answers to each of the following questions:

Who would you talk to if you were:

- feeling sick?
- worried about your school work?
- feeling like you were letting your sports team down?
- being bullied or teased by someone?
- unhappy with something a friend had said to you?
- unhappy with what your brother or sister said or did?

Back in the large circle ask students for examples of the people they would talk to for each scenario. Then ask different students to give one example of a time when they were able to talk to someone about a problem and the person helped them to bounce back. Ask how that person helped them see things differently.

Stress the importance of getting another person's opinion, and collecting and checking facts. Use the **BOUNCE BACK! e-tool** and refer to the BOUNCE BACK! statement for this session: *Other people can help if you talk to them. Get a reality check.*

Read one of the suggested books to discuss how talking to others can be helpful.

Discussion questions

- Who did the character talk to about the terrible thing that has happened?
- Did the character find it helpful to talk to others?
- How did the character feel after they talked about the terrible thing that has happened?
- Why is it helpful to talk to other people if you have a problem or are feeling unhappy? (You feel cared for and supported; it feels safer to have two people sharing a problem; other people help us to get a reality check, i.e. some evidence about what is really true and not just imagination, exaggeration, panicking or jumping to conclusions.)
- Who are some of the people we could talk to about a problem we have?
- Do we talk to different people depending on the kind of problem?
- Who are the people whose job it is to help others by talking to them, helping them to solve problems and helping them with a reality check? (Doctors, nurses, counsellors, psychologists, ministers, priests, teachers, police.)
- What is a reality check? (Checking your facts, looking for evidence, finding out what other people think.)
- Why is it good to check your facts?

Activities

- Students complete **BLM Who Would I Talk To?** Discuss students' responses.
- Students make lift-up flaps (see page 103). On the outside they write: 'How does a … help us?' Underneath they write the answer, e.g. 'How does a doctor help us?' 'By giving us medicine to make us feel better when we are sick.'
- In pairs students write a reality-check checklist to refer to.

Unhelpful thinking makes you feel more upset - think again

Resources

✦ Books

Downsized

A father loses his job because his company has downsized and the family's life changes, with everything becoming 'smaller' (e.g. their house). Dad seems to get smaller too and becomes quite depressed. Then the main character gets Dad involved in building a garden.

Terrible Tuesday

Terry overhears his mother saying to a friend on the phone that Tuesday will be a terrible day. His imagination runs wild with all the terrible but funny things that could happen on Tuesday, but in the end he discovers that it's just his obnoxious little cousins who come to visit.

Circle Time or classroom discussion

Write a statement such as one of the following on the board:

- When I read aloud in class, I didn't know how to read some of the words.
- I messed up my project/story and didn't do what I was meant to do.
- I went to a new school or joined a new team/club and no-one played with me.

Discuss with students that how you think affects how you feel and how you act (what you do). Talk about how they can choose to think in a helpful or unhelpful way. Use the **Bounce Back! e-tool** or refer to the BOUNCE BACK! statement for this topic: *Unhelpful thinking makes you feel more upset. Think again.* Then refer to each sentence on the board. Give an example for each sentence of an unhelpful way to think ('I'm not clever enough', 'I'm always unlucky', 'No-one will ever like me'), and then a helpful way to think ('Other students find things hard too', 'It's hard when you are new but other students would have problems too'). Use a resource to discuss helpful and unhelpful thinking.

Discussion questions

- What was some of the unhelpful thinking in the book?
- What was some of the helpful thinking in the book?
- What happens when you use unhelpful thinking? (You get more upset.)
- What would happen if you used unhelpful thinking all the time? (You would often feel unhappy.)

Use **BLM The Dos and Don'ts of Helpful Thinking** and **BLM Unhelpful and Helpful Thinking**. Display each statement and ask different students to give examples of unhelpful thinking and helpful thinking in relation to each of the statements on the board.

- In **BLM Unhelpful and Helpful Thinking** what is an example of:
  - thinking something is the end of the world when it isn't?
  - not doing a reality check and checking your facts?
  - putting yourself down (i.e. always finding negative things to say about yourself)?
  - jumping to bad decisions or wrong conclusions?
  - trying to read someone's mind and thinking they are thinking something mean about you?
  - generalising from one small negative thing to thinking it happens all the time or in every situation?
- What happens when you think again and use helpful thinking? (You feel better and more hopeful, you have more energy to make things better, you are more likely to ask for help.)

Activities

- Complete the **Helpful and Unhelpful Thinking e-activity** with the class.
- Students write an imaginative text or cartoon about someone who started off with unhelpful thinking and then learned how to think again and use helpful thinking.

Group posters or thought bubbles

In groups of three, students make two posters featuring the same person using helpful and unhelpful thought bubbles, similar to **BLM Unhelpful and Helpful Thinking**. Alternatively, students could use a digital photo of themselves with an unhelpful thought bubble and then another bubble titled 'Think again: Helpful thinking'.

Drama

In groups of three, students make up a brief two-minute puppet play or skit (see page 105) where one puppet/person uses unhelpful thinking, another puppet/person thinks again and uses helpful thinking, and a third person is the narrator who highlights the unhelpful and helpful thinking.

Nobody is perfect – not you and not others

Resources

◆ Books

The Girl Who Never Made Mistakes

Beatrice has never made a mistake. She never forgets to do her homework and her socks always match. She spends a lot time worrying about the possibility that she might make a mistake. But when Beatrice does make a mistake, she discovers that she can cope with it.

Nobody's Perfect: A Story for Children About Perfectionism

Sally Sanders is very good at most things that she does, but she is driven by her unhelpful thinking that if she can't do something well, or be the best, she will feel and look like a failure. Gradually, Sally realises that making mistakes is a part of learning and that nobody is perfect.

◆ Poems

Joshua

Perfect Peter Paul

Circle Time or classroom discussion

Read one of the books or poems. Ask students to raise their hand if they know anyone who is perfect and gets everything right and never, ever makes any mistakes (no names). Use the **BOUNCE BACK! e-tool** or refer to the **BLM BOUNCE BACK! poster** for this lesson and the statement: *Nobody is perfect – not you and not others*.

Discussion questions

- How is the character in the book/poem 'perfect'?
- Tell us of a time when you made a mistake or forgot to do something important or behaved inappropriately.

- Can anyone do everything perfectly all the time? (No)
- What is the difference between trying to do something very well and aiming for a high standard, and trying to be perfect? (Aiming high is about trying to do the best job you can and putting in all the effort that you can, but not stressing out if the outcome isn't perfect.)
- What's not good about thinking you can be perfect? (You will be too hard on yourself, you will lose your confidence, you will worry a lot about things not being perfect.)
- What's not good about expecting other people to be perfect? (You will be too critical of them and unfairly angry with them, it can hurt your relationships with your family and friends.)
- How is it helpful to make mistakes and get things wrong sometimes?
- Would you want to invite someone who was perfect to your home? Why/Why not?

Activities

- Students complete **BLM Absolutely Perfect**. They could also turn the story into a dramatic enactment or draw Polly with thought bubbles showing what she was worried about that made her try to be perfect.
- Students work with a partner to create a similar imaginative text or comic strip about Pandora or Preston Perfect.
- Students write in their **Bounce Back!** journal (see page 101) about what they have learnt about 'nobody's perfect'.
- Students write a poem (similar to the poem *Joshua* or *Perfect Peter Paul*) about a child who is perfect.

Concentrate on the good and funny bits when things go wrong

Resources

✦ Books

The Tenth Good Thing About Barney

See page 149.

Sunday Chutney

See page 144.

Circle Time or classroom discussion

Read one of the books to the class and discuss it, focusing on the good things or funny parts in a not-so-good situation in relation to the character. Use the **Bounce Back! e-tool** or refer to the **BLM BOUNCE BACK! poster** for this lesson and the statement: **C**oncentrate on the positives (no matter how small) and use laughter.

Discussion questions

- What is one good thing about a match that your team lost, being sick on the day of an excursion, being away for your best friend's birthday party etc.?
- How does finding the good things in an unhappy situation make us feel a bit better?
- How does finding any small, funny parts in an unhappy situation make us feel a bit better?
- How does having a bit of a laugh sometimes help if we are feeling sad or worried?

Activities

Story writing

Students write an imaginative text about:

- a child who can't go on a planned holiday (because there has been a natural disaster where they were to have their holiday) and who finds some good things about the cancellation
- a pet, in the style of *The Tenth Good Thing About Barney*.

Journal writing

Students write in their journal about:

- a time when something went wrong in their family but there were some positives as well (or a funny side to it)
- a funny book, video clip, poem, game or song that helps them feel happier – ask a student to share their item with the class when things might not be going so well for other students.

Everybody has setbacks sometimes

Resources

✦ Books

Today Was a Terrible Day

Ronald Morgan's day begins by his teacher asking why he is crawling around under his desk like a snake, and all the children call him Snakey. The day gets worse – he gets into trouble and struggles to read. At the end of the day, the teacher assures him that tomorrow will be better.

Alexander and the Terrible, Horrible, No Good, Very Bad Day

Alexander wakes up to the start of a 'terrible' day, and from there everything that can go wrong, does go wrong. Some things are simply bad luck and others are a result of his own actions. At the end of this humorous story, the author normalises having bad times in your life.

✦ Film

Alexander and the Terrible, Horrible, No Good, Very Bad Day

Circle Time or classroom discussion

Prior to Circle Time, ask students to fill out **BLM Postbox Survey: Have You Ever?** You could also use the Bundling strategy (see page 91) and ask students to write down three things that make children their age feel really upset. Use one of the resources to discuss setbacks.

Discussion questions

- What are some of the bad things that happened to the character?
- How did the character manage the bad times?

Use the **BOUNCE BACK! e-tool** or refer to the **BOUNCE BACK! poster** for this lesson and the statement: *Everybody experiences sadness, hurt, failure, rejection and setbacks sometimes, not just you. They are a normal part of life. Try not to personalise them.*

- Write each of the following words on a card: sadness, hurt, failure, rejection, setbacks. Students take turns at pulling a card out of a box. Explain the concept where needed (e.g. rejection) and ask students to give an example of a situation where someone their age might experience this.

Unit 3 People bouncing back

- Ask each group to present their postbox survey results. How many people said yes? How many said no? What were some of the yes examples? (no names)
- Was anyone surprised at how many people said yes for the different questions in the postbox survey? What do the results of our survey show? (Everyone has problems, worries, setbacks and unhappy times sometimes.)
- Are there any people who never experience unhappy times, problems or worries? (No, it is normal to have them. No matter how hard you try to always have a good life, it is likely that you will face some problems sometimes.)
- If a day starts badly, will it be bad all day? (Not necessarily, but sometimes one or two things going wrong makes us look more for the bad things than for good things.)
- Why do people sometimes think they are the only ones who have problems or unhappy times in their life? (If people don't talk to other people about their hard times, they might think only they have problems and not notice other people's problems.)
- What are some of the unhappy things that occasionally happen to children your age? (Stress that life is mostly pretty good and often full of joy.)
- Some children think they are jinxed. What does this mean? (You wrongly think that lots of bad things only happen to you because of who you are.)
- Is it true that some children are jinxed? (No, it is just a result of unhelpful thinking. They are personalising instead of normalising; they are looking only for bad things and ignoring the good things that happen to them too.)
- Some children get an attack of 'I-can't-stand-it-itis'. What do you think that means? (It means they convince themselves that if they missed out on something, e.g. not going to the movies when promised, or something bad happened, e.g. their bike was stolen, that it would be the worst thing that could happen.)
- Is 'I-can't-stand-it-itis' another example of unhelpful thinking? What would be a more helpful way of thinking when you are disappointed?
- What do we mean by personalising a bad event? (Thinking that it happened only to you because of who you are rather than because those things sometimes just happen to lots of people.)
- What do we mean by 'it is the kind of thing that sometimes happens in life'? (It means it is normal.)

Activities

- In groups of three, students use the Postbox survey data (see page 155) to make a class graph and write a report.
- Students complete **BLM Helen Keller** and discuss the results.
- Students write a reflection in their journal (see page 101) on times when they have been able to bounce back after something has gone wrong for them.

Collective classroom research

Use the Collective classroom research strategy (see page 91) to research the many different ways in which people have bounced back from disabling conditions e.g. Paralympians. This could form the basis of an inquiry topic.

Blame fairly

Resources

◆ Books

Alexander and the Terrible, Horrible, No Good, Very Bad Day
See page 155.

But It's Not My Fault
Norman David Edwards, the young narrator, explains that sometimes things happen to him that get him into trouble when it's not his fault. When things go wrong, Norman always has an excuse but his mother teaches him the importance of being responsible for his actions.

Circle Time or classroom discussion

Read the following situation to students:

> Nicki and Khan are good friends. They are in the same basketball team and play together every Saturday. Recently, their team lost a semi-final by two points and they weren't able to get into the finals. After the game, they were all disappointed, but they thought differently about why they had lost the game. Nicki said it was all her fault that the team had lost, because she missed an important three-point shot. Nicki was really angry with herself. She was surprised to hear that Khan thought they had lost because two members of the team arrived late for the game and did not play well. Also, Khan thought it was bad luck that their team's best player was sick and couldn't play.

Explain that when things go wrong for you and you are trying to understand why, there are nearly always three kinds of reasons for it. Some of it happens because of:

- **Me** – what you do. What did Nicki do that could have been part of the reason for their losing the game? (She missed the shot.)
- **Others** – what other people do. What did other people do that could have been part of the reason for their losing the game? (Two players came late and didn't play well.)
- **Bad luck or the circumstances** – what was happening at the time. What bad luck or circumstances could have been part of the reason for their losing the game? (One of their best players was sick.)

Draw three columns on the board and label them:

- Me
- Others
- Bad luck or circumstances.

Ask students to pretend they are Nicki.

■ Does Nicki think her team lost because of what she did, or because of what others did or because of bad luck/circumstances?

■ How much does Nicki blame herself for the team not getting into the finals? A big amount, a middle amount or only a little amount?

Show on the board that Nicki says 'all me', 0 for others and 0 for bad luck, then draw a line across the columns.

■ How does Nicki feel when she thinks it's all her fault? Is she blaming herself fairly?

Then ask the students to pretend they are Khan.

- Does Khan think his team lost because of what he did (0), because of what others did (two team members late), or because of bad luck/circumstances (best player sick)?
- So, what does this show us? (Different people can see the same event in different ways.)

Use the **BOUNCE BACK! e-tool** or refer to the **BLM BOUNCE BACK! poster** for this lesson and the statement: *Blame fairly. How much of what happened was due to you, to others and to bad luck or circumstances?*

Discussion questions:

- What would happen if we always blamed ourselves unfairly when things went wrong in our lives? (We would be unhappy, we would give up and not try.)
- What would happen if we always blamed others when things went wrong in our lives? (We would not learn from our mistakes, we would not learn to take our share of responsibility, it might negatively affect our relationship with that person.)
- What would happen if we always blamed things on bad luck? (We'd think that there is nothing that could be done to control the situation or make things better.)
- What would happen if we always blamed fairly when things went wrong? (We'd look at three things: what we did wrong, what others did wrong and how much of what happened was due to bad luck or circumstances.)
- Can we always know why bad things happen? (No, sometimes there are reasons that we don't know about.)

Activities

▶ Have students individually work through **BLM Blame Fairly!** and discuss their answers. Students could also use the scenarios for role-plays using Good genie/Bad genie (see page 92).

Book analysis

Read *Alexander and the Terrible, Horrible, No Good, Very Bad Day* and discuss which things happened to Alexander: because of him, because of others and due to bad luck/circumstances. In pairs, students then find two things that were mostly Alexander's fault, two things that happened because of others and two things that happened because of bad luck/circumstances. Does Alexander blame fairly? How does he feel when he blames unfairly?

Responsibility Pie Chart

Students draw or make a Responsibility Pie Chart (RPC) (see page 107). They use the RPC to demonstrate how Nicki and Khan saw the situation differently. Students can also use the stories on **BLM Blame Fairly!** to draw an RPC for each story, or use their self-made RPC to show how much was due to themselves, due to others or due to bad luck/circumstances.

Embed it

Consider using the RPC to help students to take responsibility for their behaviour. Consider having a RPC for teachers on yard duty to use to help students take fair blame and accept responsibility for issues that occur during recess time.

Accept what can't be changed (but try to change what you can change first)

Resources

✦ Books

Emmanuel's Dream: The True Story of Emmanuel Ofosu Yeboah

Although he was born with one misshapen leg, Emmanuel Ofosu Yeboah accepted what he couldn't change and pursued life with a tenacity that helped him accomplish all that he set his mind to. Encouraged by his mother, he pursued his dreams regardless of his disability.

Since Dad Left

When Sid's parents separate, he feels very sad; but he starts to accept the fact that his Dad has left and his mood improves. Sid still has ambivalent feelings, but he starts to come to terms with the new arrangements.

Sometimes We Were Brave

In this book exploring courage, Jerome has to accept that his mother is a sailor in the navy and that her ship goes to sea for long periods of time. His dad and teacher help Jerome accept what he can't change when Mum is away, and bounce back when he's feeling down.

✦ Songs

'Que Sera Sera (Whatever Will Be, Will Be)'

> **Teacher reflection**
> Before this lesson, think about a time in your own life when you had to deal with a major change like moving house or starting a new job. What were some of the difficult aspects as well as positive aspects of this change in your life? What would you be comfortable to share with your students about your story?

Circle Time or classroom discussion

Begin the circle by asking students to quickly pass a greeting such as a smile and a handshake. Use the **BOUNCE BACK! e-tool** or the **BLM BOUNCE BACK! poster** for this session and the statement: *Accept what can't be changed (but try to change what you can first)*. Use a resource to introduce the topic.

Discussion questions

- What was something the character in the story couldn't change?
- What do we mean by 'accept'? (Understand that something won't change and acknowledge we have to live with it.)
- What was it that the character in the book couldn't change and just had to accept?
- Did the character do anything that helped them to feel better?
- Do you have a special place (or one in your head) where you can safely go when you feel upset so that you can be in a calmer place for a while?

Talk about how sometimes, when we can't change a situation we don't like and which has been upsetting us, we need to 'get away' from things for a while. But we need to do it in a useful not dangerous way. Sometimes getting away from what's worrying us helps us to keep things in perspective. Emphasise that really running away from what's worrying us isn't helpful and is very dangerous, but that sometimes you can 'run away' in your head by finding other things to think about or useful things to do. Sometimes you can find a special safe place to go to (e.g. your bedroom, a sunny corner of the garden).

- Was there anything the character could do to change the event they didn't want to happen? (No, they had to accept what they couldn't change. It is often hard to deal with something we don't like but sometimes we just have to.)
- How did they deal with the situation? Were these helpful or unhelpful things? Did they make things better or worse? (The main thing the character has control over is how they think about and how they deal with the situation.)
- What do we mean by 'making the best of things'? (Accepting things and finding any positives or good bits in a situation that we don't like.)
- What can we do if something happens that we don't like, but which we have no control over and have to accept? (Instead of being sad, angry or hurt, we can say to ourselves things like: 'That's the way things are and I will just have to put up with it. There's nothing else I can do to change things', or 'What's done is done and can't be undone. I will have to live with it, or 'I may find the good bits in this situation.')

Activities

▶ Complete the **What You Can and Can't Change e-activity** as a class.

Finish the reflections

In the circle students take it in turns to finish the sentences:

- One thing that I don't like but I have had to accept is …
- One thing I like to do that helps me feel better is …

Drama

▶ Students act out a scene from one of the books. They can use one of the BOUNCE BACK! statements and incorporate it in their dramatic enactment.

Puppet play

In small groups students can write a simple script and present a puppet play (see page 105) that demonstrates accepting an event that they can't change (e.g. having to have a disliked cousin share your room for a month, moving to another city, going to the dentist or doctor, having an operation).

Embed it

Journal writing: My quiet thoughtful place

Students write in their journal about their 'special place' where they go for comfort (in their heads or a special physical place) to manage something they have had to accept.

Catastrophising exaggerates your worries

Resources

✦ Books

Blossom Possum: The Sky Is Falling Down Under

In this Australian reworking of *Chicken Little*, something falls on Blossom Possum's head. Certain that the sky is falling, she races off to tell the Prime Minister. Along the way, Blossom Possum meets up with her friends, then the predatory By-Jingo Dingo tries to trick them.

But What If? A Book About Feeling Worried

Daisy and her family are about to move to a new house, which means a new school for Daisy. She is very worried about all the things that could go wrong. Her grandfather has some strategies to help her to stop catastrophising.

Circle Time or classroom discussion

Use the resources to introduce the concept of catastrophising. Bring some balloons and a pin to pop them with. Ask a student to come to the front of the class. Tell them you are going to need their help to show the class how you can make yourself feel really upset by catastrophising. Explain that this means thinking about the worst thing that could happen and believing that it will happen. Each time you say something catastrophic, the student blows up the balloon a bit more. These are the 'catastrophic' statements you make to illustrate that when you are catastrophising you keep imagining things getting worse and worse. For example:

- We are going on a boat to a nearby island.
- I'll probably feel sick on the boat. *(blow)*
- I'll probably throw up. *(blow)*
- I'll probably make a mess on somebody. *(blow)*
- There will be mess all over the floor. *(blow)*
- I will probably start to cry and feel embarrassed. *(blow)*
- The captain will get cross. *(blow)*
- They'll ban me from the boat. *(blow)*
- I'm not going on that boat! *(POP!)*

Try the scenarios of speaking at assembly, staying overnight at someone's house, going to camp, etc. Use the **BOUNCE BACK! e-tool** or refer to the **BOUNCE BACK! poster** for this session and the statement: *Catastrophising exaggerates your worries. Don't believe the worst possible picture.*

Discussion questions

- How did the character catastrophise their worries? What is catastrophising? (When we imagine the bad things that could happen, then convince ourselves that they will happen and start to behave as if they have already happened.)

- Why do we catastrophise? (We exaggerate how serious it is, we haven't been in this situation before so our imagination takes over and thinks the worst, we don't do a reality check by looking for evidence or asking other people or getting some more facts, we don't think of it as a problem that can be solved if we try.)

- How can we try not to catastrophise? (Do a reality check, check the facts, look at the good possibilities too, think about how likely something is to really happen, look at how to solve the problem so you don't make it worse and 'make mountains out of molehills'.)

Activities

- Students work in groups of three to act out one of the situations in **BLM Catastrophising!**
- The BLM situations can also be used as 'choose your own adventure' stories where students write two versions of an imaginative text on a theme. At some point, they give the reader two choices of decisions (e.g. the character does catastrophise or doesn't) and then the reader turns to the section with the ending that matches their choice.
- Students use the **Catastrophe Scale e-tool** to rate the seriousness of the situations in **BLM Don't Worry About the Small Stuff**.
- Students write an imaginative text about a character who catastrophises or create their own version of *Chicken Little*.

Keep things in perspective

Resources

✦ Book

Did I Ever Tell You How Lucky You Are?

This Dr Seuss classic is based on the advice of a wise elderly man who helps readers realise just how lucky they really are.

Circle Time or classroom discussion

Draw five circles on the board and label each circle: 'School', 'Family', 'Friends', 'Sports team', 'Hobbies'. Ask students to think about when one thing has gone wrong e.g. struggling with reading (represented by the 'School' circle). Does that mean everything else goes wrong too?

Read the book and use the **BOUNCE BACK! e-tool** or refer to the **BOUNCE BACK! poster** for this session and the statement: *Keep things in perspective. It's only part of your life.*

Explain that a person's perspective is their way of looking and thinking about something. Keeping things in perspective means keeping things in balance, and understanding that if one bad thing happens in their life, it does not mean that everything else in their life is spoiled. They may have a problem with a friend, but their family life is still fine, their pets are still terrific, their school work is still good, and their netball team is still playing well. Bad times are like a few threads in a jumper that have come loose. But the whole jumper hasn't fallen apart.

Activities

- Students make a poster, cartoon or painting that communicates the saying: 'Don't sweat the small stuff!'
- Students work in pairs to find as many small words as possible in the big word 'perspective'.

Keeping things in perspective circles

Students draw many small circles to show the different parts of their lives (e.g. school work, family, sport, clubs, pets, friends). Ask them to colour in one circle that represents a situation in which they have been worried or unhappy about something (e.g. they are worried about reading out loud in class). Then each student can turn to a partner and say, 'One part of my life in which I sometimes feel a bit worried is ____, but I'm not worried or upset about ____' and they read all the other categories in the circles that include things they are not worried about.

Don't worry about the small stuff

Make a copy of **BLM Don't Worry About the Small Stuff** for each student on light cardboard and ask them to cut out the statements. Ask them to make labels 'Small stuff', 'Middle stuff' and 'Big stuff' and then individually sort the cards into the three categories. They then compare their categories with two other students. What do they agree on? What don't they agree on? What does this tell us about the different things that people worry about?

Consolidation

Activities

- Ask students to write the ten coping statements in their own words and using their own design.
- Students make a door hanger for their bedroom door or a poster with the BOUNCE BACK! acronym. This could be a good ICT activity.
- Use the TEAM coaching strategy (see page 97) to help students to learn the BOUNCE BACK! statements to mastery level so they recall each statement correctly.

What do we think NOW?

Revisit **BLM People Bouncing Back: What Do You Think?** (pasted in their journals or collected) and ask students to complete the second column. As a follow-up, students write a summary of what 'Bouncing back' thinking has stayed the same and what 'Bouncing back' thinking has changed.

Bounce Back stories

Use **BLM Bounce Back Stories**. Students read one story in a group of three (alternatively, use the story in a whole-class setting). The students talk about how the BOUNCE BACK! statements can help the character in the story with their problem. Each group records their ideas and takes turns at telling the story and presenting the ideas to another group with a different story.

Students then write an imaginative text of their own in two ways:

- without using BOUNCE BACK! (like the stories provided)
- using BOUNCE BACK! statements.

Sequencing BOUNCE BACK! statements

Redo the **Missing Words: BOUNCE BACK! e-activity**, in which students correctly insert the words in each BOUNCE BACK! statement. Alternatively, give each pair of students five envelopes with two BOUNCE BACK! statements (cut into two or three parts) in each envelope. They paste their completed statements in order onto an A3 sheet.

Throw the dice

For more on this strategy, see page 98. Alternatively, use the **Reflections** or **Animal Asks e-tools** (and see pages 97 and 90) with this activity. The prompts are:

- Who are you most likely to talk to when you are worried about something?
- What is one way in which you are not 'perfect'?
- What is one thing in your life that you have learnt to put up with but you don't like?
- Tell us about someone you know who had a bad thing happen to them but who 'bounced back' from it (no names).
- What is one good way for someone to stop themselves from thinking about unhappy things when they can't sleep?

- Have you ever worried about something that you thought might happen, but it never did happen? What did you learn from that experience?
- Why is it helpful to concentrate on the good bits in a not-so-good situation?
- What do we mean by unhelpful thinking?

Games

Play these games with the whole class or in groups.

- **Cross-offs e-game** (see page 91). The secret message is 'It's normal to have setbacks and disappointments sometimes.'
- **Before or After? e-game** (see page 90).
- **Memory Cards e-game** (see page 93). Students match nouns with verbs or adjectives. The words are:

  bounce – bouncing

  concentration – concentrate

  perfection – perfect

  acceptance – accept

  thought – think

  sadness – sad

  fairness – fair

  help – helpful

  catastrophe – catastrophise

  trust – trustworthy

  exaggeration – exaggerate

  laughter – laugh

Bingo strips

Play Bingo strips (see page 90) or Bingo for pairs (see page 98) with a selection of these words:

again	helpful	problem
accept	luck	reality
back	mistakes	setbacks
bounce	nobody	support
catastrophise	normalise	talk
change	other	temporary
exaggerate	people	think
fairly	perfect	unhelpful
feelings	personalise	worries
gloomy	perspective	

BOUNCE BACK! game

Materials needed:

- two ping-pong balls for each student
- four large cardboard boxes (one for each team)
- paints or marking pens.

Steps:

- Before the activity, cut out ten holes in each box so they are large enough for the ping-pong balls to pass through easily. Label each hole with a large painted letter of B^1-O-U-N-C^1-E B^2-A-C^2-K.
- Divide the class into four teams and have them name their teams.
- Give each student two ping-pong balls. Allow students to take turns tossing the balls into the different letters. If they get the ball through the hole, they must say the BOUNCE BACK! statement for that letter accurately to get a point for their team.
- The team with the most points wins the game.

Bounce Back! award

Present the **Bounce Back! award** to students who have best demonstrated the capacity to bounce back after a setback.

UNIT 4

Courage

KEY MESSAGES

Everyone feels frightened sometimes.
Everyone feels frightened sometimes, even if they don't show it. When you feel scared, it is because you feel unsafe. There might be some danger. Don't ignore unsafe feelings. Tell someone you trust if you are feeling unsafe. They can help you work out whether the danger is real. Sometimes you need to be ready to move away or avoid real danger. At other times you need to face the fear, because there really isn't any danger – it has become exaggerated in your mind.

We don't all feel frightened by the same things.
We are all scared of some things and brave about other things. But different people are scared by different things. One person may be scared of going up a tall building, but not scared of speaking in front of the class. For another person it might be the other way round. You feel more nervous if you don't have the skills you need to do something. When you learn the skills, you feel less scared and more confident about doing it. For example, if you practise your speech at home before speaking in front of the class, you will feel less nervous and more confident about doing it.

Everyone feels nervous and worried sometimes too.
Anxiety is another word for feeling nervous or worried. It is a feeling that something bad might happen later. We often make ourselves nervous by exaggerating what could happen in our mind. (The issue of worry and anxiety is dealt with more extensively in Unit 6: Emotions.)

What is courage?
Courage means feeling anxious or frightened about something that you need to do, but finding a way to face your fear and deal with it and doing it anyway. Being brave doesn't mean that you have no fear. It's about facing your fear and not letting it beat you. Each time you overcome a fear you get braver and stronger and become more confident.

There are different kinds of courage.
There are three main types of courage:
- everyday courage
- one-off acts of courage
- heroism.

Everybody often needs 'everyday courage'. This is the courage you show when you have to do something that is 'ordinary' but it makes you feel a bit scared or anxious (e.g. trying something new). One-off acts of courage are more unusual situations where the risk is a bit higher (e.g. speaking up when an older student is teasing you). Heroism is when you risk your own safety or wellbeing so that somebody else can be safe (e.g. stopping other students from bullying someone). Often the best thing to do in this situation is to get help from an adult.

Some 'tough self-talk' is needed when you want to be brave.
'Tough self-talk' is when you say things to make yourself feel strong and brave, like:
- 'just do it'
- 'this is important'
- 'you have to do it'
- 'I know I can do this if I try hard'.

Being foolish, trying to show off or looking for silly thrills are not being brave.
Being foolish is doing something that is scary and dangerous to impress others. This is a foolish form of courage because it is not worth it. An example could be feeling scared but walking on a steep and slippery roof because somebody dared you. The risk is too high and you could be seriously injured, because you probably don't have the skills to do it properly. All you get is a chance to brag or show off, or to try to prove something. You don't have to prove anything to other people.

> **Learning objectives**
> In this unit, students will further develop their understanding that we:
> - all feel worried or frightened at times
> - need courage to face our fears.

Resources list

A complete list of resources including references for core and additional books, films, video clips, poems, songs and websites is available.

Everyone feels frightened sometimes

Resources

♦ Books

I Feel Frightened

The main character talks about his many fears, like spiders, the dentist and certain TV shows. The story includes strategies for managing fear, e.g. singing, telling yourself not to be silly, imagining yourself as a superhero and talking to someone you trust.

Caterpillar and Butterfly

In this tale, told in the tradition of Aboriginal teaching through fable-like stories, Caterpillar is always scared. One day she hides away by building a chrysalis around herself. When she emerges, she finds she is a beautiful butterfly and decides to try lots of exciting things with her friends.

Circle Time or classroom discussion

Read one of the books to the class.

Discussion questions

- What are some other words that mean 'scared'?
- What does fear feel like in your body? (Heart beating fast, flushed face, shaking.)
- What are some of the things the character was afraid of?
- What are some of the strategies the character used to manage their fear?

Ask students to pair up and discover one thing that they both find scary and one thing (each) that one of them finds scary but the other doesn't. Alternatively, they could complete a Venn diagram. Debrief back in the circle.

In the discussion that follows, emphasise the following points:

- Although some people try to impress others by acting as if they are never scared, everyone feels afraid or nervous at times.
- Fear is necessary to our survival as it warns us that there might be something dangerous that we need to deal with.
- You can talk yourself through most of your fears if you try.
- It is helpful to focus on what you will gain once you can deal with a fear.
- Having the skills to deal with a situation makes that situation less scary (e.g. a firefighter usually isn't afraid because they have the skills needed, and they have procedures to follow, so there is less danger).
- Many people surprise themselves and others by being braver than expected when it really matters or under certain circumstances.
- Why do we all feel scared sometimes? How is it helpful to us to feel scared? (It warns us that we might be in danger and that we should do a reality check – see Unit 3: People bouncing back.)

- What is one thing that you were scared of when you were younger that no longer makes you feel scared?
- Were you a bit scared when you first tried something new? Why? How did you make yourself feel braver?
- How have you helped someone in your family when they felt scared about something?
- When have you surprised yourself and been braver than you expected to be? How were you able to do that? Did you use 'tough self-talk'? What are some examples of 'tough self-talk'? (This isn't too bad. I can do this.)

The **Animal Asks e-tool** can be used with the questions above.

> **Teacher reflection**
> No matter how old we are, we all have times when we need everyday courage to have a go at something that we feel anxious about. Often teachers find it very easy to speak to a group of students but a lot more intimidating to speak to a group of parents. What situations do you find challenging and what strategies do you employ to deal with them? Do you use 'tough self-talk' and if so, what would you say to yourself? Are you comfortable to share one example with your students?

Activities

- Students make a class book (see page 101) about one thing that scared them when they were young but not now. They could write about this in their **Bounce Back!** journal (see page 101).
- Students draw what they think fear looks like.
- Students draw a two-frame picture to show themselves first being scared and then being the boss of their fear. They should add speech balloons to show their 'tough self-talk'.
- Students draw caterpillars and write a message about being brave and having a go.

Relaxation activities

Discuss with students how relaxing your body can help you to feel calm and better able to use 'tough self-talk' and face your fears. The following activities will help students to relax.

- Ask students to practise calm deep breathing (see Unit 6: Emotions).
- Students act like a floppy teddy bear and make every part of their body go limp.
- Ask students to tense and then relax one part of their body at a time (e.g. first relax your right foot, then your left foot, then each leg, your chest, your arm, and your eyes).
- Students choose a word (e.g. glad) and then go through the alphabet naming all the words that rhyme with that word (e.g. add, bad, dad).
- Students think about something that makes them feel happy (e.g. baby animals, going on holiday)

Take-home tasks

Night-time relaxation and reflection card

Students make up a 'night-time' card with these questions written on it. They can think about these things just before they go to sleep. The card might help someone else in their family to relax too:

- What was one nice thing that happened today?
- What is one thing I am looking forward to tomorrow?
- What is one good thing about my life right now?

- What is one good thing about my family?
- What is one safe thing about where I am?

Relaxation practice

Ask each student to select one of the strategies from the Relaxation activity on page 168 to practise at home until they get good at it. Encourage them to talk to their parents about their strategy and how they think it helps them to be braver.

We don't all get frightened by the same things

Resources

◆ Books

Not Afraid of Dogs

Daniel isn't afraid of spiders, snakes or thunderstorms, and constantly tells his family that he is very brave. But he *is* scared of dogs. When his mother agrees to mind her sister's dog Bandit, Daniel finds himself 'trapped', but manages to cope with his fears.

Come Down, Cat!

Nicholas's cat refuses to come down from the roof where she loves to sit late at night. He tries to catch her and bring her inside but with no success. Although he is frightened by what might be up on the roof, he gets a very long ladder to try to get his cat.

◆ Poems

Exploring

Screaming

The Longest Journey in the World

Circle Time or classroom discussion

Read one or more of the resources, then ask students, 'What helped the character overcome their fear?'

Use the People pie strategy, the Movers and shakers strategy or an anonymous Postbox survey (see pages 95, 94 and 96) and ask:

- Are you afraid of spiders?
- Would you bungee jump?
- Would you keep a snake as a pet?
- Do you like to have a night light?
- Can you swim in deep water without feeling scared?
- Do you feel nervous about speaking at assembly?
- Do you feel nervous when you have to go to the dentist?
- Do you feel nervous when you visit a friend's place for the first time?

In the discussion, stress that people feel more frightened of doing something if they don't have the skills to do it, or if they have had bad experiences before.

The **Animal Asks e-tool** (see page 90) can also be used with these questions or the ones below.

Discussion questions

- Why are some people frightened of things that other people don't find scary?
- Which animal do you think is the most scary?
- Are there any things that scare you that others aren't afraid of?
- Are there any things that don't scare you that many other children are afraid of?
- Does what has happened in your life (your experiences) make a difference to what does and doesn't scare you?
- What skills could help someone your age to feel brave and not be scared?
- Does a successful experience make a difference to how brave you can be? (e.g. if you have been able to put up with some pain when you fell over once before, is it likely that you can do so again?)
- If you don't already have the skill that would make a situation (e.g. giving a talk to the class) less frightening, what could you do about it?
- What kind of 'tough self-talk' could help someone who is scared, for example, of thunderstorms (see page 169 for other situations)?

Activities

- Ask students to write an illustrated reflection about where or when they have already been brave and where or when they would like to be braver.
- Have students complete the ranking activity in **BLM Which Is the Most Scary?** Students complete the task individually and then compare their answers with a partner. They could also discuss examples of 'tough self-talk'. Alternatively, choose any four of the situations on the BLM as a Four corners activity (see page 92).

Take-home task

Students take their illustrated reflections home and ask families to add their comments on where or when the adult family members themselves have been brave.

Everyone feels anxious sometimes

Resources

✦ Books

Clare's Goodbye

Clare's family is moving to a new house and she is very sad and anxious about what they have to leave behind. She returns to her old bedroom and dances a sad but cathartic dance to help her to find the courage to cope with her losses and to face the changes to come.

Don't Think About Purple Elephants

Sophie finds it difficult to go to sleep because her mind focuses on minor worries. Her mother suggests Sophie shouldn't think about purple elephants at night no matter what. Of course, Sophie can't stop thinking about cute purple elephants, and falls asleep more easily.

The Worry Glasses: Overcoming Anxiety

MJ worries all the time, until she learns how to take off her 'Worry Glasses' and take control of her anxious feelings.

♪ Song
'Open the Fear Door'

Circle Time or classroom discussion

Use one of the resources and discuss them with students. Introduce the concept of a 'wobbly'. Explain that a wobbly is a kind of anxious or worried thinking that everyone uses sometimes, but which is exaggerated. A wobbly often starts with 'What if?' Stress that it is important for people to argue with and challenge a wobbly, so they can make better and braver choices. Explain that people have two options for responding to a wobbly. One option is to let the wobbly beat them, i.e. they are overwhelmed by their worry about something that may never happen. The other option is to argue with it and use 'tough self-talk', e.g. 'Thunder is loud and scary but it's not going to hurt me.'

Discussion questions

- What are some of the wobblies the character had?
- What are some ways the character beat the wobblies?
- What might be some other examples of wobblies?
- What are some ways to stop your wobbly from beating you? (Talk to someone about it, remember a time when you were scared of the same thing but nothing bad happened.)
- What are some 'tough self-talk' words you can use? ('Bad times don't last.' 'Things always get better.' 'Unhelpful thinking makes me feel more upset.' 'I can do this; just do it', etc.)

Activities

- Follow up with students drawing a 'wobbly' that is trying to make someone feel scared about something. Then they can add a stick figure with a dialogue balloon that describes the person's 'tough self-talk' to argue with the wobbly.
- Students make a 'wobbly' from a variety of craft materials with a sign, such as 'My wobbly won't beat me'.

What is courage?

Resources

♦ Books

Courage

This book focuses on the many different kinds of courage. It stresses that most courage is of the everyday kind, like learning to ride a bike; protecting a brother, sister or friend; being asked to spell a really difficult word; or being the first to make up after an argument.

I Don't Want to Go

Joey is visiting his grandparents on his own for the first time and feels very scared about being away from home. But as a result of being brave and going, he ends up having some wonderful experiences.

♦ Song

'All About Courage!'

Circle Time or classroom discussion

Start by reading one of the books to the class. Then use the Bundling strategy (see page 91) and ask students to write down three things they can say about courage. Make a summary on the board. Ask students to take it in turns to tell of a time when they or someone else was brave. In the discussion that follows, stress that courage isn't about not having any fear. It's about feeling fearful or anxious, but then facing and dealing with the situation that is causing the fear or anxiety.

Courage can be:

- doing something that is difficult for you despite feeling fearful or anxious that you might not be able to do it well
- coping with new situations that you haven't been in before (e.g. staying overnight at someone's house)
- facing a new situation that might be a tiny bit risky, despite feeling a bit scared about it (e.g. learning to use the rock-climbing equipment at an outdoor school camp)
- managing to stay calm in an emergency in order to protect or help yourself and/or someone else.

Discussion questions

- What were some of the things the character was afraid of?
- What do we mean by courage?
- What is another word for 'courage'? (bravery)
- What was one thing the character did that showed courage?
- Who has seen a movie or read a book in which one of the characters was very brave? What was it called? How were they brave?
- When might someone your age feel fearful and then have to overcome that fear in order to be brave?
- Why do many very young children find it harder to be brave than older children? (Because they have fewer experiences of successfully being brave.)
- What is one thing that someone could say to themselves to help them to be brave when they are about to try something new, such as a new sport?
- What is one thing that someone could say to themselves to help them to be brave when they are about to do something, such as perform in a concert or speak at assembly?

The **Animal Asks e-tool** (see page 90) can also be used with the questions above.

Activities

- Make a class book with each student contributing one page about a time when they felt scared but they were brave (see page 101). It is important to stress that you can't be brave if you aren't scared to begin with.
- Have students write a 'choose your own adventure' story with a partner. Include two different options for the ending of the story. The imaginative text should feature a point where the character is faced with a fearful situation and has to decide whether or not to be brave.
- Have students make posters that say: 'Courage is not letting fear beat you.'

Drama

Showing courage

Act out scenarios that require courage (use students' ideas) and use the Good genie (you can do this if you try)/Bad genie (it's too scary, give up) strategy (see page 92).

Animals can be brave too

Resources

📖 ✦ Books

Herbert the Brave Sea Dog

This book tells the true story of a young boy, Tim, and his beloved dog, Herbert. One day they are on a boat with Tim's father, but the weather turns rough and Herbert is thrown into the sea. Thirty hours later they find him still paddling in the sea.

The Bravest Dog Ever: The True Story of Balto

When the train carrying medicine to an Alaskan town in the depths of a diphtheria epidemic was unable to get through the blizzards, a dog sled relay, led by Balto, travelled for nearly 24 hours without rest to get the medicine to the children.

🎞 ✦ Film

Balto

❄ Circle Time or classroom discussion

Read one of the books to the class and/or show the film or an excerpt. Use the Partner Retell strategy (see page 95) where students share a story about an animal they have seen or heard about who has acted bravely, even in a small way. It could be an animal they have seen on the news, in the newspaper, in a TV story or in a film (but not a cartoon character).

Discussion question

- Why would animals be brave? (Sometimes to take care of themselves, sometimes to help or protect other animals, their owners or other people.)

✏ Activities

- ▶ Students write and illustrate an imaginative text about a brave animal.
- ▶ Students complete **BLM Not All Heroes Are People** about Daisy the canine hero and share their responses. This could also be a take-home task.

Courageous animals

Students undertake an Inquiry-based learning project (see page 92) or prepare a talk on animals who have shown courage. Remind students to apply the definition of courage accurately (i.e. overcoming fear because something is worth it).

There are different kinds of courage

Resources

📖 ✦ Book

Rebel

A general invades a small village in Burma. As he is giving his speech to the unhappy villagers, he is hit by a child's thong. He orders his troops to search for the child who is wearing only one thong, but all of the children, and the teachers, have taken off their thongs and are now bare-footed.

✦ Song

'Courage Song'

Circle Time or classroom discussion

Read the book and explain to students that there are three different types of courage:

1 Small acts of 'everyday courage'

Everyone uses this type of courage to cope with some mildly challenging situations in their lives that happen quite a lot and are very ordinary. For example:

- speaking in front of the class
- meeting new people
- trying a new food
- owning up to something you have done wrong
- having the courage to be yourself
- telling someone who is being slightly annoying towards you to 'please stop it'.

2 Acts of 'one-off' courage or courage in an unusual situation

Explain the concept of 'one-off' to students. We may sometimes need to use this type of courage in an unusual or one-off situation where the level of risk or the chance of injury or hurt (this can include feelings) is a bit higher. For example:

- climbing over a fence to get a younger brother's lost ball
- performing a song by yourself at a school concert
- asking an older student to stop teasing you.

3 Being a hero (heroism)

Use the Lightning writing strategy (see page 93) ask students to write what they immediately think of when they hear the word 'hero'. Then explain that when someone is a hero it means that they risk their own safety or wellbeing so that somebody else can be safe. Standing up for someone who is being mistreated or who is being bullied is one example of this kind of courage. Sometimes it is foolish and dangerous to try to save someone else if the person does not have the skills or resources to do it, e.g. if you try to carry someone who is injured you could both get hurt. Often the best thing to do is to warn someone that there is danger or quickly get help from an appropriate adult.

Emphasise that very few people are ever in a position to be a hero. When someone is a hero, they are being selfless because they believe that it is worth risking their own life to save somebody else's life. These situations are very rare.

Discussion questions

- What is a hero?
- Who was a hero in the book? How did all the villagers work together to be heroes? What was the 'danger'?
- Who do you think is a hero? Why?
- Who do you admire or look up to? Are they a hero? (Gently challenge nominations of people who may be admirable or high achievers but who haven't done something that required overcoming fear and self-risking to help someone else. Often sportspeople are mentioned as 'heroes' in the media.)
- Can anybody become a hero?

- What is one act of everyday courage that you have done recently?
- Can you think of a time when either you or someone in your family had to do something that required 'one-off' courage?

Activities

Everyday courage

Students keep a diary for a week listing acts of 'everyday courage' that they do, for example:

- inviting a classmate that they don't know very well to their house
- putting up their hand to answer a question when they are not sure that they know the correct answer.

One-off courage

Students work with a partner to write a brief imaginative text about someone their age in a situation where they need to use 'one-off courage', for example:

- grabbing their pet dog to stop it from running on to the road
- yelling out to warn someone that there was a hole in the footpath they were about to step into
- telling a teacher that someone in your class was being teased and made fun of by other children and they needed support.

Hero talk

Students work in pairs to undertake an inquiry-based learning and/or class talk on someone they think is a hero. Before they begin working, make sure that students have understood what a hero is and have not just chosen someone whose achievements they admire. Emphasise that these people are worthy of admiration too but that 'hero' is not the right word (use the terms 'someone I look up to or admire' instead).

What type of courage is this?

Using **BLM Courage Cards**, ask each student to categorise the type of courage on the back of each card into everyday courage, one-off courage and being a hero. Students can then cut them out and decorate them.

The courage to be yourself

Resources

✦ Books

The Only Boy in Ballet Class

Tucker loves dancing. Uncle Frank tries to convince him that dancing isn't for boys, and pressures Tucker to play in a junior football game. Tucker manages to catch the ball and then uses dance moves across the oval to avoid being tackled and score the winning touchdown.

Spaghetti in a Hot Dog Bun: Having the Courage to Be Who You Are

Lucy enjoys unusual food such as spaghetti in a hot dog bun. One of her classmates, Ralph, makes nasty comments about how weird she is. Lucy's papa has taught her to treat others how you wish to be treated, so despite Ralph's nastiness, Lucy helps him when he's in trouble.

◆ Film

Babe

A farmer wins a piglet named Babe at a county fair. Babe is taken under the care of a sheepdog called Fly, who teaches him to herd sheep. The other animals don't readily accept him. The farmer enters Babe in a sheep-herding contest and, with a little help from the sheep, they win the prize.

Circle Time or classroom discussion

Read one of the books to introduce the topic. Alternatively, show *Babe* over two sessions or show relevant excerpts of the film. After each session, ask students to recount the story. Use the Think–ink–pair–share strategy (see page 97) and ask students to tell each other one way in which they are brave enough to be who they are, even if that means they are different to others in some ways in regards to things like:

- what they like
- how they think about things (e.g. specific films or preferred sports to play in or watch)
- what they enjoy doing.

Select some students to report back to the circle.

Discussion questions

- What do we mean by 'being brave enough to be yourself'?
- What did the character do that showed they were brave enough to be themself?
- How did the character have the courage to be themself?
- Why might it sometimes be a bit scary to 'be yourself'?
- Why do you sometimes have to be brave just to say what you really think, feel or like, or to dress the way you want to? (Emphasise that if you do have a different point of view, you still need to say it in a socially skilful way, not in an aggressive, antagonistic or stubborn way.)

Activities

Partner Retell about being yourself

Use the Partner Retell strategy (see page 95) with students describing one or more ways in which they have needed the courage to be themselves. Examples might be:

- having a preference for a specific kind of music (or film) which other students think isn't 'cool'
- playing a different kind of sport (e.g. water polo) or hobby from most of their peers
- preferring a food that other students don't like.

Survey on thinking differently

Conduct a classroom survey on students' perceptions of, for example, the:

- most interesting hobby or sport to play
- most interesting sport to watch
- best show on TV
- best type of lunch to take to school.

After results have been tallied, ask selected students whether or not their response was the same as, or different to the majority response on specific questions. If it was different, ask them to explain why they thought differently. After each example say, 'Thank you. It is always okay to think differently and have the courage to be ourselves.'

How to become braver

Resources

◆ Books

The Deep

Alice, the youngest of the family, is normally quite a brave little girl. However, she is afraid of the 'deep' water off the jetty where her family swims every day. One day she accidentally finds herself swimming beside some dolphins and this helps her to momentarily forget her fear.

Singing Away the Dark

Each winter, a young girl has to walk alone for some distance in the dark, often in a strong howling wind, so she can catch the school bus. Whenever she starts to feel scared, she finds courage by singing to herself as she walks.

Jess Was the Brave One

When Claire and Jess go to the medical clinic to have injections, it's the younger sister, Jess, who is the brave one. Claire is scared of dogs and many other things. But when Jess's teddy is stolen by some older children, Claire shows how brave she can be by standing up to them.

Circle Time or classroom discussion

Read one or more of the books to the class.

Discussion questions

- In *Singing Away the Dark,* how did the girl find the courage to complete her long walk?
- In *The Deep,* why was Alice able to feel braver when she found herself swimming with the dolphins?
- In *Jess Was the Brave One,* what did Claire do that was brave? What was the fear that she had to overcome?
- How did they talk themselves through her fear? What kind of 'tough self-talk' did they use?
- Did anyone else act bravely in this story?
- Is there anyone in your family who has helped you to be brave? What did they do?
- Did you ever have a toy or something from home that helped you to feel brave?
- How do you make yourself act bravely when you go to the dentist or the doctor?
- Does it help to have some skills, that is, to know how to do things? For example, would you feel braver about deep water if you could swim well? (Yes, because one of the solutions to being fearful is having the skills and practising them.)
- Who feels a bit nervous if they have to talk in front of the class? How about at assembly in front of the school? What could you do to help yourself be braver if you had to do this?

Ask selected students to tell of the kind of 'tough self-talk' that they sometimes use to help them to feel braver when they feel scared. Emphasise that 'brave builds brave'. Each time we overcome fear we get stronger and are more likely to be braver when we are next faced with fear.

Ask students to give examples of occasions when they have used one of the following strategies to feel more brave:

- Think about the good things that will happen if they can overcome their fear.
- Remind themselves of the previous times that they have succeeded at being brave.
- Stay calm and say to themselves, 'This is not so bad. I can do this.'

- Say, 'Just do it!' or, 'I can do this. It will be okay.'
- Go slowly and take it one step at a time.
- Consider whether they might be exaggerating the danger to themselves. Get a reality check. Find out the facts. What is the real truth? How dangerous is this really?
- Think of something funny, happy or safe to take their mind off the problem (e.g. night-time relaxation or relaxation activities such as reading).
- Take something with them (e.g. to camp) that makes them feel braver, such as a favourite thing or a photograph of their family or pet.

Activities

- Use the Quick quotes strategy (see page 96) with students commenting on what they do when they are scared and want to feel braver.
- Display and provide students with **BLM Giving a Talk**. Go through all the presentation tips. Then complete **Giving a Talk e-activity** with the class. Students then work with a partner and give a class talk on a topic linked to a current curriculum topic using the suggested hints in the BLM. Together they reflect on how well they did at each step.
- Students make a booklet about 'Good ways to help yourself be brave' using the ideas from Circle Time above and adding their own.
- Complete the **How to Be Brave e-activity** with the class or in groups.
- Individually or in pairs, students complete **BLM How Did They Do That?** and selected students share their responses with the class.

Embed it

Encourage students to remember to use 'tough self-talk' when they may be challenged by a situation, whether it is a difficult task, a performance, a presentation, etc. Practising or rehearsing the situation will also build confidence.

Being foolish and showing off is not being brave

Resources

✦ Book

Help Me Be Good: Showing off

This book highlights the inappropriateness of showing off by doing stupid or dangerous things and then boasting about them. It suggests more socially appropriate behaviours for enhancing social acceptance and friendships.

Circle Time or classroom discussion

Read the book and ask selected students for examples of people acting foolishly and taking risks in dangerous activities (e.g. diving into unknown water, riding a bike too fast, climbing onto a high roof, not swimming between the flags).

Differentiate between foolhardiness and risky sports. Emphasise that even though some sports are a bit risky, the people doing them usually have the skills, experience and equipment to reduce that risk. Foolhardiness is when you don't have the skills or experience, the danger level is unknown, and what you get out of it simply isn't worth taking that degree of risk. It isn't worth the risk just to get a 'thrill' or to show off and impress others.

Activities

- In pairs, students make an illustrated poster urging fellow students to think carefully before doing foolhardy things. Assist by giving examples such as: 'What do we do when we're at a surf beach? We always swim between the flags.'
- Students work in groups, select a sport or activity and research it to find tips on reducing risks. They can present their findings as a checklist, e.g. When riding a bike, wear a helmet, ride on bike paths, etc.

Consolidation

Activities

- Students complete **BLM Cross-offs** individually or in pairs (see page 91). The secret message is 'Even if you feel scared, have a go.'

Naming different kinds of courage

Use the **Animal Asks e-tool** (see page 90) with a selection of the following situations.

Ask students to first name the kind of courage (answers in brackets) they would use in the following situations, then ask what kind of tough or sensible self-talk would be useful. You may want to display a list of possible answers (see below) for students to select from.

- giving a classroom talk on a new topic *(everyday courage)*
- a strong swimmer and you jump into a pool to save a small child in trouble *(being a hero)*
- dressing in your own style despite two classmates laughing at you *(having the courage to be yourself)*
- playing inside a large drain with other children when there is fast-flowing water inside the drain after a storm *(being foolish not brave)*
- giving an opinion in class which no-one else agrees with *(having the courage to be yourself)*
- admitting to doing something wrong when asked about it *(having the courage to do the right thing even if there is a price to a pay)*
- answering a question when you are not sure you are correct *(using everyday courage)*
- having a go at a sport you haven't tried before *(having the courage to try something new)*
- putting up with the pain and discomfort of getting stitches *(having the courage to cope with something painful that could also scare you)*
- having the courage to let a teacher know when someone keeps teasing you in a nasty way *(having the courage to stand up for yourself when you are being mistreated)*
- having the courage to stand up for someone else who is being bullied *(standing up for what is right)*
- having the courage to admit when you are wrong *(having the courage to do something you find hard)*
- having the courage to say 'no, I don't want to' when someone wants you to take part in something that is against the rules *(having the courage to do the right thing)*
- stealing something because someone dared you to *(being foolhardy)*
- auditioning for the class play despite being nervous about performing *(having the courage to do a hard thing that scares you)*

Note: some of these could have different answers.

Key vocabulary

Use the Whisper game, Mystery square or the TEAM coaching strategy to assist students to learn vocabulary and spelling related to courage to a reasonable level of mastery (see pages 98, 94 and 97). Examples:

anxiety/anxious	nervous
brave/braver/bravery	risk/risky
courage/courageous	safe/safety/unsafe
danger/dangerous	scared/scary
different	self-talk
fear/fearful	skills
foolish	strong
fright/frightened	try
hero/heroism	worried/worry

Classroom statistics

The class collects and then graphs class statistics about aspects of courage and fear, such as:

- Which animal do you think is the scariest?
- Who is the first person you think of who has shown great heroism?
- What fears or worries might cause some students to be a bit nervous about going to a school camp?

Ensure that students can give their responses anonymously and privately.

Reflections

Using the Reflections strategy (see page 97) ask students the following questions:

- What used to frighten you when you were younger? How did you learn to deal with that fear?
- Tell us about a younger child you have seen being brave.
- Tell us about a time when you felt scared about something but did it anyway. How did you convince yourself to do it?
- What is the scariest thing you could be asked to do?
- What could you say to a younger child to help them feel brave when they need to have an injection or blood test?
- Are there some good things that you might have missed out on because you felt scared about making a mistake or looking silly?
- Tell us about a risk you took (even though you felt scared) and it made something good happen for you.

The media and courage

Students collect newspaper articles that reflect people using everyday courage, one-off courage, the courage to be themselves, heroism or being foolish. They are then displayed under the appropriate heading on the bulletin board. Ask students:

- How might this person have felt?
- Why did they do what they did?
- How do you think they made themselves be brave?

Courage survey

Use the PACE strategy (see page 95) to conduct a class survey on 'Which one of these five things would you need the most courage to be able to do?'

- speaking in front of a very large audience
- having an operation
- disagreeing with your friends about something
- auditioning for a role in the school musical or trying out for a team
- doing an important test at school.

Musical stop and share

Use the Musical stop and share strategy (see page 94) to ask questions such as:

- What do you think 'brave' means?
- What is another word for 'brave'?
- When do you feel a bit nervous?
- How do you feel about going snorkelling?
- Who is the bravest person you know?
- Who is the bravest person you have ever heard about or seen?
- When have you had to be brave?

Reflective journals

Students write in their **Bounce Back!** journals (see page 101) about times when they have been scared or nervous, when they have needed courage, and when they have been able to act courageously (and how they did so). They can also write about their observations of when others have shown courage (e.g. family members, classmates). Remind them that courage is about overcoming fear and doing something you would rather not do because it is scary, difficult or painful.

Cut-up sentences

Cut up the sentences below or use the **Cut-up Sentences e-activity** (see page 92).

- You need courage to do the right thing.
- It takes courage to stand up for someone who is being treated badly.
- Sometimes you need to use tough self-talk so you can be brave.
- Everybody has fears but not always the same ones.
- Sometimes it takes courage to be yourself.
- ▶ Play Big words, small words (see page 98) with one of these words: courageous, frightened or overcoming.

Drama

A sound story about fear and courage

Together with the class, create a fear and courage sound story. This is a story told only in sound effects. Two students leave the room for five minutes or so. The class then puts together and rehearses a story of courage and fear told entirely in sound effects. The two return to the room, hear the story and then work out the plot. The sound effects are performed in groups. Each group produces a different sound effect and tells the story in sequence. For instance, use a story about being frightened about going to the dentist, but then going anyway and handling it with everyday courage. There could be sound effects (but no acting) for the following:

- relaxation (ordinary heartbeats)

- the initial fear (rapid heartbeats) after a parent says it's time to go to the dentist (drill noise)
- travelling in the car (car door slamming, car travelling noises and then car stopping sounds)
- entering (door noises) the dental surgery with great fear (very rapid heartbeats)
- taking a deep breath and then walking in (deep breath and then walking noises)
- dentist says you have no cavities because you have been cleaning your teeth so well (positive 'mmm, mmm' noises and admiring by clapping)
- relief (sighs of relief).

Students can then create their own ideas for other sound stories based on the theme of fear and courage.

Puppet plays

Use puppets (see pages 105–106) with role-plays to act out situations in which 'everyday courage' is used to overcome fear (see page 174). Encourage the actors to make 'asides' to the audience to explain how they are thinking at each stage of the scene. Students could be asked to act out two ways to deal with the scenario – the courageous way and the non-courageous way. Then the class can guess which version was which. The Freeze frame and rewind strategy can also be used (see page 92). Here are some situations to use:

- You see other students saying mean things to someone in your class and blocking their way.
- You have to get along with an older cousin you have never met who comes to stay at your house for two months and shares your room.
- You do poorly on a test and then have to do another one the next day.
- You are a slow runner but you are expected to enter all the races for your age group at the school sports.
- You have to give a class talk on a hobby and you are very nervous about it.

Games

Play one of these games with the whole class or in groups.

▶ Play the **Before or After? e-game** with the class (see page 90).

▶ Play the **Memory Cards e-game** with the class (see page 93). The words are:

afraid	difficult	protest
bold	facing	risks
brave	fail	scary
bravery	fear	sensible
challenge	fearful	stupidity
choice	foolish	survive
courage	hero	worried
courageous	mistake	uncomfortable
dangerous	nervous	

Bounce Back! award

Present the **Bounce Back! award** to students who have shown everyday courage and had a go at something that made them nervous.

UNIT 5

Looking on the bright side

KEY MESSAGES

Bad times don't last. Things always get better. Stay optimistic.
Unhappy things and bad feelings always go away again, although it might take a bit of time for this to happen. Being optimistic means thinking that things will get better and that good things are more likely to happen than bad things.

Being optimistic means expecting that good things are more likely to happen.
You can get over unhappy, sad or worrying times in your life more easily if you look on the bright side. Because an optimist expects things to get better, they cope better and bounce back more quickly. If you think pessimistically, you don't expect things to get better and you are likely to stay upset longer.

Optimists use bright side thinking and pessimists use down side thinking.
When things go wrong, a pessimist says to themself: 'This happened because of me (I'm dumb, stupid, always unlucky). It will make everything in my life bad and it will keep on happening.' An optimist says to themself: 'I don't like this but it happens to other people too, not just me. Everything else is okay – it's just this bit that isn't good right now but it won't go on forever.' If you change how you think, you can become more optimistic and cope better.

Be a positive tracker and look for the good things.
A positive tracker is someone who is optimistic and always tries to look for the good things in themselves, in others, and in what happens in their life. Positive trackers are happier.

Positive trackers look for the small good bits in the bad things that happen.
Sometimes things happen that you don't like. You can usually find something good in the situation if you try. Sometimes the good thing is that it could have been worse. Sometimes the good thing is what you learnt from what happened.

Be thankful and grateful.
Be thankful for the kind and helpful things that other people do for you. Thinking about the good things that happen helps us feel happier and cope better.

It's important to stay hopeful when you have unhappy times.
Even the most optimistic person can find it hard to stay positive. Sometimes it takes a while to feel better. You will get over unhappy times in your life more easily if you stay hopeful and look on the bright side. If you stay hopeful, you are less likely to give up.

Good memories help us to bounce back.
We feel sad when we lose someone we love. Remembering some of the good times we shared with them will help us feel a bit better. (See also Unit 3: People bouncing back.)

Just because one unhappy thing has happened, it doesn't mean that everything else is spoiled too.
When one thing in your life goes wrong and you feel unhappy or worried, try to remember all the things that are still good in your life. It is just one thing that is not going well for a while, not everything. (See also Unit 3: People bouncing back.)

Make your own good luck.
People can help to create their own 'good luck' by:
- being hopeful that things will work out
- working hard
- using positive tracking.

These things can turn a not-so-good situation into a better one.

Give yourself credit for good results too.
If you are optimistic, you understand that good things happen because of the things that you did, not just because you're lucky. If you are pessimistic, you think that when good things happen, you just got lucky for a change and it was nothing to do with what you did.

> **Learning objectives**
> In this unit, students will learn to:
> - think positively and learn from their mistakes
> - be grateful for all the good things in their lives.

Resources list

A complete list of resources including references for core and additional books, films, video clips, poems, songs and websites is available.

Bad times don't last

Resources

◆ Books

Gleam and Glow

Two children, whose father has gone to fight in the Bosnian War, are given goldfish, Gleam and Glow. The children slip the fish into a pond when they must flee their home and on their return, find Gleam and Glow miraculously alive and well.

Baseball Saved Us

In this true story, a young boy called Shorty and his Japanese-born American parents are sent to an internment camp in Idaho during World War II. Shorty struggles to deal with the hardships, until he and his father create a baseball diamond and organise internee baseball teams.

Circle Time or classroom discussion

Read to the class and discuss one of the books. Use the **BOUNCE BACK! e-tool** and/or **BLM BOUNCE BACK! poster** and refer to the first BOUNCE BACK! statement: *Bad times don't last. Things always get better. Stay optimistic.*

Discussion questions

- What was the bad time or bad thing that happened in the story?
- How did the character(s) feel about this bad time?
- What positive steps did they take to try and make things better?
- Did it take a long time for things to get better?
- What might happen if you only focus on the bad time and what you have lost? (You continue to feel sad and unhappy.)

In pairs, students share with their partner one time they experienced a setback, sadness or disappointment but it didn't last forever and eventually went away. Ask some students to share their experience with the class, and emphasise that at the time they probably felt sad and unhappy, but eventually things did get better. Remind them not to be too disclosing. Debrief as a class and reinforce how good memories can help us bounce back. Things will get better and other parts of life are still good.

Activities

- Students write a personal reflection in their *Bounce Back!* journal based on the Circle Time discussion.
- Students complete a T-chart, identifying how bad times don't last and things get better. For example:

Bad time	Things get better
I have a bad cold.	If I rest, I will feel better soon.
We lost our match.	If we train hard, we can do better next time.

Bright side versus down side thinking

Resources

✦ Poems

I Asked the Zebra

Sour Face Ann

I'm Thankful

> **? Teacher reflection**
> Do you tend to be an optimist or a pessimist? Refer to page 187 to understand the research benefits in developing your skills in being optimistic and a positive tracker. Can you think of some opportunities to model these skills for your students?

Circle Time or classroom discussion

Read one of the poems to the class and explain that we can look at the same situation from two different sides: the 'bright side' or the 'down side'. Refer to Key messages (see page 183) to explain the idea of thinking optimistically and pessimistically. Emphasise that pessimists see life as mostly negative (the down side) while optimists see life as mostly positive (the bright side).

In pairs, students take turns reading the stories of Jack and Ryan from **BLM Bright Side Versus Down Side Thinking** or read them as a whole class.

Explain these stories show that people have a choice about how they think. They can use 'bright side' (positive and helpful thinking) or 'down side' (negative and unhelpful) thinking about a setback.

Jack and Emily think like a pessimist. They think:

- **Me**: This unhappy situation has happened because of 'me'. (No-one likes me so it must be my fault.)

- **Everything**: It is affecting everything in a bad way. (Jack hates everything about his new school and Emily glares at everyone.)

- **Always**: The situation will go on and on and can't possibly get better. (Jack does not expect that the situation can be changed by anything he does and Emily thinks it's never going to get any better.)

Christie and Ryan think like an optimist. They think:

- **Not just me**: This type of unhappy situation is sort of normal and happens to others too. (It's not just happening because of 'me'.)

- **Not everything**: This isn't affecting everything in my life; some of it is going okay. (I have made friends in the street.)

- **Not always**: This situation won't last forever. Things will get better soon, especially if I try some strategies to see if I can make a difference.

Use the **Animal Asks e-tool** (see page 90) with a selection of the discussion questions that follow.

Discussion questions

- What were the bad times that happened to the characters?
- Which characters are positive and expect things to get better? (Ryan, Christie)
- Which characters are negative and expect things not to change or even get worse? (Jack, Emily)
- Who thinks he/she will never make friends? (Jack, Emily)
- Who thinks other people would find it difficult to make new friends at a new school too? (Ryan, Christie)
- Who makes this one bad situation affect everything else in their life? (Jack, Emily)
- Who is able to think of some things that are okay in his/her life? (Ryan, Christie)
- What did Ryan do differently to Jack? (Ryan brings a ball to school, looks friendly, talks to other kids, cooperates. Jack looks glum, glares, says he hates school, is uncooperative.)
- What did Emily and Christie do differently?
- Did the 'bad times' last for all the characters?
- Who stayed hopeful in this story? How did they show that they were still hopeful that things would get better? (Ryan, Christie)
- What happened as a result of the different ways that each person acted?

Activities

▶ Play Big words, small words (see page 98) with one of these words: pessimist, optimist.

Story writing

▶ Students write an imaginative text or a poem or create a simple script for a dramatic performance on bright side versus down side thinking.

Drama

Each scenario on **BLM Drama: Looking on the Bright Side** has a positive and a negative version. Photocopy them onto card. With a partner, students take turns at pulling out a card from a lucky dip box and then acting out that response. The class guesses whether the student is using bright side optimistic thinking or down side pessimistic thinking.

Being a positive tracker

Resources

✦ Books

Rain Brings Frogs

Nate is a boy who always finds a way to see the bright side of life. When others complain that it is raining, Nate is happy about the frogs that the rain brings. Other people might not be able to find anything to do but Nate is always happy to just enjoy the view.

Zen Tails: Are You Sure?

Gilbert B. Beaver experiences some unhappy situations but finds that sometimes there is something good in them. You never know how things are going to turn out.

♪ Song
'Accentuate the Positive'

> **Teacher reflection**
> Are you a positive tracker? A positive tracker hunts the good things in their day, even the small good things such as really savouring a nice drink, reflecting on getting a good run in the traffic so you get to work with time to spare, enjoying a conversation with a student or a colleague. Focusing on the small good things in your day has shown to be a reliable way of boosting your positive emotions and hence your sense of wellbeing.

Circle Time or classroom discussion

Use one of the resources to start a discussion about positive tracking. Discuss what 'being positive' means. Talk about positive tracking (finding the positives in oneself, in another person or in a situation, no matter how small).

Discussion questions

- Which character used positive tracking and when?
- When could positive tracking have been used?

In the circle students practise being positive trackers by sharing some of the good things that have happened in their day so far. Start by giving an example from your own day. Then ask each student around the circle to share one good thing that has happened for them today (tasty breakfast, got to school early, played with their dog etc.).

- What are some reasons why it is better to be a positive tracker? (They are liked more by other people, they feel more confident, they do better in their school work because they don't give up when faced with a problem, they are better able to cope with 'bad patches' in their life, they have better health.)

- What are some of the reasons why it is not good to be a negative tracker? (We don't warm to them as much because we know that they're watching for our mistakes or what we are not good at, not our strengths, and we tend to avoid their company; they tend not to do as well as others at school work because they give up easily when they can't do something; they don't feel confident.)

Do a Multiply and Merge (page 94) where everyone writes four good things about the class. Emphasise that the positive things might be quite little, such as having a particular story read, singing a song, playing a game, doing a favourite or fun activity, or doing something for someone.

> **Teacher reflection**
> **Giving positive feedback**: It's quite natural to like some students more than others. However, how you verbally and non-verbally communicate with different students can reveal biases that you may not even be aware of. Consider tracking the following over time:
> - Who do you call on (based on gender, ethnicity, etc.)?
> - What is the tone of your responses (i.e. the ratio of positively to negatively worded comments)?
> - What is the content of your feedback (i.e. specific and concrete responses vs. general and/or dismissive responses)?

Activities

- Students complete **BLMs What Would a Positive Tracker Think Here?** and **What Kind of Tracker Is This Person?** These could also be take-home tasks. Discuss responses as a class.

- Each group presents their Multiply and Merge (see page 94) findings from Circle Time on the best things about the class. They then make a class poster called 'The best things about our class (or school)'. Alternatively, each group can provide two slides of positive images (scanned photos of good activities, class celebrations etc.) or illustrations and write captions for a class digital book (see page 101).

Positive tracking colour quiz

Have students complete **BLM Positive Colour Quiz**. Photocopy one copy onto white card for each student. Each student will need coloured pencils to colour in the 18 cards as indicated. Then they cut out the cards. For each number, they choose the card which is more like them and put it in a pile. Then they paste all their chosen pink, red or purple cards in one column and all the green, blue or yellow cards in another column. They record how many cards they have in each column. Are they more like a positive tracker (i.e. they chose six or more reds, pinks and purples) or a negative tracker (i.e. they chose six or more blues, greens and yellows)? They can then write how they will use positive tracking more in their **Bounce Back!** journal. Stress that many students are already doing a good job, but we can always improve.

Positive tracking Inside-outside circle

Use the Inside-outside circle (page 93) or **Animal Asks e-tool** with this positive tracking activity (see page 90).

Repeat regularly with different positive questions.

- What is one good thing about today?
- What is one good thing about different seasons?
- What is one good thing about this month? (or term)
- What is one good thing about going to school?
- What is one good thing about our class/classroom?
- What is one good thing about our school?
- What is one good thing about living in the town/city where we live?
- What is one good thing about our country?

Be a class positive tracker detective

Conduct a Partner Retell (see page 95) at the end of a unit of work or at the end of the day. Ask students to track the good things about the topic or day and share with a partner:

- one new thing they learned
- one thing that interested them
- one thing that was fun to do
- one way someone helped them or shared something.

The negative aliens Negabelle and Negatar

Ask students to imagine that a spacecraft has crashed and two aliens from the planet Neg have landed in your school playground. These two aliens, a girl called Negabelle and a boy called Negatar, can speak English. They have one antenna on their heads that can 'track' only the bad things in a situation. They have no ability to track positives. Your class has been asked to teach them how to become positive trackers so they can live with people for a while and then find a way to get back to their planet. Build drama, writing, arts and technology activities around this theme, whereby two members of the class accompany the aliens through different situations acting as their 'positive translator'.

For example, Negabelle and Negatar:

- spend a day at school
- attend a party
- come along on a school excursion, e.g. to the zoo
- go swimming
- play a sport or join in on one of your hobbies
- attend school camp
- go shopping
- try to make friends.

Game

Positive tracking game

Each student draws a picture with ten items in it. Then, without showing their picture to their partner, they instruct them to draw the same picture by giving only positive instructions and feedback as to where the items are located in the picture. They can say, 'Draw the trunk of a tree on the right side of the picture. Yes, that's right, now draw three branches'. They can't say, 'No, the tree is all wrong' or other negative feedback. Emphasise that being positive is a more helpful and successful way to teach someone something. You could use the **Coin toss e-tool** to decide which person in the pair goes first.

Take-home tasks

Track the good things in your day

Send a note home to families asking them to encourage their child to think about positive things in their day: 'Just before they go to sleep, ask your child: "What were three good things that happened for you today?" If they can't think of anything, ask them some prompting questions, e.g. "What did you laugh about? Who did you enjoy being with? What activity did you like doing?" Remind your child that it can be any little good thing like playing outside, etc.'

Journal: Family positive tracking

Have students record in their **Bounce Back!** journals the positive incidents that occur in their family. Follow up in Circle Time or as a Partner Retell (see page 95) with each student sharing one good thing that happened in their family this week.

Embed it

On-the-spot positive tracking

Whenever possible, use situations that occur in the classroom or playground to keep students practising positive tracking (hunting the good things), e.g. when no-one remembers to feed the class budgie for a day, say: 'Well, it wasn't a good thing to happen. Let's see if we can use some positive tracking here. Any ideas?' (At least there was some seed in his feeder left over from the day before.) Have we learnt anything useful here? (We've learnt that we have to come up with a better way of reminding ourselves to feed him.) Encourage students to do the same by asking about any negative event they encounter: 'Was there any good side to this that you can see?'

Give positive feedback

Teach students to give positive feedback on classmates' performances in class (e.g. morning talk, drama, role-plays, talks). After each performance, ask the class only two questions:

- What did this person do well?
- What is one thing they could do next time to make it even better?

It is also helpful to develop simple rubrics as a class related to each classroom activity/task (e.g. writing an imaginative text or doing an oral presentation) and ask students to use these to give peer feedback.

Partner Retell: Two good things in your day

Regularly conduct a Partner Retell (see page 95) at the end of each day where students share two good things about their day. Remind them that they only need to be small good things like sharing a fun game with someone, enjoying a classroom activity, etc.

Being thankful and grateful

Resources

✦ Books

And Here's to You!

This book focuses on the diverse things in the world that we can be grateful for and celebrate.

For All Creatures

This picture book celebrates the beauty and wonders of all animal life.

My Gratitude Jar

Miss Lane's students fill a gratitude jar with strips of paper describing everyday small things they are grateful for. One student having a bad day, bounces back after reading the paper strips in his jar.

✦ Video clips

What Does it Mean to Be Thankful?

A video clip about all the things we are thankful for – family, music, friends, etc.

My Gratitude Jar

✦ Songs

'The More We Get Together, the Happier We'll Be'

'I Am Thankful'

(to the tune of 'Yankee Doodle Dandy')

> I have some special favourite foods
> My mum cooks them for me
> She always treats me very well
> I'm thankful for my mum.
> (*Chorus*)
> There are lots of special things
> We can all be thankful for
> People, places, pets, police
> And many many more.

I am thankful for my sister
Even though she stirs me
She always lets me share her drink
Whenever I feel thirsty.

I am thankful for my teacher
Telling us great stories
He also tells us awful jokes
But he's never boring.

I am thankful for my dad
He comes to see my games
He always yells out far too loud
I love him just the same.

I am thankful for my gran
She likes to play Monopoly
She shows me how to clean my shoes
So I can do them properly.

I am thankful for my dog
He takes me for a walk
Though when he stops at every tree
I feel like such a dork.

I am thankful for the beach
In sunshine and in rain
The sand gets in my bathers but
I wash it out again.

I am thankful for police
They're trying to stop the crime
They help us all to feel more safe
It takes a lot of time.

Circle Time or classroom discussion

Begin the topic with the video clips and ask students to look for two good reasons for keeping a gratitude jar. Share the following examples:

- When we take time to be grateful, we feel happier.
- We can bounce back more quickly when we feel unhappy if we go back to our gratitude jar and think about the things that make us grateful.

Discuss what gratitude is. Explain that there are two kinds of gratitude:

- appreciating and feeling grateful for what another person has done for you, e.g. by being kind, helping you
- being grateful for the good things in your life, e.g. your home, your family, your class, your pet, going on holiday.

Go around the circle and ask each student to share one thing they are grateful for. Then ask each student to trace around their hand and then write four things they are grateful for (one on each finger and a smiley face on the thumb). Encourage them to focus more on the actions and behaviour of people rather than on material things. Also encourage them to be specific: what did the person do that made things better for them? For instance, instead of 'I am grateful for my family', they could write:

- I am grateful to Dad for picking me up from school because it was raining.
- I am grateful to Aisha because she helped me when I tripped and grazed my knee.
- I am grateful for my dog because he's fun to play with.

Activities

- Each student writes one thing they are thankful for on a large piece of paper. Take a picture of the student holding up their paper, frame the photo and send it home as a holiday gift.
- Students cut out pictures of things they're grateful for and then use the pictures to create their own collage or to decorate a classroom gratitude bulletin board.
- In pairs, students make a two-minute video of the people they feel grateful to, showing examples of grateful thinking.
- Make a group or class collage display of 'People we are thankful for', using pictures or drawings of people from the school and wider community.
- As a class, sing 'I Am Thankful'. In pairs students write a verse for the song, or a verse for a poem similar to the song.
- Read the book *And Here's to You!* (see page 190) and follow up with students making a class 'Here's to ...' book along the same lines.

Embed it

Appreciation station

Have a weekly classroom 'Appreciation station' in Circle Time where students chant, 'Two, four, six, eight, who do we appreciate?' or sing the song 'The more we get together, the happier we'll be'. Then each student shares one action that they are grateful for and specify the person involved, for example:

- I appreciate my dad taking me to sports training.
- I appreciate Samir and Emma from Year 6 helping me with my story.

Letters of gratitude

Encourage students to prepare and send emails, cards or letters to express their gratitude for what others have done for them or the class, or for the love, friendship or support they have shown them. For example:

- Thank you for being my friend and waiting for me if I am late getting out of class.
- Thank you, Mum, for looking after me when I was sick.
- Thank you for being my grandma. You always have time to play card games with me.

Whenever an opportunity arises, send a whole-class message of appreciation and gratitude (e.g. to helpers on an excursion, to the IT staff for the speedy repair of malfunctioning equipment, to another teacher for the extra work they did, to a local business for the donation they made to the class stall at the fête etc.). This could be extended to include the local community, e.g. police, hospital, tradespeople etc.

Appreciation notice board

Create a class 'Appreciation notice board'. Keep sticky notes or circles of coloured paper that students can pin on the board. Students write a note to someone in the class who are grateful to and stick it on the board.

Gratitude jars

Follow up on *My Gratitude Jar* by asking students to bring a plastic jar to school (suggest a particular size). They could decorate it with paint, stickers, etc. Have lots of slips of different coloured paper for students to write their gratitude notes.

Classroom gratitude book

Create a gratitude book to send home with a different student each week. Ask each student's family to add a page of pictures and descriptions of what they're grateful for. At the end of the year, celebrate the completed classroom gratitude book.

Being hopeful

Resources

◆ Books

I Want My Hat Back

Bear has lost his hat but he is hopeful that he will get it back. He asks each animal he meets if they have seen it, but when none of them has, Bear starts to lose hope. A deer asks him to describe his hat, which triggers Bear's memory of seeing another animal wearing it.

The Spirit of Hope

This book is about a family that is ordered to leave their home to make way for a new factory. They desperately struggle to find a new place before the deadline, keeping up the 'spirit of hope'.

◆ Songs

'Somewhere Over the Rainbow'

'Rainbow Connection'

Circle Time or classroom discussion

Use the resources to discuss the concept of 'hope'. Explain that hope is linked to optimism or 'bright side thinking'.

Discussion questions

- What does 'hope' mean? (The belief that something you want to happen is still possible, even if it doesn't look as if it will.)
- In what ways were the characters in the books or songs hopeful? Did they give up?
- Tell us about a time when you stayed hopeful that things would turn out okay and they did.

Point out examples where staying hopeful meant that the student didn't give up.

- What are some things that you can do to help you feel more hopeful? (Remember the BOUNCE BACK! acronym, talk to someone about the thing that is troubling you, 'picture' in your mind things turning out as you'd like.)
- Why is it important to have hope when things are difficult? (You're more likely to stay optimistic and not give up.)
- How does staying hopeful help you to plan for something and hence make it more likely that what you want to happen will happen? (Having hope that something will happen helps us to set goals and to think about what we can do to make those goals happen.)

Activities

Partner Retell
Students do a Partner Retell (page 95) about something they are hoping will happen and share one thing they could do to help make it happen and achieve their goal. Remind the partner to be a good listener as they will share their partner's answer to another pair or to the whole class if time. (Goal setting and planning are addressed in Unit 10: Success (CHAMP).)

Hope mobile
Students make a collage or a class poster featuring drawings of something in their future turning out the way they'd like, such as passing a swimming test or a pet recovering from being sick.

The hopeful book
Students make a book which shows a 'before' picture and then a positive 'after' picture. They can draw their own pictures or find pictures in magazines or on the internet. You could also make lift-up flaps or circular rotating lids with this activity with a 'before' image on the top lid or flap and an 'after' image underneath (see page 103). Here are some suggestions:

Before	After
rainy miserable day	a rainbow and the rain starting to ease
new at school and lonely	happy and playing with others weeks later
being unable to swim at start of holiday	swimming okay at end of holiday
drought (dead plants and animals)	rain (new growth, animals thriving)

Rainbows as symbols of hope
The experience of seeing the beautiful and vivid colours of the rainbow in the light that occurs when the sun is shining after it has been raining is magical and uplifting. Students make rainbows using digital drawing/painting software.

Class rainbow
Students, working in pairs or threes, make a big class rainbow on the floor with rainbow-coloured objects. They start first by arranging the red objects in a big arch, then the yellow objects, and so on until the rainbow is completed.

Class handprint rainbows
Materials needed:
- red, orange, yellow, green, blue and purple construction paper or paint in these colours
- a large roll of neutral-coloured paper or space on a bulletin board
- scissors and glue to share
- pencils.

Steps:

Each student traces their hand on one piece of construction paper. Make about ten handprints of each colour. The students cut out the handprints and put their name in the centre. Glue the handprints onto the paper (or staple onto the bulletin board) in a rainbow shape.

Alternatively, students can paint their own hands and press them directly onto the roll of paper in a rainbow shape. Or they can paint their own hands, press them on light card and cut out the shape of their hand. The hands can then be arranged in the rainbow shape.

Rainbow mobile

Materials needed:

- white paper plate per student
- felt pens/crayons in rainbow colours, plus paper and some coloured paper
- glue, scissors and a hole punch to share
- string.

Steps:

1 Cut a white paper plate in half and draw a rainbow on it.
2 Punch three holes in the plate: one at the top, and one at each end of the rainbow. Attach a piece of string to the top hole.
3 Students make different things from coloured paper, such as a cloud, a shamrock, a pot of gold and a sun (with a smiley face), and hang them from each end of the rainbow using the string.

They could also make a mobile with the sun at the top, then a cloud, and finally the rainbow.

Making your own good luck

Resources

✦ Books

The Duck with No Luck

A duck oversleeps and misses flying south for winter with the rest of the flock. He tries to find his way south, but no matter what he does disaster follows him and he eventually arrives at the North Pole instead! He always stays optimistic and is able to make the best of a bad situation.

Sarindi and the Lucky Bird

When Sarindi's father has an accident and loses his contract as a becak (auto-rickshaw) driver, his solution is to buy a lucky bird to change their luck. Sarindi's mother's solution is to make their becak more attractive to customers. Together the family works to change their luck.

Circle Time or classroom discussion

Begin the topic by asking: 'Do you think there is such a thing as good luck?' Explain that scientists have found lucky people make their own luck. Lucky people do four things to help themselves be 'lucky'. Write the four luck factors on the board and unpack unfamiliar vocabulary:

1 A lucky person is open to new experiences and opportunities.
2 They listen to and act on hunches.
3 They expect good things to happen (hope).
4 They turn bad events into good ones.

Read *The Duck with No Luck* and use the **Animal Asks e-tool** (see page 90) to ask the questions over.

Discussion questions
- What was the bad event?
- How did the duck turn that bad event into a good event?
- How could things have been worse for the duck?
- In what way was the duck hopeful that things would work out?
- In what way was he open to new experiences and made the best of a bad situation?

Read *Sarindi and the Lucky Bird* and discuss the following questions.

- Although Sarindi's family was poor, they felt there were many good things in their lives. What were some of these good things?
- Was the new work that Father found a result of good luck or good planning and hard work?
- What might have happened if Father had just kept on worrying and not doing anything?
- What are some of the good things in your life?
- What are some of the good things you and your family like doing together?
- How have you helped yourself to be luckier? (e.g. wanting to get into a team so practising harder; wanting to be friends with someone so making an effort to talk to them.)

Emphasise it's important to credit yourself for good results. Good outcomes or results are often because of what you did (rather than didn't do), e.g. I'm really proud of myself because I worked really hard on my project. That's why I got a good mark.

> **Teacher reflection**
> Are you an optimist who expects good things more than bad to happen? Do you maximise opportunities and are open to new experiences and opportunities e.g. networking and meeting people that might help you? Do you listen to your intuition and act on hunches and gut feelings about what seems the right thing to do? Can you turn a bad event into a good one? Can you think of a time when you made your own good luck? Can you share this story with your class and link it to the four luck factors?

Activities

- Give each student a sheet of A4 paper. Get them to fold it into four sections, and label each with one of the four luck factors. Then they write in each section the things the duck or Sarindi's family did to show each luck factor.
- Students complete the sentence stem, 'I am lucky because …' and illustrate their responses. Encourage students to refer to the four luck factors. Display students' work around the classroom.

Consolidation

◆ Films

There are many suitable films with themes of hope and optimism. Ask students to recommend optimistic videos to show when the class needs a 'positive boost'. Ask them to outline why they think the film is optimistic. This reinforces their understanding of positive tracking and staying hopeful. Some suggestions:

- *Paulie* – the story of a talking parrot who is separated from his owner but who never gives up hope of finding her.
- *Annie* – the film version of the stage musical in which the little orphan girl, Annie, is perpetually hopeful.

Encourage students to look for the positive trackers and what they do when they are positive tracking, as well as where the characters stayed hopeful. Make the link between any happy endings and the fact that the characters stayed positive.

Activities

▶ Whenever a student comes up with a good idea, place it on a 'bright ideas' board, written on a cut-out light globe with the student's name.

Reflections

Use the following questions to run a Reflections activity (see page 97) or use the **Reflections e-tool**. You could also use the **Animal Asks e-tool** or Throw the dice with this activity (see pages 90 and 98).

- Why is it helpful to concentrate on the good bits in a not-so-good situation?
- What is one thing you can say about optimistic thinking?
- What is one thing you can say about pessimistic thinking?
- What is meant by 'the harder you work, the luckier you get'?
- What is a positive tracker?
- What is a negative tracker?
- What is 'gratitude' and why is it important to show it?
- Why do people like positive trackers more?

Key vocabulary

Use the Whisper game, Mystery square or the TEAM coaching strategy to assist students to learn vocabulary and spelling related to looking on the bright side to a reasonable level of mastery (see pages 98, 94 and 97). Examples:

bad	grateful	luck	pessimistic	think
better	happier	lucky	positive	tracker
bright	happy	negative	right	unhappy
cope	helpful	optimism	sad	upset
down	hope	optimistic	sometimes	worse
good	hopeful	pessimism	thankful	wrong

Games

Play one of these games with the whole class or in groups.

▶ **Before or After? e-game** (see page 90)

▶ **Memory Cards e-game** (see page 93) – students match synonyms and antonyms. The words are:

lucky – unlucky

bright – dark

optimistic – pessimistic

up – down

positive – negative

happy – sad

better – worse

sometimes – never

good – bad

hopeful – hopeless

grateful – ungrateful

helpful – unhelpful

▶ Complete the **Cross-offs e-game** (see page 91). The secret message is 'It feels good to be a positive tracker.'

Bounce Back! award

Present the **Bounce Back! award** to students who have best demonstrated being optimistic, using positive tracking, showing gratitude or being hopeful.

UNIT 6

Emotions

KEY MESSAGES

Feelings are important and needed, even the unpleasant ones.
Everyone has lots of different feelings every day. Feelings are natural, important and useful to us, even the unpleasant and uncomfortable ones. Pleasant feelings (such as pleasure, pride, excitement) help you to understand the things that make you happy. Happy feelings also help you to cope better when you make a mistake or have a setback. Angry feelings act as alarms that tell you that you might need to defend yourself because you are being treated badly. Feeling scared warns you about possible danger and makes you protect yourself by telling someone.

Understand yourself better by knowing how you are feeling and how to name your feelings.
Sometimes you might make a mistake about the name of the feeling you are having. For example, you might think you are feeling angry when you are really feeling scared. The feelings in your body can be similar. Sometimes you can make a mistake about how strong a feeling is too. For example, you may think you are really, really angry when you are just annoyed or disappointed. Giving the right name to your feeling helps you to better manage your feelings, or to be the boss of your feelings.

You can boost positive feelings.
The more you feel pleasant emotions, the happier you will be. You will also be able to bounce back from any mistake or setback more quickly, and more people will want to spend time with you.

You can change a bad mood into a good mood.
Feeling sad, disappointed, angry or worried are normal feelings. But sometimes you can help yourself feel a little better if you do something or think about something that helps you to feel happier.

You can be the boss of your own feelings.
Trying to change your bad mood into a good mood and trying to calm yourself down when you are angry are examples of being the boss of your own feelings. If you let your unpleasant feelings control you, then they can hurt you and hurt others.

If anger is the boss of you, people may not want to be friends with you. Be aware that you are feeling angry and then calm yourself down. Then speak up for yourself in a calm but strong way. 'No hitting or hurting and no name calling' is the rule.

If fear (feeling scared or worried) is the boss of you, you may not have a go at something new.

Practising mindfulness helps you to be the boss of your feelings.
Practising mindfulness can help you to be the boss of your feelings by staying calm before acting. Being mindful also helps you notice and really appreciate what you are feeling.

You need to ask 'Did they really mean it?' when you feel hurt and angry.
You may get upset and angry over something that a person has done. But sometimes it is an accident and they did not mean to hurt you or your feelings.

Unhelpful thinking makes you feel worse.
You can feel worse if you say unhelpful things to yourself. Sometimes it is understandable to feel sad or angry about things that happen, but that event or person hasn't *made* you have that feeling. One of the best ways to be the boss of your feelings is to use more helpful thinking and helpful 'self-talk'. (See also Unit 3: People bouncing back)

To understand other people, work out how they are feeling.
Working out the feelings of other people is called 'empathy'. Empathy is important for making and staying friends and for supporting other people.

> **Learning objectives**
> In this unit, students will further develop their understanding that:
> - all feelings are important
> - it is important to name their emotions correctly
> - it is important to try to understand and respond positively to another person's emotions.

Resources list

A complete list of resources including references for core and additional books, films, video clips, poems, songs and websites is available.

Describing and understanding feelings

Resources

✦ Books

My Book of Feelings

This book describes a variety of situations that trigger different emotions.

My Many Coloured Days

A deceptively simple book that introduces the notion of how our feelings can change a lot and how different feelings can be linked to different colours.

✦ Song

'That's Why I'm Asking You'

(To the tune of 'Oh My Darling Clementine')

> I feel worried, I feel worried
> And that's why I'm asking you
> When you're feeling very worried
> What's a good thing to do?
> Talk it over with a friend
> That's a good thing to do
> When you're feeling very worried
> That's our advice to you
>
> I feel angry, I feel angry
> And that's why I'm asking you
> When you're feeling very angry
> What's a good thing to do?
> Tell the person why you're angry
> That's a good thing to do
> When you're feeling very angry
> That's our advice to you
>
> I feel sad, I feel sad
> And that's why I'm asking you
> When you're feeling very sad
> What's a good thing to do?
> Remember all the good bits
> That's a good thing to do
> When you're feeling very sad
> That's our advice to you

Circle Time or classroom discussion

Read one of the suggested books and sing the song. Ask students to give examples of some 'feelings' words (happy, sad, worried, angry). Then ask them to turn to the person on their left and say one word that describes how they felt before they came to class this morning. Discourage physical sensation words such as hungry or sleepy. Ask some students to share their responses. Then ask for words that describe:

- how they felt on their last birthday
- when they had their favourite food for dinner
- when someone hurt their feelings
- if they were lost in a shopping centre
- if they lost their pet.

Discussion questions

- What are some of the other words for feelings? (emotion, mood)

Point out that feelings can have everyday names like 'angry', 'happy' and 'sad', or more descriptive names like 'stormy', 'bubbly', 'fiery' and 'empty'.

- Does everyone have feelings? (yes)
- What feelings were mentioned in the books/song?
- What does your body do when you're having an uncomfortable or unpleasant feeling?' (Blushing, dry mouth, feel like crying, butterflies in the tummy, feel sick, feeling sweaty, giggling, going pale, clammy hands, hot face, jelly legs, lump in the throat, pounding heart, shaking, tingling skin.)
- Why do we have feelings? (Pleasant feelings tell us when something feels good; unpleasant feelings can warn us that we might need to stay safe or find ways to solve our problems.)
- What colours can we link to feelings? (feeling blue or sad; green with envy; fiery or angry red; yellow for sunny or happy)
- What sounds can we link to feelings? (groaning, whining, giggling)
- Can we change our feelings? (Yes, but sometimes it's hard to do – to change our feelings we have to use our brains and try to think differently.)
- Why is it important to be the boss of our feelings? (So that we don't hurt others or their feelings, so that we don't hurt relationships, so that we don't hurt ourselves.)

In the discussion emphasise:

- how it is important to use the right word for your feeling
- that sometimes your body feels pretty much the same when you are scared as it does when you are angry, and sometimes you can get the two feelings confused
- that it is also important to pick the word that is the right 'strength' for your feeling.

Sometimes we use different words for a weaker or stronger feeling, and sometimes we add words to make them less strong (e.g. a bit, a little, slightly, somewhat) or to make them even stronger (really, so, very). Give selected students two words in the same feeling family but of a different intensity and ask which is the stronger feeling. For example:

- If one person is annoyed and another is angry, which one has the stronger feeling?
- If one person is pleased and another is thrilled, which one has the stronger feeling?

Emphasise that we need to make sure that our unpleasant feelings do not take control of us, because if they do, then we might hurt others or ourselves. We have to be the boss of our unpleasant feelings.

> **Teacher reflection**
> Teaching is complex and many interactions with students, parents or colleagues can be stressful and even contribute to teacher burnout. See the section on managing 'emotional labour' (pages 78–9) to help you better manage stressful relationships and enhance your own wellbeing.

Activities

- Students use a digital camera or phone to photograph classmates who are acting out certain expressions. They then make a labelled collage of the different feelings or a class book, e.g. 'Here is Adam acting very proud when he received an award at assembly,' or 'Here is Lucy acting out being worried because her pet is unwell.'

- Use drawing software where students construct several faces showing different emotions. They then print them and make a collage of the different images.

- Draw or cut out magazine pictures that reflect feelings. Students use them to make a class display around a specific feeling, or categorise them into pleasant and unpleasant feelings. Students could also compete in groups of three to see how many pictures of three specific emotions (such as happy, sad, angry) they can find in magazines and newspapers within 15 minutes. You could use the **Timer e-tool**.

- Make a class A to Z picture dictionary of feelings. Students work in pairs, with each pair working on several different letters.

- In pairs, students complete **BLM Feeling Faces**, cutting out and pasting each 'feeling face' onto a large sheet of paper and then pasting the appropriate label beneath it. Students compare their responses with a partner.

- Ask students to select four feelings and then to write those feeling words in the colours they think match them.

- Students draw or paint one page for a class 'colour and feeling' book using *My Many Coloured Days* (see page 200) as the inspiration. The pages could be scanned into a digital book or made into a class book (see page 101).

Feelings word ladders

Students make four-rung ladders using craft sticks and glue. Mix up the word families of emotions (below) and then ask the students to sort them into order from least to most intense or strong. They write the words in order of intensity onto the steps of the ladder or they paste them on, with the most intense at the top of the ladder.

- angry feelings: annoyed, cross, angry, furious
- sad feelings: unhappy, sad, miserable
- scared and worried feelings: nervous, worried, scared, terrified
- unpleasant surprised feelings: puzzled, surprised, stunned, shocked.

Intensity sentences

After the word ladder activity, ask students to write sentences about each emotion word that reflects the intensity of the feeling. For example:

- I was annoyed when …
- I was cross when …
- I was angry when …
- I was furious when …

In pairs, students see if their partner agrees that the situation matches the intensity of the emotions.

Feelings quiz

Give students a number of situations and ask them to indicate non-verbally how strongly they might feel. They communicate their response by:

- holding up both hands (very)
- holding up one hand (some)
- making an 'X' with both index fingers (not at all).

Some questions you might use:

- If you called your principal by the wrong name, how embarrassed would you feel?
- If you were expecting to go to a school camp for a week and it had to be cancelled because of floods or bushfires, how disappointed would you feel?
- If you moved into a new street and no-one seemed friendly to you, how lonely would you feel?
- If a friend accidentally damaged something of yours, how angry would you feel?

After each question ask selected students for their reasons. Emphasise that different people can feel differently about the same situation. What might be some reasons for this? Ask students in groups of three to create some situations for another similar quiz at a later point.

'Most' books

Students make individual flip books (see page 102) where they write and draw their response to 'The most [feeling word] I have ever felt was when …' Feeling words could be 'surprised', 'worried', 'happy', 'embarrassed', 'disappointed', 'excited', 'frightened'. Students write 'The most' on the top half pages and the feeling word and text on the bottom half. Alternatively, make several class books or a digital class book with each student contributing a page about just one feeling for each book (see page 101).

Drama

Acting with feeling

Write 'happily', 'excitedly', 'sadly', 'angrily' and 'worriedly' on five cards, one word on each. Write one action on new cards, such as:

- hammer a nail
- sit down at the table and start eating
- dig the garden
- hit a tennis ball several times
- eat an apple
- dance
- blow your nose
- brush your hair.

Students draw one 'feelings' card from a container and one action card from another container which tells them what action to do in that way (e.g. brush your hair *angrily*).

Embed it

✦ Songs

'Sing, move and groove' time

Group singing and movement increases positive mood and builds relationships. Whenever there is an opportunity, take five minutes to have a 'sing, move and groove' session with students singing songs that could be described as happy, inspiring, celebratory, joyous or just plain loud! Here are some suggestions:

- 'I Like to Sing!'
- 'Why We Sing'

- 'Supercalifragilisticexpialidocious'
- 'What a Feeling'
- 'Doing the Penguin'
- 'New Way to Walk' (Sesame Street)
- 'Bounce Back Wriggle Jive'
- 'Locomotion'
- 'Monster Mash'
- 'YMCA'
- 'Walking on Sunshine'
- 'Crocodile Rock'
- 'Prehistoric Animal Brigade'

Feelings change a lot

Resources

✦ Books

Feelings

This book uses many styles, including narratives, poetry, monologues and comic strips. A rich variety of emotions is portrayed, and many feelings words are used. Empathy is also apparent in some of the stories.

Lizzy's Ups and Downs: NOT an Ordinary School Day
See page 144.

Circle Time or classroom discussion

Prior to Circle Time set up six stations for a Circuit brainstorm (see page 91), with six large pieces of paper. Write the following question on each sheet with one of the emotions: What is one situation where many children your age might feel happy/sad/lonely/angry/worried/jealous?

Read one or two of the suggested books. Discuss the different feelings identified and the situations that triggered those different feelings.

Then form groups of four students (in class of 24). Ensure that students understand each feeling, for example, that feeling sad is different to feeling lonely, angry, worried or jealous. Each group moves clockwise from station to station when asked. Each group is to come up with a different situation so at the end each sheet has six situations that might trigger that feeling. When each group gets to their original station, they sit down with their sheet. Each group then takes turns at reading the different situations that evoke different emotions. Follow up with the discussion questions.

Discussion questions

- Do our feelings change a lot in a day? (yes)
- Can you have different feelings in the same day e.g. happiness, disappointment, worry? (yes)
- Why do you think feelings change a lot? (Lots of different things happen in our day.)
- Why is it helpful to know the kinds of situations that might trigger different feelings? (It helps us to be the boss of our feelings.)

Drama

Lucky-dip miming

Make one set of separate situations cards and one set of feelings cards (using the words and/or pictures in **BLM Feeling Faces**) and place them in separate containers. Use the following for the situation cards:

- airport/school/sporting match
- a wedding/birthday party/funeral
- at the zoo/beach/camping ground/caravan park/park/playground.

Each student draws out one feeling card from the first container and then one situation card from the second container. Then they:

- say what could happen in that situation which might lead to having that feeling in that situation
- write or dramatise a scene in which someone has that feeling in that situation.

Charades: Guess the feeling

Students all contribute (in pairs) to making a class set of paper plate masks (see page 105). The masks each have different emotions, based on the feelings cards from Lucky-dip miming above. Students take turns drawing out a feelings card and using the appropriate mask to act out that feeling in some way. The class then tries to guess the feeling. The faces/cards can also be used for many other activities, for example:

- draw out two faces or cards and write an imaginative text based on the feelings
- copy the expressions onto faces in your own 'story picture'.

Activity

Students choose two feelings from the feeling cards container (see Lucky-dip miming above) then plan and write a short imaginative text about a day in the life of someone whose feelings change from one of those feelings to the other.

Boosting positive feelings

Resources

✦ Book

The Jar of Happiness

Meg believes that there is a 'recipe' for being happy and she collects what she thinks are the most important ingredients in a jar. She uses what is in the jar when she wants to help her friends and family to be happy, and it also enhances her own happiness in different ways.

✦ Song

'Happy Dance'

Circle Time or classroom discussion

Read *The Jar of Happiness* to the class and discuss.

Discussion questions

- How did Meg's jar of happiness help others and herself to feel happy?
- What is one thing that helps you to feel happy?

After the circle discussion, summarise the types of situations that make students feel happy, stressing that if we can understand what makes us feel happy in different ways then we can help ourselves to experience more positive emotions.

- What kinds of situations make most people feel happy?
- Are we more likely to feel happy when we are doing something active (e.g. going for a walk) or when we are doing something quietly (e.g. reading)?
- Are we more likely to feel happy when we are with other people or by ourselves?

Activities

- Students write an imaginative text that includes three or four of the positive emotions.
- Each student makes their own jar of happiness or they can contribute two ideas to a class jar of happiness.
- Follow up the Take-home task below with everyone reporting on their Positive emotions challenge after one week. Look for ways to collect class data on the types of activities that boost each of the six positive emotions in **BLM Boosting Positive Emotions Challenge**.

Drama

- Make a copy of the **BLM Boosting Positive Emotions Challenge** (see above). Write the seven positive emotions on individual cards. Randomly distribute the cards so each group of students gets one card. The group then acts out a situation that would help them feel that positive emotion.

Take-home task

Positive emotions challenge

Each student takes home the **BLM Boosting Positive Emotions Challenge** and looks for ways to feel each of the six emotions over the following week.

You can change a bad mood into a good mood

Resources

✦ Books

Wanda-Linda Goes Berserk

In this humorous Australian story, Wanda-Linda wakes up in a bad mood and then proceeds to terrorise her parents and the entire neighbourhood. Her biggest tantrum involves the Fire Brigade, as thousands of people watch.

The Grouchies

A story told in rhyme of a boy who learns how to change his grumpy mood into a good mood and get along better with his family and friends.

Circle Time or classroom discussion

Ask students when they are sitting in the circle to put their hands up if, before the lesson, anyone felt cross, sad, angry, worried. Say that it's okay and natural to have these feelings if the day did not start well. Ask everyone to stand and sing 'The Hokey Pokey' and do the actions. Then ask them to put their hands up if they feel happier after the song and why they think they felt happier. (It's fun to sing together, doing fun things together gives us more energy, movement helps our brains to work a bit better, it helps us to also pay attention to the good things in our life, not just the bad things.)

Read one of the books listed. Talk about how there are different things we can do to help ourselves get into a better mood when we feel grumpy or grouchy.

Discussion questions

- Did the character(s) in the book do anything to help change their bad mood into a good mood?
- What are some of the things the characters did to change their bad mood into a good mood?
- Do you think you can change your bad mood into a good mood?
- Who likes to do something fun or active when they need to change a bad mood into a good mood? Can you give some examples? (Reading, painting, singing, dancing, swimming, playing time with your pets, riding your bike, going for a walk, hitting a ball.)
- Who likes to talk to someone to help them change a bad mood into a good mood? Who do you like to talk to? (Mum, dad, grandparent, sister, brother, friend.)
- Do you have a special place that helps you change a bad mood into a good mood? How can having some quiet thoughtful time also help?

> **Teacher reflection**
> Teachers are resilient! But we all have days that are particularly challenging. What strategies do you use to change a bad mood into a good mood? Do you call a friend, talk to a partner, exercise, connect with nature, play calming music, meditate? Did you know that exercise has been shown to be an effective anti-depressant?

Activities

- Students make a class book (see page 101) in which they each draw one thing that they like doing that changes their bad mood into a good mood.
- Students make a good mood flower with six petals. On each petal, they write one thing that makes them happy. In the flower's centre they stick their photo or draw themselves and write their name. Make a vase of good mood or 'happy' flowers or a collage on the classroom wall or in the hall.
- Students collect (from a class beach excursion or bring to school) smooth rocks which they then paint or illustrate. Varnish the final products. The small rock can be kept in a pocket as a reminder to go to their quiet thoughtful place when they feel the need to calm down. A good mood rock can also be given as a gift.
- Students draw a comic strip or write an imaginative text about a grumpy day they have had and how they saved the day.

Being mindful to be the boss of your feelings

Resources

📖 ✦ Books

Mindful Monkey, Happy Panda

In the beginning, Monkey is not mindful. Peaceful Panda helps Monkey to experience the pleasure of doing things in the moment without distraction and with a peaceful and happy mind.

Take the Time: Mindfulness for Kids

This thoughtful and peaceful book encourages children to slow down and become more mindful and deliberate with their day-to-day actions and thoughts. When a day feels stressful, it encourages children to calm down and feel better and to enjoy and savour the beauty of the world.

💻 ✦ Website

The Smiling Mind

This website (and app) has a number of guided meditations for 7–9 year olds.

❄ Circle Time or classroom discussion

Read one of the books then introduce the idea of calming down, clearing your mind and being mindful or focusing your feelings. Explain that being mindful simply means paying attention to how you are feeling now, not how you felt yesterday or last week, or how you might feel later in the day or further in the future. If people are mindful of how they are feeling now, they become more aware of the body sensations associated with their feelings and thoughts. Being mindful helps people to be better at identifying and managing their feelings, thoughts and body sensations. This is especially important when they are feeling strong and powerful emotions like being angry, sad or anxious.

Give students an opportunity to experience going into their quiet thoughtful place by using the following script:

> Let's visit the quiet thoughtful place inside our minds. Close your eyes and take some slow deep breaths. Each time you breathe in count 'one' in your head and each time you breathe out again count 'two' in your head. Try to do each new breath more slowly than the one before it. Let's do ten of them. Our quiet thoughtful place is a good place to visit if we are feeling angry, or sad, or worried or nervous. We can stay there for a while and think deeply about our feelings. Sometimes, we will become clearer about the name of the feeling we are having. Sometimes, we will find that our feelings are not as strong or as 'hot' as they seemed to be before. Sometimes, we will find some good ideas for things to do about our feelings that will help. Sometimes, if we are thinking about pleasant feelings, we will enjoy them even more than we did before. Let's try it now.

Explain that when they arrive at their quiet thoughtful place, you want them to think about how they are feeling at that time.

Discussion questions

- What did it feel like in your quiet thoughtful place?
- When might be a good time to visit your quiet thoughtful place? (When they are feeling anxious, angry, sad or agitated; when they want to feel calm and peaceful.)

Activities

▶ Students draw or paint their quiet thoughtful place, and use the colours they think fit best.

The good mood wonder walk

Periodically take the class on a good mood walk (10–15 minutes) that they have designed. It might be outside the school in a nearby park. It might be within the school but should pass as many plants as possible. The walk can be silent or just quiet. In preparation, ask students to each design and make their own (safe) 'wonder zapper' (e.g. a sun illustration on the end of a stick or ruler) that they can take with them on their walk. As they walk in single file they point to anything they see that is a thing of beauty or wonder and savour it for a few seconds, noting its colour, smell, texture, etc. They could also use a thinking routine such as 'I see, I think, I wonder' with this activity. Follow up with a writing or drawing activity based on their walk.

Take-home task

Remind students to go to their quiet thoughtful place to access happy memories if ever they have trouble getting to sleep.

When do you feel angry?

Resources

◆ Books

I Feel Angry

This is a nonfiction comic-style book about angry feelings, with metaphors for anger and management strategies.

Zen Tails: No Presents Please

This book uses animal characters to explain a moral from Zen philosophical teachings. Grizzel Bear becomes angry when Guru Walter Wombat does not do as he demands. While Grizzel becomes angrier during their meeting, Guru Walter remains calm.

The Magic Finger

An eight-year-old girl has the power of putting the 'magic finger' on people when she is really angry. When people are given this treatment, strange things happen to them!

◆ Poem

I Wonder Why Dad Is So Thoroughly Mad

Circle Time or classroom discussion

Draw an anger meter like this one on the board.

Explain that people's level of anger will relate to how important they think the situation is to them. Read one of the books and/or the poem and discuss.

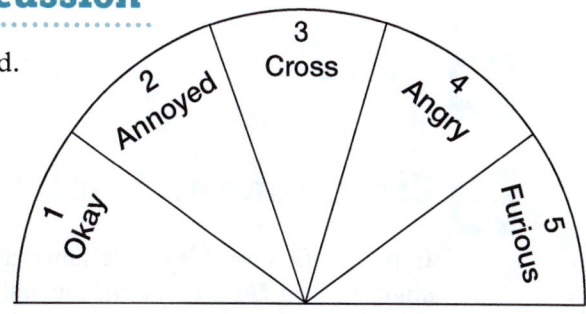

Discussion questions

- Why does the character feel angry? Does anyone or anything make them angry? (No, what others do might be annoying or nasty but we choose whether or not we will be angry by what we say to ourselves.)

Ask each student to do the **BLM Postbox Survey: The Anger Meter**. Then organise the class in groups so each group collates and reports on one item in the Postbox survey (see page 96). Ask each group to share their data for their question, i.e. how many students felt okay, annoyed cross, angry, furious. Talk about the different things that resulted in students feeling angry. Try to avoid the term 'makes me angry' and, if it is used, rephrase it as, 'Well, we can understand that you felt angry when that happened, but it didn't *make* you angry.'

- What happened or what was the situation?
- What did the other person say or do that you didn't like?
- What did you do or say when they did that?
- What does it feel like when we are angry? Is anger a hot or a cold feeling?
- How can angry feelings be helpful? (They alert you to a possible 'wrong' being done to you.)
- What did you do to calm yourself down again?
- Why is it important to be the boss of our angry feelings?
- What are some good ways to respond to someone who is angry with you?
- Were you pleased when you were the boss of your angry feelings?
- What did you do when your angry feelings had gone away?
- What would you do differently if that happened again?

Activities

- Students draw their own 'images' of anger with the caption, 'No-one *makes* me angry. I can be the boss of my angry feelings.'
- Organise for students to write up the class data from the **BLM Postbox Survey: The Anger Meter**.

How much anger?

Ask students to count the number of situations in the previous week in which they felt furious, angry, etc. If most of the answers were at the top of the anger meter, then they are not the boss of their feelings and need to develop strategies for managing their anger (see Dealing with angry feelings below).

Dealing with angry feelings

Resources

♦ Song
'If You're Angry and You Know It, Take A Walk'

Circle Time or classroom discussion

In preparation for this Circle Time, ask students to write down every time they feel cross or angry in their **Bounce Back!** journal for a week (if they haven't already done the 'How much anger?' activity above). Ask them to note what happened: what was said that they didn't like, what they did, and what happened after their anger cooled down. Use the class data gathered from the **BLM Postbox Survey: The Anger Meter** earlier to have a discussion on when they feel angry and the damage that anger can do. Focus the Circle Time discussion on the damage that anger can do when it gets out of control. For example:

- People will think badly of you (it can damage your reputation).
- It can cause loneliness (other students will not want to work with you and you could lose friends).
- It is unfair to others, doesn't respect their rights and hurts them.
- You often have guilty feelings afterwards and wish you hadn't done it.
- Your loss of control will cause you to respect yourself less.
- You will not seem 'cool' in front of others.
- You may get into trouble and be punished.

Discussion questions

- How can the way others view a person be damaged if they don't control their angry feelings?
- Why do friendships sometimes break up if one person can't control their angry feelings?
- What do you think when you see someone who is angry and out of control?
- What are some of the good ways that you have used to be the boss of your angry feelings?
- What are some of the ways that don't help and which sometimes make things worse?

Discuss with students the difference between the times when they do manage to be the boss of their feelings and the times when their angry feelings get on top of them. You could use the Smiley ball strategy (see page 97) to elicit responses. Make a list of ways of being the boss of one's angry feelings. On the board write: 'When I feel angry, I can …' and elicit responses such as:

- calmly tell the person why I am angry
- try to find a way to solve our problem and stay friends
- count my breaths from one to five – slowly breathing in and breathing out and then start again
- go to my quiet thoughtful place
- say to myself:
  - 'staying friends is more important'
  - 'keep cool'
  - 'you will get into trouble'
  - 'it's not worth it'
  - 'the person who 'loses it' is the loser'.

Activities

▶ Use the **Good Ways or Bad Ways to Deal With Anger e-activity** with the class and discuss strategies that could be used in these situations.

▶ Make a class X-chart with students about good anger management with 'sounds like, looks like, feels like, thinks like' on the four diagonal lines.

▶ Ask students to write in their **Bounce Back!** journal two statements that start with this sentence stem: 'When I feel angry next, I will …'

▶ Have students work with a partner to make a poster outlining the good reasons for being the boss of one's anger.

▶ Groups of three students can create an advertising campaign that encourages people to learn to manage their anger more effectively. This can include a jingle, sticker, slogan, poster or video clip.

▶ Using Quick quotes (see page 96), students record and display their personal comments about one good way in which they have managed their angry feelings in the past.

Sing a song

As a class, sing the song: 'If You're Angry and You Know It, Take a Walk' to the tune 'If You're Happy and You Know It.' Other verses might be:

- If you're angry and you know it, tell them why.
- If you're angry and you know it, keep your cool.
- If you're angry and you know it, think again.

Embed it

As a school, designate some spaces for students (and staff) for quiet reflection. Provide opportunities for students to practise accessing their quiet thoughtful place.

Take-home tasks

Family interview

Students interview an older family member about their two best ways they stay in control of their angry feelings. Collate their information and make a whole-class poster: 'The Best Ways Our Families Are the Boss of Their Angry Feelings'.

Fridge magnet

Students make a fridge magnet (see page 103) which contains an important message about emotions such as, 'We need to be the boss of our own feelings', or one of these quotes:

- If you can stay calm in a moment of anger, you will save yourself sadness.
- When you feel angry, count backwards from 20 before you say or do anything.
- When you feel angry, always think of what you might lose if you hurt someone.
- What starts in anger, usually ends in shame.
- Anger is like a stone thrown into a wasp's nest. (proverb)

Helpful thinking - check your facts

Resources

✦ Book

Lucky

Leo and his brother are told there will be a surprise for dinner and jump to all sorts of conclusions. They discover that what you already have is enough to make you feel 'lucky.'

Circle Time or classroom discussion

Introduce this lesson by making the point that a lot of our angry feelings happen because we don't check our facts (do a reality check) or wait to find out what really happened. Then read the book, which reminds students to wait for more information before they react.

Discussion questions

- What do the boys think the surprise will be? Describe the boys' feelings.
- How does the story make you feel?
- Why is the book called, *Lucky*? What did the boys learn?
- Turn to your partner: Have you ever made a mistake because you jumped to the wrong conclusion? (e.g. got angry with a friend or a brother or sister because you thought they had done something but you got it wrong)
- What does this tell us? (That sometimes we make mistakes and get angry at unnecessary things.)
- What could be the consequences? (It could mean that you lose a friendship because you haven't checked the facts.)

Activity

▶ Students can write an imaginative text about ruining a friendship because they got angry when they jumped to the wrong conclusion that their friend had done something to hurt them.

Drama

Use Good genie/Bad genie (see page 92) to act out various scenarios where the good genie encourages the person to check their facts, while the bad genie encourages them to jump to incorrect conclusions. For example:

Maddi is in a really grumpy mood and cross with me. Bad genie: 'I must have done something to upset her.' Good genie: 'Actually, she's feeling grumpy because she didn't sleep well.'

Be an intention detective

Resources

✦ Book

Just Kidding

D.J. is often on the receiving end of classmate Vince's nasty comments at school. When he goes too far, Vince says he was just kidding, but D.J. correctly recognises that Vince's intention is to be nasty and to put him down.

Circle Time or classroom discussion

Introduce the topic by asking students to imagine lining up at the canteen and being knocked over by someone playing nearby. How do you know whether it was an accident or whether they meant to knock you over? Intention detection is the ability to work out someone's motive or what they really intended to do. What signs tell you what their intentions were?

Read the book and discuss what Vince's intention was. Ask students to think about how good they are at being an intention detective? On the board or a poster entitled 'Intention Detective' draw up a sounds like/looks like/feels like/thinks like X-chart for both 'accident' and 'meant it'. As students answer the following questions, record their answers on the two charts. Elicit a number of different answers to each question.

Discussion questions

- What tone of voice does someone have when they are trying to upset you by what they are saying? (Sounds like: sarcastic, laughing, not genuine.)

- What kinds of things do they say to you? (Sounds like: nasty words)
- What kind of look do they have on their face when you are upset and they are pleased because they meant to do it? (Looks like: a smirk, smiling at other people.)
- How do they act when they meant to upset you? What do they do next? (Looks like: not sincerely apologising, not helping you, just walking away.)
- How do you feel when someone means to hurt you? (Feels like: upset, sad.)

Activities

- Students work with a partner to write two stories about the same incident, one in which someone means to hurt someone else and another in which it was an accident. They emphasise the 'intention detection' signs each time.
- Students create a 'Be an Intention Detective' poster. They incorporate examples to illustrate the key differences between Hurtful behaviour and Unintentional behaviour.

Drama

Students write and perform a puppet play (pages 105–106) that shows the two types of intentions, i.e. accidental or intentional. The class guesses which one it is.

Dealing with disappointment

Resources

✦ Books

Gorilla

A lonely young girl is disappointed when her father is too busy to take her to the zoo. In her imagination, she goes to the zoo with a gorilla wearing her father's clothes.

Pooka

Everyone loves Pooka, a lost dog that is discovered on the doorstep. Grandad warns about getting too attached, but of course the children do and then become very disappointed. This book also links to empathy.

Circle Time or classroom discussion

Read one of the books and discuss who was disappointed and why.

Discussion questions

- What is disappointment? Why do we feel disappointed? (Our hopes are not met.)
- Why were the children in the book disappointed?
- Is 'disappointed' often a better word than 'angry' to describe how someone feels? (Yes, especially if we know they couldn't help it or it was a result of something out of their control.)

Use the Partner Retell strategy (see page 95) and ask students to share a time when they felt disappointed and say why.

- How can you be the boss of feeling disappointed? (Focus on the positives, accept what can't be changed, distract yourself in a good way, realise everyone feels disappointed sometimes and this feeling will pass.)

Activities

- Students use the Good genie/Bad genie strategy (see page 92) to act out scenarios such as:
  - your team lost the grand final
  - you didn't do as well has you thought you would in a school project or test
  - your grandparent becomes sick and your family has to change their holiday plans
  - you're not invited to a classmate's birthday party.
- Students write a persuasive text on 'It's important to get over feeling disappointed and move on'. They could use one of the above scenarios.

Dealing with jealousy

Resources

✦ Books

Gertrude McFuzz

Gertrude is a bird who is full of envy about the two beautiful tail-feathers of Loll-Lee-Lou. She nags her uncle, who is a doctor, into telling her where to find the pillberry plant that will give her another beautiful feather. After finding it, she eats more than she should.

I Feel Jealous

The cartoon-style character talks about what makes him jealous and some ways that jealousy can be dealt with. There are some nice visual metaphors that students can work with and develop.

Alexander and the Terrible, Horrible, No Good, Very Bad Day

See page 155.

Circle Time or classroom discussion

Read *Alexander and the Terrible, Horrible, No Good, Very Bad Day*. In groups of three, students brainstorm and write down all the occasions when the character showed jealousy. Then each group nominates an example to be written up on the board (e.g. Alexander was jealous because: there was no toy in the cereal box, he could not find a seat by the window, the teacher liked Paul's picture best, he was only the third-best friend, there was no dessert at lunch, he was the only one to have a cavity, the only one with plain white sneakers and the cat slept with Anthony). Alternatively, read one of the other books and use it as a starting point for groups of students to brainstorm different reasons for jealousy. Use students' examples to categorise the kinds of situations when people might feel jealous such as:

- when they want something that someone else has
- when they are worried about losing something they have to someone else
- when good things happen to someone else that they wish had happened to them
- when others get more attention than they do so they feel neglected/unimportant.

Discussion questions

- What is jealousy?
- Why is jealousy called the green-eyed monster? (It is scary and can control you if you aren't careful.)
- When have you felt jealous?
- Does everyone feel jealous sometimes? (Yes, it's normal.)

- How can you be the boss of your jealous feelings? What kind of helpful thinking could you use? (Talk to your family or a friend, focus on the good things that happen to you, feel happy for the person and celebrate or share their happiness, use tough self talk such as, 'Stop feeling jealous!')

Activities

▶ In groups of three, students make a chart of 'Helpful thinking to stop the green-eyed monster'.

▶ Students create their own green-eyed monster to remind them that jealousy can be harmful.

Drama

Students write and act out a puppet play (see pages 105–106) about jealousy or adapt one of the books for Reader's theatre (see page 96).

Dealing with embarrassment

Resources

✦ Books

The Terrible Underpants

This book has a very simple storyline and pictures. When all your good underpants are in the wash, what can you do but wear your tacky old ones? But it is embarrassing when everyone gets to see them!

Tiger Trouble

Eric's mother is a little bit eccentric and slightly accident prone, and Eric often finds himself in embarrassing moments with her.

✦ Poem

Remember Me

Circle Time or classroom discussion

Read and discuss one or more of the books or poem.

Discussion questions

- What is embarrassment?
- Why was the character embarrassed?
- What does your body do when you're embarrassed?
- Does everyone feel embarrassed sometimes?
- How can you be the boss of feeling embarrassed? (Remind yourself that everyone embarrasses themselves sometimes, trying to laugh about it, talking to someone who cares about you, reminding yourself it's temporary and most people won't even remember it in a day or two, keep it in perspective and say 'It's no big deal – it's not the end of the world.')

Tell students that another strategy for dealing with embarrassment is to not keep thinking about it. They could have another 'TV channel' ready in their head that they can switch over to and think about. This could be a zoo channel, a baby animal channel, a sports channel, a perfect holiday channel. When they want to switch to another channel, they blink hard to make the change.

Next, use the Bundling strategy (see page 91) with students writing down three situations in which children their age might feel embarrassed (tripping in front of assembly, forgetting lines in a play etc.). Each group shares their responses and then reinforce about how they might handle their embarrassment.

Activities

- In groups of three, students make a collage or painting of situations in which children their age might feel embarrassed or images representing embarrassment. The collage incorporates messages of what they can do to manage being embarrassed.
- In pairs, students write and illustrate a comic strip about someone their age who finds themselves in a number of embarrassing situations.

Dealing with feeling lonely and being left out

Resources

◆ Book

A Bit of Company

Christopher is lonely, and his mother is too busy with the new triplets to find time for him. His neighbour Molly is not busy and a relationship develops between them. This story is a useful resource for discussing family relationships and friendships.

◆ Poem

Picking Teams

Circle Time or classroom discussion

Using the Lightning writing strategy, students write what comes to mind when they think of feeling lonely (see page 93). Then read to the class the book or poems. Ask for examples of situations in which people might feel lonely or left out. Link this topic to Unit 2: Social values (including others).

Discussion questions

- Why was the character lonely? Why do people feel lonely?
- Does everyone feel lonely sometimes?
- What can you do about feeling lonely? (Problem-solve, keep busy, do physically active things, e.g. 'move and groove', do something for someone else, reach out to someone, say 'this feeling won't last', go to their quiet thoughtful place for a short time.)

Activities

- Students write and illustrate responses to 'Loneliness is like …'
- Students work in pairs or groups of three and come up with one idea on how recess and lunchtime can be less lonely.

Dealing with sadness

Resources

✦ Books

The Sound of the Sea

See page 149.

The Boy Who Didn't Want To Be Sad

A boy who didn't want to be sad decides to do everything to avoid sadness, e.g. when his sister knocks down the tower he made, he decides that he won't build any more in case it happens again. Eventually, the boy realises that by trying to avoid sadness he also misses out on happiness.

✦ Poems

What Dads Do

Since Hanna Moved Away

Circle Time or classroom discussion

Read to the class and discuss one or more of the books or poems listed.

Discussion questions

- What was the character sad about?
- Is sadness normal? (Yes, everyone in the world experiences it because everyone experiences loss or potential loss of someone or something they care about.)
- How can you cheer someone up when they are sad?
- Do sad feelings last forever? What helps them to go away again?
- How can you be the boss of feeling sad and cheer yourself up? (Music, keeping busy, being with others, laughter, playing sport, cuddling a soft toy, playing with a pet.)

Stress that sadness always goes away, and it may take some time depending on the reason you are sad, but you can use your thinking to get over it and remember happy memories.

Activities

- Ask students to bring in photos from home of soft toys or pets or activities that have helped them cope with feelings of sadness, and make a digital story book (see page 101).
- Make a 'How can you cheer someone up when they are sad?' collage or write a checklist.

Drama

Sad feelings

Students put together a puppet play (or dramatic scene) about sad feelings (for puppet ideas see pages 105–106). They start by working in groups of three to brainstorm all the situations in which people feel sad (e.g. a pet dies, a friend moves, a grandparent goes home). They then list ways for feeling better about their sad feelings for each situation. Students choose one to develop into a short drama performance.

Dealing with worries

Resources

◆ Books

The Huge Bag of Worries

Jenny worries about absolutely everything – her school marks, her weight, her friends and so on. Her bag of worries gets bigger and bigger and follows her everywhere. Eventually, the old lady next door helps to sort out Jenny's worries.

What If?

Joe is nervous about his first big party, and as Mum walks him along the darkening street to his friend's house, his imagination starts to run wild. They search for the right place, looking through the windows, wondering 'What if…?' while making surprising discoveries along the way.

◆ Poem

Whatif

Circle Time or classroom discussion

Read one or more of the books or poem listed. Then use the Bundling strategy and ask students to write down three things children their age often worry about (see page 91). In the discussion that follows, emphasise that everyone worries sometimes and different things worry different people.

Discussion questions

- What did the character/s worry about?
- What are the kinds of things that children your age worry about? What are examples of imaginary worries, school-based worries, everyday worries?
- Does everyone have the same worries?
- What are some examples of big worries, small worries?
- Do you share any of the worries that the characters had? (Make the point that many people share similar worries.)
- Do you sometimes worry about things that are not your worries? (e.g. parents' worries)
- Do you sometimes worry about things that are happening in other places in the world? (e.g. war, natural disasters)
- Do you sometimes think you are the only kid with that worry? (Link to the BOUNCE BACK! statement: *Everyone experiences sadness, hurt, failure, rejection and setbacks sometimes, not just you.*)
- How can you be the boss of feeling worried? (Talk to someone about your worries; take big deep breaths and visit your quiet thoughtful place; practise if you are worried about doing something; go and do something you enjoy doing; challenge any of your 'what ifs' by asking how likely they are to happen, using helpful thinking, not unhelpful thinking.)
    - If you are worried about doing something, practising helps.
    - Visit your quiet thoughtful place.
    - Go and do something you enjoy doing (painting, playing with a ball, dancing etc.).
    - Challenge any of your 'what ifs' by asking how likely they are to happen, using helpful thinking, not unhelpful thinking.

> **? Teacher reflection**
> Research shows that teachers' stress levels are contagious (Oberle and Schonert-Reichl 2016). If teachers are stressed, then the students in their class tend to be more stressed too. On a scale from one (not at all) to ten (highly stressed), how stressed do you think you are? What strategies can you adopt to lower your stress levels?

Activities

- Students write an imaginative text about write a character who catastrophises about some things that are unlikely to happen or could happen but are unlikely. They can incorporate into their story the coping statement: *Catastrophising exaggerates your worries.*

Huge bag of worries

Make a set of cards with Jenny's worries or, if you don't have the book, make a set with a range of situations (e.g. atom bomb, bushfire, flood, cyclone, your house burns down, your house blows away, a lion escapes from the zoo, your house has no water, a big hole opens up in the garden, a dragon visits) and ask students to classify them into:

- *impossible*: could never happen
- *unlikely*: could happen but probably won't
- *likely*: but not important or awful
- *other people's worries*.

Developing empathy

Resources

◆ Books

Stand in My Shoes

Emily learns how to respond to others in her family and at school by noticing how they are feeling and letting them know that she understands and cares.

Diary of a Wombat

A humorous little story about a wombat with attitude who despairs of ever training his humans to be better 'pets'. This can be used to illustrate how different people see things differently, i.e. empathy and perspective taking.

So, What's It Like to Be a Cat?

This story is a question-and-answer interview between a child and a very clever cat, and what cats think about various things, including people.

◆ Video clip

Empathy for Students

Mojo is the director of the school musical in which the ClassDojo monsters star, but he lets his ego become the boss of his feelings.

Circle Time or classroom discussion

Read to the class and discuss one of the books listed.

Discussion questions

- How was the character(s) feeling? How do you know?

Discuss that 'empathy' means trying to understand how another person is feeling. It also means trying to put yourself in their shoes so that you can work out how they might be thinking as well as feeling. 'Showing empathy' means letting a person know that we understand how they are feeling and that we care. Empathy is important for making and staying friends and for supporting other people. Make an X-chart of what 'showing empathy' sounds like, looks like, feels like and thinks like.

- How do you know when someone in your family or a friend is feeling happy/sad/angry/worried? (Emphasise facial expression, posture, tone of voice, how the eyes look, what is said and what they do.)
- Have you ever felt glad when someone else has understood how you were feeling and let you know that? What happened? How did they show that they understood your feelings and cared about you?
- How could we let a classmate know that we understood that they felt worried (e.g. about someone in their family) or that they felt sad (e.g. about their pet dying)?
- How could we let a classmate know that we understood and cared after they have hurt themselves or have been sick?

Activities

- Students work in groups of three to write a book review or create a digital book trailer (see page 101) where they focus on how the character(s) in the story are feeling. How do they know when the character in the story is happy, sad, scared or angry? How do they think they felt when … ? What tells us that they are feeling this way? This can be completed with an older buddy.
- Students write the same story from the perspective of two different characters. For example, students could write about themselves and their sister or brother.
- Give students cards with different emotions written on them (e.g. excited, sad, happy, worried) and ask them to report back after recess if they observed that emotion in another (emphasise the 'no names' rule). Ask what they saw or heard that led them to think the other person was feeling that emotion.
- Use any books you are reading as a class to talk about what it would be like to be the different characters. Can students be Empathy Detectives and put themselves into the characters' shoes and imagine how they would be feeling at different parts of the story?

Empathy T-chart

Students make sounds like/looks like charts about showing empathy, for example:

Sounds like	Looks like
I'm sorry that you got hurt.	Patting them on the shoulder.
I'm happy for you.	Looking excited for others when they win.
That happened to me once.	Having the same look as them on your face.
I understand how you feel.	Having a sympathetic expression when someone is hurt.
I bet that really hurts.	Comforting someone.
I'm sorry you feel so sad.	Hugging someone who looks sad.
I'm really excited for you.	Doing something kind for that person.

Drama

- Adapt one of the books in this topic for Reader's theatre (see page 96).

Who walked in these shoes?

Obtain three old (but clean) pairs of shoes from an op shop: one male, one female and one child. In groups of three, students create stories about the people who walked in each pair of shoes. They perform their story wearing the shoes. Have spare socks for students to wear. Students could also write their story before the drama activity, then proofread and improve their story after the feedback from doing the activity.

Consolidation

Activities

- Students individually complete **BLM Cross-offs** (see page 91). The secret message is: 'Try to be the boss of your angry feelings.'

Feelings ABC

In groups of four, students make 23 cards, each featuring one letter of the alphabet (not 'x', 'y' or 'z'). They shuffle the cards and turn them upside down in the centre of the group. Students take turns at picking up a card and saying an emotion that starts with that letter. See **BLM A–Z of Emotions**.

Feelings Snap

In groups of four, students take turns at telling a short story and the rest of the group listens. Whenever one of the group recognises that they have experienced a similar feeling or situation, they say 'Snap!' When the first person has finished their story, the 'snappers' briefly tell of their matching experience and/or feeling.

Alternatively, instead of having the student say 'Snap', ask them to place a card with the word 'Snap' on it face up.

Reflections

Use the **Reflections e-tool** (see page 97) which asks these questions:

- A time when I felt sad was …
- A time when I felt angry was …
- A time when I felt worried was …
- A time when I felt surprised was …
- A time when I felt proud was …
- One thing you can do to be the boss of your feelings if you feel embarrassed is …
- One thing you can do to be the boss of your feelings if you feel sad is …
- One thing you can do to be the boss of your feelings if you feel angry is …

Each student can also make a 'Me too!' paper plate (see page 95). After one student has finished answering their question say, 'Now hold up your "Me too" sign if you have had a feeling like that in a similar situation.'

Key vocabulary

Use the Whisper game, Mystery square or the TEAM coaching strategy to assist students to learn vocabulary and spelling related to emotions to a reasonable level of mastery (see pages 98, 94 and 97). Examples:

angry	empathy	normal
annoyed	fear	pleasant
better	feelings	sad
boost	happier	scared
calm	happy	setback
change	helpful	surprised
control	hurt	unhelpful
cross	mindful	unpleasant
disappointed	mistake	worried
emotions	mood	

Games

▶ Play the **Before or After? e-game** with the class (see page 90).

Feelings detective

Each student has a feelings card pinned onto their back. Then they wander around asking classmates questions about their emotion for which only a Yes or No answer can be given. First brainstorm the kinds of questions that would help them to work out what emotion they have (e.g. Is it a pleasant emotion? Would I feel it at a sports game?). When they guess the emotion correctly, the person they are talking to takes the emotion card off their back. They can still stay in the activity, answering other people's questions to help them guess their emotion.

Feelings memory, Snap and Fish

Play Feelings memory, Snap and Fish using cards with the noun of a feeling on one card and the adjective on the other (e.g. amazed/amazement and anger/angry). Students could also draw a simple illustration for each card to show the emotion. Each group can play with their own set of 20 cards or swap with other groups. Students can also make their own sets using **BLM Feeling Faces**.

Bounce Back! award

Present the **Bounce Back! award** to students who have best demonstrated the ability to be the boss of their unpleasant feelings or to behave with empathy towards other students.

UNIT 7

Relationships

KEY MESSAGES

Getting along well with others makes you feel happier.
When you get along well with others, you feel happier and have more chance of making friends. Having friends means you can have fun together. Friends are people who will support you when you need help.

Everyone can learn friendship (social) skills.
Social skills are ways of getting along well with others. We are not born with good social skills. We all need to first learn them and then to practise them, so we are comfortable using them with different people.

Some social skills are really important for getting along with others.
The most important social skills for getting along with others are:

- being positive
- being a good listener
- finding things in common
- being a good winner and a good loser
- playing fairly
- having an interesting conversation
- standing up for yourself
- cooperating
- negotiating and sorting out disagreements.

Some social skills are really important for being a good friend.
The most important social skills for being a good friend are the ones listed above, plus:

- being thoughtful
- being loyal
- sharing information about yourself
- being kind and caring.

Friendships can change and that's normal.
Friendships change because we change. It's normal for some friendships to last for only a short time and for other friendships to last for much longer. Sometimes friends also move away.

Every friendship is different.
You can have lots of different friends and care about and be close to them for different reasons. You might like to play sport with one friend but you share a different interest, such as reading or building things, with another friend.

No friendship is perfect.
No-one is perfect, so no friendship is perfect. Everyone makes mistakes, and gets things wrong sometimes – that's normal. Being too critical of a friend can hurt your friendship. Learning to apologise or say sorry is important.

Sometimes it can be hard making new friends.
Sometimes it can be hard making new friends if you are in a new situation, such as a new class or team, and friendship groups have already been formed. Using good social skills can help you to make friends, even if it takes some time to do it.

Stand up for yourself. Don't be afraid of disagreements.
Standing up for yourself is an important skill for getting along well with others and also for being a good friend. It shows you have self-respect and builds trust within your friendships. Having a disagreement every now and then is part of a normal friendship. It is important to handle disagreements in a way that doesn't hurt anyone and that still allows you to be friends.

Be the boss of your angry feeings to handle disagreements well.
The main reason why people don't deal well with disagreements is because they let their angry feelings be the boss of them. Out-of-control, angry feelings will make you forget about trying to stay friends. It is important to be the boss of your angry feelings before you try and sort things out. Apologising is also an important part of this. (See also Unit 6: Emotions.)

> **? Learning objectives**
> In this unit, students will further develop their understanding of how to:
> - get to know others and be a good friend
> - respond effectively to disagreements with friends.

Resources list

A complete list of resources including references for core and additional books, films, video clips, poems, songs and websites is available.

Getting along well with others

Resources

✦ Books

Look What I've Got

This is a modern morality tale. Jeremy has everything – a new bicycle, a pirate outfit and an enormous bag of lollipops. But he won't share anything with Sam and boasts about what he has. Jeremy's selfishness and unkindness have negative outcomes for getting along well with others.

One of Us

Roberta is starting at a new school and hopes to find some new friends. She investigates various groups but realises that she is different in some way to all of them. She begins to worry she might not fit in anywhere, but then finds a group who is happy to be all different.

Circle Time or classroom discussion

Prior to this topic, give each student a list of the names of all the students in the class. Then ask them to place a tick against the names of the people they know very well, a dot against the names of the people they know reasonably well, and a question mark against the names of those people they don't know well.

Begin the circle with a name game, for example, where students introduce themselves and then the person on their right and left. Then read one of the books and discuss the ways in which the character tried to get along with others. Use the **What Works and What Doesn't? e-activity** to introduce the skills of getting along well with others.

Then ask the students to imagine they are meeting someone for the first time. Write down:

- three things you could tell them about yourself
- three things you could ask this person to find out more about them.

Write some of the ideas on the board.

Then organise students in pairs, based on the 'Classmates I don't know well' data above so that they are carrying out a Partner Retell interview (see page 95) with someone they don't know well.

Steps:

1. One person interviews their partner and asks them three things to find out more about them.
2. The pairs reverse roles and the second person does the interview.
3. Each student in the circle shares one new thing to the whole class they learnt about their partner.

> **? Teacher reflection**
> What importance does your school executive place on collegial relationships at your school? Are there any structures or processes that are designed to enhance these relationships? Are they effective? What approach to enhancing staff relationships have you seen or heard about being used in other schools?

Activities

- Use a digital camera to take photographs of people in the class getting along. Use captions such as 'Sally and Marie are cooperating', 'Dev and Adam are sharing the basketball' and 'Alisha and Simon are having an interesting conversation and both are listening well'. Make a photo display with captions on your class bulletin board.

- Complete **The Getting Along e-quiz** with the class.

Being a good listener

Circle Time or classroom discussion

Play a quick greetings game where one student starts by saying hello to the person on their left and start a ripple hello around the circle. Then ask all students who have a dog to swap places, then all who play basketball/netball, etc. to change places so students are mixed up.

Organise students into pairs. Use the **Coin toss e-tool** to determine which student is person A and person B. Person A is the first to talk while B pretends not to listen well. Then they reverse roles and B talks while A doesn't listen well. You might like to choose a topic such as 'Things you like to do on the weekend'. Allow the pairs to have one conversation where person A talks and person B acts as a good listener.

Back in the circle, gain student feedback on their experience with their partners and develop a 'Good Listening Dos and Don'ts' chart.

Discussion questions

- How did you know that the other person wasn't listening well? (Fidgeted, interrupted, didn't look at them or pay attention.)
- How did it feel when you were not being listened to? (Ignored, unimportant, like you want to stop talking to them.)
- What does someone do if they are listening really well? (Pay attention, not fidget or do something else, look at you, smile, summarise what you said, ask a good question.)
- How did it feel when you were being listened to? (Valued, important)
- What jobs require people to be excellent listeners?

Repeat the exercise with students practising 'listening well'.

Activities

- Students create an advertising campaign to encourage better listening.

Interviews

Students work in pairs, where one person is being interviewed and the other person is the reporter. They prepare questions and responses, and perform their interviews, with the class judging how well the interviewer listened to the interviewee. Use a toy microphone or a foil tube with ball attached. Topics could include:

- your ideal future job
- the prize you would most like to win
- your dream holiday
- your favourite book, writer, television show or computer game
- the best party you have ever been to.

Picture listening

Each student cuts out and pastes five different magazine pictures of people onto five cards. Mix the class set up and give each group of three a container of 15 pictures and a container of 'picture listening questions' – one question per card (see below). One student draws one picture out of the container without looking. Then the person on their left draws out a question. The first student answers the question in relation to the picture. Then the person on their right gives a simple summary of what they said. The next student then has a turn and so on.

Picture listening questions:

- What is this picture about and why do you think this?
- Do you like this picture? Why or why not?
- How does the picture make you feel and why?
- Do you like the colours? How do they make you feel?
- What might have happened before this photo was taken?
- How is each person in the picture feeling and behaving?
- What does the picture make you think about?
- How would you change this picture if you were asked to make it better?
- Does this picture remind you of anything in your own life?

Having an interesting conversation

Resources

✦ Poem
I'm the Single Most Wonderful Person I Know

Circle Time or classroom discussion

Begin by sending a greeting around the circle. Each person takes turns at saying hello and shaking hands with the person on their right and the person on their left. Read the poem and discuss why no-one seems to like the person described in the poem. Then give everyone a copy of the **BLM Relationships People Hunt**. Remind students to look at each person they talk to, smile and then ask their partner if they can help in answering one of their questions. Allow students time to talk with six different people, and they sit down in the circle when they have completed their people hunt. Debrief and discuss.

Discussion questions

- What makes conversations boring? What do the people do? (They talk too much, they talk about themselves, they might boast about what they are good at, they don't ask you any questions, they don't show any interest in you, they don't use any expression.)

- What happened in your people hunt? (Took turns in talking and listening, asked good questions, used good listening and recorded your partner's answers, answered the questions you were asked i.e. practised having an interesting conversation.)

- What are the skills of having an interesting conversation?

Ask for ideas, then show the **BLM Having an Interesting Conversation Chart** and discuss.

Talk about the difference between Yes/No and Tell-me-more questions. Yes/No questions are ones that invite a short, factual and simple answer such as 'yes' or 'no'. Tell-me-more questions are used by good conversationalists to draw the other person out.

Yes/No questions	Tell-me-more questions
Involve short, simple answers like yes/no, e.g.: • Where did you go? • What colour was it? • Did you like it? • Had you been there before?	Often start with 'how', 'why' or 'what', and keep the conversation going, e.g.: • What did you do when your cat ran away? • What do you like to do? • How did you find him again? • Why did you like it?

- What questions in the people hunt were examples of Yes/No questions?
- What questions were examples of Tell-me-more questions?

Then pair students up so they have a three-minute conversation on a topic written on cards that they select from a container (e.g. pets, the beach, dessert, parties, music, movies). Their task is to practise the skills of having an interesting conversation using the skills outlined in the BLM.

At the end of the conversation, students take turns to give their partner feedback on two things they did well (from the chart) and one thing they could do better next time from the chart.

Activities

- Students make a Tell-me-more and Yes/No questions poster about the two types of questions, using speech balloons.
- Students write two 'I will …' statements in their **Bounce Back!** journal about improving their conversational skills.
- Using the poem *I'm the Single Most Wonderful Person I Know* as stimulus, students write an imaginative text or draw a comic strip about the Big Head Family, who end up on their own without any friends because of their boring and boastful conversation.

There-and-back conversation

Provide real-life opportunities for students to practise their conversational skills. Organise students into pairs with someone who isn't a close friend. Mark out a walk such as from the library to the bicycle racks (there) and back (back). Specify a conversational topic (e.g. good games to play) and ask each student beforehand to prepare a few interesting questions to ask about it and a few interesting comments to make about it. One student talks about the topic while they are walking there, while the other listens and asks good questions. Then they swap over as they walk back.

Getting-to-know-you

This activity helps students to both get to know some of their classmates better and also practise conversational skills and listening skills.

Materials needed:

- one dice
- a full-page sheet with six numbered squares for each group of five students. Each square contains a different question that students can answer about themselves such as:
  - What is your favourite dessert? (or ice-cream flavour, sport to play, sport to watch, etc.)
  - What has been your best holiday and why?
  - Who is someone special in your life and why?
  - What is your favourite season and why?
  - Name a book you have really enjoyed reading and say why.
  - What TV show do you look forward to watching?
  - What do you think is the best kind of pet to have and why?
  - What present would you really like to receive and why?

- If you could visit any country you wanted for one week, which one would you choose?
- If you could be an animal for a day, which one would you choose to be?
- What kind of adult job do you think sounds most interesting and why?
- What is something you have done that you are proud of and why?
- What do you most like to do on a Saturday?

Ask students to suggest ideas for other questions by writing them on a card and posting them into a suggestion box.

Organise students into groups of five. Each student has a turn to throw the dice and answer the question that corresponds to that number. If they throw the same number twice, they can throw the dice again until they get a number they haven't yet thrown.

Embed it

Use teachable moments in Circle Time or when a student is telling a story or giving a response to stop and ask, 'Was that a Yes/No or a Tell-me-more question?'

Take-home task

Send home some brief notes such as the 'Dos and Don'ts Chart of Having an Interesting Conversation' for families outlining the class focus on the specific skills associated with good conversation, and include some information from **BLM Having an Interesting Conversation Chart** (see pages 227–8). Ask them to look for practice opportunities to have a conversation with their child and give them feedback on those skills. Good opportunities for conversation can be around the dinner table or driving in the car.

Being a good winner and a good loser

Resources

✦ Book

Sally Sore Loser: A Story About Winning and Losing

Sally always wants to win and she reacts badly if she loses. Her teacher and her mum help her to cope with losing and teach her to just have fun.

Circle Time or classroom discussion

Read the book and discuss.

Discussion questions

- How does Sally behave? What do you think of her behaviour?
- What sorts of games do you like to play with others?
- What does a poor loser do when they lose a game?
- How do you feel if you're playing with a poor loser?
- What does a good loser do?

Refer to **BLM Being a Good Winner and a Good Loser Charts**.

Randomly organise students into groups of four (see page 88 for ideas). Follow up with a Cooperative games round robin (see next page).

Activity

▶ Use the **Good and Bad Ways to Play a Game e-activity** with the class to review the social skills of being a good loser.

Games

Cooperative games round robin

Students practise being good winners and good losers while playing a reasonably quick game in pairs against another pair. Each pair plays the same game (e.g. Hangman) against three other pairs, not necessarily on the same day. Before each round robin, ensure that students know how to play the selected game and are familiar with the content in the game. It can be helpful to first play the game as a whole class and remind them of the strategies that are most effective in playing well. Give each pair **BLM Pair 'Good Playing' Rubric** and discuss it with the class.

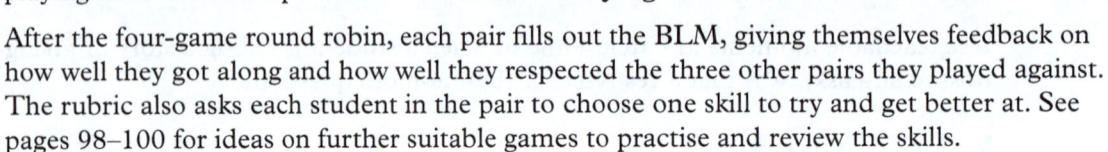

After the four-game round robin, each pair fills out the BLM, giving themselves feedback on how well they got along and how well they respected the three other pairs they played against. The rubric also asks each student in the pair to choose one skill to try and get better at. See pages 98–100 for ideas on further suitable games to practise and review the skills.

Take-home task

Ask parents to play age-appropriate card games and board games with their children and to give their children positive feedback when they play fairly and are good winners and good losers. Stress that they shouldn't let their child win just to make them feel good.

Embed it

Relationship committees

Organise students to work on a committee for at least one term that:

- liaises with the teacher to organise the Cooperative games round robin (see above)
- organises and oversees lunchtime clubs that are available once a week or once a fortnight (the term one committee will need to plan the clubs based on students' interests, e.g. board games, conversation, dinosaurs, guinea pigs, swap-a-book, science)
- looks for good ways for students to practise their conversational skills
- identifies activities and structures that enable all students to feel included and have a happy and fun time in the playground at lunchtime.

Making and keeping friends

Resources

✦ Books

Rosie and Michael

This book looks at the ways that Rosie and Michael are friends, despite recognising that each of them has faults and likes doing things differently.

Best Friends

Kathy and Louise are best friends who do everything together, both at school and at home. Louise goes away with her family over the summer holidays, has a great time and also makes some new friends. When she returns, Kathy feels hurt that Louise had such fun without her.

Pearl Barley and Charlie Parsley

Pearl Barley is loud and loves to move and talk, while Charlie Parsley is quiet and shy and likes to watch his garden grow. They are good friends who, although very different from each other, care for each other and help each other when the other feels down.

A Couple of Boys Have the Best Week Ever

Friends James and Eamon stay with Eamon's grandparents while attending a week-long nature camp. They have fun and enjoy grandma's special treats. They seem to merge into one person, leading grandpa to nickname them both 'Jameon'.

◆ Songs

'Reach'

'You've Got a Friend in Me'

◆ Poems

Harvey

Phyllis

> **Teacher reflection**
> Fifty years of happiness research shows that our happiness and wellbeing is best predicted by the quality and quantity of our relationships with others – our friendships, our relationships with family members and colleagues, and our closeness with neighbours. We lead such busy lives that often it's very challenging to find time to spend with friends, but it's worth making time for those relationships since our relationships with others are the key to our happiness. Also refer to the discussion in Unit 7: Relationships and in Chapter 2 of the Handbook about how good relationships benefit children.

Circle Time or classroom discussion

Read one or more of the books and poems and discuss issues around friendships. Write students' ideas on the board.

Discussion questions

- What were some of the things the good friends in the books did?
- Can you have more than one friend? (Yes, it's good to have a number of friends. We have different interests that we can share with different people.)
- Is it okay to have friends that are very different to each other?
- What are the good things about having different friends? (Having different friends means you can enjoy different things with each one of them.)
- Can you have or be the perfect friend? (No, no-one is perfect.)
- What kinds of problems do friends sometimes have?

Then review **BLM Being a Good Friend Chart**. Ask students to explain why each item is important for being a good friend.

- Why is being honest with your friends important? (Trust)
- Why is being loyal (e.g. standing up for friends, being on their side, defending them, not bad-mouthing them) important? (Trust, you get what you give.)
- Why is it important to try to use both of your ideas when you are working on something together?
- Why is feeling comfortable about being yourself important? (Closeness, trust, support.)
- Why is being happy in each other's company important?
- Why is it important that when something good happens in your life, your friend is happy for you?
- Why is it important to try to find a solution that you are both happy with when you disagree? (Being fair, trust.)

Activities

- Complete **BLM Friendship Similarities** and **The Friendship e-quiz**. The quiz could also be completed as a lead-in to the topic.
- Make posters on 'What are the friendship facts?'
- Create Quick quotes (see page 96) about friendship.
- Students do a word hunt to find as many words as they can that mean 'friend'.
- Sing one of the suggested songs together.
- Write and illustrate a 'Wanted' sign for a good friend listing desired attributes or qualities.
- Draw a cartoon strip, create an illustrated imaginative text or write a script for a short puppet play to be acted out for the class about 'The Really Good Friend' or 'The Disappointing Friend'.
- Using the Pairs rally, pairs compare strategy (see page 95) ask students to respond to the topic question 'What are things we do to be a good friend?'

International Friendship Day

International Friendship Day is held around the world every year on the first Sunday in August. The United Nations has appointed Winnie-the-Pooh as its friendship ambassador. Have students make friendship kits or craft items with a friendship theme to prepare for and celebrate the day. Some students may not currently have someone they would call a friend. Remind them that they could make the items for a friend who is also a relative (see book below) or an adult friend. Here are some suggestions:

- Make posters about the day or have a school-wide celebration.
- Make digital friendship cards. Students can design a friendship card (with an appropriate greeting plus illustrations and graphics) and friendship wrapping paper.
- Make a placemat with a friendship theme. Students can draw or paint on A4 paper and then slide paper into a plastic A4 sleeve, or they could be laminated.
- Make a calendar on the computer with important dates for students and their friends or record them in the school diary.
- Make a friendship mobile or collage, using drawings or pictures cut out of magazines to illustrate the joys and benefits of friendship (see page 105).

Paper friends

Students make paper friends holding hands. Using two coloured sheets of A4 paper folded into four, students make two sets of four teddies, hearts with arms, or animals with their hands joined. They draw their 'friends' first, making sure they are large enough to write a sentence on. Then on their 'friends' they write good friendship behaviours.

Journal writing about friendship

Students write in their **Bounce Back!** journal about the ways in which they could be thoughtful towards a friend. For example, what could they do to make a friend feel special and cared for? Students can write using particular situations to make their writing more specific. For example, what could they do when their friend is sick and couldn't come to school, or what could they do when their friend is excited about their upcoming party?

Friendship wall

Students work in groups of three to make a wall of friendship. Use tissue boxes covered in paper or painted so that the boxes look like the bricks in a wall. On each 'brick' they write a good friendship behaviour. They could also complete this activity with a partner using bricks drawn on a large sheet of paper.

Friendship sunshine wheel

Students work with a partner to make a sunshine wheel. In the circle they write 'a good friend' and on the spokes they write how a good friend behaves and what they do and don't do, for example:

- helps you if you need help
- waits for you if you are running late
- saves you a seat
- helps you carry heavy things
- remembers your birthday
- stands up for you if someone teases you
- shares things with you
- shares things about themselves
- tells you what you do well.

Stress that nobody can be a perfect friend who does all these things all the time!

Dealing with friendship problems

Resources

✦ Books

Our Friendship Rules

Alexandra and Jenny have been best friends for a long time, and Jenny feels hurt when Alexandra seems to be dazzled by a new girl to the school who is very 'cool'. To impress her, Alexandra foolishly tells the new girl some private information about Jenny.

Trouble Talk

A new girl, Bailey, arrives at school and Maya is asked to help her settle in. But Maya soon discovers that Bailey is very prone to using put-downs, saying hurtful things, spreading malicious rumours and sharing private information without permission.

✦ Poems

Sad Underwear

It's a Puzzle

Circle Time or classroom discussion

Read one or more of the books or poems to the class and discuss. Stress that all friendships have problems sometimes, but things can often be sorted out if you try hard. However, sometimes a friendship changes. When friendships start to change, it doesn't always mean that one of you has done something wrong or that one of you is a bad or unlikeable person. It just means you start to develop different interests.

Discussion questions

- How did the friendships in the books/poems change?
- How did the character/s feel? (Sad, nervous, lonely.)
- What kinds of problems can friends have? (Arguments, misunderstandings, growing apart, jealousy, competition from potential new friends.)
- Why do friends sometimes start to grow apart?

Discuss that there could be two kinds of reasons friends drift apart:

- As you grow, you become different and you both might not have as much in common anymore; you each become involved in new interests; you don't get to spend much time together.
- One person can do something that hurts the friendship; sometimes you find out things about a person which make you less keen to stay friends; the other person wants to boss you around; the friend wants you to break the rules or be mean.

Ask selected students to say one thing that can hurt a friendship.

Activities

- Students write a similar poem to *Sad Underwear*.
- Using the PACE strategy (see page 95) ask students to respond to the question 'What is the most common problem that happens between friends?'
- Students draw pictures, create cartoons or write stories about 'friendship shakers' (i.e. people who can make a friendship 'shaky' if they don't mend their ways). For example:
  - Petra or Pedro Promise-Breaker who makes promises to friends but doesn't follow through
  - Tabitha or Tyrone Two-Face who talks about friends behind their backs and says critical things about them
  - Brianna or Bailey Big-Mouth who tells a friend's secret to impress others
  - Janey or Jeremy Joker who thinks that teasing friends and playing mean jokes is funny
  - Queenie the Queen Bee or Kyle the King who bosses their friends around and tries to control them, including saying who else they can be friends with.

Dealing with friendship disagreements

Resources

◆ Books

The Sandwich Swap

Lily and Salma are best friends. They always eat lunch together, but one day they get into an argument over sandwiches – Lily prefers peanut butter and Salma likes hummus. This 'difference' starts to threaten their friendship, but they are able to sort things out.

Pink Tiara Cookies for Three

Sami and Stella have been best friends for some time. Then Jasmine and her family move into house near Sami's, and Jasmine wants to be friends with Sami. This causes friction between Sami and Stella, but they find a way to include Jasmine in their friendship.

✦ Poems

Best Friends

The Quarrel

Circle Time or classroom discussion

Use the Lightning writing strategy (see page 93) and ask students to write down everything that comes to mind when they think about the words 'argument' or 'disagreement'. List all the words they associate with arguments or disagreements. Count how many words and phrases are positive (e.g. solve problems, sort things out) and how many are negative. This activity can be repeated three months later to see if students use more positive words and fewer negative words than they did the first time.

Read one of the books or poems to the class and discuss. Talk about different versions of events or different 'points of view'. When relevant, ask 'whose version of things is the correct one?'

Explain that it's normal in any healthy friendship to sometimes disagree. Give students a copy of **BLM Healthy Disagreement Cycle** and discuss the cycle of a normal healthy friendship.

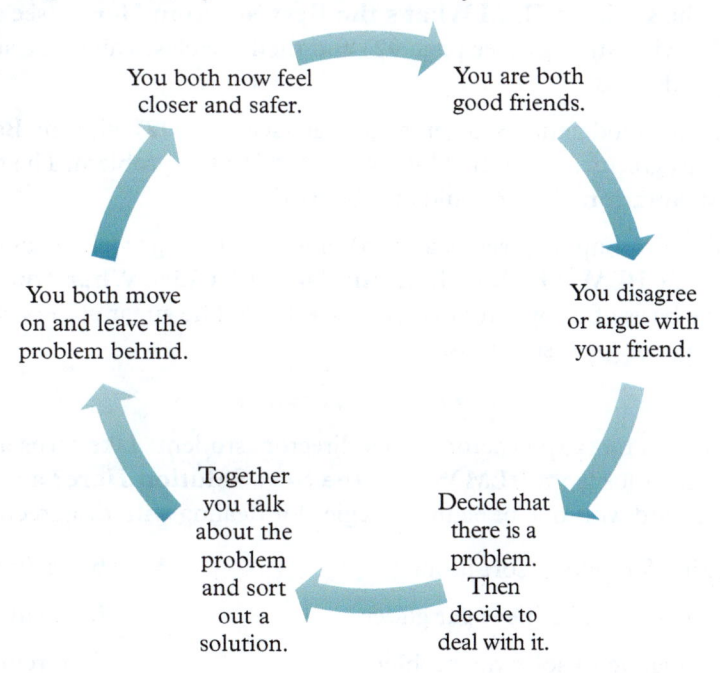

Cycle diagram:
- You are both good friends.
- You disagree or argue with your friend.
- Decide that there is a problem. Then decide to deal with it.
- Together you talk about the problem and sort out a solution.
- You both move on and leave the problem behind.
- You both now feel closer and safer.

Discussion questions

- What is a disagreement? (A disagreement is when two people both want the same thing and only one can have it their way, or two people don't agree on what should happen or did happen, or when one person thinks the other is being unfair.)
- Is an argument the same as a disagreement? (An argument is a heated or angry discussion that you have where you each say why you disagree and what you want to happen.)
- Is a fight the same as a disagreement? (A fight usually happens after an argument when things haven't been sorted out well and someone still feels upset and angry.)
- What did the characters disagree about?
- How did the characters sort out their disagreement?

Display or give each student a copy of **BLM Which Animal Are You Most Like When You Disagree?** Ask students if any of the characters were like these animals. Then ask them to turn to the person next to them and share which animal they are most like when they disagree with a friend. Emphasise that being like a sugar glider is the best way to deal with disagreements.

Give each student **BLM Disagreement Memory Jogger** and go through each tip. Ask students which strategies the characters used. Students colour in the picture of the tip they need to practise and paste the BLM in their *Bounce Back!* journals.

Activities

- Complete **Which Way Did They Sort Out Their Disagreements? e-activity** as a class.
- Undertake Inquiry-based learning (see page 92) into foxes, sugar gliders and wombats.
- Students complete **BLM What's the Best Solution Here?** and share their responses in groups.
- Use the Round table strategy (see page 97) and ask students to categorise the strategies from the **BLM What's the Best Solution Here?** into Fox, Wombat or Sugar glider. Include other strategies such as hurting others (fox), thinking only about winning (fox), ignoring that there is a disagreement (wombat) and thinking only about being liked (wombat).

Drama

- Use the stories in **BLM What's the Best Solution Here?** (see above) with the Freeze frame and rewind strategy (see page 92) and then the class can make suggestions as to what they might do next.
- Use the Good genie/Bad genie strategy (see page 92) with the Bad genie forcing and avoiding the disagreement and the Good genie solving the problem. The scenarios in **BLM What's the Best Solution Here?** could also be used.
- Make stick puppets (see page 105) of wombats, sugar gliders and foxes (use enlarged pictures from the **BLM Which Animal Are You Most Like When You Disagree?**) and use these as the basis of puppet drama (see page 105). The sugar gliders can arrive and give advice on sorting out good solutions.

Strategies for resolving disagreements

In groups of three (two actors and a director) students take turns at drawing a card with one of the scenarios from **BLM What's the Best Solution Here?** and from a separate container taking a card with one of eight strategies for dealing with disagreements:

1. asking for help to sort it out
2. being smart like the sugar glider
3. negotiating to solve the problem
4. avoiding or being wishy-washy like the wombat
5. saying 'Okay, let's do it your way'
6. speaking up firmly
7. forcing like the fox
8. saying sorry.

Students draw a story map first, then act out their story. Classmates guess whether they are being a fox, a wombat or a sugar glider and which strategy they are using.

Embed it

Have a box in the classroom where students can write out and post conflict situations that they would like to be used as pretend (hypothetical) examples to be acted out or discussed. In groups of three, students prepare two enactments: a good solution to the conflict, which is more likely to maintain the friendship, and a bad solution, which is more likely to end the friendship.

Fixing friendship problems

Resources

📖 ✦ Book
Louise and Andie: The Art of Friendship

Louise has a new neighbour, Andie, and they both love art. During a shared art session they disagree about what is good art. Angry words are spoken and drawings get torn up. But they manage to successfully negotiate and collaborate in ways that help them to remain friends.

🎬 ✦ Video clip
Ramon Learns to Resolve a Conflict

This video clip teaches students about communicating feelings and resolving conflicts.

🎵 ✦ Song
'Kids Rap – Conflict Resolution and Respect'

Circle Time or classroom discussion

Read the following dialogue to students or ask two students to act it out. Alternatively, use one of the resources to start discussions.

> Amira: Let's play handball at lunchtime.
>
> Matthew: No, I don't feel like it. Let's play basketball instead.
>
> Amira: No, I don't want to play basketball.
>
> Matthew: Well, I don't want to play handball. We play handball all the time.
>
> Amira: No, we don't!
>
> Matthew: Yes, we do!
>
> Amira: You're so annoying.
>
> Matthew: You're even more annoying. I don't want to play anything with you.

Discussion questions

- How do you think the characters are feeling? Did this situation end well? Who won the disagreement?
- How did they say what they thought? Did they respect each other's opinion? Did they listen to what the other person was saying?
- How could they have sorted out their disagreement?
- What does negotiate mean?

Explain that negotiating means making sure that everyone feels they have been heard and that the final decision/outcome is one that everyone can live with, even if it's not exactly what they would have chosen by themselves. It means problem-solving and finding ways for everyone to 'win' at least some of what they wanted to happen so that everyone 'maintains face'. It's a win/win approach.

Record students' ideas on how the disagreement could have been sorted out, for example:

- Listen to others' views.
- It's okay for others to have a different point of view.
- Don't be angry.

- Don't ignore others.
- State your view in a friendly way.
- You should never force someone to agree to your point of view or just give in to another person's point of view.
- Give good reasons for your point of view.
- Be open to other points of view.
- You need to be respectful when disagreeing and avoid put-downs.
- Problem-solve and offer other options.
- Can your view and other views join up?
- Aim to reach a win/win situation.
- You might have to give up a part of what you want to reach a decision.
- Even if you're not totally happy, can you live with the agreed decision?
- Ask for help from a teacher to sort things out, but try to sort it out yourself first.

Display **BLM How to Negotiate Well Chart** and ask students for examples of each tip. Give students a copy of the BLM to paste into their *Bounce Back!* journals to refer to.

Activities

Finding great gifts

Give each pair of students a store catalogue. Their task is to negotiate the best way to decide on three presents – one for a parent, one for a friend, and one for a three-year-old girl or boy. They cut the chosen presents out and paste them onto a sheet of paper and then tell the class why they have chosen them. Students write down three skills of negotiation they practised.

Ranking

Ask groups of three to rank a list of things. Choose lists that have some preferences involved, not just factual characteristics. For example:

- Rank these four animals in terms of how good they would be as a pet: dog, fish, cat, rabbit.
- Rank these four foods in order of how good they would be as a party food: pizza, hot dogs, pies, sandwiches.
- Rank these four games in order of how good they would be to play at a sleepover: Bingo, Hide and Seek, Snap, Charades.

Ask students to give their results and what skills they practised to negotiate a decision.

Friendship rap

Play 'Kids Rap – Conflict Resolution and Respect'. Students write their own rap song about fixing friendship problems.

Drama

Students use puppets (see pages 105–106) to act out various scenarios using negotiation skills, for example:

- One student in the group wants to present their project as a slide show while others want to do a poster.
- One student wants to use the computer/a book/pens, but another person is using it/them.
- Everyone wants to watch a different film at a friend's sleepover.

Embed it

Use Class meetings to allow students to practise the social skills of cooperation (e.g. listening, taking turns to speak, negotiating, sharing the work, sorting out disagreements). Rotate the positions of chairperson and secretary (see page 89).

Peace mat

Use a large mat or piece of carpet and section off the room in some way if possible. Send students there to sort things out. If they can't resolve things, then the teacher mediates. The peace mat or room is where students can sort out solutions to disagreements. Create laminated posters of **BLMs Which Animal Are You Most Like When You Disagree?**, **BLM Disagreement Memory Jogger** and **BLM How to Negotiate Well Chart**.

On-the-spot conflict resolution support

Make laminated copies of the BLMs above and use them to talk to students who become involved in conflict situations in the classroom and playground (e.g. 'Are you being a fox, a sugar glider or a wombat?', 'What strategy have you used here?', 'What other strategies could you try?', 'How can you build bridges here?').

Peaceful solutions slogans

Use some of these slogans on a rotating basis during disagreements. Students make their own class posters.

- Nobody is a loser here. We use a win/win approach.
- Look for peaceful solutions to your problem.
- Hurting does not solve problems – talking, listening, negotiating and caring do.
- Peacemakers are welcome here.
- No matter how serious or silly, most disagreements can be fixed if you are prepared to try.
- It takes courage to sort things out or build a bridge back again.
- Nobody wins if you never speak to each other again.

Building bridges and saying sorry

Resources

✦ Poems

Apology

I'm Going to Say I'm Sorry

There Are Only Two Kinds of I'm Sorry

The Hardest Thing

Circle Time or classroom discussion

Read one or more of the poems and discuss them. Talk about how a gap can open up between people when they have a disagreement. People can grow apart from each other which means that they don't feel comfortable being together. Ask students to draw this to show what 'emotional distance' looks like visually. Explain that once there is a gap between people, they need to build a bridge to get back to each other and be friends again.

Discussion questions

- What are some good ways to build a bridge and cross back over to your friend, family member or classmate? (Apologising for anything you did that added to the disagreement, saying 'I'm sorry we had an argument', being kind to them, spending time with them, telling them how important the relationship is to you, saying how pleased you are that the argument is over, having a laugh together.)
- What is the best thing to do if the other person doesn't want to cross over the bridge you try to build? (Wait a while, say that you're sorry they feel like that now and that you hope they will change their mind.)
- Tell us about one time you said sorry to someone or someone said sorry to you. Did it make things better? How did you feel when you got or made an apology?
- When is it good to apologise? (When you have done something unfair, unkind or thoughtless, or when one small thing you have done has added to a disagreement or an argument, even though that wasn't the only thing that led to it – you can say sorry for your bit.)
- What makes it hard sometimes to apologise? (Pride, wanting to win, not wanting others to think we are losers, fear that the other person will make us feel bad and use the apology against us.)
- What can you lose if you don't say sorry when you have done something wrong? (Friendship, self-respect.)
- What do we mean by 'swallowing our pride'?
- What is the best way to say sorry to someone? Does it depend on who was mostly wrong? (Emphasise that usually both people have added to an argument or fight, even if it is just by the way in which they have responded.)
- What would you say to yourself? What would you say to them?
- What sort of voice would you use? What words would you use?

Elicit responses from students and record them. Some examples are:

Dos	Don'ts
If you were in the wrong, say so and explain why you did it. (e.g. 'I'm sorry I said that mean thing to you. I was having a bad day.')	Don't be too stubborn or too proud to say sorry.
Say, 'I'm sorry, I didn't mean to hurt your feelings.'	Don't say, 'I'm sorry … but you …' and then say that it was really their fault.
Use a friendly tone of voice to show that you mean it.	Don't use a tone of voice that says you are not really sorry.
Even if you think the other person was in the wrong, you can still say, 'I'm sorry we had a fight.'	Don't think that being right is more important than being friends.
If someone has said sorry to you, accept that everyone makes mistakes and let them know that they are forgiven.	If someone has said sorry to you, don't refer to what happened again. It is in the past.

Activities

- Students make a bulletin board display of drawings of two people crossing over a bridge back to their friendship. Speech and thought balloons can be used to show what they are saying in order to build the bridge, or they can write these things in the building blocks of the bridge.

- Students create Quick quotes on apologising (see page 96).
- Create a puppet drama (see pages 105–106 for ideas) around good and bad apologising.
- Students make a class poster of 'How to Say Sorry', using the table on page 240 as a guide.

Dealing with being separated from a friend

Resources

✦ Book

Amber Brown Is Not a Crayon

Amber and Justin are best friends, but Justin's family decides to move to the USA, leaving Amber upset and angry because she thinks that Justin doesn't care that their friendship is to be interrupted. After some distance between them, Amber sorts her feelings out.

✦ Poem

Since Hanna Moved Away

Circle Time or classroom discussion

Read to the class the book or poem. Use the discussion questions below to discuss how students may feel when they are separated from a friend and how they can deal with these feelings.

Discussion questions

- How did the character feel when their friend moved away?

- In the book *Amber Brown Is Not a Crayon*, why is Amber angry with Justin? (She feels Justin is letting her down and doesn't understand the impact that his moving to the USA will have on her, she feels that she has lost her best friend and will have no-one to support her any more.)

- What reality check could Amber have used? (She could have checked to see if they could stay in contact in other ways and still be friends, she could have asked him whether he felt as sad about the move as she did.)

- Tell us about a friend you've had who moved from your street or school. Do you still keep in touch with them?

- How does someone feel if their friend moves away or they move themselves? (Lonely and sometimes angry; scared that they will make new friends and forget about you, that you will no longer be special to anyone, that you will never see your friend again, or that you won't find any other friends.)

- What could you do to stay in touch with them? (You can email, write a letter, phone them, have a 'Me too!' day where you arrange to do the same thing at the same time on the same day, send souvenirs or photos of things you have done, or make and send video clips, connect via technology.)

- What helpful thinking and self-talk could you use to help you feel better? ('It doesn't mean that everything in my life has been spoiled', 'There are many exciting new things to come now that I have moved', 'Others will like and care about me when they get to know me', 'The sad feelings will go away again and things will get better', 'I will see them again', 'I can stay in touch with them', 'I will find new friends but it might take a bit of time.')

Activities

- Students make a Lift-up flap wall chart (see page 103) of all the things they can do to stay in touch with a friend who moves away. On the front of their flap, they can write, 'This is one good way to stay in touch with a friend'.
- Make a class book (see page 101) on 'This is one good way to stay in touch with a friend'.
- Students write a letter to an absent friend.
- Students write a poem similar to *Since Hanna Moved Away* (see page 241).

Consolidation

Embed it

The cooperative learning strategies and Circle Time discussions throughout **Bounce Back!** are all designed to build positive classroom relationships. See Handbook Chapter 1 for a summary of teaching students in their social and emotional wellbeing class about the social skills of working and playing well together.

Activities

Throw the dice

Use the Throw the dice strategy for this activity (see page 98), with the following questions:

- How could someone try to make new friends if they moved to a new school?
- Talk about a friend you had before you came to this school.
- What do you think is the most important quality in a good friend?
- What advice would you give to someone who wants to have more interesting conversations?
- What do you think most arguments are about?
- What do you and your family argue about and how do you sort it out? (Stress the privacy rule.)

These questions could also be used with Musical stop and share (see page 94) or Inside–outside circle strategies (see page 93).

Cut-up sentences

Cut the following sentences into individual words and place each cut-up sentence into an envelope (see page 92). Make enough sets for each pair of students to have one set of the six sentences. Each pair reconstructs the six sentences. The **Cut-up Sentences e-activity** can also be used.

- A good friend is loyal, caring and thoughtful.
- Try to sort things out in a friendly way.
- Disagreements are normal so don't be afraid of them.
- You can't sort things out well if you stay angry.
- Being a good listener is important for getting along.
- People can be very different and still be friends.

Drama

Let's act it out

Students can use puppets to act out any of the scenarios mentioned in this unit. This can be done in pairs or as a whole class.

Reflections

Use the **Reflections** or **Animal Asks e-tools** (see pages 97 and 90) to ask these questions:
- Why is friendship important?
- What is one thing that children like about other children?
- What is one thing that can be difficult when you try to sort out disagreements?
- Why is saying 'sorry' important?
- What is meant by 'building bridges'?
- Why is it a good idea to try to sort out a disagreement and not just try to avoid it?
- Can you think of something that could be negotiated when students are working together on a task?
- What is one thing that people expect a friend to do?

Key vocabulary

Use the Whisper game, Mystery square or the TEAM coaching strategy to assist students to learn vocabulary and spelling related to relationships to a reasonable level of mastery (see pages 98, 94 and 97). Examples:

apologise	friendship	negotiate
argument	happy	negotiation
boring	honesty	support
change	interesting	relationships
conversation	kind	respect
disagree	listener	social
disagreement	loser	sorry
fair	loyal	thoughtful
friend	mistake	winner

Games

Play one of these games with the whole class.

▶ **Before or After? e-game** (see page 90).

▶ Complete the **Cross-offs e-game** with the class. The secret message is: 'To have a friend you must be a friend.'

▶ Bingo strips (see page 90) or Bingo strips for pairs (see page 98) using some of the words listed above.

▶ Big words, small words (see page 98) using one of these words: friendship, relationships, conversation, negotiation.

▶ **Memory Cards e-game** (see page 93)– students find the matching synonyms:

negotiate – work things out

apologise – say sorry

respect – treat well

argument – disagreement

boring – not interesting

conversation – talk or chat

honest – tell the truth

interesting – not boring

support – help

thoughtful – think about others

different – not the same

kind – nice

Bounce Back! award

Present the **Bounce Back! award** to students who have best demonstrated the social skills that have been taught in this unit.

UNIT 8

Humour

KEY MESSAGES

Humour is enjoyable.
Finding something funny and having a good laugh is fun. It makes you feel relaxed and happy. It puts you in a good mood.

Everyone has their own sense of humour.
Everyone's sense of humour is different as we all find different things funny.

Humour is good for your health.
When you laugh a lot, you are more likely to stay healthy. Laughter helps our bodies to fight disease and illness and repair our bodies. Laughter helps us to cope with stress and worries by sending messages to our bodies to relax.

Humour can help us to cope and feel more hopeful when things aren't going well.
Laughing can often make you feel a bit better when you are feeling sad or worried. It can take your mind off what is troubling you for a while. It can help you put things into 'perspective' and see that everything isn't sad or difficult. This doesn't make the problem go away. But finding the funny side helps you to feel more hopeful about solving problems and dealing with things.

You can use humour to cheer someone else up.
Being funny can help to cheer someone up when they are feeling sad or worried. But you need to be careful about how you do this. If the other person lets you know that they are not enjoying it, then stop.

Humour can help friendships to grow stronger.
One way friends can get closer to each other is by sharing laughter. But laughing together about someone else in a mean way is not a kind thing to do. Share good laughter, not nasty laughter.

Humour can be hurtful if you use it to make fun of others or put them down.
There is a big difference between friendly teasing and nasty teasing. It is not kind to laugh at:

- someone else's bad luck
- or make fun of the way another person looks, thinks, speaks or acts.

Humour should not be used as a way of being nasty or to hurt someone's feelings or embarrass them. This is unkind and must stop quickly.

> **Learning objectives**
> In this unit, students will further develop their understanding that humour can:
> - help us to feel better
> - make others feel better as long as it isn't hurtful.

Resources list

A complete list of resources including references for core and additional books, films, video clips, poems, songs and websites is available.

Everyone has a different sense of humour

Resources

◆ Books

The Book with No Pictures

The book has no pictures, but everything written in it must be spoken aloud by the person reading it. This is the source of the humour, as they have to say nonsense words and phrases that will have young listeners laughing.

Little Penguin Gets the Hiccups

Little Penguin has eaten too much chilli and now has a very bad case of the hiccups. His friend Franklin suggests that a 'good scare' usually gets rid of hiccups. Little Penguin asks for some help from those reading and listening to the book to give him a sudden scare.

One More Sheep

This is a funny rhyming story about Sam the shepherd who can't count his ten sheep without falling asleep. He needs to ensure that all ten are safe. He is so sleepy one time that he almost fails to recognise that the 'sheep' knocking at the door is really a wolf in a woolly costume.

◆ Video clips

Show your favourite age-appropriate video clips. Those involving an animal being cute or silly are often popular with students.

Circle Time or classroom discussion

Read two of the books above and/or show a video clip, then ask students to say which one they thought was the funniest. Count their show of hands and then ask selected students why they thought their choice was the funniest. Stress that everyone has their own sense of humour, and that is okay.

Ask students to each say one funny thing they have laughed at recently. Make a chart on the board of the categories they mention (e.g. poetry, movies, TV shows, cartoons, illustrations, jokes, riddles, stories, performances). Identify and discuss similarities and differences.

Discussion questions

- What is humour?
- Why were the books or video clip/s funny?
- What type of cartoon do you find funny and why?
- Can you name a book that you think is funny? Why is it funny?
- Can you remember thinking a picture or drawing was funny? Why was it funny?
- Do you sometimes find something funny when someone else doesn't?

Activities

- Students write a review about a funny book, computer game or television show and why it makes them laugh.
- In groups of three, students make a class riddle book. Use a format whereby the answers to the riddles are mixed up on a separate page and students have to 'find' the correct match.
- Adapt one of the books for Reader's theatre (see page 96).

Take-home task

Students interview one or two family members about some of the things that make them laugh (e.g. books, TV shows, movies, cartoon shows). They could also ask each family member to provide an age-appropriate funny joke or riddle that the student can bring back to contribute to a class collection.

Embed it

Fun zone

With the help of a rotating class committee, create and maintain a humour zone in the classroom. You could include comic strips, funny books, funny poems, a class compilation of riddles and jokes, and cartoons around the wall.

Humour is enjoyable and is good for your health

Resources

✦ Books

Bad Kitty

Bad Kitty is a different sort of alphabet book. There is an A to Z of the types of food that is available for Kitty to eat when the family runs out of cat food (asparagus to zucchini) and the naughty things that Kitty gets up to when her family is out.

Oh No, George!

George is a curious but somewhat naughty dog. He really wants to be good, but he struggles with temptation.

✦ Song

'The Quartermaster's Store'

Circle time or classroom discussion

Read one the books listed, or sing 'The Quartermaster's Store'. Explain that laughter helps our bodies to relax so we can think more clearly, feel happier and be less stressed and worried. It also helps us to feel closer to other people when we laugh together about something we have shared. Make the point that laughter also helps our bodies to fight disease and illness.

Laughter:

- makes the brain release 'feel good' chemicals and we feel happier
- helps us to fight infection and disease
- lowers the heart rate so that we feel fitter
- helps to make our bones stronger, especially if we have been stressed for a while
- helps our bodies to grow and repair themselves when they have been damaged.

Discussion questions

- Why were the books or song funny?
- When have you laughed more than any other time?
- How does your body feel after listening to a funny story? What feelings do you have in your head? (The body feels less tense, more floppy and relaxed; you feel happier.)
- Who has a pet at home? Describe something funny that your pet does (or did) that makes you laugh.
- Does it feel good when your pet does something funny and makes you laugh? How is this healthy?
- Do you laugh more when you are on your own, or when you share something funny with others? Why do you think this is so?

Enlarge a copy of the **BLM Laughter Is Good for the Body and Mind** and discuss how laughter helps our bodies. Ask students to match the labels to the parts of the body affected.

> **Teacher reflection**
> Reflect on some of the ways you share humour informally with your class. Are there students in your class who stand out for their sense of humour and, if so, how might they contribute to the enjoyable use of humour in your classroom?

Activities

- Each student makes up their own rhyming verse in the style of the song 'The Quartermaster's Store'. Use the names of the students in the class.
- Follow up on the *Bad Kitty* book by asking students to make an A to Z of both the good and bad things (combined in the A to Z) that a pet or a character from a book, film or TV show gets up to.
- Give students the same squiggle (a short line that curls and loops in an irregular way) on a sheet of paper and ask them to make a funny creature or picture from it.

Rating jokes

Give each student a copy of **BLM Jokes**. Get students to rate each joke as they read them in pairs. Tally the results for each joke. Students can make a class chart and graph the results or write a report on the findings. Invite other classes and teachers to be involved in the ratings as well and make comparisons. Consider inviting older students to provide jokes for students to rate.

Games

The Wright Family's Picnic

This fun physical activity can be used to reinforce direction, enhance concentration and re-focus attention. Students stand where there are no obstacles close by. Read the following story slowly, and have students react in the following ways to the action words:

- Each time the word 'Wright/right' is said they take a side step to the right.
- Each time the word 'left' is said they take a side step to the left.
- Each time the word 'up' is said they wave both arms in the air.
- Each time the word 'down' is said they squat down and get up again quickly.
- Every time the word 'dog' is said they say 'woof'.

> Mr and Ms **Wright** and their children Cindy and Bobby decided to have a picnic **down** by the river. They were taking their **dog** Fred with them too as he didn't want to be **left** behind. Cindy **Wright** took the picnic basket **down** the stairs to the car and Bobby cleaned **up** the mess that was **left** after they had made their sandwiches. The **Wright** family finally **left** home at 10 a.m. and headed for their favourite picnic spot **down** by the river. When they arrived, the **Wright** family set **up** their chairs and table to the **left** of the bend in the river. Mrs **Wright** looked a bit cross and Bobby said 'What's **up**, Mum?' His mother replied that she was disappointed that the people before them had **left** their rubbish behind. They all helped to clean it **up**. Mr **Wright** took the **dog** for a walk. The children played on the playground equipment to the **left**. When Mr **Wright** and the **dog** returned from their walk, the children **left** the play area and came back to the picnic table where they enjoyed the lunch they had helped to prepare.

After the activity, ask students:

- How well were you able to concentrate on the story?
- What strategies did you use to pay attention?
- How much did this activity make you laugh and why?
- ▶ Follow up with students working in groups of three to develop another Wright family story. Remind them that a right direction should be followed by a left, because too many steps in the same direction could lead them right out of the classroom!

Laugh for the Joker

This is a silly group card game that helps develop concentration and memory. Everyone is usually laughing so hard that the game rarely gets finished. The aim is to be the first person to get rid of all their cards. You will need one pack of cards including the two Jokers for each group of 6–7 students. One additional student acts as a non-playing referee for each group.

One student deals out all the cards face down so that each student has the same number of cards; any cards left over are put aside.

The player to the left of the dealer turns up the first card (in a way that doesn't show everyone what's coming) and places the card face up in the centre. Then all other members of the group go round the circle and take turns at turning up one of their cards (the next one in the pile). When one of the following cards is turned up, everyone together has do a certain action:

- For a King, they all stand up, bow and say, 'I bow to the King.'
- For a Queen, they all stand up, curtsy and say, 'I curtsy to the Queen.'
- For a Jack, they all kneel and salute and say, 'I salute the Jack.'
- For an Ace, they all put their hand on the ace and say, 'I slap the Ace.'
- For a Joker, they all stand up, do a funny head wobble with their arms flapping and say, 'I laugh for the Joker, hee haw.'

The person who is the last to do the required action (as observed by the referee) is then given an additional card by the referee as a penalty. Then the game resumes.

Embed it

Giggle gym

Have a short (5–10 minute) Giggle gym session twice a week, if possible. It could be linked with literacy, language, music, dance, maths or any relevant learning area. Introduce the laughter break by reviewing with students why it is good to have some laughter in your day (to help you feel relaxed, to help you cope, to give you hope, to keep you healthy, to make you feel less anxious and to build friendships). Select a humorous or silly dance, game, song, poem, story or book from the suggestions in this unit or from your own collection.

Consider making a file with humorous poems, books, songs, activities, etc. and asking students to draw one out for each Giggle gym session. Remove the activity when they have been drawn out. Replace them every six weeks to make sure of a good mix.

You could also offer students the chance to vote on what will be in Giggle gym each week. You can combine this with behaviour management or practising social skills. Provide points (or point cards) for specified behaviours. Students who earn three points during the previous week can participate in the selection of a Giggle gym sessions during the following week.

Humour helps us cope better and feel more hopeful

Resources

✦ Books

First Grade Dropout
A boy in first grade feels totally humiliated when he accidentally calls his teacher 'mommy' in class, and his best friend laughs about it with the class. But after his best friend embarrasses himself too, they both laugh about their mistakes and keep them in perspective.

The Terrible Underpants
See page 216.

✦ Song

'Nobody Likes Me, Everybody Hates Me (I Think I'll Go Eat Worms!)'
(The tune is similar to 'Polly Wolly Doodle All the Day'.)

Circle Time or classroom discussion

In the circle, read one of the books listed or sing the song together. Ask students to think of a time when they were feeling sad or worried, but something made them laugh and feel just a little bit better. Emphasise that funny things remind us that what makes us feel sad or worried isn't going to go on forever and things will get better. They also remind us that there are still lots of other good things in our life.

Talk about how it can be helpful to say, 'We'll laugh about this next week' or 'This will be a funny story later', as a way of dealing with unhappy times.

Discussion questions

- How could the song 'Everybody Hates Me . . .' help us to feel more hopeful if we were feeling lonely or left out?
- What is the message in the book *First Grade Dropout*? (We all embarrass ourselves sometimes; try to find the funny side to help you feel less upset when you are feeling embarrassed.)
- Can you think of funny things that can cheer us up if we feel unhappy and make us feel more hopeful that things will get better? (A baby being silly, a clown, a pet doing something funny, a funny cartoon show, a funny book.)
- Do you think children in their first year of school would enjoy and understand the book *First Grade Dropout*? What are the reasons for your answer?
- Can you remember a time when you were very embarrassed about something that happened when you were younger? How did you cope with it? Was there a funny side to it that helped you to cope? Can you see the funny side of that situation now?
- Can you think of times when you have seen someone fall over or trip and some people laughed? Why do people sometimes laugh when they see someone have a fall? (There are some nasty reasons, e.g. they don't stop and think about how the other person feels, and some kind reasons, e.g. they want the other person to feel better by seeing the funny side of the situation.)
- Why is it helpful sometimes to laugh at yourself when you embarrass yourself? (It helps you to cope better, others think you can deal with things in a cool way and are confident.)
- How could you help someone else feel better by using humour in a kind way when they are feeling embarrassed?

> **Teacher reflection**
> How is humour used within staff meetings at your school and what impact do you perceive that it has on staff connectedness and wellbeing?

Activities

Crazy hats

Students make crazy hats, decorating the hats with anything that will help to make them bizarre or funny (feathers, buttons, torn pieces of gift wrap, recycled rubbish, google eyes). Have a crazy hat parade with a fashion commentary.

Design a clown

Show students some photos of clowns as stimulus. Students create their own clown character, designing and drawing the make-up and clothes on paper.

Drama

In groups of three, students prepare and perform small plays about doing something embarrassing, finding the funny side and then feeling a bit better about what happened. Some examples are:

- burping loudly during school assembly
- getting the hiccups in a test

- stepping on your own toe in a sporting match/dance
- bringing your pet dog into class for a talk. Your dog is so excited and wets the carpet.

Take-home task

Students interview a family member about a time they felt sad or worried but having a laugh helped them feel better. Students follow up by writing a brief recount (Stress the importance of privacy and the 'no names' rule.)

Embed it

A clown day

Have a 'clown day' where the students dress up and perform as clowns. They can put on make-up and work with a partner to perform a clown act for the class. They could juggle, be a terrified tightrope walker hit by a gust of wind, pretend that a balloon on a string tries to lift them into the air, and make exaggerated gestures and expressions (e.g. hold a big smile for a long time and then collapse the smile into a sad look).

Following are some suggestions for props.

To make dumbbells (and pretend they are very heavy).

Materials needed:

- a long piece of wood such as dowelling
- two balloons
- paint and sticky tape.

Blow up the balloons until they are about the same size. Sticky tape the balloons to the ends of the dowelling. Paint the dowelling.

Pretend to have an invisible dog with a lead.

Materials needed:

- pipe cleaners
- stiff wire or stick.

Make a lead with a collar made out of pipe cleaners on the end of a piece of stiff wire or a stick so that it looks like you are walking an invisible dog. If you are using wire instead of a stick, you can bend one end of the wire into a large loop to look like the dog collar.

You can use humour to cheer someone up

Resources

◆ Video clip

Clown Doctors Australia

The Clown Doctors provide some humour that helps sick children, their families, and hospital staff.

♪ Song

'The Duck Song'

Circle Time or classroom discussion

Play the video clip or song.

Discussion questions

- What do you think of clowns trying to cheer up sick children in hospital?

Discuss how the very exaggerated (and hence funny) facial expressions that the clown doctors use to show excitement, fear, embarrassment, pleasure, or sadness help cheer up the sick children, as well as the tricks and music they play.

- What was funny about the song?

Ask each student to think of an experience that made them very scared or sad or excited. Examples might include going on a scary theme park ride, their first day at school, when they were lost, etc. Ask selected students to briefly tell their story accompanied by exaggerated and funny facial expressions related to that story. After each story, ask students to raise their hand if they felt more cheerful after hearing and 'seeing' the story. Consider telling a story of your own.

Activity

Students write one or two brief one-paragraph stories from their own lives accompanied by drawings of exaggerated and funny facial expressions that reflect the emotions in each part of their stories. Students could also act out their story and students have to guess what happened.

Embed it

I need an extra laugh today

Prepare a number of copies of **BLM I Need a Laugh**. Leave them near a box that students can use to communicate with you without their classmates being aware of it. Make sure it is a sealed box. Tell students that when they feel sad or bothered about something, they can ask for some help to be cheered up. This allows you to get some idea about what is happening in the students' emotional lives. You may need to follow up with some one-on-one discussion using the BOUNCE BACK! acronym. Provide a very brief extra five-minute activity if this is asked for and if you can fit it in. Silly songs, brief games and poems are probably the quickest things you can select from or draw something in the room with their non-preferred hand, make funny faces or adopt funny walks that everyone copies. Refer to Giggle gym on page 250 for ideas. If more than one student asks on a given day, use the same 'extra' session for all of them. This is another way of encouraging students to talk to someone if they are feeling down or something is bothering them.

Humour can help friendships grow stronger

Resources

♦ Books

My Uncle's Donkey

The narrator's uncle lets his donkey live inside the house and do whatever he pleases. The donkey talks to his friends on the phone, eats from the fridge, does hoof-stands in the kitchen and cartwheels in the living room, takes long baths and stays up as late as he wants to.

Little Hoot

Little Hoot likes to go to bed early and his parents insist that he has as to stay up late and play because he is an owl. They tell him that they don't give 'a hoot' about what his friends are allowed to do.

Little Oink

Little Oink is a naturally tidy and clean pig, but his parents insist he improve his behaviour by unmaking his bed, wearing a dirty shirt and messing up his room. Little Oink laments that when he becomes a parent he's going to let his kids clean their room as much as they want!

Circle Time or classroom discussion

Read one of the books and ask students whether they would enjoy sharing the book with a friend, and why.

Use the Bundling strategy (see page 91) and ask students to share a time when they laughed with their friend(s). Draw together some categories of the kinds of humorous activities that friends of this age share.

Ask whether any of the students have a joke they could tell (one that is appropriate!), and let them tell it. Stress that telling a joke well is a social skill that anyone can learn if they try. Telling a joke well can also help with the development and support of friendships.

Discussion questions

- Why do we like laughing with our friends? (It feels good, we share something special, we feel more relaxed with each other, we discover if we laugh at the same things.)
- Do you think people who laugh a lot are well liked? If so, why? (They seem more friendly, they are more fun, they seem more positive.)
- What are some ideas about how to tell a joke well? (Practise before telling the joke, speak clearly, use expression and deliberate pauses to tell the 'story'. And don't forget the punchline!)

Activities

- Each student contributes one illustrated page of a riddle, a joke, a limerick or funny poem to a class book on 'Laughing with Our Friends'.
- Students draw three other activities that the donkey from *My Uncle's Donkey* might enjoy doing in the house, but hasn't thought of yet.
- Students write a similar imaginative text to *Little Hoot* or *Little Oink* using a different animal e.g. a little snake that wants to make friends, a little duck who doesn't like water.
- In groups of three, students make a funny machine with moving parts. You can give directions to follow, such as, 'one bottom, three legs and two hands must touch the ground'. Then put the groups together to create a collection of funny machines in a funny factory.

Tell a joke well

Students make a 'Dos and Don'ts' list about how to tell a joke well. For example:

- Do get to the punchline fairly fast.
- Don't get too bogged down in detail. A good joke is a reasonably quick joke.
- Do use expression in telling the 'story' in the joke.

- Do make sure you know the joke and the punchline before you tell it!

Students then practise the skill with the four jokes in **BLM Jokes**.

Drama

▶ Students select one of the jokes on **BLM Jokes** and act it out as a funny drama performance.

▶ Students perform funny mimes, using cards drawn from a lucky-dip container. The rest of the class tries to guess what is happening. For example:
- picking flowers and discovering a bee or caterpillar on them
- eating an apple and discovering half a worm inside it
- lifting a weight that is too heavy and nearly dropping it on your foot
- slipping on a banana peel
- picking up a cactus or an echidna to move it from one place to another
- being in a lift that smells really bad
- getting stuck in quicksand.

▶ Have a class competition in which students create and perform funny ways of walking. The funniest two or three can then be practised by the class so that the whole class can then perform them in unison.

Take-home task

Create and send home a one-page handout: 'How to Tell a Joke'. Encourage families to share jokes and give each other feedback on their joke-telling skills.

Humour can be hurtful if it makes fun of others

Resources

✦ Books

That's Not Funny

One day, just for a joke, Hyena puts a banana skin on Giraffe's path. When Giraffe slips and collides with a tree, a chain of unfortunate events begins which involves all the other animals. Hyena laughs and laughs at their misfortune. But the other animals have the last laugh.

The Tease Monster

When Purple and Green tease One-of-a-kind in a mean way, his mother explains that everyone has to learn how to manage being teased. One-of-a-kind learns there are different types of teasing – laughing at someone (mean teasing) and laughing with someone.

Circle Time or classroom discussion

This Circle Time can also be used as part of Unit 9: Being safe.

Read one of the books to the class. Explain that friendly teasing and joking around can be enjoyable and fun, but some teasing can be unkind. Talk about nasty humour, explaining that not all humour is good and that when someone is funny in a way that hurts someone else, they are using bad humour. Examples of nasty humour include:

- mean practical jokes (a practical joke is a trick played on someone, e.g. leaving a plastic spider

on their chair if they are very scared of spiders)
- nasty put-downs that are intended to make someone look bad (e.g. making fun of someone who looks different or who made a mistake)
- name calling
- mimicking someone's speech or behaviour (point out that comics often mimic well-known people and this can be funny)
- laughing when someone makes a mistake or hurts themselves.

Stress these key points:
- It is not kind to laugh at someone else's misfortune.
- It is not kind to laugh at or make fun of the way another person looks, thinks, speaks or acts.
- Humour should not be used as a way to hurt someone's feelings or embarrass them.
- Unkindness can become a habit if you don't stop it quickly.

Use the chart below to bring out the key points when asking the discussion questions that follow. Select students to act out specific scenarios that are examples of either 'friendly teasing and joking around' or 'nasty teasing'.

	Friendly teasing and joking around	**Nasty teasing**
Behaviours and intentions	Exaggerated joking is used to show you like someone. The other person laughs with you, not about you, and you both think it's funny. The other person thinks carefully about what they say to you and about you.	Insults, put-downs or nasty comments are used in a nasty way or to make fun of the other person. The aim is to make others not like, respect or include them. When nasty teasing is repeated towards the same person, it becomes bullying. The nastiness may be about how the person looks, speaks, their background or their skills.
The other person's response	The person who is the target is usually smiling, enjoying it and sometimes joining in.	The person who is the target is clearly not enjoying it, looks upset, is likely to avoid eye contact and may try to leave.
Body language	The teaser has a warm and genuine smile and friendly eye contact.	The person teasing has a false smile or a smirk and a 'cool' stare.
Tone of voice	The teaser is warm and shows they like the person they're joking with.	The teaser is cold, mocking and mean.
Attitude towards others watching	The teaser focuses mostly on the person who is part of the 'joking around' rather than on any people watching.	The teaser focuses a lot on the reactions of other people who are watching.

Discussion questions

- What sort of teasing happened in the book/s? Was it friendly or unkind?
- What is the difference between 'friendly teasing' and 'nasty teasing'? (See the table above for answers.)
- What is a put-down? (An insult used to mock or tease someone.)
- Why do children sometimes use 'mean' humour or nasty teasing? (To make others think that they are tough, to show off, to make someone look stupid so others won't like them, because they don't realise that they are hurting someone else's feelings.)

- What could our class do to make sure that there is no nasty or hurtful humour? (Remember how it feels; don't laugh if someone has hurt themselves; tell anyone who uses nasty humour that you don't like it, e.g. say, 'Stop it, I don't like that'; have a class rule/contract about not using unkind humour.)

Activities

▶ As a class, develop the message 'No hurtful humour in our class, thank you!' using the Quick quotes strategy (see page 96).

▶ Make a class book (see page 101), with each student contributing one page of speech balloons and cartoons about using kind humour.

Consolidation

Activities

▶ Students make word-family charts based on words connected with humour (e.g. funny, humour, laugh, comedy, amuse).

▶ Students complete **BLM Cross-offs** individually or with a partner. The secret message is 'Have a laugh and you'll feel better.'

Throw the dice

The following questions can be used with the Throw the dice strategy (see page 98) or with the **Animal Asks** or **Reflections e-tools** (see pages 90 and 97).

- Name a cartoon series that makes you laugh and say why.
- Who makes you laugh the most in your family and why?
- What do you think it means to have a good sense of humour?
- What is a funny movie you have seen and why was it funny?
- Have you ever seen a clown perform in a circus or live show? What made you laugh?
- Has your pet or an animal ever done something that made you laugh?
- Describe a funny commercial that you like and tell us why you think it's funny.
- If you had to choose an activity for this coming weekend where you would be sure to laugh a lot, what would it be?

Collective classroom research

Organise a Collective classroom research (see page 91), and collect examples of:

- humorous animals and birds (ones that act in funny ways)
- animals that laugh (or seem to) or make us laugh (e.g. hyena, kookaburra, dogs or dolphins who seem to smile)
- humorous items or novelties, funny books, songs or DVDs.

Tongue twisters and limericks

▶ Students practise these tongue twisters:
  - 'Seven sleepy sheep slept shoulder to shoulder in the shepherd's shadow.'
  - 'Rubber baby buggy bumpers rubbed the bugs off the rugby jumpers.'

- Read some limericks and then ask students to write their own. Students could also write their own tongue twister. Display the results.
- Students perform a funny poem, tongue twister, or limerick of their choice, including their own work.

Funny writing

Students work individually or with a partner to write a:

- news report about something that happened in their family that they found funny; they model the features of a news report, and could also read it out as a news reporter would
- self-reflection about a funny thing that happened to them, which they laughed about later but not at the time
- character profile about someone they know or have met who made them laugh a lot.

Silly instructions

Students draw a picture according to the instructions read aloud, for example:

- Draw a man who is walking upside down and taking a duck for a walk on a lead.
- Nearby, draw a woman with a teapot on her head.
- On the right-hand side, draw a tree with fish instead of leaves.
- On the left-hand side, draw a dog dancing with a bird.
- Overhead, draw a flying pig that is eating an ice cream.

People scavenger hunt

Use the People scavenger hunt strategy (page 96) to find someone who:

- can tell you a limerick
- can tell you a riddle or joke
- knows what 'slapstick' means
- can explain what a punchline is
- can name characters from a funny TV show
- likes the same funny TV show as you
- has seen a clown in a real circus
- has had a pet with a funny habit.

These questions can also be adapted for use with the **Animal Asks e-tool**.

Key vocabulary

Use the Whisper game, Mystery square or the TEAM coaching strategy to assist students to learn vocabulary and spelling related to humour to a reasonable level of mastery (see pages 98, 94 and 97). Examples:

cartoon	exaggerate	illness
cheer up	friendly	joke
chuckle	funny	kind
circus	giggle	laugh
clown	healthy	limerick
embarrass	hopeful	mean
enjoy	humour	nasty

relax	silly	tickle
riddle	surprise	worries
sharing	tease	

Make and draw funny things

Students make or draw the following:

- funny incongruities (things that don't really go together) such as a cold snowman/polar bear, a cow with wool, a cat that barks, a car that flies, the top and bottom part of two different animals to make one new animal
- a class mural of photographs of students in the class with funny expressions on their faces
- a mobile of illustrated riddles plus the answers, or cartoon characters cut out of magazines and newspapers (for ideas for mobiles see page 105)
- a 'feely box' containing things that are harmless and inoffensive but will make people laugh or smile
- lift-up flaps using knock-knock jokes or riddles (see page 103)
- funny creatures using vegetables and fruit such as turnips, oranges and carrot tops with toothpicks or anything else; or decorating cookies or small pizzas with funny faces
- funny puppets or balloon puppets with which to perform a funny puppet play (see pages 105–106).

Games

Play one of the following games with the whole class.

▶ **Before or After? e-game** (see page 90)

▶ **Memory Cards e-game** (see page 93) – students match the verb with its past tense. The words are:

laugh – laughed	smile – smiled
embarrass – embarrassed	tease – teased
enjoy – enjoyed	tickle – tickled
worry – worried	chuckle – chuckled
exaggerate – exaggerated	have – had
joke – joked	relax – relaxed
share – shared	feel – felt
cheer – cheered	help – helped
giggle – giggled	make – made

▶ Play Bingo strips (see page 90) or Bingo for pairs (see page 98) using the humour words on page 258.

Bounce Back! award

Present the **Bounce Back! award** to students who have best demonstrated the values in this unit, such as using positive humour to help others.

UNIT 9

Being safe

KEY MESSAGES

It is important to be clear about what bullying is.
Bullying means trying to hurt another person on purpose and more than once. It may involve:

- hurting someone physically
- calling them nasty names
- using put-downs or embarrassing them in front of others
- saying mean things or spreading nasty rumours about them
- playing nasty jokes on them
- trying to make sure they are left out
- trying to stop others from liking them.

When technology is used to bully, it is referred to as cyberbullying.

Bullying causes great harm.
Bullying is very harmful. Bullying hurts the person being bullied. They may not feel safe at school and their schoolwork is often affected too. Students who take part in bullying are likely to behave badly later in their lives.

Bullying is not okay in our school.
It is unkind, cruel and unfair to bully. Everyone in our school has the right to feel safe. Put-downs are also not okay as they can lead to bullying.

Bullying is everyone's problem.
If someone in our school is being bullied, it spoils things for all of us. Nobody can feel safe and happy if bullying is happening. It hurts both our classroom and our school. We can all help to make sure that there is no bullying.

Teachers want to be told when bullying is happening.
Teachers care about students and want to know when bullying is happening so that they can stop it and help the students involved. Be responsible and let a teacher know if you are being bullied or if someone else is being bullied. It takes courage and kindness to do this.

If someone gets bullied, it is not their fault.
Nobody deserves to be bullied. The person who is doing the bullying is the one doing the wrong thing. It is not the fault of the student who is being bullied.

Why do some children bully others?
Some children have not yet learnt that bullying is wrong. Some may not yet have learnt empathy and kindness. Some children may wrongly think that bullying is a good way to be popular.

Think for yourself and don't just follow others.
If you take part, even in a small way, in bullying others, you are behaving badly. You will get into trouble. If you watch or laugh at bullying behaviour by others, then you are part of the problem. Think for yourself and don't take part in bullying.

Try to be an 'upstander', not just a 'bystander'.
Our school wants students to stand up for others who are being bullied. If you are worried about your own safety when you are an 'upstander', talk to a teacher.

If you are being bullied, tell the person to stop. If they don't stop, ask a teacher for help.
If someone tries to hurt you, firmly tell them to stop. If they keep doing it, then it becomes bullying. Ask a teacher to help you solve the problem. This isn't dobbing or telling on someone, it is asking for help.

Be a friend to someone who is being bullied.
Children who are being bullied feel better if you tell them that what's happening is unfair and wrong. Invite someone who is being bullied to join your game or conversation. They will feel included, safe and supported. Go with them to tell a teacher what's happening. Even doing something small to help someone being bullied can make a big difference.

> **? Learning objectives**
> In this unit, students will further develop their understanding of:
> - what bullying is and isn't
> - why bullying is never okay
> - how to deal with bullying.

Resources list

A complete list of resources including references for core and additional books, films, video clips, poems, songs and websites is available.

Classroom organisation

Postbox Survey: Bullying

Photocopy **BLM Postbox Survey: Bullying** for each student. Cut the questions into strips and use only one or two with each Circle Time as specified in the following topics. Give them out before the relevant Circle Time and ask a different group each time to collate them and then report back at Circle Time.

Follow up with graphs and report writing. Suggested responses are included.

1. Do children who are bullied deserve it? (No. It is always the person doing the bullying who is in the wrong. No-one ever deserves to be bullied. Even if you feel annoyed by someone, this is no reason to mistreat them. Find a better way to deal with your feelings.)

2. Should children who are bullied be responsible for stopping it from happening? (No. It is very hard to stop it by yourself and most children need the support of other children or help from an adult to do it.)

3. Is it dobbing if you tell a teacher that someone is being bullied? (No, this is an example of being responsible and helping someone who is in trouble.)

4. If you try to help someone who is being bullied, will you probably get bullied too? (Sometimes, but there are some better ways to do it which make it less likely that you will also be bullied. If that happens, ask a teacher to help you solve the problem.)

5. Would you ever bully another child? (no)

6. Would you ever help someone else to bully or pick on someone else? (no)

7. Would you try to help someone who was being bullied? (Yes. How?)

8. Would you help an animal who was being treated cruelly? (yes)

Repeat the full activity (with all questions on the BLM) at the end of the year and see if the percentages have changed for each question. If there is a change in a positive direction, then give the students positive feedback on their improved understandings, attitudes and commitments about bullying.

What is bullying?

Resources

✦ Films

A Bug's Life

A colony of ants is intimidated and tormented by bullying grasshoppers who make the ants give them the food the ants have worked so hard for. The ants, under the leadership of an inept but lovable ant, find some unusual ways to reclaim their rights.

For the Birds

In this short film, a group of birds are sitting on a telephone wire, and they mock and taunt a friendly but unusual-looking larger bird who makes a funny honking sound. But their bullying backfires when they try to physically force him off the wire.

> **Teacher reflection**
> Bullying is often referred to as a relationship problem that requires relationship solutions. What experiences (if any) have you had in managing challenging situations with colleagues or parents? You may find the guidelines on managing challenging situations useful. **Bounce Back!** aims to build positive student–peer relationships, parent–school relationships and a positive school culture that supports positive relationships in your school community.

Circle Time or classroom discussion

Show *A Bug's Life* over several sessions prior to Circle Time. Before and after each section is shown, ask students to recount what has happened in the story so far. Alternatively, show *For the Birds*.

Discuss the bullying in the film. Ask students for any examples of bullying (no names). Make sure they understand that it isn't just mean behaviour – emphasise that bullying behaviour is when mean things are deliberately done to someone repeatedly in order to try and upset or hurt them. It is about continuing to tease someone and mistreat them. Emphasise that doing any of these things even once is still mean and wrong, but we only call it bullying if a person is regularly being treated badly.

Ask students when the character/s were being bullied, whose fault was it? Stress that it is never the fault of the person who is being bullied. Bullying is always bad behaviour by one or more people (or in the case of the films, grasshoppers and birds). They may find someone a bit annoying or different but it is *never* okay to bully someone for any reason.

Discussion questions

- How does the person who is being cruelly treated feel? (Scared, sad, lonely, unwanted, less confident, angry.)
- How might the person doing the bullying feel? (Superior, happy, confident about their power to make others do mean things.)
- How do the children who are seeing it feel? (Scared, ashamed, worried, distressed, unsafe.)
- How might teachers who find out about it feel? (Shocked, ashamed if it is a member of their class, disapproving, worried about the child being bullied, worried about those doing the bullying.)
- How might the family of the child being bullied feel? (Angry, worried, like they want to go and see the principal to let them know who is bullying their child and how upset the whole family is because of it.)
- How might the family of the child who gets into trouble for bullying someone at school feel? (Ashamed, angry with their child, worried that they might do it again.)
- Is it true that 'sticks and stones may break my bones but names will never hurt me?' (No, awful names can be very hurtful.)
- How is friendly teasing different to nasty teasing? (Friendly teasing occurs between friends, is intended to be funny and communicate affection, the tone of voice used is warm and 'joking' rather than mocking or hostile.)

The **Animal Asks e-tool** or strategy (see page 90) can also be used with the questions above.

Note: Sometimes nasty bullying-type behaviours may also occur between friends (e.g. during an argument) but the other features are different (e.g. it isn't one-sided or a repeated pattern).

Next, write examples of bullying behaviour on cards or paper and mix them up in a container for students to select randomly. For example:

- physically hurting someone
- name-calling or insults
- trying to embarrass or humiliate
- playing nasty tricks
- taking, hiding or breaking/hurting their things
- telling lies about them or their family
- making sure they are left out and not allowed to join in
- making them do things they don't want to do
- using a mobile phone to bully someone
- using emails to bully someone.

Remind students about the 'no names' rule. Students take turns to give an example of bullying in the category they have drawn from the container.

Use opportunities from their responses to offer advice about dealing with each bullying situation.

The person who is being treated badly can:

- keep in mind that what is being said usually isn't true
- say something like: 'I don't know why you are putting me down, but I want you to stop doing it'
- give a secret smile, break eye contact, shake their head a few times and then walk away
- look away, keep doing what they are doing and say, 'Whatever.'
- move to a safer place which is more visible to others and/or closer to a teacher
- firmly but politely ask them to stop and keep repeating their request (e.g. 'Back off, please', 'Just go away', 'Haven't you got anything better to do?')
- loudly but calmly shout, 'Stop it!' while staring at them and not breaking eye contact
- ask 'What is your problem?'
- ask a teacher for support to deal with the problem.

Support someone who is being bullied in one or more of the following ways:

- distracting the person or people who are bullying
- saying 'Cut it out. None of us thinks that what you are doing is okay/cool.'
- calling a teacher if someone is being hurt
- asking a teacher for advice about what to do
- finding subtle ways to move them away from the situation (e.g 'Hey, let's go over to the climbing frame.')
- including them in games and conversation in a way that takes them out of the situation.

Strategies on how to deal with bullying are explored further on pages 274–6.

Activities

- Students draw a sunshine wheel – a simplified sun drawing with a central circle and 'sun ray' lines drawn from the edge of the circle outwards, like wheel spokes. In the circle students write 'bullying' and on each of the rays they write what they know about what bullying is, e.g. repeated, nasty words or actions.
- In pairs, students write a list of action points or steps based on the discussion of what to do if a person is being bullied.

Anti-bullying posters

- Make anti-bullying posters that emphasise how the person being bullied and their classmates feel.
- Make a class poster that says: 'We don't bully in this classroom or school. We care and support.'

Rights and responsibilities chart

Develop a rights and responsibilities chart like the one below for display in the classroom. These will need to be discussed beforehand.

Rights	Responsibilities
To be treated with respect.	To treat others with respect and to show respect for yourself.
To ask a teacher for support if you are being bullied or feel unsafe.	To let a teacher know what is happening.
To *feel* safe and *be* safe at school.	To not behave towards others in ways that lead to their feeling unsafe.
To be supported by your classmates.	To support your classmates.

What is cyberbullying?

Resources

✦ Website

Office of the Children's eSafety Commissioner

A useful collection of primary school level educational activities can be found on this Australian government website. The site also enables young people to report cyberbullying. Similar sites are located in most countries.

Circle Time or classroom discussion

Start by asking students to volunteer to say one thing they know about cyberbullying (using the 'no names' rule). You may wish to refer to the website. The key points to make are that some people bully others by repeatedly doing or saying nasty things using technology, such as email, the internet or a mobile phone. They might:

- try to trick someone by pretending that they are someone else and then saying nasty things to them or about other people
- spread lies and rumours or say mean things using email or text messages
- trick people into revealing their personal information via an email or text message and then send it to other people by email or text message without permission

- send or forward mean text or email messages about someone to other people and find a way to make sure that the person knows about these messages
- take embarrassing photographs of people without the person agreeing and then text or email them to other people or put them up on a website.

Discussion questions

- **What is cyberbullying?** (Emphasise that the behaviour must be repeated.)
- **What are some ways in which people can cyberbully?** (See points in Circle Time.)
- **Why do some people cyberbully?** (For the same reasons that people bully offline, they think they won't get caught because they can lie about who is doing it by using another email address etc., they don't have to face the person they send nasty messages to or do nasty things to when online.)

Activities

▶ In pairs students create simple concept maps that define cyberbullying.

▶ Students cut out pictures from magazines and newspapers of different technology that could be used to bully someone. They add labels and an appropriate caption.

Bullying causes great harm

Resources

✦ Books

Sorry!
Charlie regularly puts classmates down and gets away with it because he always says 'sorry' afterwards. When Charlie deliberately damages a model made by another classmate, he says 'sorry' as usual to her but she won't accept his false apology.

My Secret Bully
Katie claims to be Monica's friend, so Monica is surprised and distressed when Katie starts to humiliate her and put her down in front of other kids. Initially, Monica feels sad and isolated but, with support from her mother, she copes with the situation and moves on.

✦ Website

Stop Bullying
This US government website provides information and short animated video clips for children about bullying situations, including follow-up quizzes after each video.

Circle Time or classroom discussion

Use one of the resources and then discuss the following questions.

Discussion questions

- **Can you name some ways in which being bullied could hurt or harm someone?** (They might feel worried and not want to go to school, they might feel unwell when they are at school because they no longer feel safe, they might not have any friends, they may not be able to concentrate on their schoolwork as well as before and this might affect their learning, they might not want to go to school or might want to go to another school.)

- How could students who bully others cause harm to themselves? (Other students might not want to spend time with them in case they get bullied too, when they are older they might often be mean and nasty to some of the people they work with and this might mean they lose their job, they might be nasty and mean to their partner or children if they become parents.)
- How might bullying behaviour by students in our class cause harm to our class and school? (People might say bad things about our class or school and families may not want to send their children to our school.)

Activities

▶ With older peer buddies, students review a video clip or book about how bullying causes harm. A digital book trailer could also be created (see page 102).

▶ Using the cube pattern (see page 102), students write 'Bullying causes great harm' on one side and five short statements on how bullying causes harm on the other sides.

Embed it

Student safety and friendship advisory committee

Establish a group of students who work with their Year 3 and 4 teachers in one or more of the following ways:

- Identifying 'hotspots' in the playground where bullying might be occurring out of sight of the teachers on duty.
- Identifying students who might be socially isolated and vulnerable and finding ways to include them in organised activities, such as lunchtime clubs and sport.

Bullying is not okay in our school and is everyone's problem

Resources

✦ Book

Each Kindness

Despite attempts by Maya (a new girl at the school) to be friendly, Chloe and her friends deliberately reject and isolate her, because they think her clothes are shabby. Maya stops coming to school. When her teacher gives a lesson on kindness, Chloe feels shame about their bullying of Maya.

✦ Song

'BULLY-FREE ZONE! (Anti-bullying song for kids!)'

Circle Time or classroom discussion

Read the book or play the song and stress that some of the behaviours mentioned would only be examples of bullying if they happened more than once. Explain that teachers always want to know about any bullying that occurs at their school.

Discussion questions

- What is the message in the book or song?
- What do we mean when we say that 'bullying is not okay in our school'? (All students are expected to treat each other with respect and not bully anyone, any student who bullies another will get into trouble, their families will be asked to come to the school to discuss with their teacher and the school principal what their child has done and what can be done about it.)
- Why do you think teachers want to know about any bullying that is happening in the school? (They care about every student's wellbeing and learning and they want to be able to help and protect any students who are being bullied so they can help them to feel safe again; they also want to help any students who are bullying to stop doing it, show kindness and get along well with others, and have better relationships both now at school and later in life.)
- Why do we say that 'bullying is everyone's problem'? (Bullying makes our school an unsafe place, we can all do something to help stop bullying, everybody in our school is harmed in one way or another when bullying is happening, we can all have better relationships with each other and concentrate better on learning if we can stop bullying from happening.)
- How is our school a bully-free zone?

Activities

- Students write an information report on 'How our school is a bully-free zone'.
- Students create signs for display about how 'Bullying is not okay' and 'Bullying is everyone's problem'.
- Students make badges (see page 108) that display messages such as, 'Bully-free zone' 'No bullying zone' 'Bullying is not cool'.
- Students complete **BLM Cross-offs** to find the secret message: 'Bullying spoils things for all of us.'

Embed it

Circle of friends

Set up several 'circles of friends'. These are groups of two or more students who are prepared to seek out and include and/or move near and support a specific student when they are being mistreated/bullied. They don't need to directly confront those who are doing the mistreatment, just find a way to remove the student on the receiving end. Sometimes all they have to do is stand near the student and stare at the offenders so that they know they are being observed and that the mistreatment is being witnessed. They can also be asked to let the teacher know when mistreatment is happening. This is also a good peer buddy strategy.

Put-downs are not okay in our school

Resources

✦ Book

Simon's Hook: A Story About Teases and Put-downs

Simon is being teased and put down in a nasty way by some of his classmates. Grandma Rose helps him to manage the situation by using a fishing metaphor, focusing on him not taking the bait so that he doesn't get 'hooked in'.

Circle Time or classroom discussion

Read the book and discuss the concept of a put-down. Explain that put-downs can be words or expressions on our face (e.g. smirking or rolling eyes) or the way we use our voice (e.g. using a nasty or sneering tone of voice). Explain that put-downs very often lead to bullying behaviour.

Discussion questions

- What are some examples of put-downs from the book?

- What are some other examples?

- What do put-downs sound like? ('That's stupid/ridiculous/silly/dumb!', 'What would you know?', 'That's rubbish!', 'You're such an idiot!', 'She is so thick!', spoken in a nasty or smirking tone of voice.)

- What do put-downs look like? (Nasty smile (smirking), mean eyes, laughing at the other person, looking at someone else and laughing about something another person said, acting bored when they say something or deliberately not listening, copying someone's mannerisms, laughing at someone's mistakes.)

- What do put-downs feel like when you receive them? (You feel 'small', you feel embarrassed, you feel as if you are not a likeable or clever person.)

- What are some good ways to let the other person know that you know they are trying to put you down? (Say something like 'I don't know why you are putting me down, but I want you to stop doing it'; just give a secret smile, break eye contact, shake your head a few times and walk away.)

- Why do some people use put-downs? (They haven't yet learnt how to be kind and caring; they think if they make others look bad, they will look good; they want others to think they are cool and tough; they want to try and stop others from being your friend so that you will like them more; they have not yet learnt positive values.)

- What would happen if put-downs happened all the time in our classroom? (No-one would feel safe enough to say anything, we would always be arguing, we wouldn't like each other, we wouldn't be as kind as we are now, we wouldn't want to be in this class.)

- What's the difference between having a joke and using a put-down? (A joke is between friends; if it is a joke, both people think it is funny, not just the person saying it.)

- What is a 'lift-up'? (A comment, expression or gesture intended to lift someone's spirits and confidence.)

Activities

Put-downs X-chart

Make a class X-chart about put-downs. On each of the four lines write what put-downs look like, sound like, feel like (if you are put-down), and think like (i.e. what you think if someone puts you down). Repeat for 'lift-ups'.

Posters

- Students make posters that list typical put-downs. The title of the poster can be 'Beware! Put-downs are poisonous! Don't use them!'

- Students make posters that say 'In our classroom put-downs are OUT and lift-ups are IN.' They can add 'lift-up' speech bubbles.

- Give each student **BLM No Put-Down Zone Poster** to decorate and display them in the classroom.

Put-down garbage bin

Students make a class put-down garbage bin. They can write about any put-down they receive and then throw the piece of paper into the garbage bin where it belongs.

Embed it

Reducing put-downs

- If a student is using put-downs, have a private talk with them and tell them that what they are doing is *not* okay. To help them stop using put-downs, consider giving them a private daily count of how often they do it. If there are just one or two main offenders, this often solves the problem. A daily class count can be used in the same way.

- Draw ten circles on the board. Each circle is equal to one minute's free time. Every time you hear or see a put-down during a discussion or game, silently cross off one circle. The class records the number of circles that are left at the end of the week, which equates to the period of free time (or class 'games time' they have earned). The following week try to better the score until the full ten minutes of free time is earned.

If someone gets bullied, it is not their fault

Resources

✦ Book

The Bully and the Shrimp

Noah Shrimpton is small for his age and when he moves to a new school one of the boys starts picking on him. Noah works hard to make some new friends and finally gets the confidence to stand up to the boy who is bullying him.

Circle Time or classroom discussion

Before this Circle Time, give out Postbox survey questions 1 and 2 (**BLM Postbox Survey: Bullying**) and ask students to answer them.

Discuss the responses to the questions. Emphasise that although we can make it less likely that we will be bullied, if we are bullied, it is not our fault. The person doing the bullying is in the wrong. Emphasise that if you act confidently and 'cool' when someone starts to pick on you, you might be able to discourage them. However, once they have been bullying you for a while or if there is more than one person doing it, you need to ask a teacher or an adult for help with the problem. Read the book and discuss.

Discussion questions

- Was it the character's fault when they got bullied?
- Why do you think the bully teased the main character?
- Is it a person's own fault if they get bullied? (No, the person bullying is always the person who is to blame.)
- Why do some people get teased? (They are different in some way – but it is okay to be different; they don't seem to have friends or support; others may be jealous of them; they get more nervous about things and don't seem very confident, so some students notice this and think they are easy to push around and hurt.)

- Why don't children always tell a teacher what is happening when they are being bullied? (They think that asking for help is the same as dobbing or telling on someone; they are worried there will be pay back, but they can ask the teacher for help with this; they are not sure if the teacher will believe them or help them. Emphasise that teachers will help them and there are ways of stopping bullying that make it less likely that there will be pay back.
- What do we mean by acting confidently? (Stand tall, smile, look into people's eyes, speak in a strong voice, say your own opinion, don't laugh if people put you down.)
- How can acting confidently help protect you against being bullied? (People who are looking for someone to bully will think you might be too hard to upset and that you might give them a hard time if they bully you.)

Activities

Choose the right behaviour

Students complete **BLM Behaviours That Do and Don't Protect You**. Discuss these behaviours afterwards. Talk about good ways for becoming better at acting confidently (see above), looking at people in a brave way, not letting others make a fool of you, being a good loser etc.

Journal writing about support groups

Students write in their **Bounce Back!** journal the names of three people at the school who are in their support group, i.e. they are people students could go to if they needed help because they were being bullied.

Why do some children bully others?

Resources

✦ Books

Is It Because?

A boy who is being bullied asks himself questions to try to understand why a classmate is bullying him. He concludes that his classmate is unhappy and jealous of him. This is an over-simplistic view of bullying, but it can be used to discuss this complex issue.

Confessions of a Former Bully

When nine-year-old Katie gets caught bullying some of her classmates, she is required to have sessions with the school counsellor. She is not keen on going, but the sessions help her realise how much harm her bullying behaviour has caused and she finds ways to make amends.

Be a Buddy, Not a Bully

While travelling on the school bus, Kate notices Jesse looking teary and sad because he is being teased by two fellow students, Benny and Mason. Later, Kate and Jesse find Mason crying in the playground and they offer him support, with a reminder about the importance of kindness.

Circle Time or classroom discussion

Read one or more of the books above and discuss the following questions.

Discussion questions

- Why do some children bully others? (They may not have learnt yet that bullying is wrong and unkind; they may need to work harder at showing kindness to others; they don't understand that what they are doing is cruel because they aren't sure yet about what's right and wrong; they don't have positive values; they don't think about other people's feelings; they might be jealous of someone else and want to make others not like them or respect them; to show off, to look tough, to look popular.)

- **Why are most students kind to their classmates and not cruel?** (They know bullying is wrong; they have good positive values, such as being fair and kind; they would feel ashamed; they realise that bullying someone makes the other person feel very sad and worried; they know that their family would feel unhappy if they were cruel to others; they have better ways to make others respect them, e.g. using good social skills and being good at things.)

- **What are some better ways than bullying people for children who want to try and impress their classmates?** (Start good games, use positive tracking [see Unit 5: Looking on the bright side], tell good stories, be very good at something, help others, use good humour, do some difficult things that require courage and hard work, achieve their goals, cooperate well with others, treat other people well.)

Activities

'Why Do They Do It?' Match-up

Students individually complete **BLM Why Do They Do It?** Photocopy the sheet, cut up the squares and mix them up. Organise students into pairs, and give one set of squares in an envelope to each pair. Ask them to paste them on a sheet and match up one column with the other. Remember to insert the headings of the two columns into the envelopes.

No bullying brochure

Students work with a partner to make a 'No bullying' brochure using slogans such as 'Bullying spoils things for everyone', 'Bullying is everyone's problem', or 'Bullying is OUT and respecting is IN'.

Think for yourself – don't just follow others

Resources

◆ Books

The Recess Queen

Mean Jean is the recess queen and she dominates all of her classmates at recess. A new girl, Katie Sue, is warned by the others to do whatever Jean wants, but she decides to do her own thing and ignores Jean. The ending is rather glib, but can be one of the issues discussed.

Nobody Knew What To Do: A Story About Bullying

The theme of this story is that sometimes peer pressure can cause students not to do anything about a bullying situation. Ray is being bullied at school and although other children are upset about it, no-one does anything to help. One boy eventually becomes brave enough to speak up.

Circle Time or classroom discussion

At the start of the discussion, students complete the quiz on **BLM Do You Think for Yourself?** Debrief with the class and ask students to write in their **Bounce Back!** journal what they found out about themselves and what plans they can make to think for themselves more often.

Read one of the books to the class and discuss it. Talk about how we all like to feel we belong to a group. Often we try to copy other people so that we feel as if we belong. Friends remain important throughout our life, but being part of a group and always acting just like them becomes less important as we get older.

Give out Postbox survey questions 4, 5 and 6 from **BLM Postbox Survey: Bullying** and ask students to answer them.

Discuss the responses to the Postbox survey questions, and the following discussion questions.

Discussion questions

- Why do some students like to be a 'queen' or 'king' and rule over others?
- What makes it hard sometimes to be brave enough to be a friend to someone who is being bullied? (Fear of rejection, fear of attracting the same mistreatment.)

Ask students to imagine that twins – a boy and girl from a different town – are joining the class.

- Are there unspoken 'rules' about games, how we dress or behave at our school that only students know about?
- Who makes 'kids' rules'? Are they really that important? (Sometimes they are made by students who think they're more powerful or popular than others; sometimes the rules are part of the school's traditions e.g. sporting preferences, lunchtime activities. It can be helpful to know these rules and in some cases, try them out. You don't need to agree with these students, and it is important that you think for yourself.
- How important is it for everyone to follow these 'kids' rules'? (Not important if you don't agree with them.)
- How could students who don't want to follow these rules still fit in? (Make up their own mind and think for themselves but still treat others with kindness and respect their preferences.)
- How do you know when something is the right thing to do? (When it affects somebody else's wellbeing and feelings, e.g. bullying and being nasty; when it relates to your own sense of who you are.)
- What does it mean to exclude someone? How is that bullying?

Stress that staying silent when you know someone is being bullied gives the message that it is okay to bully. Refer to **BLM Being a Friend to Someone Who Is Being Bullied** and run through the Do and Don't strategies with the class.

- Which of these strategies would work best and why?

Activity

End-of-the-week reflection

At the end of the week, ask students write a reflection in their *Bounce Back!* journal. Ask them to think about the last week as if they were running a movie of the week again in their head.

Reflection questions:

- When did you think for yourself and make up your own mind this week?
- Did you think for yourself even when someone else wanted you to agree with them?
- Did you do anything to support someone who was being treated badly this week, no matter how small your action was? Which strategy did you use? How did it make you feel to support someone else?

Drama

In groups, students create a drama based on the skills and behaviour described in **BLM Being a Friend to Someone Who Is Being Bullied** (see above).

What can someone do if they are being bullied or cyberbullied?

Resources

✦ Books

'Please Stop, I Don't Like That!': 6 Magic Words to Be Respectfully Assertive

This picture book consists of a series of situations at school where Joey stands up for himself using the statement in the book's title, followed up with a comment and a resolution. The book concludes with five situations where children may need to be assertive.

Simon's Hook: A Story About Teases and Put-downs

See page 267.

I Am Jack

A chapter book in which George starts to call Jack names, and many of the other boys join in and torment Jack further. The boys Jack usually plays with succumb to peer pressure and stop playing with him. After a classmate speaks up, the bullying is successfully dealt with by an anti-bullying campaign.

Circle Time or classroom discussion

Give out question 3 from **BLM Postbox Survey: Bullying** before Circle Time and ask students to answer it. Then read one of the books above and discuss ways in which the character/s being bullied could protect and defend themselves.

Discussion questions

- In each of the books, where was courage shown in the story?
- How was the bullying kept going in the stories?
- What happened in the end to help everyone at the school feel safe?

Display **BLM Protecting Ourselves from Bullying** as a basis for discussion.

- How can we stay away from trouble?
- What does 'putting on a protective shell or shield' mean?
- What other things could we say or do to stop the person from bullying?
- What kinds of proof of being bullied are there? (Taking notes, screen shots, photos with dates.)
- Where could we go?
- What is the difference between asking for support, being responsible and dobbing? (Asking for support is asking a teacher to help you solve a serious problem that you haven't been able to solve by yourself. Being responsible means telling a teacher when something bad is happening to someone else so that you can help that person. Dobbing is just trying to get someone into trouble, often over a very small issue.)

Strongly encourage students to seek support from a teacher if they are being bullied.

- When would you let a teacher know if you were being treated badly?
- Which teacher would you approach and why (e.g. your class teacher, the teacher on playground duty)? What could you say?

Students individually complete **BLM Is This Dobbing?** Use this as the basis of discussion, emphasising that it is okay to ask for support if a student is being bullied. The correct answers are:

1. acting responsibly
2. dobbing
3. asking for support.

Discuss the responses to the Postbox survey and ask each student to say one kind thing we can all say and/or do to be a supportive friend when someone is being bullied.

Drama

Students prepare scenes for a puppet play using **BLM Protecting Ourselves from Bullying** to help them prepare assertive and strong responses that the puppet being bullied can use to stand up for themselves. Use the following scenarios:

- Two children do mean things to Yannis whenever they see him. They have called him nasty names, thrown rubbish at him, hidden his hat so that he can't go out to play in the sun, stepped on his things and broken his lunchbox. What could Yannis do?

- Ava tries to stop the other girls liking Ruby. She tells them that if they play with Ruby, they can't be in her group. If they do talk to Ruby, Ava and her best friend Mila make sure that they get the silent treatment for a while too. Ava tells lies about Ruby, saying that she steals things from other people's bags. Whenever she sees Ruby, she holds her nose, meaning 'you smell bad'. What could Ruby do?

After each role-play, debrief and discuss these questions:

- How do we know that bullying was happening here? (The nasty behaviour was repeated, cruel, and meant to hurt or put the person down.)
- What are some actions that worked well for the person defending themselves against this bullying? What else could the person have tried to do to stop the bullying? (Tell them to stop, move away and stand near other people or a teacher, ask a teacher for support.)

Activities

▶ Do Quick quotes (see page 96) on what students can do if they are being bullied and display them in the classroom.

Choose your own adventure

Students write a 'choose your own adventure' imaginative text with a partner on the theme of someone being bullied. The two options are 'the person asked for support' and 'the person didn't ask for support'.

Take-home task

Students complete and discuss with their families **BLM We Can Stop Bullying**.

Dealing with cyberbullying

Resources

✦ Website

Office of the Children's eSafety Commissioner

See page 264.

Bounce Back! Years 3–4 Curriculum Units

Circle Time or classroom discussion

Recall the different examples of cyberbullying from the discussion on pages 264–5.

Discussion questions

- What are some good rules for using email or text messages? (Don't use them to be nasty and insulting, don't spread lies and rumours or mean things or give personal information about other people, don't pretend to be someone else to trick people.)
- What is a good rule about taking photographs of other people? (Always ask for their permission.)
- What can you do to protect yourself from cyberbullying? (Don't give anyone your password information, only give your email address or mobile phone number to people you know you can really trust, don't give anyone your mobile phone to use unless it is an emergency and you can watch what they do with it.)
- What is one thing you could do if someone sent you a nasty email or text message? (Save the message and the contact details as proof – explain how to cut and paste or screen capture, block the sender etc. See the Office of the Children's eSafety Commissioner website for more information.)

Activity

Rules for staying safe and respecting others

Students work with a partner to write an illustrated page of simple rules for staying safe and respecting others when using technology, such as social networking sites on the internet and mobile phones.

Embed it

Family forum evening with students teaching families about cybersafety

Conduct further workshops for students on cybersafety. Then hold a family forum evening at the school in which the students teach their parents and carers about bullying, cyberbullying and staying safe online. (Thank you to Sue Cahill at St Charles Borromeo, Templestowe, for this idea).

Useful information for cybersafety workshops can be found on the **Resources list** for this unit.

How can we all help with the problem of bullying?

Resources

✦ Book

Juice Box Bully: Empowering Kids to Stand Up for Others

Pete arrives at his new school and very soon he starts to bully some of his new classmates. But all his classmates had made a promise to their teacher that they would take care of each other. So instead of being mean back to Pete, several of them act as supportive bystanders.

✦ Websites

Kids Helpline: Bullying

This webpage includes classroom activities, e.g. an anti-bullying superhero activity.

Comic book covers

In 2014, Marvel Entertainment used its biggest comic superheroes for 'National Bullying Prevention Month' in the USA. Their superheroes supported and stood up for children who were being bullied. This was framed as another example of superheroes working for 'good' and against 'bad'.

♦ Song

'Heroes (We Could Be)'

Circle Time or classroom discussion

Give out questions 7 and 8 from **BLM Postbox Survey: Bullying** before Circle Time and ask students to answer them. Collate the answers, and discuss them as a class.

Read the book *Juice Box Bully* and explain that a bystander is present when bullying occurs but an 'upstander' is someone who is present but also offers support and help to the person being bullied.

Discussion questions

- How did the students honour the promise they had made with their teacher?
- Do you think it would be a good idea if everyone in this class agreed to take care of each other as happened in the story?
- What could you do to help someone who is being bullied? (Help them to move away from the person/people who are doing the bullying, ask the people who are doing the bulling to stop doing it, invite the child who is being bullied to join your game or conversation.)

As an alternative to reading the book, show the anti-bullying comic book covers to the class and discuss the following questions.

- What are superheroes? (Modern fictional characters who have special skills and/or superhuman powers and who work on making things fair and protecting the public.)
- Who can name some superheroes and what they do?
- If there was a superhero whose job was to protect and support children who are bullied at school, what kind of superpowers and skills would this superhero need? (Stress that these superpowers or skills cannot cause physical harm or aggression. Examples of possible skills might be *super-hearing* so they could listen when they suspected that someone was saying nasty things or making put-down remarks to a student, *becoming invisible* so that they could move near to someone who was being bullied and whisper useful advice about how to respond to the nasty things being said to them e.g. 'Just smile and then turn around and walk quietly away to another part of the playground.')

Explain that HERO stands for **H**elping **E**veryone **R**espect **O**thers. None of us can be superheroes like Spiderman or Wonder Woman because they are just enjoyable fictional characters. However, everyone in the class can become 'everyday heroes' who behave in ways that support and include others children who are being bullied or excluded. Everyday heroes need skills for being kind and supportive and for helping others to be included. They also need skills for asking students who are mistreating someone else to stop doing it a way that doesn't make things worse for either themselves or the student they are trying to help.

Remind students that it is never okay to hurt someone (physically or verbally) in order to prevent them from bullying or excluding another student, even though they are being mean and unkind.

Activities

Hero posters

Students make posters about standing up for each other with the phrase 'Everyone can be an Everyday HERO' (using the HERO acronym **H**elping **E**veryone **R**espect **O**thers).

Everyday hero

Students work with a partner to write down some good ways to be an 'everyday hero' and support students who are being bullied or excluded. For example:

- What could you say to someone who was being mean to another student that might get them to stop doing it?
- How could you support a student who was being excluded? What could you say? What could you do?
- How could you help someone who was being treated badly to move away to a safer place within the school? What could you say? What could you do?

Each pair acts out one of their ideas in front of the class. Discuss with the class what strategies are most likely to work.

We can be superheroes

Students work in groups of four or five to create a superhero who has superpowers for protecting, supporting and including children who are being bullied. Aim for a mix of male and female superheroes.

Materials needed:

- cloth for capes
- cardboard for masks, shields badges
- dress up caps, hats, boots etc. brought from home.

Steps:

1. In groups, students give their superhero a name e.g. Playground Ranger, Guardian Girl or The Shield. They can also decide to have a team of superheroes (e.g. the Kindness Crew).

2. Students decide what superpowers and skills their superhero has (stress that physical and verbal aggression is unacceptable). For example:
   - super-hearing or super-vision
   - invisibility for quickly moving someone away from a difficult situation
   - all-seeing power to check and see if anyone is in trouble and needs help
   - super-kindness for comforting someone who is upset
   - super-assertiveness for calmly asking someone to stop it
   - having immediate access to very wise people (e.g. teachers)

3. Based on the powers of their superhero, the students design and draw their superhero as a cartoon figure.

4. Together, they make a costume for their superhero (e.g. a cape, mask, hat, symbol, belt, shield, badge, boots etc.). One student in each group will dress up in the costume.

5. Each group introduces their superhero to the class by presenting the student in the costume to the class.

6. Each group creates a dramatic action scene (approximately one or two minutes in length) in which their superhero protects or supports a child who is being bullied. Stress that no verbal or physical aggression can be used. Debrief after each performance.

Superhero cartoons

Students develop their own 'superhero' similar to the 'We can be superheroes' activity. Then they draw a four or five-frame cartoon story about their superhero in action supporting someone who is being bullied.

Take-home task

Students will love to take home their work on their Superhero to share with their families, or they could even make their costumes at home. Prepare students to explain what bullying is, why it is everyone's problem, the power of their superhero and how they help stop bullying.

Consolidation

Activities

Be a cyber detective

Use **BLM Be a Cyber Detective!** – a fun activity where students use their detective skills to decipher the code and work out the answers to questions about cybersafety.

Cut-up sentences

Cut these sentences into individual words and place each cut-up sentence into an envelope. Make enough sets for each pair of students to have one set of the six sentences. Each pair reconstructs the six sentences. The **Cut-up Sentences e-activity** can also be used.

- Put-downs and bullying are not okay in our school.
- If you wouldn't say it to their face, don't say it in a text message or email.
- Don't send on anything nasty that has been sent to you about someone else.
- Bullying is everybody's problem and affects all of us.
- Have the courage to speak up if someone is being treated badly.
- Arguing is different to bullying but we need to sort it out peacefully.
- If we stay silent when bullying happens, we are saying it's okay to do it.

Reflections

Use the **Reflections e-tool** to ask these questions:

- Why is bullying unacceptable in our classroom and our school?
- What is bullying behaviour?
- What do we mean by cyberbullying?
- How can students in our class be a friend to someone who is being bullied?
- What do we mean when we say that 'silence says bullying is okay'?
- What is one thing you can do to stand up for yourself if someone treats you in a nasty way?
- What can you do to get support if someone keeps bullying you?
- Why is it important to let a teacher know if you or if someone else is being bullied?

Creating slogans

Students make posters or fridge magnets (see page 103) with a slogan such as:

- Do whatever you can to stop bullying, no matter how small.
- Be an upstander against bullying.

- Working together to stop bullying makes a big difference.
- Stop bullying and help those in trouble.
- Silence says bullying is okay.

Key vocabulary

Use the Whisper game, Mystery square or the TEAM coaching strategy to assist students to learn vocabulary and spelling related to bullying to a reasonable level of mastery (see pages 98, 94 and 97). Examples:

bullying	hurt	safe
bystander	include	safety
courage	kindness	support
cyberbullying	mean	teacher
embarrass	mistreat	tease
exclude	nasty	unfair
fault	put-down	unkind
friendly	responsibility	wrong
harm	rumour	upstander

Games

Play one of these games with the whole class or in groups.

▶ **Before or After? e-game** (see page 90)

▶ **Memory Cards e-game** (see page 93) – students find the following matching words:

bullying	mistreat	tease
upstander	name-calling	understanding
cyberbullying	nasty	unfair
unfair	rumour	courage
exclude	responsibly	harm
kindness	put-down	safe
unkind	support	

▶ **Cross-offs e-game** (see page 91) to find the secret message, which is 'Speak up if someone is being bullied.'

▶ Bingo strips with students playing in pairs (see page 98) using some of the words above.

▶ Big words, small words (see page 98) using one of these words: kindness, cyberbullying, upstander, supporting.

Bounce Back! award

Present the **Bounce Back! award** to students who have best supported any other students within the school who may have needed to feel safe.

UNIT 10

Success (CHAMP)

KEY MESSAGES

Think like a CHAMP.
You can train yourself for success by using the CHAMP acronym.

Challenge yourself, set a goal and make a plan.
A challenge is something that is new or hard to do. You have to work hard when faced with a challenge. To achieve a goal, start by making a plan about how you will do it. When you do achieve a goal, you will feel happy with what you have done. However, nobody achieves all of their goals.

Have a go! Take a risk! Believe in yourself.
Challenging yourself means pushing yourself to do something that you are unsure you can do. You may need to risk making a mistake or not being able to do it to begin with. Having a go shows that you believe in yourself.

Always look for and use your strengths.
The things you are best at are called your 'strengths'. Everyone has different strengths and no-one is good at everything. Usually you really like doing the things you are best at. However, you can still improve in things that are not your strengths through hard work.

There are two kinds of strengths.
We all have two kinds of strengths:

- **Character strengths** are the ways in which you behave, such as being kind.
- **Ability strengths** are things you are good at, such as reading, maths, art or sport.

Use your strengths to help others.
When you use your ability and character strengths to help others, then you are helping to make both yourself and other people happy.

Mistakes help you to learn. Don't be afraid to make them.
Everybody makes mistakes when they try to do something that is new or challenging. Making a mistake or failing is useful because you can learn from them. Try to learn from your mistakes as well as your successes.

Persist, work hard and use willpower.
Keep on trying. There will be some things you can't do YET. But you will mostly be able to do them if you persist. 'Grit' is a word we use for trying and not giving up. Using willpower is also part of grit. This means doing what you have to do or what is most important rather than just what you feel like doing.

The harder you work, the smarter you get.
Every time someone uses their brain to work hard (e.g. by thinking of new ideas, solving problems, practising new skills, creating new things), their brain gets 'smarter'.

Don't give up when you face a challenge, problem or obstacle.
Everyone faces some obstacles when they challenge themselves and try to achieve their goals. That's normal. Be clever or resourceful to solve problems – use other people or information to help you.

Manage your time and be organised.
If you want to succeed at something, then you need to manage your time and be organised, e.g. by making a plan with a timetable.

Think about yourself and your behaviour.
Thinking like a CHAMP means you learn to think about:

- what you are good at (your strengths)
- what you are not good at (your limitations)
- what you have learnt
- what was easy for you to do
- what was challenging and needed lots of hard work
- what you still need to learn
- how your mistakes helped you to learn. It helps to get feedback from others.

> **Learning objectives**
> In this unit, students will further develop their understanding of how to:
> - use their strengths
> - develop grit and use a growth mindset.

Resources list

A complete list of resources including references for core and additional books, films, video clips, poems, songs and websites is available.

Train your brain for success and think like a CHAMP

Resources

✦ Video clips

Growth Mindset Animation

A short animation explaining the theory of a growth mindset.

Growth Mindset for Students – Episode 1

Mojo has trouble keeping up in his maths class and is ready to give up. Mojo thinks you are either born smart or you're not – and he's not. Kate tells him that your brain is like a muscle and you can exercise it to become stronger and smarter.

Circle Time or classroom discussion

Begin the discussion by getting the class to do a Values line up. Explain that you are going to ask students to choose where to stand in the line to show what they think about the idea: 'Some people are really smart, others are not so smart, and no-one can change how smart they are.'

- Standing at one end of the line indicates that students strongly agree that you can't change how smart you are.

- Standing in the middle of the line indicates that students are 'not sure'.

- Standing at the other end the line indicates that students strongly disagree. Anyone who stands at this end of the line believes that people can make themselves smarter if they persist and work hard. Even if they are not very good at something, they can train to become smarter.

When students have lined up according to their point of view, ask different students to explain why they took that position in the line. Depending on their answers, make the point that we can all become smarter by putting in extra effort and that being prepared to make mistakes and learn from them will make a difference. Show one of the video clips about growth mindset.

Discussion questions

- What is a growth mindset? What is a fixed mindset?

- Did Mojo have a growth or fixed mindset?

- 'What happens if we don't water a plant and leave it in a dark cupboard?' (It withers and dies.)

Explain that our brain is like a plant. If you don't try to learn new things, then your brain doesn't improve and get better. Emphasise that the more you try to learn and the harder you work, the more your brain makes new connections between its brain cells and the smarter you get. If you are not challenging your brain and learning new things, then it doesn't grow.

Organise students to work in pairs in the circle. Give each student a sheet of recycled A4 paper. Ask one student in each pair to fold their paper twice. Ask the other student in the pair to tightly scrunch the paper as many times as they can. Then get them both to open up their paper.

- **What do you notice?** (One sheet of paper has only a few fold lines whereas the other sheet of paper has lots of fold lines.)

Explain that all the creases are like the connections between the brain cells in your brain. Our brain cells communicate with each other through such connections (like lines) when we ask them to do hard things.

- The first sheet of paper is what someone's brain might be look like if they haven't challenged their brain and worked hard. They would have fewer brain cell connections.
- The second sheet of paper shows lots and lots of creases, which is like having lots of brain cell connections because you have challenged your brain to do hard things. The more you work at things that are challenging, the more brain cell connections you create and the smarter you become.

Then introduce the CHAMP acronym using the **CHAMP e-tool** and talk about how the class is going to learn about each of the CHAMP messages:

Challenge yourself, set a goal and make a plan.

Have a go! Take a risk! Believe in yourself.

Always look for and use your strengths.

Mistakes help you to learn. Don't be afraid to make them.

Persist and put in effort. Don't give up.

Activities

▶ Students create and illustrate a poster with the headings: 'I will train my brain for success' or 'The harder I work, the smarter I become.'

▶ Students write in their journal, 'I need to train my brain for success. The harder I work, the smarter I become.' They can add a sketch of themselves with a brain that is getting smarter and write one way they challenge it with something that is new or difficult for them to do.

▶ Organise students into groups of five and explain the BRAIN strategy (see page 90), using the **BRAIN e-tool** to think about some ways to improve the classroom. In follow-up discussion link back to the CHAMP acronym and highlight how the use of the **BRAIN e-tool** helped them to 'stretch' their brain by thinking of new ideas.

Take-home task

Students make a CHAMP bookmark or fridge magnet to take home (see page 103). As they learn more about the meaning of each statement, they can teach their family members the CHAMP messages and how each statement helps them to train their brain for success.

Embed it

Self reflections

Throughout this unit there are many opportunities for students to use their **Bounce Back!** journal to think about themselves, to record their goals, progress, challenges, strengths and limitations, and to reflect on the unit's Key messages (see page 280).

Challenge yourself, set a goal and make a plan

Resources

♦ Books

Nadia: The Girl Who Couldn't Sit Still

This book tells the story of Nadia Comaneci, a young Romanian gymnast who became an Olympic champion in 1976 after years of practice and dedication. Although she faced difficult times, Nadia worked hard and picked herself up and persisted even after failures.

The Librarian of Basra: A True Story from Iraq

This is the true story of Alia Muhammad Baker, a librarian in Basra, who feared that the library and the 30 000 books within it would be destroyed when war broke out in 2002. Alia and her friends made a plan to save the books, storing them safely before the library was destroyed.

♦ Songs

'Keep a Dream in Your Pocket'

'High Hopes'

'Let's Do a Bit Better Than Best'

(to the tune of 'Popeye the Sailor Man')

> Let's do a bit better than best
> Yes, do a bit better than best
> We won't just say
> We'll do our best
> We'll do a bit better than best

> **Teacher reflection**
> Think about a time when you set a goal for yourself that was new or challenging. How did you plan to achieve your goal? How challenged were you to do something that was new or difficult for you? What risk-taking was involved? What strengths did you use? What mistakes did you make? What obstacles did you encounter? How hard was it at times to persist? How frustrated were you at times? How happy, proud and satisfied did you feel when you succeeded?

Circle Time or classroom discussion

Read one of the books to the class and help students identify the goal or challenge faced by the characters, and their plan to achieve their goal. You could also use the songs.

Discussion questions

- **What is a 'goal'?** (Something you want to achieve or have happen, e.g. to improve your swimming and win a race at your swimming club, or to get better at using fractions in maths.)

- **What is a dream?** (Usually a bigger goal that takes more time and more steps to achieve than a short-term goal, e.g. to represent your country in the Olympics or to go to university.)

- Why is it good to have goals? (Goals help you to work out what you want to do and can help you to get what you want; you can check how you are going along the way; you feel successful and more confident when you achieve your goal; you become more resourceful.)

Ask students to discuss with a partner one thing that they have learnt to do that was really challenging or hard for them to do (e.g. riding a bike, doing a difficult maths problem, giving a class presentation). Ask a few students to share their challenge. Talk about the difference between short-term goals (this morning, tomorrow, the next day, or in the next week or so) and long-term goals (six months from now, one year from now, two years from now, or longer).

Then plan and implement a whole-class goal that is quick and easy to achieve. For instance, implement one or more of the students' ideas from the BRAIN activity on page 90.

Before starting:

- clarify the goal with students
- together make a plan of what will be done, the steps in order, when and by whom.

As a class, put the plan into action.

Then in a follow-up Circle Time, discuss the planning process the class went through and how it was useful in achieving the goal. Discuss what went well and what could have been done better.

Activities

Be a CHAMP

Show the CHAMP acronym using the **CHAMP e-activity** or **BLM You Can Be a CHAMP** and explain that students are going to learn how to challenge themselves, set a goal and make a plan.

Each student chooses a goal to pursue. Focus on short-term goals that are very concrete, specific and fairly immediate. The following are examples of suitable individual goals for students to work with:

- sporting goals (e.g. learning to kick or throw a ball more accurately)
- social goals (e.g. asking a classmate home to play, getting to know someone, becoming better at conversations, becoming a better winner and loser)
- goals associated with creative or performing arts (e.g. learning to play a new song, improve drawing faces, improve a particular dancing skill)
- academic goals (e.g. reading a longer book, making less errors in a piece of work)
- financial goals (e.g. earning and saving money for a specific purpose)
- self-discipline goals (e.g. getting fitter, going to bed earlier, reading more)
- wellbeing goals (e.g. eating a piece of fruit each day, walking the dog each day)
- family goals (e.g. tidying room weekly, setting the table for dinner)
- independence goals (e.g. making own bed, school lunch or breakfast).

Give each student a copy of **BLM CHAMP Goal-Setting Chart** to help them to choose one goal that is challenging for them and make a plan to direct their efforts. The goal should be something they can do rather than something they can stop doing, e.g. 'do more exercise', rather than 'watch less TV', 'eat more fruit' rather than 'stop eating junk food'. When they have made their choice, ask them to share the selection with a partner.

Discuss these questions to help them to start working towards their goal.

- What is something small that you can do straight away that will be the first step towards reaching your goal?

- What kind of lists could you make (e.g. things to read, things to do, things to find) that would help you to make sure you don't leave anything out that needs to be done?
- What can you do every day, or often, that will take you closer to reaching your goal?
- Is there anyone you can ask for help or advice?
- Are there any tools or things that you need to help you achieve your goal?

▶ Make CHAMP lift-up flaps (see page 103) when students achieve their goal. On the top they write their name (e.g. Zara) and the sentence 'Guess what Zara can do now?' Underneath, Zara writes what she can now do.

Award a **BLM CHAMP Certificate** when students have achieved a goal.

CHAMP class goal posts

Each student draws and cuts out a number of footballs or basketballs on which they write their names and a personal goal. Make a large set of cardboard class goal posts or a basketball/netball ring. When they have achieved the goal, they attach their football, between the goal posts or in the basketball ring. On the back of their football, they list three things they did that helped them to achieve that goal (e.g. 'I worked really hard', 'I challenged myself', 'I followed my plan').

CHAMP challenges (in pairs)

Materials needed:

- a box with a lid
- blank cards on which you write challenges that the students can undertake in pairs to practise goal-setting.

Make up the challenge cards and put them in a large closed box. Ask students for suggestions for challenges. Once a week organise students into pairs. One of the pair pulls a card out of the box. They take the card away, copy the task down and then return the card to the box so all cards are available all the time.

Students can then choose to take up the challenge or not. When the pair completes three challenges (i.e. they achieve their goal), they are a CHAMP.

Some ideas for challenge cards:

- sing a song of your choice to the class
- organise a dance routine to music and perform to the class
- learn a poem off by heart and recite it together in front of the class
- learn ten hard spelling words and then take turns at spelling them out loud without looking
- pick a maths concept that you both find difficult and practise it until you both improve
- invite someone who is not a good friend to play a board game with both of you
- read a simple chapter book and present a brief book review to the class
- make a Cross-off with a secret CHAMP message to give to classmates (see page 91)
- go as far as possible (each helping the other to practise and improve) playing the game of Sevenies (see page 286).

Do a bit better than your best

When students push themselves to improve their current personal bests, they gain confidence and gain a deeper understanding that effort and motivation, as well as ability, play an important role in achievement and goal attainment. If they are told 'just do your best', then they are not being challenged to push themselves and they will think this is the best they can do. Every now and then get students to sing 'Let's Do a Bit Better Than Best' and then ask them to 'do a bit better than best' on a nominated or self-selected task. Ask them to write in their **Bounce Back!** journal about their 'bit better than best' goal, what they did to try to do a bit better and what the outcome was. Debrief with them one-on-one and/or give written feedback on their reflections.

Game

Sevenies

Students play in pairs and try to go through their sequences for each player in ever faster times. Each player uses a tennis ball against a rebound wall and completes a sequence of seven plays. If they make a mistake, they must pass the ball to their partner and, when it is their turn again, they must start from one. Alternatively, they can just keep trying to improve their own personal best time for completing all seven sequences.

- Sequence 1: Throw the ball against the wall and catch it. Do this seven times.
- Sequence 2: Throw the ball against the wall and catch it after one bounce. Do this six times.
- Sequence 3: Throw the ball against the wall, turn around once and catch it. Do this five times.
- Sequence 4: Throw the ball against the wall and catch it after one bounce and one clap. Do this four times.
- Sequence 5: Throw the ball so that it bounces once before it hits the wall and then catch it. Do this three times.
- Sequence 6: Throw the ball so that it bounces once before it hits the wall, clap once and then catch it. Do this two times.
- Sequence 7: Throw the ball against the wall but under one leg, clap once and then catch it. Do this once.

Have a go, take a risk and believe in yourself

Resources

✦ Books

Drum Dream Girl: How One Girl's Courage Changed Music

This is an inspiring story about a girl who dared to dream of being a drummer in a culture that said girls could not. She practises in secret and never gives up on her dream. Ultimately, her risk taking and her belief in herself changes a culture and reverses a long-held taboo.

Salt in His Shoes

Michael Jordan almost gave up basketball when he was a child as he feared he would never be tall enough. He even put salt in his shoes to make himself taller. Finally, he succeeded because his parents urged him to have a go, persist and work hard.

✦ Song

'I Have a Go'

> **Teacher reflection**
> Think about a time when you wanted to achieve or learn something that you had never done before. You wondered if you would be able to do it, then you thought about what you can do and thought it was worth 'having a go'. For instance, you wanted to learn to ski but you had never been skiing before. You knew you were fit and good at other sports, so you believed in yourself and had a go. You were also sensible in the risk you took because you had lessons to learn how to ski. Thinking about how self-belief applies in your own life will help you more effectively teach these skills to your students.

Circle Time or classroom discussion

Begin by reading one of the books and discuss the following questions.

Discussion questions

- What was challenging for the character in the story?
- How did believing in yourself (or lack of it) affect them?
- What is a risk?
- What would have happened if they did not take a risk and have a go? What risk(s) did they take? (Most risked failing or making a mistake.)

In pairs, students discuss an example of when they believed in themselves and had the confidence to take a risk. Ask students how can someone turn 'I can't do it' into 'I'll have a go' or 'I'll try to learn how to do it'? Use the **CHAMP e-tool**.

In the discussion that follows, stress these points:

- You need to accept yourself and believe that who you are is okay, even though we are all different in many ways.
- It is helpful to 'positive track' yourself a lot (see Unit 5: Looking on the bright side). This means focusing more on the positive things about yourself than what you can't do or what you're not good at. Pat yourself on the back for every success or achievement, however small.
- You can't succeed if you don't believe that you can.
- You usually can do something if you decide to and if you work hard and keep at it.
- All successful people that you admire started just as you are starting, i.e. with a dream and the will to do it.

Use the **Animal Asks e-tool** (see page 90) to discuss the following questions:

- What motivates students to try to be like others rather than be themselves? (The desire to belong, to copy people they admire.)
- Should we listen to people who tell us that we have to be like them?
- How can we believe in ourselves when others try to stop us?
- What can happen to our thinking if someone says to us, 'You can't do that' or 'That's not worth doing'? How can we stop that effect? (Say to ourselves, 'They are not always right'; 'Try to turn "I can't do that" into "I'll have a go".')
- Why is it more helpful to concentrate on getting better at the things that are important to us than on comparing ourselves to other people?

Activities

- Students read and complete **BLM Amelia Earhart**.
- Organise students into groups of three to prepare a book review or digital book trailer (see page 102) that focuses on how the character in the selected book 'had a go, took a risk, believed in themselves'.

Always look for and use your strengths

What are your ability strengths?

Resources

✦ Books

Counting on Frank

Frank has a fascination with numbers and calculations, and he is very good at it – it's one of his top brain strengths. This fascination and ability with numbers pays off for him in an unexpected way when he uses his skills to win a competition.

Crow Boy

A boy with no friends is teased at his school in a small village in Japan. They call him 'Chibi', or 'tiny boy'. A new teacher realises that the boy has amazing skills in the area of 'naturalist intelligence', and gives him opportunities to show the other children his skills.

✦ Film

Matilda

Matilda is an exceptionally intelligent child. She looks forward to starting school, only to find that the tyrannical headmistress, Miss Trunchbull, makes school life awful. When Matilda discovers she has an amazing superpower, she's able to give Miss Trunchbull her just desserts.

Circle Time or classroom discussion

Start by reading to the class and discussing one or more of the books or showing part of the film where Matilda shows her talents.

Discussion questions

- In what way was the character smart?
- What are some of the things they did that showed us they were smart?
- How hard did they work?
- Was there anything they weren't able to do well?
- What is one thing you are good at?

Stress that there are different ways to be smart. Ask each student in turn to say one thing they are good at. After each contribution, reframe it as a strength, as follows: 'So, Liam, one of your strengths is organising others. Can you tell us one way in which you have used that strength well?' Emphasise that no-one is good at everything and that we all have different combinations of strengths.

- Why is it important to know what we are good at and not good at if we want to be successful? (We can use our strengths to achieve our dreams and goals, we can try to get better at the things we are not good at, or we can find ways to avoid having to do too many of the things we are not good at.)
- Why is it important to be able to do a reality check and find some proof or evidence for what we think we are good at? What might happen if we didn't look for evidence? (We might feel upset when we can't do what we thought we could do.)

Activities

▶ After reading *Counting on Frank*, follow up with maths activities that are based on some of Frank's comments.

▶ After reading *Crow Boy*, follow up with Inquiry-based learning (see page 92) into Japanese geography, culture, art etc.

Multiple Intelligences

Introduce different ways in which people can be smart, making links with Howard Gardner's eight Multiple Intelligences. Photocopy **BLM Multiple Intelligences Symbols** (four copies per student), and have students cut out the 32 squares.

Place eight containers of symbols in the centre of the class circle. Label each container to show which symbol is in it. Give each student an A3 sheet and a glue stick to share. Explain that you will be reading some questions to them (see below) and if they can answer 'yes' then they pick up the symbol that goes with that question and paste it on their sheet in a picture graph. Encourage them to think carefully about the statement and about whether they could provide evidence of what they can do to support the statement. Every now and then, when a student chooses a symbol, ask a question that checks for evidence of a strength in that intelligence, e.g. 'What musical instrument do you play?' or 'Have you danced in a concert?'

The questions are:

1. Can you get along well with lots of different people? (people)
2. Can you say what things you are good at and what you are not so good at? (self)
3. Are you good at making things with your hands, e.g. models or things that require cutting and pasting to make something? (body)
4. Can you remember songs well and quickly work out what songs they are when you hear them? (music)
5. Can you draw or paint well? (space and vision)
6. Do you find it easy to do tricky maths problems and puzzles? (logic and maths)
7. Are you a good reader who reads quickly and confidently? (word)
8. Are you good at recognising many animals and insects and remembering their names? (naturalist)
9. Do you know more facts about science than most people your age because you are really interested in why things happen? (logic and maths)
10. Are you really interested in why people behave the way they do? (people)
11. When you have a goal (i.e. something you want to achieve, like saving money to buy something), are you good at making a plan to get it and then sticking to it? (self)
12. Can you play a musical instrument well? (music)
13. Are you good at working out which things look better than others because of their colour, their shape and their decoration (e.g. clothes, cars, paintings, designs)? (space and vision)
14. Are you good at writing or telling stories? (word)
15. Do you know a lot of facts about animals, birds, insects or plants because you are really interested and have found out about them yourself? (naturalist)

16 Do you find it easier than many students to learn a new sporting skill? (body)

17 Do you sing well and know more songs than most people your age? (music)

18 Are you good at remembering the details of how things looked after you have seen them? (space and vision)

19 Have people said to you that you are really good with pets and looking after them? (naturalist)

20 Are you good at working out how other people are feeling and then helping them if they need help? (people)

21 Do you think a lot about why you behave and feel as you do, and feel confident that you know a lot about yourself? (self)

22 Are you good at acting or miming? (body)

23 Are you really interested about how things work (e.g. taps, machines, tools and appliances) and do you spend time trying to find out about them? (logic and maths)

24 Are you good at word puzzles and word games? (word)

Students then complete **BLM Multiple Intelligences Record Sheet** to work out their strongest intelligences. You could also use the Paper plate quiz strategy with these questions (see page 95). As you read out each question, students show 'yes' or 'no' on their answering device. It's a quick way of demonstrating that everyone has different strengths and weaknesses and no-one is good at everything.

A 'class strengths' book

Make a class book in which each page of the book contains one student's drawing of them doing something that shows an ability strength. On the page they can write a statement such as:

- My name is …
- My best ability strength is …
- My evidence for this is …

What are your character strengths?

Resources

◆ Books

Ish

A book about a boy who is highly creative. He feels light and energised (in flow) when he is creating. However, feedback from his siblings has a significant impact.

Iggy Peck, Architect

Iggy's strength in building and constructing is not valued by his teacher, until he saves the whole class using creative problem-solving when he builds a bridge across a fast current.

Best Friends

See page 231.

> **Teacher reflection**
> Prior to this topic, complete the free VIA character strengths inventory (see **Resources list**.). It will take 10 to 15 minutes. You will then get a rank order listing of your strengths based on the VIA's 24 character strengths. See page 291 for more information about character strengths.

Circle Time or classroom discussion

Begin Circle Time by explaining that we not only have 'clever' or 'smart' strengths, but we also have personal or character strengths, such as being brave, being kind, being well organised and so on. Share one of your personal strengths from the inventory you completed and talk about how this strength is a character strength, i.e. it is about the kind of person you are trying to be. Explain how you know that this is a personal strength for you by giving one example of how you have used this strength as a teacher. Explain that Aristotle, the famous thinker, once said, 'You are what you repeatedly do.' Ask them what that means (that you can develop the character strengths you want to have by taking certain actions over and over until they become a habit). For instance, if you want to have the character strength of kindness, then you can develop this by taking many opportunities to act in a kind way towards others.

Read one of the books and discuss.

Discussion questions

- What are the character strengths of the character/s in the book? How do you know?
- Did the characters have to practise these over and over again or were they just good at them?

Make 'Strengths cards' using the strengths listed in **BLM My Personal Strengths List**. Place all the strengths cards in the middle of the circle. Ask each student to choose one strength card and to think about one thing they may have done that demonstrates that strength. Then go round the circle and ask each student to read out their strength and share one time they have demonstrated that strength. If any student indicates that they can't think of an example for a particular strength card that they have drawn, ask the rest of the class for an example or ask the student to choose another card.

Students then complete the **BLM My Personal Strengths List**.

- Why is it important to have evidence of what people say they are good at?

Encourage students to look for evidence and to ask you, other teachers, a family member or a friend to write examples of when they have demonstrated these behaviours.

When students have completed **BLM My Personal Strengths List**, they take turns showing their strengths list to a partner and comparing similarities and differences. Back in a new Circle Time, each student takes turns at saying one strength they had in common with their partner and one thing that was different from their partner. Alternatively, they could do a Venn diagram before they share in the circle.

Activities

▶ Students reflect in their journals about what they found out about their strengths.

Digital 'class strengths' photo album

Make a digital photo album and include photos of students doing different things that show their different strengths. Students can write a brief description of what they can do or have done as evidence of that strength.

Ability and character strengths showcase

Set up opportunities to showcase your students' ability strengths, for example:

- Let students demonstrate some of their learning in different ways such as by a flow chart (spatial), a three-dimensional model (body), a rap or song (music), a cooperative mime and so on (people and body), according to their strengths.
- Create opportunities for students to contribute stories, poems and drawings and scanned photos of their work to a class newsletter or a bulletin board in a high traffic area of the corridor.

- Hold a special 'showcase' day when students choose items, creations or performances to display or present their ability strengths or their character strengths. Students can take on the planning for this day as a whole-class goal. Don't forget to make a program/catalogue.

Embed it

Classroom directory

Make a classroom directory and establish a student committee to create and maintain it. List all the skills you can think of from A to Z and ask students for ideas too. For example, for J you might have jewellery making, jumper knitting, jelly making, joke telling and juggling. In a note home, ask families to provide additional information about their child's skills.

Write the names of students who believe that they have a reasonable degree of competence or knowledge for that listing. Each student should have several entries. For example, one student might have listings under 'kite flying', 'drawing' and 'cooking scrambled eggs'. You may need to teach a specific skill to some students (e.g. using a particular software program or game, making a pop-up card). Encourage classmates to teach each other. Give a copy to other staff in the school and encourage them to draw on students' expertise for different projects in their classrooms or the whole school.

Business cards

Show students a range of different business cards. Talk about how and when people use business cards. Students then design their own business card, which includes their name, class, phone number and information from the classroom directory on what skills they can offer. Use the Inside–outside circle strategy (see page 93) to enable students to take turns at showing a partner their business card and talking about their skills.

Using your strengths to help others

Resources

◆ Book

Randy Riley's Really Big Hit

Randy Riley knows everything about science, the solar system and space, but very little about baseball. One night Randy sees a fireball through his telescope and it's headed towards his town! Randy uses his knowledge of maths and space to save the town.

Circle Time or classroom discussion

Read the book and discuss the questions.

Discussion questions

- What were Randy's strength?
- How did he use his strengths to help others?

Ask students to share one of their top ability strengths, followed by one of their character strengths. Then students (who volunteer) tell the group about a time when they did something for someone else using one of their strengths, e.g. a student who draws well might have helped someone else to draw something, a fluent reader might have read a book to a sick grandparent or a younger sibling.

- How did you feel when you helped someone else?

Stress that when we do something for others we feel happy and they feel happy too. Knowing what our strengths are can help us to decide how we can help others.

Negotiate with the class to set a whole-class goal that helps others such as a community or fundraising project (see suggestions below and on page 294). Use the process of achieving the goal to illustrate the steps and skills involved, e.g. goal setting, planning, etc. Assign different responsibilities using people's different strengths. Use the CHAMP acronym and **CHAMP e-tool** to help students to formulate the plan and evaluate progress along the way. Make and use an advent-style calendar that shows the countdown to the final goal. Highlight the need to solve problems resourcefully as they arise using the next topic, 'Mistakes help you learn – don't be afraid to make them'.

Follow up on the whole-class goal to help others with individual student reflections. You could use the **Animal Asks e-tool** here (see page 90).

- What did you do to help someone else?
- What ability strength did you use?
- What character strength did you use?
- What is one thing you learnt from others?
- How do you feel about this project?
- How do you think the people we helped feel?
- What is one thing you might do differently next time?
- How successful were you at achieving your goal?

Activities

Using our class strengths to help others

▶ Students help their classmates, e.g. using a Classroom directory (see page 292).

▶ Organise an event to share with another class. Students can brainstorm ideas for being kind and supportive to another class in the school, e.g. inviting another class to share a picnic and games, conducting a class competition of games, participating in a tabloid sports event the class has organised, sharing a special morning tea.

▶ Students can buddy up with a younger class to:
  - read one of the books recommended in **Bounce Back!** and teach a key BOUNCE! message (see **Bounce Back!** Years F–2)
  - act as a reading tutor using 'pause, prompt, praise'
  - make a bounce-backer (see page 101)
  - make a STAR badge or STARfish for younger students in the school (see **Bounce Back!** Years F–2 Unit 10: Success)
  - conduct a puppet show of a **Bounce Back!** story
  - play a board game
  - make up a **Bounce Back!** word game for younger students, e.g. Cross-offs, Mystery word.

▶ Fundraise for a charity. The class can pursue goals that involve the need for some understanding of people and systems outside the classroom by raising money for a particular cause e.g. a World Vision child or a local homeless youth charity. The students could:
  - hold a stall to sell things they have made
  - have a sausage sizzle

- prepare a three-dollar lucky dip stall
- make badges or fridge magnets to sell, perhaps featuring CHAMP or BOUNCE BACK! (see pages 108 and 103)
- hold a read-a-thon, walk-a-thon or dance-a-thon: each student collects pledges from family, friends and community members for each hour or kilometre students walk or dance, or for each book read
- organise a junk food fast where they give up junk food for one week and donate the money they would have spent on the food to a cause
- organise a school talent show where students perform, dance, sing, recite, play a musical instrument, demonstrate acrobatic skills etc.
- make a class cookbook to sell.

Mistakes help you learn – don't be afraid to make them

Resources

✦ Books

Rosie Revere, Engineer

When Rosie's attempt to build a flying contraption for her aunt doesn't turn out quite as she plans, she feels like a failure. But as her aunt explains, mistakes are a normal part of creating something and you only fail if you give up.

Don't Put Yourself Down in Circus Town

Ringmaster Rick, the Ringmaster in Circus Town, calls an emergency meeting after overhearing several performers put themselves down for mistakes they made while rehearsing their acts. The message is that anyone can make a mistake.

✦ Song

'Power of Yet!'

Circle Time or classroom discussion

Begin by reading one of the books.

Discussion questions

- What mistakes did the character/s make?
- What was the message in the book about making mistakes?

Then ask students to put their hand up if they have ever made a mistake. Conduct a Partner Retell (see page 95) where students take turns to interview their partner with the following Yes/No questions. They keep a record of their partner's answers and then pool all their answers to the ten questions when they join another pair.

1. Have you ever made a mistake when playing sport?
2. Have you ever fallen off your bike?
3. Have you ever messed up a painting?
4. Have you ever misspelt a word in your schoolwork?

5 Have you ever made a mistake in doing a maths problem?

6 Have you ever made a mistake when reading out loud?

7 Have you ever got the words mixed up when singing a song?

8 Have you ever called someone by the wrong name?

9 Have you ever made a mistake when playing a board game or card game?

10 Are you more likely to make mistakes when you start learning something new?

Ask each group of four to share their data, then discuss the following questions.

- **What do the results from your ten questions show?** (Everyone makes mistakes, especially when we are learning to do new things.)
- **What might happen if we always worried about making mistakes?** (We wouldn't have a go at learning new things, we wouldn't learn from our mistakes.)

Play the song and discuss the power of YET (e.g. 'I can't do it yet. When I'm learning something new, I will make mistakes').

Activities

▶ Students use digital software to make posters using one of the following slogans:
  - My mistakes help me learn
  - F.A.I.L. means **F**irst **A**ttempt **I**n **L**earning
  - The power of YET: I can't do this yet / This doesn't work yet / I don't know yet / It doesn't make sense yet / I'm not good at this yet, but I will get there.

▶ Give each student a sheet of A4 paper. They fold it in half. One the left side they write six things they can do. On the right-hand side they write three things they can't do YET and include the message: 'Mistakes will help me learn.'

Drama

In groups of four, students create and present a two-minute skit on the 'Power of Yet!' They start by making mistakes and then learning from their mistakes. The skits could be recorded.

Use grit – persist, work hard and don't give up

Resources

✦ Books

The Streets Are Free

This book is based on the true story of the children of San José de la Urbina in Venezuela, who had nowhere to play. A group of them visited the mayor to ask for some land for a playground, but he just made empty promises. The children persisted and eventually achieved their goal.

The Dot

Vashti sadly sits in class looking at her blank sheet of paper and wails, 'I just can't draw'. Her teacher suggests that she start with a dot and see where it takes her. Vashti does this and puts in lots of effort, finally coming up with something that pleases her.

✦ Video clips

Sesame Street: Persistent

Elmo and David Beckham demonstrate the quality of persistence.

Katie Discovers the Dip

With Mojo's help, Katie persists with an art class.

✦ Song

'Perseverance'

> **Teacher reflection**
> Do you give mostly 'process praise' that emphasises how much effort students have given to the task or 'person praise' that emphasises how 'smart' they are? (See page 281 on growth mindset.) Use the CHAMP messages to help you give process praise:
> - I noticed that you didn't give up when you felt frustrated.
> - I saw that you tried a number of ways to solve the problem.
> - Your strength of drawing really helped your team make a great poster.
> - I noticed that you really challenged yourself to achieve something that was difficult for you.
> - It's great that you learned from your mistake and tried again.

Circle Time or classroom discussion

Start the discussion by giving a specific example of a time when you had to work hard and not give up in order to do something or learn something. Emphasise that it can take time to become good at something and that people might be not so good at it at the start and for some time afterwards. Explain that this is called persistence. Stress that persistence and effort allow people to find out what they can really do when they try hard. Also stress how others can provide help and support as people learn.

Use one of the resources and discuss, linking back to the CHAMP statements.

Discussion questions

- How did the character/s think like a CHAMP in that they were determined to reach their goal?
- Did they plan and work hard and persist even when they had problems?

Then ask students to use the Think–ink–pair–share strategy (see page 97) to talk about a goal they achieved that was hard for them at first and for which they had to practise a lot. Select some students to report to the circle and ask them the following questions.

- Did you find it hard to do at first?
- Did you make any mistakes?
- Did you have to practise a lot?
- Did you experience the 'dip'? (Refer to the video clip *Katie Discovers the Dip*. The 'dip' occurs when things start to get harder and you start to lose a bit of the initial excitement and enthusiasm for your goal and have thoughts of giving up.)
- What might be some good ways to get yourself past the 'dip'?
- What helped you to persist and put in effort and not give up?

Activities

▶ In pairs, students create a short imaginative text about someone who persisted, didn't give up, dealt with problems and achieved what they set out to do. Use the **CHAMP e-tool** with this activity.

Which fairy tale characters are CHAMPs?

Organise students into groups of three or four. Give each group a different fairy tale to analyse, e.g. *Hansel and Gretel*, *Snow White*, *Cinderella*, *Three Little Pigs*, *Red Riding Hood*, *Sleeping Beauty* and *The Ugly Duckling*. Each group uses the CHAMP acronym statements to analyse the behaviour of the main character(s).

- What was the challenge for the main character(s)?
- Was this character a CHAMP or not? Were they determined? Persistent?
- Did they take a risk? Work hard and put in effort?
- Did they believe in themselves and accept themselves as OK?

Each group presents their analysis to the class.

Success keys

Students make their own key to success. They trace around a key and enlarge it to A4 size on light and bright cardboard and cut it out. Each student has one cardboard key for each goal they set for themselves. The keys can be displayed on several large ring-binder rings attached to the wall or cupboard door. Each time a student puts in time or effort into stepping closer towards their goal, they write it on their key to success (e.g. 'I finished reading the book that showed me how to make the model I am planning to make for my project'). Encourage students to write on their key when they learnt from their mistakes or failures relating to their goal (e.g. 'I forgot how to play a guitar chord but I learnt that I need to practise more often' or 'I didn't eat any fruit yesterday because I don't like apples, so I will ask dad to buy fruit that I do like'). Encourage them to include any new 'risks' they take as the move towards their goal (e.g. 'I wasn't sure I could remember the words of the poem before reciting it in front of the class because I was very nervous, but I managed to do it'). Each new goal will need a new key.

(This activity is adapted from McGrath, H. & Francey, S., 1991, *Friendly Kids, Friendly Classrooms*, Pearson Australia, Melbourne.)

Progress chain

Each student makes a progress chain using strips of coloured paper. Each time they progress towards their goal, they write what they achieved on a strip of paper and add a link to the chain (like a Christmas decoration chain). Remember to encourage them to include the effort they put towards the goal and the lessons learnt from mistakes, rather than focusing only on success. Some of the links could simply celebrate 'not giving up'.

Take-home task

Interviews with people who have achieved an important goal

Each student interviews someone they know who has achieved a goal that was challenging and meaningful to them (e.g. an older sibling who has bought their own car, someone who has won an award, a parent who has finished a training course, a grandparent who has completed a project).

Students complete **BLM An Interview with a Person Who Achieved Their Goal**, to record their findings.

Make a class book of the interviews. Organise students into groups of three to look for common features in their interview results and report them to the class.

Embed it

Learning journeys

At the end of the day, each student shares with a different partner one reflection. For example:

- One new thing I learnt today was …
- Something I finished today was …
- One thing I found hard to do today, but I tried and didn't give up, was …
- The activity I liked doing best today was ____. I liked this best because …
- One goal I have for tomorrow is …

Students can then record their reflection in their journal and date it.

At the end of term students can use the information in their learning log to help them draw their learning journey for the term. Encourage them to record the ups and downs as hills and valleys or stops and starts. Remind them to include personal learning as well as academic and other kinds of learning. Ask them to draw a more inclusive journey at the end of the year. Alternatively, they can, at the end of each term, list the ten most important things they learnt this term (either in general, or just about **Bounce Back!**).

Using willpower

Resources

✦ Books

Will Powers: Where There's a Will There's a Way

This story focuses on a young boy, Will Powers, whose ambition is to play music. He achieves his goal through commitment, hard work and believing in himself.

Alexander Who Used to Be Rich Last Sunday

Alexander receives some money on Sunday, but by the end of the week he has managed to squander the lot!

✦ Poems

Homework! Oh, Homework!

Credit

Circle Time or classroom discussion

Use the poem *Credit* as a starting point to talk about how you don't get any credit for things you plan to do but don't do. Read one of the books and use the **Animal Asks e-tool** (see page 90) to discuss the following questions.

Discussion questions

- What is willpower or self-discipline? (Making yourself do what you don't really want to do because there is a good reason; doing something you should do but don't want to.)

Give some examples of willpower from your own life (e.g. getting out of bed on a chilly morning, preparing work for the next day, not eating too many foods that are bad for you even though they taste good, not wasting money on unimportant things).

- Did the character use willpower? If he had, what might he have done differently?

- **What is one way in which you use willpower?** (Getting out of a nice warm shower so that others can have hot water too, going to netball training when you are tired, finishing a project instead of watching TV.)
- **Why is it hard to use willpower or self-discipline?** (The alternatives offer immediate pleasure or satisfaction and it's hard to give them up for a bigger satisfaction that may take a bit longer. However, it's worth it.)

Activities

▶ Students write in their **Bounce Back!** journals a checklist of the ways in which they show willpower and self-discipline when they have to do something they don't enjoy.

▶ Students use one of the poems as a stimulus to write their own poem.

Solving problems and being resourceful

Resources

✦ Books

What Do You Do with a Problem?
This is the story of a child learning the truth about what it really means to have a problem. He learns not to run from it, but to face the fear of it head on. He learns, therefore, that problems are not necessarily troubles or obstacles, but rather opportunities for growth.

Doctor De Soto
Doctor De Soto is a mouse who, with his wife, has a dental practice with one rule: they won't see patients who might eat them! However, because they are also very caring, they treat a fox with a terrible toothache. But they make a good plan to ensure that he doesn't eat them!

Hansel and Gretel
The themes in this book are courage, perseverance, creative problem-solving and setting goals. Anthony Browne's illustrated version of this classic portrays a home of extreme poverty, child abandonment and hopelessness. Encourage students to 'read' the drawings as well the text.

✦ Poem

Today Is Very Boring

Circle Time or classroom discussion

Read to the class and discuss one or more of the books listed. You could also read the poem then ask students to answer the following questions. The **Animal Asks e-tool** (see page 90) can also be used.

Discussion questions
- Where was/were the character/s persistent?
- What difference did their persistence make?
- What does being resourceful mean? (Finding new creative ways to solve problems, thinking of new plans if an old one doesn't work, using available resources to achieve your goals.)
- Where did the character(s) solve a problem or deal resourcefully with an obstacle that was in the way of achieving their goal (i.e. what they set out to do)? How did they do this?
- Do plans always work? (No, sometimes we have to make a new plan.)

- What do you need to do when you encounter obstacles and problems in following your plans? (Persist and try to solve the problem, put in effort, not give up, be resourceful.)
- What happens if you don't try hard and you give up too easily? (You don't feel satisfied, you don't achieve your goals, you aren't as happy or as confident as you would like to be.)

Activities

▶ Guide students to map a story, showing the problem of the story and how it was resolved.

▶ Students photocopy the images in a fairy tale, e.g. *Hansel and Gretel*, and make stick puppets. Each group take turns to re-tell the story, with a narrator emphasising where the main character set goals, persisted and solved problems.

▶ Students read and complete **BLM Thomas Edison**.

Survive a disaster

Use some realistic disasters for which students can offer resourceful solutions. They could act them out as a drama. For example:

- What could you do if you were separated from your family during a crowded event?
- What could you do if the water supply was shut off to your house without warning and you had to survive without it for three days?
- What could you do if you were lost in the bush in winter with a friend and had to spend the night there? You have nothing but the clothes you are wearing.

Students can make up some of their own 'disasters' for the class to discuss.

Being resourceful when you are bored

Read the poem *Today Is Very Boring* and discuss: What is boredom? What does it feel like? Why do we get bored? Does everybody get bored sometimes? (Yes!) When have you felt very bored? How did you solve that problem? You could also use the **Animal Asks e-tool** with these questions.

Follow up by using the Bundling strategy (see page 91) to ask pairs of students to write down ideas about what they could do to be resourceful if they are bored at home and can't watch TV, play music or use the computer. They choose their best five ideas and make a poster to display. At a later time, repeat the activity with 'five things to do in the playground if we are bored'.

Managing time and being organised

Managing time

Resources

✦ Book

See You Later, Procrastinator! (Get it Done)

Humorous cartoons are used to teach children how to motivate themselves to get things done. The book also contains 12 strategies for dealing with procrastination.

✦ Poem

All My Great Excuses

Circle Time or classroom discussion

Begin the discussion by telling one anecdote about your own time management, e.g. what time you get up, how you make sure you don't sleep in, how you make sure you have enough time to do the things you have to do before you go out.

Discussion questions

- What would happen if:
  - people came to school at different times of the day?
  - different classes went to recess and lunchtime any time they felt like it?
  - the teacher let students spend as much time as they like doing the same activity?
  - the teacher did not plan different lessons for the day?
  - we didn't have any clocks or watches?

Read the suggested book and poem.

- What tips does the book give you about managing your time well?

Stress the need for everyone to cooperate with time. Students can then take turns at sharing information about their own time management, e.g. what time they go to bed, what time they get up, how much time they spend watching TV, playing sport or doing their homework. They can also share how they make sure they do their homework, get up on time, go to bed on time etc.

Activities

Keeping a time-management log book

Students keep a log book to improve their time management. They record and graph how much time they spend doing different activities at home and school every day for a week. They can also record what time different lessons or activities start and finish, what time they start and finish watching TV, and what time they go to bed and get up.

Setting short-term goals for time-management

Students' time monitoring can be part of their own short-term goals of better time management (e.g. watching less TV, going to bed earlier, getting up more reliably, having a shorter shower, getting to school five minutes earlier).

Time-management poster

Discuss good ways to manage time and then ask students to make a poster with a partner with time-management tips (e.g. use clocks or watches, ask people to remind you about the time, estimate how long each thing will take before you do it, make a timetable, record times that things have to happen, don't get distracted by other things that will waste time).

Take-home tasks

Family interviews: Time management

Students interview other members of their family about how they manage time and also how they make sure they get up on time (and don't go back to sleep!). They record their answers and bring to class for collation and conversion to class graphs.

Good ideas for remembering things (or storing things)

Students interview people in their families about how they remember things. Record responses in light bulb shapes on a bulletin board.

Being organised

Resource

✦ Book
Get Organised Without Losing it

A practical, humorous book that provides strategies to help children manage 'their tasks, their time and their 'stuff'. Topics covered include prioritising tasks, managing homework, preparing for tests and planning projects.

Circle Time or classroom discussion

Start by reading the book and discuss.

Discussion questions

- What tips does the book give about being organised?

Then use the Paper plate quiz strategy (see page 95). Ask the following questions and count up the number of people who respond to 'yes' to each question. Alternatively, use the **Animal Asks e-tool** here (see page 90).

- Do you pack your own school bag?
- Have you ever used a list to help you remember what to buy at the shops?
- Does your home have a calendar displayed to remind people when things are on?
- Do you have a special box in your bedroom to keep things that are important to you?
- Do you have a special place in your home where keys are put?

All these questions are about being organised. Emphasise that good organisation means that people can find things because they are stored in a predictable place and not messed up with everything else. Good organisation also means that people can remember what has to be done. Then use the Lightning writing strategy (see page 93) and ask students to write about the phrase 'being disorganised'. Ask each student in turn to say one thing they wrote about and discuss the following:

- What do people in your family do to help them remember things?
- How does your family store things so they can be easily found? (Labelled containers, special cupboards, sorted by size or colour, always in same place.)
- What are the things we need to remember to take to school each day?
- What are some good ways to remember what we have to do? (Lists on the fridge, 'stickies' on the computer screen, a diary, a bright sticker in the diary, a prompt e.g. a coat-hanger to remind us to take our blazer.)
- What are some good ways to remember what to do for homework?

Sum up by making a list on the board of all the things that people who are organised do. For example:

- Use ways to record and remember important information (e.g. diaries, calendars, online calendars).
- Make lists of things that have to be done and prioritise them by highlighting those that are more urgent.
- Use reminders for things that must be remembered (e.g. a sticky note stuck on the bathroom mirror).

- Storing and labelling things so that they are easy to find again, e.g. by using broad categories when making computer folders and using keywords in the name of files, having a separate drawer for certain things. (Link this with good analytical thinking; i.e. deciding what things go together and using a category name for it, e.g. the category of 'celebrations' might be used to store birthday cards, souvenirs etc.)

Activities

- Students set a goal to improve the way they store and label one thing, e.g. their computer, their stationery or their toys.
- Students make a prompting card with visual symbols that lists the things they need to take to school each day.
- Students make a personal storage box using a shoebox covered in images from the internet or cut out from greeting cards, magazines or wrapping paper.
- Students work with a partner to find and record the different ways in which things are stored in their classroom (or another classroom). They then make suggestions for improving things and write up a recommendations report for the teacher.
- Students design and create a collage on the computer or make a mobile (see page 105) of different ways that things can be stored so that they can be easily located again. They can use illustrations from magazines and advertising literature from office suppliers and furniture shops or produce their own drawings or use clip art.

Take-home task

Each student investigates how things are organised, stored and accessed in their homes (e.g. different foods, cleaning supplies, clothes, jewellery, tools, books, CDs and DVDs, bills, school notices).

They then contribute their ideas to the creating a giant whole-class poster with a section for each category.

Consolidation

Activities

- Use the TEAM coaching strategy (see page 97) with the CHAMP acronym to ensure the students learn and remember the CHAMP statements (see Key messages, page 280).
- Make CHAMP posters that incorporate the CHAMP messages. Make the positive statement large and the negative 'instead' statement small.
  For example, in our classroom we say:
  - I like a challenge instead of 'I won't try anything new'.
  - I set goals and make a plan instead of not having any direction.
  - I believe in myself and will have a go instead of not trying.
  - I know my strengths instead of 'I'm not good at anything'.
  - Mistakes help me learn instead of 'I failed'.
  - I persist and keep working hard instead of 'I give up'.

Reflection

▶ Students complete **BLM CHAMP Reflection Sheet** when they successfully achieve a goal. These Reflections questions (see page 97) could also be used as a Throw the dice activity (see page 98).

- What is one goal you have achieved?
- What is one dream you have for your adult life?
- What is one of your ability strengths and what is your evidence for that strength?
- What is one of your character strengths and what is your evidence for that strength?
- What is one thing you do to help you remember things you need to bring to school?
- What is one thing you have in your bedroom that keeps your things organised?
- Do you find it difficult or easy to get up in the morning? Why?
- Name someone you know who has achieved a goal similar to one you would like to achieve.

Games

Play one of the following games with the whole class or in groups.

▶ **Before or After? e-game** (see page 90)

▶ **Memory Cards e-game** (see page 93) – where students match Multiple intelligences with corresponding symbols.

Key vocabulary

Play Bingo strips (see page 90) with a selection of these words:

achieve	ability	problem
challenge	character	remember
clever	learn	resourceful
determined	manage	risk
effort	mistakes	self reflect
fail	obstacle	solve
finish	organise	strength
goal	persist	success
grit	persistence	time
improve	plan	willpower
		work

CHAMP celebration ceremony

Students who have achieved their goal (or their 'bit better than best' goal) can choose to choreograph their own congratulations ceremony where they receive their **BLM CHAMP Certificate** using any of the movements/chants on **BLM Congratulations Ceremony** in any order. They can do this individually, in pairs or in groups of three with others who have achieved a goal. They prepare a written sheet of the ceremony/movements (or show slides) for their classmates. The ceremony should be optional, not obligatory. The student can wear a royal blue championship sash (with 'Champion' written on it) or any other ceremonial clothing during the ceremony. Ask students for their ideas on this at the start of the year.

CHAMP trophy

Students could also choose to make a collection of CHAMP trophies. One way of doing this is to use disposable plastic gloves and play dough (or similar). They write messages on the gloves, fill them with play dough and then sculpt one or more gloves into different congratulatory shapes, such as:

- thumbs-up
- a handshake
- a high-five.

Bounce Back! award

Present the **Bounce Back! award** to students who have worked hard and achieved a challenging goal.

Index

ability strengths 35, 280, 288–290, 304
acceptance 143, 159–160
adaptive distancing 45, 54, 55–56
'After the 2012 Riots' (Riots Communities and Victims Panel) 3
AI *see* Appreciative Inquiry
anger 199, 202, 203, 209–212
Animal asks 88, 90
animals
    bouncing back 147–148
    bravery of 173
    fear of 169, 170
    kindness to 129–130
anxiety 170–171, 172
Appreciative Inquiry (AI), five stages 75–77
assessment tools 11, 72–74; *see* ebook
Australian Curriculum 29
Australian Temperament Project 65
Australian Values Education Good Practice School Projects 16
Autism Spectrum Disorder 67

bad moods 61, 62, 199, 206–207
bad times, surviving 142, 184–185, 186
ball bouncing *see* Elasticity (ebook) 3-7
Baumeister, Roy 49
Beck, Aaron 8, 54
Before or after? 90
behaviour management 64, 67, 69, 107, 270
Bingo for pairs 98
Bingo strips 90
blame 61, 63, 143, 157–158
Bloom's taxonomy 43
boss of your feelings 199, 201, 208–209, 210–212, 216, 217, 218, 219, 224
BOUNCE BACK! acronym 2–3, 17, 60–67, 74, 103, 142–143, 145, 146, 150, 163, 193, 253
BOUNCE BACK! e-tool 145, 150, 151, 152, 153, 154, 156, 158, 159, 161, 162, 184
BOUNCE BACK! journal 72, 73, 101
BOUNCE BACK! program 33
    benefits 4–6
    curriculum differentiation 35–37
    implementation and maintenance 68–79
    Key message prompts 87
    key principles 4–6, 10, 61
BRAIN 90–91
brain training/elasticity 54, 90–91, 281–282, 284
bravery 172, 173, 177–179
bright side thinking 183–199
British Cohort Study 19
building bridges 239–241
bullying 21, 22, 41, 57, 67, 75, 260–279
    bystanders 260, 276
    upstanders 260, 276
Bundling 91
Bushfire Recovery Project 3

Cameron, David 15
Canada 6–7
card challenge 99
CASEL *see* Collaborative for Academic, Social and Emotional Learning

catastrophising 54, 61, 64, 143, 161–163, 220
challenges 78–79, 280, 285, 297
CHAMP acronym 103, 108, 280–305
change/s 159–160, 204–205
change assessment 74–75
'Character Education in UK Schools' 18
character strengths 43–44, 280, 290–292, 293, 304
cheating 111-12
cheering up 218, 245, 250–253
Circle Time 5, 9, 20, 21, 30, 32, 35, 36, 71, 73, 81–82
Circuit brainstorm 91
Class Assessment Inventory (F-6) 73, *see* ebook
class book 101
class meetings 89, 239
class or school rules 115
classroom resources 101–108
    bounce-backers 101, 145
    Bounce Back! journal 72, 73, 101
    class books 101
    cube pattern 102
    digital book trailers 102
    digital class books 101
    digital stories 102
    flip book 102–103
    fridge magnet frame 103
    lift-up flaps and circles 103–104
    masks 105–106
    mobiles 105
    puppets 105–106
    Responsibility Pie Charts (RPC) 107–108, 158
    wax-resistant badges 108
clowns 251, 252, 253, 257
Cognitive Behaviour Theory (CBT) 8, 17, 54, 61
collaboration 71, 72, 134
Collaborative for Academic, Social and Emotional Learning (CASEL) 5–6, 28, 40, 42
Collective classroom research 91
confidence 22, 28, 73
confidentiality 85
conflict management 31, 57, 73, 239
connectedness 7, 30, 33–4, 71, 82
conversational skills 227–229
cooperation 124, 133–134, 135, 239
Cooperative games round robin 98–100, 230
    Before or after? 90
    Big words, small words 98
    Bingo for pairs 98
    Card challenge 99
    Four Kings 99
    Greedy pig 99
    Multiplication challenge 99
    Speedy Gonzales 99
    Ten circles 100
    Word detective 100
    Yes/No 100
cooperative learning 8, 17, 36, 72, 73, 133–136, 242
Cooperative number-off 91
coping skills 17, 40–59, 61, 65, 66, 75, 245, 250–252
core values 6, 15–17, 29, 34, 36, 56, 57, 109–123
counselling 64, 66
courage 5, 15, 17–18, 43, 87, 166–182
critical and creative thinking 29, 64, 86
Cross-offs 91

cube pattern 102
cultural diversity 85, 119, 120
Curriculum correlation charts *see* ebook
curriculum differentiation 35–37
curriculum integration 10, 61, 69, 71
Cut-up sentences 92
cyberbullying 21, 22, 41, 264–265, 273–275, 278

Deakin University 2
death 41, 149–150
Departments of Education (Australia) 3, 22
developmental stages, childhood 55
difference 35–37, 109, 119–121
digital book trailers 102
digital stories 102
disagreements 78, 224, 234–239, 243
disappointment 199, 214–215
dobbing 273–274
down side thinking, bright side thinking and 185–186
drama 85, 189, 236, 237, 272
    Accept what can't be changed (but try to change what you can change first) 160
    Being a positive tracker 189, 190
    Being honest 111
    Being tactful 113
    Boosting positive feelings 206
    Bright side versus down side thinking 186
    Building bridges and saying sorry 241
    Dealing with friendship disagreements 236
    Dealing with jealousy 216
    Dealing with sadness 218
    Describing and understanding feelings 203
    Developing empathy 222
    Feelings change a lot 205
    Fixing friendship problems 238
    Helpful thinking – check your facts 213
    How can we all help with the problem of bullying? 277
    Humour can help friendships grow stronger 255
    Humour helps us cope better and feel more hopeful 251
    Mistakes help you learn – don't be afraid to make them 295
    Nobody is perfect – not you and not others 154
    Solving problems and being resourceful 300
    Think for yourself – don't just follow others 272
    Unhelpful thinking makes you feel more upset – think again 153
    Unit 4 consolidation 181
    Unit 7 consolidation 243
    What is courage? 172
    What can someone do if they are being bullied or cyberbullied? 274
dreams and goals 283–286, 287, 304
Drug Education section, Victorian Department of Education 2
Duckworth, Angela 56

early schooling 7
elasticity (Extra unit) *see* ebook
Ellis, Albert 8, 54
embarrassment 203, 216–217, 251, 265
emotions 5, 6, 15, 19–20, 29, 35, 36, 40–59, 67, 71, 78, 87, 199–223, 239
empathy 10, 56–57, 78–79, 87, 199, 220–222
energy 44, 82 *see* Elasticity (Extra unit) 1
environments promoting student wellbeing and resilience 32–34
ethical understanding 29, 31, 57

European Career Learning for Lifelong Learning 3
everyday
    courage 18, 108, 166, 174, 175, 179, 182, 276, 277
    optimism 188, 189
    stressors 41, 67
evidence-based thinking 2, 7–9, 36, 50, 54, 70
explanatory style 45, 46–8, 49

F.A.I.L. (First Attempt In Learning) 295
failure 65, 66, 295
fairness 16, 109, 112, 114–116, 157–158
families 7, 41, 69, 72, 75, 136, 247, 252, 262, 274, 278, 282
    difficulties 155
    extended 33
    kindness and support from 126–127, 129
    support 126–127
fault, bullying and 269–270
fear management 166, 167–169, 172, 177–178, 180, 181–182
feedback 100, 228, 230
feelings 75, 78, 87, 145, 199, 223
    describing and understanding 200–203
    changing 204–205
    boosting positive 205–206
films *For details see* Resources lists ebook
fixed mindset, growth mindset and 52–53
flexibility *see* Elasticity (Extra unit) 1
flip book 102–103, 203
foolhardiness 166, 178–179
foolishness 78
Four corners 92
Four Kings 99
Freeze frame and rewind 92
fridge magnet frame 103
friends/friendship 17, 20, 31, 57, 124, 131, 224, 230–233, 234
    bullying and 260, 263, 272, 278
    importance of 130–132
    loss of 211, 241–242
    making and keeping 224, 230–233
    problem-solving 224, 233–240
    strengthening 245, 253–255

Gardner, Howard 22, 42, 43, 289
gender, self-disclosure and 85
getting along well with others 225
Giggle gym 128, 250, 253
goals 23, 45, 51, 53, 87, 193, 280, 283–286, 289, 293, 296, 297, 298, 300, 304
    long-term 284
    short-term 284, 285, 301
good
    luck, making own 183, 195–196
    manners 136, 137, 138, 140–141
    moods 199, 206–207, 209
    outcomes 154–155, 196
Good genie/Bad genie 92
Greedy pig 99
grateful/gratitude 183, 190–193, 197
grief, and loss 149–150
grit 5, 23, 31, 50, 53, 54, 56, 87, 295–298
growth mindset 22, 52–54, 56, 87, 234, 281
guided meditation 208

happiness 206, 293
hard work 280, 295–298
harm, bullying and 260, 265–266
health, humour and 245, 247–250

Health and Physical Education (HPE) 11, 71
helpful thinking 53, 54–55, 87, 152–153, 212–213, 241
helping others 280, 292–294
heroism 166, 174, 175, 180, 276, 277
honesty 109, 110–111, 112, 113, 232
hope/hopeful 183, 193–195, 250–252
HPE *see* Health and Physical Education
humour 5, 6, 15, 21, 108, 245–259
hurt feelings 113, 199, 201, 234, 239, 262

inclusion of others 17, 35, 124
information for families *see* ebook
injury or illness 146–147, 148
Inquiry-based learning 92–93
Inside-outside circle 93
intellectual strengths and abilities 42–43
intention detective/detection 213–214
International Friendship Day 232

jealousy 215–216
Jubilee Centre 2015 report 18

kindness 16, 17, 124, 125–9, 140, 271
kinetic energy *see* Elasticity (Extra unit) 1

laughter 63, 155, 248, 254, 257
learning 28, 32, 35, 43, 52, 53, 75, 298
lies and rumours 264
lift-up flaps 103–104
lightning writing 93
LIGHTS (Laugh, Include, Greet, Help, Talk, Smile) 131
listening skills 83, 98, 226–229
literature prompts 86, 146
loneliness 203, 211, 217, 251
looking on the bright side 5, 15, 18–19, 29, 48, 53, 56
loser, being a good 229–30
loyalty 232
lucky-dip choice 186, 255

making fun of others 255–256
masks 105–106
mean behaviour, bullying and 256, 262, 274
meaning, sense of 23, 34, 51
Memory cards 93
mental health 1, 4, 27, 68
mindfulness 20, 199, 208–209
mistakes, learning from 63, 154, 180, 280, 294–295, 296
mobiles 105
moral values 50, 56
Movers and shakers 94
Multiple Intelligences framework 22, 42–43, 289–290
Multiplication challenge 99
Multiply and merge 94
Musical stop and share 94
Mystery square 94

National Declaration on the Educational Goals for Young Australians 28, 29
National Framework for Values Education in Australian Schools 30
negative tracker 187, 197
negotiation 237–239, 243
neuroplasticity, research 53–54
new situations, courage and 172, 179

OOHC *see* Out of Home Care
opinions, similarities and differences 120

optimistic thinking 19, 31, 45, 46–8, 61, 62, 64, 73, 87, 183–198
organisation 31, 75, 88, 89, 293–294, 300–303
other people, connection with 61, 62, 221
Out of Home Care (OOHC) 36

PACE (Predict, Argue, Check, Explain) 95
Pairs rally, pairs compare 95
Paper plate quiz 95–96
Partner Retell 95
PBL *see* Positive Behaviour for Learning
peer connectedness 9, 30, 32, 68, 72, 75
peer pressure, bullying and 271–272
people bouncing back 5, 6, 15, 17, 29, 49, 50, 53, 55, 56, 144, 164
People pie 95–96
People scavenger hunt 96
PEPS *see* Protective Environmental Processes Scale
perfectionism 61, 62–63, 87, 142, 153–154
PERMA *see* Positive Emotions, Engagement, Relationships, Meaning and Accomplishment
persistence 56, 87, 280, 295–298, 299
personal
    differences, fear and 166, 169–170
    goals 285
    strengths 29, 42, 45, 46, 50, 65, 175–176, 291, 292–294
perspective 143, 162–163
pessimistic/pessimism 19, 45–48, 55, 185, 186, 197
pessimistic explanatory style 19, 45–48, 55
pets 248, 257
    loss of 149–150, 201
planning 280, 283–286, 293, 300
poems *For details see* Resources lists ebook
Positive Education 2, 8, 15, 16, 22, 27, 30, 32, 33, 42, 43, 44, 66, 68, 75, 76
Positive Emotions, Engagement, Relationships, Meaning and Accomplishment (PERMA) 8
positive
    feedback 75, 190, 230
    feelings 19, 75, 87, 142, 199, 205–206
    tracking 18, 46, 61, 63, 79, 183, 186–190, 197, 271, 287
Positive Psychology 2, 7–8, 10, 14, 18, 19, 21, 22, 36, 43, 61, 73, 79, 167, 171, 180
Positivity, Relationships, Outcomes, Strengths, Purpose, Engagement and Resilience (PROSPER) 8
Postbox survey 96
PRASE *see* Protective Resilient Attitudes and Skills Evaluation
pride 240
principles, courage and 179
prioritisation 302
problem-solving 89, 233–234, 280, 297, 299–300
Program for International Student Assessment (PISA) 4
program planning 4, 69, 70, 71
PROSPER *see* Positivity, Relationships, Outcomes, Strengths, Purpose, Engagement and Resilience
Protective Environmental Processes Scale (PEPS) 74, *see* ebook
protective environments 30–32, 55, 66, 74, 85, 274
Protective Resilient Attitudes and Skills Evaluation (PRASE) 74, 75, *see* ebook
psychological wellbeing 23, 45, 51, 66, 72
puppets 105–106
    play 145, 153, 160, 182, 214, 216, 218, 232, 238, 241, 243, 259, 274, 293
push and pull *see* Elasticity (Extra unit) 1

put-downs 81, 83, 255, 256, 267–269, 278

quality implementation, five stages 70
Quick quotes 96, 178, 212, 232, 241, 274
quiet thoughtful place 208–209, 219

Rational Emotive Behaviour Therapy (REBT) 8, 54
rational thinking 54–55
Reader's theatre 96
reality check 87, 142, 150, 152, 178, 241, 289
   anger 212–213
   talking to other people 150–151
REBT, see Rational Emotive Behaviour Therapy
Red Cross 116, 117
reflections 97, 122, 140–141, 163, 180, 197, 212, 222, 243, 257, 272, 278, 293, 298, 304
refugee background, students of 36, 37
relationships 5, 6, 15, 20–21, 29, 31, 36, 57, 73, 87, 224–244
relaxation 168–169, 178, 247–248
religious beliefs 30–31, 34, 71
resilience 3, 23, 26–39, 40–59, 64–67, 73–74
resourcefulness 299–300
Resources lists see ebook
respect 16, 17, 50, 78, 83, 124, 136–139, 238, 273–274, 275
responsibility 6, 16, 31, 57, 107, 109, 117–118, 261, 269–270, 273–274
Responsibility Pie Chart (RPC) 107–108, 158
risk-taking 179, 180, 280, 286–288, 297
role-plays 85, 115, 182, 274
Royal Society for the Prevention of Cruelty to Animals (RSPCA) 116, 148

sadness 202, 218
SAFE see Sequenced Active Focused Explicit elements
safe class discussions 82–85
safe environment 36, 61, 73
   bullying and 260–279
scared feelings 167, 202
school committees 89
school effectiveness strategy 4, 6, 26, 69
Schoolwide Positive Behavior Support (SWPBS) 16, 51, 68
science 51, 71 see Elasticity (Extra unit)
Scope and sequence charts see ebook
'Scoping Study into Approaches to Student Wellbeing' (Australian Government) 27
SEL see Social and Emotional Learning
self-acceptance 49, 50
self-awareness 5, 10, 31, 34, 42–54, 55, 61, 64, 73
self-belief 280, 286–288, 297
self-blame 63
self-confidence 11, 31, 34, 45, 49, 55, 65–66, 78, 270
self-discipline 298, 299
self-disclosure, difficulties of 84–85
self-management 5, 11, 23, 31, 49, 50, 54–56, 73, 74, 280, 302–303, 304
self-respect 17, 22, 49–50, 73, 138–139, 224, 268
Seligman, Martin 7–8, 34, 42, 43, 51, 56
Sequenced Active Focused Explicit (SAFE) elements, SEL programming 5, 35
setbacks, dealing with 144–145, 155–156
Sevenies 286
showing off 166, 178–179
Smiley ball 93, 97
Smith Family, The 116, 117
Social and Emotional Core Competencies (CASEL) 5–6
Social and Emotional Learning (SEL) 2, 4, 5, 7, 8, 9, 10, 14, 28, 36, 40, 68, 69, 70, 81

social justice 116–17
social skills 6, 8, 21, 31, 35, 40–59, 68, 78, 89, 224, 230, 239, 254
social values 6, 15–17, 34, 36, 29, 50, 56, 57, 124–141
songs For details see Resources lists ebook
sorry 239–241, 243
speech difficulties 36, 72
Speedy Gonzales 99–100
springs see Elasticity (Extra unit) 2, 5, 7
Stanford Youth Purpose Project 51
storage systems 303
Strath–Haven Positive Psychology program 44
strengths 22, 37, 42–45, 280, 288–294
stressors 41, 55, 67
student organisation 3, 36, 51, 74, 88
Students' Perceptions of Classroom Connectedness (SPOCC) 74, 75 see ebook
student wellbeing 4, 26–39, 68, 69, 70, 71, 76
success 5, 15, 22–23, 42, 45, 49, 50, 51, 53, 56, 280–305
support 124–128
   groups 270
SWPBS see Schoolwide Positive Behavior Support

tact 112–114
talking prompts 82, 83
talking to other people 150–151
Teacher Assessment of Resilience Factors In their Classroom (TARFIC) 73–74 see ebook
teacher reflections 117, 134, 145, 149, 159, 168, 185, 187, 196, 202, 207, 220, 225, 231, 248, 251, 262, 283, 287, 290, 296
teachers
   bullying and 260, 261, 262, 263, 264, 266, 267, 270, 273, 278
   connectedness 30, 32–3
   kindness and support from 127–128
   optimism 48
   resilience and 3, 66
   wellbeing 6–7, 27, 73, 76
teaching strategies 32, 35, 64, 81–100
   Animal asks 90
   Before or after? 90
   Bingo strips 90
   BRAIN (Beautify, Replace or recognise, Add or remove, Increase or decrease, Name differently) 90–91
   Bundling 91
   Circle Time 81–82
   Circuit brainstorm 91
   Collective classroom research 91, 156, 180, 257
   Cooperative number-off 91
   Cross-offs 91
   Cut-up sentences 92
   Four corners 92
   Freeze frame and rewind 92
   Good genie/Bad genie 92
   Inquiry-based learning 92–93
   Inside–outside circle 93
   Key message prompts 87
   Lightning writing 93
   Literature prompts 86
   Memory cards 93
   Movers and shakers 94
   Multiply and Merge 94
   Musical stop and share 94
   Mystery square 94
   PACE (Predict, Argue, Check, Explain) 95

Pairs rally, pairs compare 95
Paper plate quiz 95
Partner Retell 95
People pie 95
People scavenger hunt 96
Postbox survey 96
Quick quotes 96
Reader's theatre 96
Reflections 97
Round table 97
Safe class discussions 82–85
Secret word 97
Smiley ball 97
TEAM coaching 97
Think-ink-pair-square (TIPS) 97
Throw the dice 98
Whisper game 98
TEAM coaching 97
teasing 255, 256, 262, 269
technology 9, 11, 264–265
Ten circles 100
text messages, cyberbullying and 275
thankfulness 190–193
thinking skills 9, 35–36, 43, 271–272
Think-ink-pair-share (TIPS) 97
Throw the dice 98
time management 280, 300–301
tough self-talk 166, 168, 170, 171, 177, 178
trauma, effects of 36, 40, 41

unhappy situations, good things and 62, 154–155, 250
unhelpful thinking 61, 62, 87, 142, 152–153, 164, 199

United Kingdom Jubilee Centre for Character and Virtues survey 15–16
United Nations Convention on the Rights of the Child 116
unpleasant feelings 199, 201, 202
unrealistic thinking 48

values 15, 18, 42–44, 140, 281
VIA character strengths inventory 290
Victorian Department of Education 2, 3
video clips *For details see* Resources lists ebook

wax-resistant badges 108
websites *For details see* Resources lists ebook
wellbeing 6–7, 27, 76
    measurement of 73–74
    students' sense of 2, 4, 26–39, 40–59, 68, 69, 70, 71, 76
    teachers' 6–7, 27, 76
what ifs 171, 219
Whisper game 98
whole-class goal/s 284, 293
whole-school approach 6, 69
willpower 280, 298–299
win/win approach 237, 238, 239
Wildlife Information, Rescue and Education Service (WIRES) 148
Word detective 100
World Health Organization (WHO) 27
World Vision 116, 117, 293
worries 161–162, 219–220, 250

Yes/No 100